THE HOWLING

Ely heard the rustle of leaves behind him. He spun around, his heart hammering in his chest. He heard a growl, but it was not exactly an animal growl. He'd never heard anything like it. Something was definitely in that underbrush.

"You surrender, now, you hear?" Ely hollered.

The creature lunged out at him, ugly and snarling. Ely emptied his .45 at the charging beast. Two big .45 slugs, hollow-nosed, tore into it and knocked it back as they hit big bones with tremendous shocking power. With shaking hands Ely ejected the empty clip and slammed in a full one, jacking a round into the chamber.

Monroe and Jim Bob and Luther crashed through the brush and came to a panting halt by Ely's side. They stood and stared at the creature lying dead on the ground.

All of them jerked their heads up and stood rooted to the spot as wild cries began echoing all around them, cries like nothing any of them had ever heard before.

"Sounds like there must be a hundred of them damn things," Jim Bob said.

Fingers of fear danced up their spines as the howling moved closer.

THRILLERS BY WILLIAM W. JOHNSTONE

THE DEVIL'S CAT   (2091, $3.95)

The town was alive with all kinds of cats. Black, white, fat, scrawny. They lived in the streets, in backyards, in the swamps of Becancour. Sam, Nydia, and Little Sam had never seen so many cats. The cats' eyes were glowing slits as they watched the newcomers. The town was ripe with evil. It seemed to waft in from the swamps with the hot, fetid breeze and breed in the minds of Becancour's citizens. Soon Sam, Nydia, and Little Sam would battle the forces of darkness. Standing alone against the ultimate predator—The Devil's Cat.

THE DEVIL'S HEART   (2110, $3.95)

Now it was summer again in Whitfield. The town was peaceful, quiet, and unprepared for the atrocities to come. Eternal life, everlasting youth, an orgy that would span time—that was what the Lord of Darkness was promising the coven members in return for their pledge of love. The few who had fought against his hideous powers before, believed it could never happen again. Then the hot wind began to blow—as black as evil as The Devil's Heart.

THE DEVIL'S TOUCH   (2111, $3.95)

Once the carnage begins, there's no time for anything but terror. Hollow-eyed, hungry corpses rise from unearthly tombs to gorge themselves on living flesh and spawn a new generation of restless Undead. The demons of Hell cavort with Satan's unholy disciples in blood-soaked rituals and fevered orgies. The Balons have faced the red, glowing eyes of the Master before, and they know what must be done. But there can be no salvation for those marked by The Devil's Touch.

WATCHERS IN THE WOODS

WILLIAM W. JOHNSTONE

ZEBRA BOOKS
KENSINGTON PUBLISHING CORP.

ZEBRA BOOKS

are published by

Kensington Publishing Corp.
475 Park Avenue South
New York, NY 10016

First printing: April, 1991

Printed in the United States of America

BOOK ONE

A little season of love and laughter,
Of light and life, and pleasure and pain,
And a horror of outer darkness after,
And dust returneth to dust again.
                    Adam Lindsay Gordon

1

"I think it's a great idea!" Susan said, getting so excited she almost spilled her coffee. She placed the cup on the counter and sat down in a chair. "The class of '67 rides again—yeaaa!" she yelled.

"Susan!" The voice that originated three thousand miles away tried to sound stern but failed miserably, trailing off into a schoolgirlish giggle. Talking to an excited Susan was infectious. But then it always had been. "Susan!" she yelled, finally getting her attention. "How about Tom? You remember him, don't you? He's your husband."

"Oh, he'll go along with it, Nance. I'm telling you, girl, it's fate, pure and simple fate. It has to be. Milli calls about a reunion and tells me they have a six-week vacation coming. Well, Tom had planned to take six weeks off. And then you tell me that you and Wade are taking six weeks off. It's fate!"

"Six, six, six," Nancy Lavelle said. "Three sixes. That means something, doesn't it?"

"I don't know. Is it supposed to mean something?"

"Oh, I guess not. Fate it may be, kid, but hold onto your socks, 'cause there is more."

"So tell me!"

"You remember Norman Hunt?"

"Sure, I remember him. He married Polly Simpson."

"They're taking six weeks' vacation too."

Susan squealed with delight. In San Jose, California, Nancy grinned and held the phone away from her ear. "Susan! There's more!" she yelled.

"Well, tell me!"

"Frank and Cathy Nichols are also taking their vacation then. Oh, Susie, I think you're right—it *is* fate."

The women giggled like teenagers for a few minutes. Finally Susan got herself under control. "Ok, Mrs. Lavelle, now listen up."

"Yes, ma'am!"

"The kids."

"Oh, shit . . . and we were having so much fun."

"Camp."

"What about it?"

"I can maybe stick one of mine in camp and drag the other along."

"That's an idea. We still have time to make arrangements. Your oldest is . . . ?"

"Traci is seventeen, Tommy is eleven. Oh, I think they'd like to come along. They're both good sports."

"Ok. My two boy-heathens I can farm out. Sara I'd better bring along."

"She's ten now, isn't she?"

"Eleven. And very tomboyish. She likes camping."

"How about the others?"

"That, dear heart, is up for grabs. I know that Milli and Dennis have some brats. They told me that themselves. Norm and Polly waited late and have two darling kids; they'll take them, I'm sure. Frank and Cathy had two early on, when they were both still in college, and they're both off at school."

"OK. How about vehicles?"

"Well, we're flying into Lewiston and renting vehicles

for the drive over to that quaint-sounding lodge. From there I guess we'll walk in or ride horses, or something. I tell you what: you get a Norm Thompson or L. L. Bean catalog and start outfitting you and yours. This is going to be such a kick, girl. Oh, Susan, before I forget . . ."

"Yes?"

"The last invitation was returned today, only a couple of months late. Matt will be there."

Susan had fixed another cup of coffee after hanging up and took it outside to drink by the pool.

Matt Jordan. God! Talk about a name from the past! What a crush she'd had on him. Nothing had ever come of it, although it was not because she didn't pursue him with all her teenage wiles. Matt was one of those rare young men who, when not in school, was working to help out at home. His parents had not been destitute, but neither were they quite middle class . . . just good, decent, hard-working people—both of them. Matt had dropped out of school at the start of his second year of college, after his parents were killed in a house fire. She'd heard he'd gone into the army, and then to work for the CIA around 1970. He would have his twenty years in.

Susan Dalton hadn't thought about Matt Jordan in years.

Well—months, anyway.

"What?" Tom Dalton said, turning slowly from the wet bar in their nice Westchester County home, the drink he had just fixed forgotten. He blinked at Susan. "You want to do *what?*"

"Go camping for two weeks in Idaho," she repeated. "After the class reunion. You and me and Nance and Wade and all the rest of our group."

"Our group? No—that's your group, Susan, not mine. I am not a happy camper. I don't like the woods. I don't like bugs and snakes and other things that slither and crawl around on the ground."

She could not help herself: she laughed at the expression on his face. "Tom, you were a Boy Scout!"

"Not a very happy one, I assure you. And not for very long. No, I think I'll pass on this venture, Susan."

She looked at him, defiance in her eyes. "What are you going to do for two weeks?"

He sat his martini glass on the bar. "What do you mean, Susan?"

"I mean, Tom, that the day after the dance at the reunion, a group of us are flying out to Idaho and going camping in the wilderness area. For two weeks."

"With or without my permission?"

She blinked. "Your . . . permission?"

"Susan, I, uh, I didn't say that right. Certainly you don't have to have my permission to do anything. I was just assuming that you would not want to go camping in the woods without me."

"I would rather you *did* come with us, Tom. You're behaving as if this is the first time you've heard of the reunion and the camping trip. It isn't. You just hear what you want to hear. Traci is very excited about it, and so is Tommy. They're both coming along. Tom, it isn't as if we're going out there in a covered wagon, for heaven's sake. We'll have the best equipment available. We'll sleep on air mattresses. And there is a town just about fifty miles from the campsite."

"Fifty . . . miles?"

He was so serious she could not keep from laughing at him. "I'm sorry, honey. But the expression on your face was priceless. I . . ." She cracked up again.

He walked out of the room, his face red and his back stiff with anger. She watched him go and sobered, her laughter quickly fading. One more nail in the coffin, she thought. She walked to the bar and picked up his forgotten martini, tasting it, and grimaced. As usual, he had put too much vermouth in it.

"Idaho!" Dennis Feldman said. "You've been serious about this all along?"

Milli nodded her head. "Oh, yes."

"Idaho . . . that's where they have bears and wild Indians and stuff like that."

Milli, a member of the Denver class of '67, could not contain her amusement. Like Susan, she burst out laughing at the expression on her husband's face. Dennis was city born and city bred. His idea of roughing it was an outing to the zoo.

Dennis and Milli were a physical mismatch if ever there was one. Milli was tall and slim and elegant and lovely. Dennis was built like a fireplug. But unlike Tom Dalton, Dennis was game for just about anything. He had grown up in a tough neighborhood in Brooklyn and was just as good with his fists as he was with a law book. He had met Milli in college and they were married after he got out of law school. In less than fifteen years he had become one of the most feared and respected lawyers in southern California. And one of the wealthiest.

"I can see it now," Dennis said, trying his best to look mournful. He didn't quite make it; his natural good humor prevented it. "Los Angeles attorney attacked by wild Indians and eaten by bears."

Milli laughed at him. "You're going to love it, Dennis."

"Of course I will. Sounds like fun. I've always looked forward to being infested with fleas and chiggers and attacked by porcupines."

*   *   *

"Dennis and Milli still driving down for the weekend?" Wade Lavelle asked his wife as he came in from work.

"Sure. We've got to get started on what to take on our wilderness outing."

"OK. We boys will cook the steaks and you ladies can make the salad. We'll all help with the dishes."

"You have a deal, tiger."

He fixed them weak drinks and took off his jacket before sitting down on the sofa. He loosened his tie and kicked off his shoes. "Made up your mind about our thundering herd, baby?"

"Yeah. The boys we can farm out. I've already made arrangements. We'll take Sara."

"Sounds good to me. Oh, by the way, when you order the equipment, be sure and get me one of those jackets like Stewart Granger used to wear in the jungle movies. I've always wanted one."

She grinned at him and the love they shared for each other was evident. "My husband, the great white hunter."

He returned the grin. "Who has never fired a gun in his life. And never intends to," he added. He lifted his glass. "Cheers, darling."

In Denver, Cathy Nichols sat on the couch with her husband and watched the news with Peter Jennings. During a commercial break, she said, "Looking forward to our vacation, honey?"

"I sure am," Frank said. "It'll be good to see the old gang again. Most of them. Is Matt Jordan coming to the class reunion?"

"That's what Nancy told me."

"I wonder if the rumors are true that he works for the CIA."

"According to her, yes. He just retired as chief of station of a South American desk . . . whatever in the world that means."

Frank grinned. "I wonder if Susan still has a crush on him."

"Now *that* would be interesting."

"How so?"

"Nancy implied that Susan's marriage is pretty shaky. They've split up a couple of times, for a week or so. Nancy says that Tom is a real jerk."

"Is he coming along on the camping trip?"

"I don't know. But I do know one thing: Susan will definitely be there."

In Virginia, the assistant director of central intelligence walked into Matt Jordan's temporary office within the confines of the CIA complex. He sat down.

"You won't change your mind, Matt?"

"No. I'm tired and discouraged and more than slightly pissed off. I've got my twenty years, my disability has been approved, and I can draw sixty-five percent and live nicely. The Company has changed and it isn't to my liking. I'm tired of having to account for every damned paper clip and pencil I use. Our hands are tied more now than they were during the Carter administration. It was pathetic then, it's worse now. I'm gone."

Richard nodded in understanding. "Are you planning on attending your high school class reunion, Matt?"

Matt did not bother to ask how the assistant DCI knew about that. "Yes. I'm looking forward to it."

The number two man at the Agency stared at Matt Jordan. He was losing another of the good ones and it irked him. Few men without a college degree—from the right school, of course—ever rose to chief of station. Matt Jordan was the exception. He possessed a high level of intelligence, was tough as a mountain goat—and could be just as hardheaded—and had a percentage of successes on assignment as high as any chief of station. Better than most, in fact. Richard hated to lose him. When South America was busting wide open—and drugs were only a part of the problem—the Agency needed all the older hands it could keep.

"I could probably arrange for more money, Matt."

"Money had nothing to do with my decision to leave. It's politics, Richard. It's always been too political and now it's getting worse. We could have taken out the Ayatollah in France long before he returned to Iran and screwed it all up. Turned down from Sugar Cube. We had the opportunity to kill that asshole in Panama a dozen times. Turned down. We could have stopped the drug crap in Colombia and Bolivia and Peru long before it ever got started. I drew up the plan. It was turned down supposedly because some innocent might get hurt or killed. *Nobody* who associates with drug lords is innocent. *Nobody* who is close to organized crime is innocent. Now look at the mess the country is in. And I'm not talking about South America, either. Jesus Christ, Richard! On my first day back here, you know what I was told? Don't walk in certain sections of DC during the day. Don't walk in any section of DC alone at night. Welcome back, Matt. Just remember you're in a combat zone here and we can't do anything because we might violate someone's constitutional rights. I've been gone twenty years, Rich. What the hell have I come back to?"

The assistant DCI waited, allowing Matt time to vent his spleen. Many of the older hands were irritated, and much of that irritation was justified. Richard knew just how deeply into the toilet American justice had slipped. The new young blood coming into the Agency were all good, patriotic young men, from all the right universities and so forth, but they didn't have the survival instinct men like Matt possessed. And Richard worried about that.

Matt summed it up. "I just want out, Richard."

"Very well. How is your debriefing going?"

"As good as that crap ever goes. And if I have to talk to one more psychiatrist and answer more dumb-assed questions, I'm going to punch somebody."

"It's for your own good."

Matt stared at him.

"Are you planning to go on the camping trip some of your old classmates have lined up?"

Matt blinked. "I don't know anything about a camping trip."

Richard grinned. "Normally, we wouldn't either."

"I wouldn't think so, unless domestic operations accidentally came across it."

Number Two shook his head. "You've been out of the country for a long time, Matt. All that has been scaled back. In some cases it was a good move, in others not so good. Tell me, what do you know about a group called CWA? The Citizens for a White America."

"Nothing. What are they, some kind of racist group?"

"Yes—racist-survivalist types, a large group—and growing. They train in central Idaho. In the wilderness." He opened a briefcase and spread a map on the desk. One large area was circled in red. "In that region, Matt."

Matt stood up and leaned over the desk, studying the map; a very good map. The area circled was wilderness, all right, a lot of it very likely never thoroughly explored except by the Indians, a long time ago. A lover and student of the outdoors, he knew this area would have magnificent mountains, beautiful valleys, wild, rushing rivers, and dark forests. He looked across the desk at Richard.

"Are any of my old classmates physically or mentally able to take a hike in this wilderness area? How did the Agency learn of their planned trip? And are any of them involved with this nutty organization that is training in there?"

"I would think they are all physically capable of a hike.

15

When we learned they were going in, we checked them out for any among them who might have some background in intelligence, but we struck out there. We learned of this trip quite by accident. Tom Dalton is an attorney just wrapping up a long and expensive federal suit—for the defense. He got rich, believe me. He won. Damn good lawyer. A dickhead, but a good lawyer . . .''

"There's no such thing as a good lawyer."

Richard laughed softly. "As good as a lawyer can be, how about that?"

"Better."

"Dalton has been bitching for a month about having to go on a 'goddamned camping trip,' quote, end quote. One of his pals has a friend in the Bureau. He mentioned the final destination to the guy and the Bureau man got interested."

"Why?"

"Why what, Matt?"

"Why did the Bureau man get interested in a bunch of middle-aged men and women going on a camping trip?"

"Because Dennis Feldman and his wife Milli are Jews. Norman and Polly Hunt are blacks. And Cathy Nichols used to be Cathy Marquez."

"The Bureau man didn't know that."

"God damn it, Matt, you just have to press, don't you?"

"Yes, I do. Now level with me."

"The Bureau has reason to believe that someone in the group going in has been secretly supporting the CWA with large sums of money."

"Which one?"

"They don't know."

"Crap!"

"I really don't think they do. For obvious reasons, we can let out Dennis Feldman and Norman Hunt. Did you know Cathy Marquez?"

"No. I think Frank met her in college. Is she suspect?"

16

"Possibly. She's Hispanic in maiden name only. Fifth- or sixth-generation American. Very well educated, old money, does not speak a word of Spanish, and shows no interest in Hispanic causes. None whatsoever. She does not look as if she has a drop of Spanish blood in her."

"Does the Bureau think this Tom Dalton is kicking up a fuss about going on the camping trip just to cover up that he's the money man?"

"Maybe. He's no supporter of minority causes."

"Neither am I, Richard. A person should be hired on the basis of experience and ability to do the job, not because he or she is black or white or pink."

"You're not blind prejudiced either, Matt. One of your buddies in high school was a black."

Matt shrugged. "Norm was and probably still is a nice guy. I never gave a damn about his color. We came from the same section of town. Both of us worked in the same greasy spoon." His grin took years off his face. "We stole hot dogs and hamburgers and Cokes together."

Richard looked pained. A product of the 'right school' before joining the Agency, he came from money. Hunger, poverty, despair were only words to him. "I don't want to hear about your sordid youth, thank you. Are you interested in going on this camping trip?"

"No."

"I think you should reconsider."

"Why?"

"Susan Benning is married to Tom Dalton."

Matt stared at Number Two. Good old Agency snooping and leverage. Matt had lost touch with the old gang, had never returned to his old neighborhood after leaving. There was never any reason to go back. He did not know Susan had married Tom Dalton, or anyone else, for that matter. But as beautiful as she had been, and probably still was, some lucky guy had been sure to grab her.

"I'll think about it," Matt said.

2

Matt Jordan in no way looked like Hollywood's version of a secret agent. Secret agents, in truth, come in all sizes and shapes, both male and female. They do not leap tall buildings in a single bound. They do not, with rare exception, confront a dozen adversaries and defeat them all without sustaining a single wound—or dying. Most do not possess extraordinary strength. They are men and women, usually of very high intelligence, who speak a foreign language or two—along with several dialects picked up along the way—and who can call upon great patience. For spying is a tedious business. They almost always have a sideline career as a cover. Engineer, writer, architect, radio or television announcer, mechanic, pilot—take your pick.

On average, they do not like stupid, shortsighted people. They are voracious readers, constantly on a quest for new knowledge. Paper tigers and pseudoheroes do not impress them, for while spying is oft times a very boring business, the men and women in special operations live constantly on the thin line of danger, knowing they are on the kill lists of many subversive groups around the world. Career field personnel almost never work under their real names—they usually have half a dozen documented and provable names—and upon leaving the Agency they change them. In appearance, there is no such thing as the typical spy. Much has been written about the spy being the type of person who can blend in with his or her surroundings. Anybody can blend in if he or she is trained to do so.

Matt Jordan requested and received everything the Agency had on the CWA. He read the reports, retained the names and other important data, and sent the files back to Records.

He buzzed Richard's office. "I want pictures and current background checks on everybody in this little group of overaged Boy and Girl Scouts."

"They'll be in your office in ten minutes."

"Had them ready for me, huh?"

Richard hung up.

Matt deliberately put Susan's file on the bottom of the stack, saving the best for last . . . or avoiding confronting old memories, he corrected himself. Back in high school, he remembered with a pang of emotion, he'd had quite a crush on Susan Benning, one that had never quite gone away.

He recalled that it was the girls who'd held their little group together. The boys had just sort of hung around. Milli had been the class character. He recalled her with a smile. There wasn't an evil bone in her body. Milli liked everyone and was hurt when people did not like her because of her religion. Matt had never really warmed to Frank Nichols. Frank had had a mean streak in him even back then. He was a rich kid whose parents owned a large chunk of Denver. Matt recalled that Frank could be cruel in his remarks.

Wade had been an all-right sort of guy, Matt remembered. Easy to be with. Could have been a superjock but could never take games seriously enough. Matt recalled the final blowup between the coach and Wade. Wade had asked, "How the hell can you take a game seriously?"

Wade was the son of a prominent Denver attorney with lots of old money behind him. The file stated that Wade was now a very wealthy stockbroker living in San Jose. It had been assumed by everyone who knew them that he and Nancy would be married.

Matt did not know the others; but their files indicated nothing out of the ordinary.

When he opened the file on Susan Benning Dalton, her face jumped out at him. The picture was a blowup from a passport print, black and white and stark. It could not hide her beauty.

Matt touched the print with a fingertip. "So how you doin', kid?" he whispered.

"Not good at all," Susan said to Nancy, when asked that same question via long distance.

"Tom still acting the ass?"

"Yes. No. In a way," she settled on one. "Nance, I was hoping this outing would bring us closer. But I have this uneasy feeling that it's going to be the old straw that broke the camel's back."

"That bad, girl?"

"We're not sleeping together. That is Tom's way of punishing me."

"You've got to be kidding! I thought it was the other way around. Not that I ever pulled anything that dumb, if you know what I mean."

"I know. If they don't get it at home, they'll find it somewhere else. And there is plenty to be had out there. No, Nance, I'm going to do my best to make this marriage work. But if it's time to finally bail out, so be it. I have money of my own, and it wouldn't put me in a financial crunch to leave him."

"Hey! How about something on a lighter note?"

"Please."

"Milli says Dennis is convinced we're all going to be eaten by bears or attacked by wild Indians. So he went out and bought a gun. He's taking lessons."

"Are you serious?"

"Scout's honor. Milli says the thing is about a foot long—I'm talking about the pistol he just bought—one of those wild west gunslinger guns. It's a .48-caliber manhunter, or something like that."

"A .44 Magnum, maybe?"

"Yeah, that's it! Hey, I didn't know you were into guns, Susan."

"Well, I'm not. But I *have* watched all the Dirty Harry movies."

"My other line is going crazy, kid. It's probably one of my heathens. I'll call you back."

"I've got to go shopping, Nance. Let me call you tomorrow."

Susan walked out to the mailbox and found a note from the post office advising her that she had several packages to pick up. She drove into town and filled up the backseat and the trunk of her car with them, all packages from sporting goods stores. When she returned home, Tommy and Traci were back from their wanderings, and the three of them had a good time opening all the packages and spreading everything around on the floor of the den. They did not attempt to set up the tents; both looked far too complicated. They would leave them for Tom to figure out.

"Right, Mom," Traci said, dryly and dubiously. "Sure. Dan'el Boone Dalton. That's Dad for sure."

Then they all recalled a recent movie about a bunch of city slickers who went camping and got all tangled up in the ropes while attempting to put up a tent. The three of them were rolling around on the carpet, nearly in hysterics, when Tom came home. He looked at the mess on the floor, looked at the three of them—without a trace of humor in his eyes or on his face—and walked into his office, located off the den. He shut the door behind him.

"Craphead!" Susan said to the closed door, forgetting her kids were listening.

"You got that right, Mom," Traci said.

"Ditto," Tommy agreed.

Matt shook his head when he finished making his notes on the CWA. He lifted his eyes as Richard entered the office and took a seat.

Matt tapped the legal pad. "This is a dangerous group of wackos, Rich."

"Very. And a large group."

"Why did the Bureau hand this to us? I'm curious."

"Why don't we just say there is a new feeling of cooperation between us?"

"Why don't we say that is a bunch of crap and then you tell me the truth."

Richard spread his hands in a gesture of "What? Me hold back from you?"

"Give, Richard. Now."

With a sigh indicative of his long mental anguish at the hands of field agents, Number Two said, "I was going to brief you on this just before you went in. Knowing you, once you hear it, you'll want to leave immediately." He punched a button on the phone. "You know where I am. Bring me the file on the Unseen, please."

Matt stared at him. "The file on the what?"

"That is not our choice of coding, Matt, believe me. Somebody with a strange sense of humor in the Idaho State Police named it that. But it is fitting . . . in a macabre sort of way."

Matt leaned back in his chair and sipped at his coffee. He longed for a cigarette, but he'd given them up six months back. Most of his friends had quit. As a matter of fact, he didn't know very many people who smoked cigarettes or watched TV. One rotted the lungs and the other rotted the brain.

"Something very strange is going on in here, Matt." Richard tapped the map of Idaho, in a large section of wilderness not far from the famous River of No Return. "A few people have gone in and never come out. Some who do come out are basket cases." He tapped the side of his head. "Babbling. Deranged."

"This is connected with the CWA?"

"No. We don't think so."

"We?"

"You remember Jimmy Deweese?"

"Sure. We went through the Farm together."

"He's one who didn't come out."

Matt thought about that. "How long ago?"

"Three months."

"How come we sent people in?"

"I told you: mutual cooperation with the Bureau."

Matt suppressed a sigh. Richard was lying, and he knew Matt knew he was lying. Maybe Number Two would get to the truth and maybe he wouldn't. It was all part of the strange games played in intelligence work. "Rescue attempts?"

"One. They couldn't find a trace of Jimmy. The Bureau lost an informant in there about a month before our man disappeared. Working together, we hauled in a dozen of the CWA's top people who had just come out of the wilderness area, and they volunteered to take PSE and polygraph tests. They all passed without a hitch. Even they admitted that they felt, at times, something really strange was going on in the deep timber. Not all the time, but, ah . . ." He cleared his throat and sighed deeply. "It all depends on phases of the moon."

Matt grinned, then burst out laughing. He laughed until his face was red and tears had formed in his eyes. Still

23

chuckling, he wiped his eyes with a tissue and shook his head. "I should have guessed this was a joke being played on me for my retirement. It's good, Rich. Who dreamed this up, Jimmy?"

The assistant DCI had not changed expression. "Jimmy is presumed dead, Matt. No. It's no joke. I wish it were. It's all true."

Matt sobered and looked hard at the man. "Rich, are you talking werewolves, for God's sake? Or Bigfoot?"

Richard shook his head vigorously. "No, no. Of course not . . . nothing like that. I don't really believe there is anything supernatural about this. Hell, Matt, we don't know what's going on in there."

"OK. All right. The people who have encountered this, these . . . whatever the hell it is, what do they have to say about it?"

"They all report that at first their camps were wrecked, ransacked. After a lot of strange noises in the night. And they all reported the feeling of being watched all the time. When the attack comes, it is very fast, very vicious. They never see their attackers."

Matt's look was filled with silent sarcasm. "What are they, Rich—invisible?"

Number Two drummed his fingertips on the desk. "Yes, Matt. Apparently so."

"You look ridiculous," Tom told his wife.

She turned to face him and the light in her eyes was anything but friendly. "Yes, Tom, I suppose I do, standing here in our—my—bedroom dressed in . . ." She picked up a shirt and checked the label. "Battle dress utility—BDUs. But they're much more comfortable than jeans, and all the others will be wearing them. Tom," she pleaded with him. "It's a joke. Can't you see that? We're all going to dress up in outdoorsy clothes and go have fun for a couple of weeks. There will be no one around to see us, if that's what you're worried about. And even if someone does see us, who cares, Tom?"

He pointed to the mound of clothing and equipment on the bed. "I hope you didn't order any of that crap for me."

"As a matter of fact, I did. But you don't have to wear the clothes. I'll pack several of your suits, your button-down shirts, and two pairs of wingtips. You can get all dressed up everyday, stand around in the woods, and look like a goddamned idiot!"

He flushed, but recovered and said, "I'll wear jeans, thank you." He walked to the bed and picked up a slender box, opening it, then grimaced. "What is this, Susan?"

"It's a knife, Tom," she said, a dead flatness to her voice.

"I can see that! Good God. It looks like something Rambo would carry."

"Not quite, Tom. But it is a good knife. You can use it for lots of things in a camp setting. I also have a couple of camp axes. Would you like to see them?"

"Not particularly. We're really going primitive on this outing, aren't we?"

"We're going to have to build fires, yes. Although a lot of the cooking will be done on camp stoves, using liquid fuel. But it gets cold in that area even in early summer."

"I've heard those pump-up stoves are dangerous."

"This is a new kind of camp stove, Tom. The man at the hardware store spent an hour with me, showing me all the new safety features."

Tom grunted. "Well, let's see what else we have here. Oh, here's a fancy compass. Do you know how to read this contraption?"

"As a matter of fact I do. Do you?"

He did not respond to that. "Here's some heavy-duty flashlights and lots of batteries." He opened another box. "Well, walkie-talkies."

"For us and the kids, Tom. They're very good ones, with

25

a range of about eight miles, probably less in mountainous terrain. But light enough to carry. I'm from Colorado, Tom. I used to spend part of each summer in the high country. You're a New York City boy. You don't know what it's like in the deep timber. And believe me, I don't mean that as a criticism."

He ignored that. "Very well-stocked first-aid kit. Bug lotion. Signal flares. A nice book on outdoor survival for the whole family. My, my, a dozen plastic whistles. You've thought of everything, haven't you? What else do we have here? British lifeboat matches. Goodness! They are completely windproof and waterproof. A wilderness signal kit in case we get attacked by hostiles, I suppose." He picked up another box, opened it, and stared for a moment, a frown on his face. "What are these strange looking things?"

"Cyalume lightsticks, Tom. They'll burn for hours without producing heat, spark, or flame."

"Very good, dear. You've prepared us for any eventuality. Let's see . . . magnesium firestarter. Excellent. All sorts of shiny cookware and little funny-looking emergency stoves that I don't have the foggiest idea how to operate, so therefore I won't even try. We have water purification tablets, tarpaulins, tent stakes, and ropes of varying sizes. Waterproof collapsible buckets . . . canvas, I'm sure. Sleeping pads and sleeping bags and some of the clunkiest-looking boots I have ever seen. I'll wear tennis shoes, thank you." He picked up an object and held it at arm's length. "What is this stupid-looking thing?"

"It's called a butt pack, Tom. Very useful when hiking. It rests on top of one's buttocks."

"How quaint. Don't get one for me. Let's see now: folding shovels, gloves, binoculars, and innumerable other items, each of them as uninteresting as the next."

"You're turning into a real shithead, Tom. Hey, Tom? I have an idea: why don't you stay home?"

26

"And miss all the fun? I wouldn't dream of it, darling."
He waved a hand at the littered bed and floor. "Where is
your rifle, dear?"

"Oh, I thought I'd wait and buy one out there," she said
sarcastically.

"It wouldn't surprise me."

"May I make a suggestion, Tom?"

"Is it highly vulgar?"

"No."

"By all means."

"I wouldn't suggest tennis shoes where we're going,
Tom. Not for hiking. They're okay in camp. But you need
ankle support. The ground is fairly uneven, and we'll be
hiking."

"I shall take that into consideration. Thanks much."
He walked out of what had once been their bedroom and
went across the hall to what was now his room.

"Tom!"

He turned around to face her.

"The children and I will sleep in one tent. You can have
the other."

"Fine." He walked into his room and slammed the door.

"Oh, happy days ahead," Susan muttered. She turned to
inspect herself in a full-length mirror.

She smiled at her image. A touch of gray in her hair.
Susan did not color her hair; if she was gray, fine. She
wholeheartedly agreed with Barbara Bush. Her figure was
still very good, and the only lines in her face were
laugh lines. She frowned. Khaki was definitely not her
color. But after consulting with the other women, they had
all decided that was what they would wear. It was good,
tough material and very suitable for a two-week stay in the
woods.

Not even Tom's crappy attitude could dampen the
excitement she felt.

She wondered how much of that stemmed from the

thought of seeing Matt again.

"How silly," she muttered. "He probably is happily married with children of his own."

She'd know in three weeks.

"If there is nothing else you can tell me," Matt said to Richard, "I'll shove off."

"I knew you would. Matt, you're going to be on your own in there. If you push the panic button, we can fly people in; there are little airstrips all over the place, but no roads to speak of." He shoved a small packet across the desk. "Updated ID's in there, along with a federal gun permit in case some cowboy deputy sheriff decides to get antsy with you. Just as soon as the campers get into the area, I'll have people ready to go down from Boise. They'll be ready to fly in immediately if you hit the button on that transmitter. The Bureau will have people there, too. We're working pretty close on this one."

"I know. I've been over to the Hoover Building several times talking with them. I've met the Bureau agents who will be standing by in Boise. Williams, Ford, Macky, and Pointer. All young and looking like they eat rocks and trees for breakfast. Very eager and sincere young men. Law-and-order by-the-book types."

"That's the price we pay when we work domestic, Matt," he was reminded.

"You know what you can do with that comment, Rich?"

"Unfortunately, yes. But it would be a very uncomfortable fit."

"Fine. Just don't tell me my hands are tied by law books and statutes and constitutional rights and all the rest of that happy crap. I defend myself when attacked or threatened with attack. Vocal intent to do harm upon my body is good enough for me to launch an

28

attack. I know right from wrong; if other people don't, that's their problem. I have advised the Bureau of my philosophy toward unfriendly people. The gentlemen appeared to be very unhappy with me. I am going hiking in the woods. The woods belong to the animals. I will avoid them, climb a tree if I'm threatened by a large animal. I gave up killing animals for sport when I went from boyhood to manhood. If I am threatened with attack by humans, I'll use whatever force is necessary to protect my person. Do we understand each other?"

Number Two looked at Matt for a moment. Matt's code name was Husky; he had worked under the name for years. Unofficially, many field personnel called him Sponge—behind his back. The reasoning for that was that on several occasions, Agency higher-ups had seriously considered sending in teams with huge sponges to mop up the blood when Matt finished an assignment.

The assistant director of Central Intelligence nodded his head. "I understand you, Matt. Now you understand me: you are not in the jungles of South America. The IDs in that packet I handed you give you full arrest powers anywhere in the continental United States, its territories and possessions. That means that the constitutional rights of those you might encounter must be protected . . ."

He paused when Matt started laughing.

"Do you find this amusing?" he asked Matt.

"The white-shoes boys at the Bureau told me the same thing. Do you know what I told them?"

"I can guess. How many people over there did you antagonize?"

"Everyone I came in contact with, probably."

3

Upon his return to the United States, Matt had gone to a dealership and ordered a new, full-sized, fully equipped four-wheel-drive on-demand Ford Bronco. This was before he knew anything about the class reunion, or the camping trip, or the CWA, or the unknown forces, whatever they were, in the deep wilderness of Idaho. He had planned to take a year out of his life just wandering the country and looking at all the changes that had occurred in America since he'd left.

He was not leaving the Company—if anyone ever really left it—a rich man. But he'd never married, he'd never had to support a family, so he'd invested his money over the years and done so wisely. With his pension and the return from his investments, he would be comfortable for the rest of his life, with extra money coming in when he worked contract for the Agency . . . something many ex-agents did from time to time.

Richard had squalled when Matt had told him how much this contract was going to cost the Company. But after he settled down, Number Two agreed to the terms, muttering about Matt being a mercenary.

Matt drew some equipment from the Agency, bought some with his own money (he would hand in requisitions later), loaded his Bronco, and pulled out, heading west. He intended to take his time getting to Denver, and once there, look around the city and make contact with the Agency man who'd been stationed there for years. Matt had not been to Denver in two decades.

Some of the equipment he'd be needing for the woods would be flown into the Denver office. He would either pick it up or it would be shipped to him at the jumping-off spot in Idaho. Now all he had to do was figure out how to get himself invited on this camping trip his ex-classmates had planned.

He drove the Interstate and marveled at how much work had been done on it since he'd left the country. He began to wonder if there was a single traffic light between Washington, DC, and Denver. He drove through West Virginia, through southern Ohio, and into Indiana. He picked up Interstate 70 at St. Louis and would stay with it all the way to Denver.

The big Bronco handled well, and with its 30-gallon tank, he could drive all day without having to fill up. At first he tried the fast-food chains that dotted the landscape, but soon found that most of the fare was unpalatable. He began to seek out the smaller home-owned cafés in the towns and found what they offered much more to his liking.

Before leaving the Washington area, Matt had requested a much more in-depth report on Tom Dalton. There wasn't that much and what there was was mostly hearsay. After reading the notes, Matt concluded the man had an enormous ego and was all but humorless, a fine attorney on the job and a tyrant at home. Matt began to dislike the man. He had to keep reminding himself that the report had been gathered in bits and pieces and was not all inclusive.

Matt drove past the Denver city limits two and a half weeks before the class reunion was to start.

He checked into his room at a medium-priced and quiet motel, in the back, on the ground floor—and immediately called his Denver contact to tell him he was in town.

"You're early, Husky."

"Just say I'm overeager. You have my gear?"

"Came in this morning. Agent-in-charge over at the Bureau wants to see you as soon as possible. His name is Simmons. He's an old Company hater from way back."

"What's his problem?"

"The usual. The Company gets too much money. We're all a bunch of thugs and lawless renegades. We don't have any respect for the rights of others and for due process of the law. Et cetera—ad nauseum."

"I'll see him later. I'll be with you in a couple of hours."

"See you then."

Matt ordered a sandwich from room service, ate, and then showered and dressed in slacks and a sport coat. He carefully knotted his tie and slipped into a shoulder holster, checking his Beretta .380 model 84BB, loaded up full, with every other round the exploding shock-type ammo; the other rounds were hollow-nosed. He fitted his twin-clip pouch on his belt, in the small of his back, and stepped in front of the mirror.

He was a shade under six feet. At first glance, one would think him slightly stocky. The second glance would reveal a naturally heavy musculature. His hands were big and flat-knuckled. His wrists were large for a man his size. He was a skilled fighter, but no kung fu or karate expert. His was the best—or worst, depending upon one's point of view—of all kinds of fighting, combined with plain old gutter tactics.

His thick hair was brown, just now beginning to gray at the temples. He wore it parted on the left, and shorter than most men his age would wear theirs. Matt did not have his hair styled. When it got too long for him, he got it cut.

His eyes were a strange light blue. Spit-blue, one lady

had described them. His face was not lady-killing handsome, but interesting. He did not smile often, but when he did it took years off him.

He left his Bronco parked at the motel and called a cab to take him over to his old neighborhood. It was now a slum.

The cabbie noticed the look on his face. "You must have lived here at one time?"

"Yeah. I did."

"Thought so. I been drivin' a cab for quite a few years. I occasionally bring someone over here like you, nicely dressed an' all. You been gone a long time, buddy?"

Matt slowly nodded his head. "Yes . . . a lifetime."

He had the cabbie take him downtown, and from there he walked to the Agency's small offices at the back of a religious bookstore. The store did a steady business and made money.

Matt said the right words and was let on through to the back. There he greeted the agent in charge, who had only one hand; he'd had to have the other amputated years back after being tortured for information. He was a bit old to still be active, which let Matt know the man had a lot of clout within the Agency. He was old enough to have crossed over from the OSS with Wild Bill Donavan in the late forties. The man waved Matt to a seat. They chatted about people they'd known over the years, some now dead, and about the pitiful image of the United States, both at home and abroad, and they talked about the way criminals were currently being treated at home.

"Well, enough of that," the older man said. "You want to know what's happening in the primitive area in Idaho."

"What is happening?"

"Well, first I'll tell you what the Company knows about it: nothing. We waited seventy-two hours past Jimmy's check-in time and then sent people in to his last known location. What was left of his camp was torn all to hell."

"What was taken?"

"Nothing that the team could tell. And that, to me, lets out outlaws. And there are some in that area. They'd take guns, ammo, food, blankets, anything of that nature. The only things missing were his camp ax and belt knife. Pistol and rifle and several hundred rounds of ammo were left behind. Put that together for me."

"He could have lost the knife during the fight, and the ax could be buried in a log he was chopping on for firewood."

"Right."

"Blood signs?"

"Not a drop. Nothing. And not a trace of Jimmy."

"Are you convinced the CWA is clean in this?"

"Yes, I am, Husky. I saw the printouts of the tests. They bobbled a couple of questions, but they were supposed to bobble them. I think they're clean on this one."

"But a dangerous group."

"Oh, yes. They're mostly ignorant and crude and loud. They're good in the woods. They hate anyone who isn't white. We know they've tossed some bombs and set some fires and killed at least two people: a Mexican and a black. But we can't prove it. That isn't our job anyway. And yes, they are dangerous."

"How about the local police and sheriff's department?"

"They were kept in the dark about Jimmy's true employer, naturally. At that time, we didn't know if the Bureau was going to squall about us working domestic."

The agent fell silent and Matt waited, knowing there was more. He walked to the ever-present coffeepot and poured himself a cup. "You have something on your mind. Something that I don't think you've told the boys back at Langley," he ventured.

"You're right about that." The man sighed and shook his head. "I came in back in '48—just after the Agency was formed. I've worked a lot of desks, and I've seen some shitstorms in my time. But this operation raises the hair on the back of my neck and gives me goosebumps. There is now, and has been for a long time, something . . . well, *unnatural* going on in the primitive area of Idaho. I got the same feeling when I looked inside that hangar down in Arizona and saw that spaceship that landed here on earth. That was back in, oh, '59 or '60, I believe. Just a couple of days before that big bastard blew up. We never could get inside that damn thing. I wish we could have—in a way, I do."

Matt knew better than to inquire further about the spaceship. He knew now that this old agent, code-named Swallow, had things in his head a science-fiction writer would gladly give his or her soul to learn.

"You believe in the supernatural?" Matt asked.

"I don't know. I'll tell you what I do believe in: I believe in the unnatural." He shook his head. "Husky, I don't think that the cause of what's happening in the wilderness area is something alien to earth. I think it's—they—are human or subhuman beings that have lived in that area for a long, long time. A tribe of beings . . ."

The old agent paused, seeing the look of incredulity passing over Matt's face.

Swallow smiled. "Yeah. I know, Husky. I know. It sounds like I've been smoking funny cigarettes. I don't even smoke regular cigarettes anymore. Hear me out: I think these beings are so far removed from the twentieth century they've never seen electric lights or television or experienced anything modern. They probably think airplanes are gigantic birds of prey and hide at the sound of one. Another guess is that they've been inbreeding for generations and are borderline cretins."

Matt leaned back in his chair. Maybe Swallow had something. It was certainly worth hearing him out. Matt also believed that this theory was not something new to the man, that he'd been working on this for years.

"I'm from Idaho," Swallow continued. "And I can tell you that a lot of that region has never been thoroughly explored. It's wild, Husky. And dangerous. As far as people disappearing in there . . . hell, that's been going on since I was a boy, and even further back than that."

"I don't doubt it. But why hasn't more press been given to it?"

"So three or four old trappers or hunters or recluses who don't come into any town more than twice a year disappear. Who cares? Odds are that most people would just think they died of old age or cut their foot off and bled to death. They have no family. No one really knows for sure where they live. No one cares. A couple of tourists a year go in and don't come out . . . that's not news, man. That happens all over the United States—every day. Husky, we're talking about thousands of square miles of wilderness area—wild rivers and deep timber and rattlesnakes and grizzly and puma. So five people a year vanish in there. Taking into account the transients and hitchers and so forth, I'd say the number is five times that. Maybe more. Let's say it's twenty-five a year. I can prove that it's been going on for more than a hundred years. Husky, that's at least twenty-five hundred people who've just vanished from the face of the earth."

"Twenty-five *hundred?*"

"Over the years, yes. And that's the low end, I believe. I don't find it hard to comprehend at all. Man, an outsider can walk five hundred yards off the trail and be hopelessly lost in some areas. You've spent a lot of time in the jungles; you know what I mean. Wait until you see that country."

Matt nodded, waiting in silence, knowing there was more.

"I think civilization is closing in on them, Husky. These . . . well, let's call them people until proven otherwise, are panicked. More and more tourists are coming into their area for a week or two; more and more airstrips are being built. Their way of life is being threatened. I'm not defending them; not at all. They're dangerous."

"Why haven't the members of the CWA been attacked?"

"Too many of them. The Unseen know they have guns, and they never travel in the woods alone. I think they prey on the unarmed, the campers and so forth. I think they lure them into the deep timber, and when they're lost, then they make their final attack."

"Why are they harassing the camps then, letting a lot of people leave physically unharmed?"

"To frighten people away. But it isn't working; more and more people just keep coming in. They've become desperate."

"This is not just a theory of yours, is it?" Matt asked. "You've got proof that these . . . whatever the hell they are, really exist, don't you?"

"Hard proof that would stand up in a court of law, under intense scrutiny? No. Nearly everybody has a hobby, Husky, whether they will call it that or not. Mine always has been collecting data on the disappearances in that area where Jimmy bought it."

"Bought it? You think he's dead?"

"Yes, I think he's dead. And I think he was eaten."

"Eaten?"

"Yes. I think the Unseen are cannibals."

"Jesus Christ, man!"

"I told you I believed them to be subhuman. What's so strange about flesh-eaters? The animal kingdom is filled with carnivores. These carnivores just happen to have some ability to think, that's all. Wait here. I brought this from home to give to you."

Matt waited for a moment, trying to digest what Swallow had told him. It was tough going.

The old agent came back into the room with a large box. "Some of these clippings go back over a hundred years.

They're copies of the originals. I found them in old trunks in basements and attics. I told you: this is my hobby. These are newspaper clippings, old personal letters, personal accounts from individuals. Read them, then draw your own conclusions. Husky, not one body has ever been found. No bones, either. And no sign of any of those who disappeared. Does that tell you anything? Does that raise the short hairs on the back of your neck? It damn sure does mine, and it has for a long, long time."

Matt expelled breath and shook his head. "Jesus, man. Have you told anybody about your suspicions?"

"Only my wife. She's from that part of the country, too. Her brother was a professional guide. A good, solid man who wasn't easily spooked and could live off the land for weeks if he had it to do. Back in the late fifties he went into an area that was mostly uncharted to check out the game. He never came back. It was like he'd dropped off the face of the earth. His horses were never found. This time there was a very extensive search. Nothing, not a clue. Not one track or hoofprint was found. Does that tell you anything? Finally the searchers called it off and a memorial service was held. End of story."

"Somebody went back and erased the tracks."

"You got it."

"Are you trying to spook me, old son?" Matt asked, meeting the older man's eyes.

"No, Husky. What I am trying to do is warn you to be on your toes when you go into that area. Whatever it is in there knows the land—every blade of grass, every tree, every rock, every trail. You don't. I don't have to tell you not to take anything for granted. That Idaho state trooper was more on the mark than he realized when he code-named this operation the Unseen. You watch your ass, Husky."

Matt shook hands with the man, picked up the box, and

said he'd be back for his equipment. He left the store and hailed a cab back to the motel. He had a lot of reading to do.

Matt stared at the box he'd placed on the dresser in his motel room. Eaten. Subhuman cannibals roaming the Great Primitive Area. Jimmy dead. Eaten.

What was that line? *Curiouser and couriouser.*

He took off his jacket and tie, kicked off his loafers, and opened the box. It was so tightly packed with documents that the contents spilled over the side when he cut the twine that held it closed. He picked up a double handful of letters and clippings and sat down.

Several hours later, he leaned back and rubbed his face, closing his weary eyes. Tomorrow he would start putting all of it into some sort of chronological order. But for now, he had to conclude that much of what he'd been told by Swallow carried some weight. Something—correction, some *things*—were working the woods and valleys of the wilderness area. Whatever they were—and Matt now believed they were human, perhaps a subspecies of human—they possessed at least some degree of intelligence and a remarkably high propensity for savagery and cunning.

And for human flesh.

The jangling of the phone woke him at seven the next morning. He had slept deeply and dreamlessly and felt good. He picked up the receiver.

"Simmons wants to see you, like right now," Swallow's voice came into his ear.

"Does he want me to come to his office in my drawers?" Matt asked, stretching between the sheets.

The man chuckled. "You'd better go see him ASAP, Husky. He's bouncing off the walls."

"I am beginning to develop a profound dislike for this individual."

"I can assure you the feeling is mutual."

"Let's set the record straight, Mister Matt Jordan, or whatever your name is," Agent-in-Charge Simmons said. "I just don't like you people."

"Any particular reason?" Matt asked. He took a sip of very bad coffee and set the cup on Simmons' desk. "When did you make this coffee, last year?"

"Which question do you want answered?"

"I don't give a damn if you choose not to answer either of them. What's with you, Simmons? I got along fine with the Bureau people who work the overseas desk. I come back stateside and find all sorts of hostility. What's your problem?"

Simmons glared at him. He was so angry his nostrils flared like a charging boar's. "Are you telling me you don't know about all the damned politicking that went on?"

Matt sat up straight in his chair and leaned forward, placing one hand on the desk. "Simmons, the only thing I know for sure is that I pulled the pin and was making plans to enjoy my still somewhat youthful retirement. Then I am asked by the Agency to take one more job. We agree to money. The reasoning behind why they wanted me, I presume, is because I went to high school with some of the people who are planning a couple of weeks camping in the area in question. I'm assuming that you know we lost a man in there."

Simmons nodded his big, graying head curtly.

"Fine. That makes it our business. Now Simmons, I know all about the Bureau throwing temper tantrums after Congress OK'd and legalized some domestic work by us a few years back. I don't know why you people elected to do so much hanky stomping about it, but we can work domestic and we don't have to have your goddamned permission to do so. Now you know as much about why I was elected to go in as I do."

Some of the steam went out of the Bureau man. He relaxed just a little. "The problem is," he said with a deepening frown (Matt had yet to see him smile), "I never can tell when you people are telling the truth."

"You want me to take a PSE test?"

"Would you?"

"As long as the questions pertained to this job only, yes. If that would help you get over your anger."

Simmons leaned back, relaxing more. "I believe you mean that, Matt." He waved a hand. "OK, OK. So you're on the level. A truce?"

"Fine with me."

Simmons picked up a folder and held it so Matt could see. "Three weeks ago, the Justice Department officially jerked us off the operation that is code-named Unseen. I questioned that decision all the way up to the top and got chewed because of it. You know we lost a major informant in there?"

Matt nodded his head.

"That made it our business."

"Yes. I can understand your anger over that. It's certainly justified."

"Thank you. What I'm about to tell you is between us and unprovable."

"All right."

"I think some people in Idaho government—and probably big guns outside of state government—pulled some political strings in order to keep this . . . situation quiet. It would be very bad for the tourist trade. It would be bad press if the network people picked up on the tourists

41

disappearing in the wilderness area."

"Yes. I can see that. But why pull you people off the case?" He knew, but decided to let the FBI man get it all out of his system.

Simmons allowed himself a measured smile. Matt was curious to see if his face would crack and fall off with the unfamiliar movement. It didn't. "Because we do things legally, Matt."

"Yes," Matt agreed. "And that by-the-book, legal crap is one of the many reasons this nation is wallowing in a crime wave unparalleled in its history."

A grimace of disgust passed over Simmons' face. "And your answer to that is lawlessness on the part of law enforcement personnel, I suppose?"

"Not necessarily," Matt said, surprising the FBI man. "As much as I might feel sorry for a rabid dog, I don't want to pet it. We are supposedly a nation of laws, Simmons. Most people obey them—or the major laws, anyway. There are those who don't and never will. If you doubt that, check the recidivism rate of people leaving our prisons. I don't advocate putting people who write hot checks in the gas chamber, Simmons. I believe in restitution and rehabilitation programs for people who commit nonviolent crimes. But there has to be a limit even there. There has to come a time when society says 'enough!' A criminal is given three or four or five chances to go straight and blows every one of them. Those who commit heinous crimes should be dealt with swiftly and harshly. That is when you either dispose of them in a humane manner—despite the fact that they didn't treat their victims humanely—or else lock them up forever."

Simmons exhaled slowly. "As much as it pains me to admit it, Matt, I agree with you. OK, so you profess not to be the ogre I expected." He held up another file. "But this says you are. This report says that when an organized crime family out of New York City tried to move into a South American country where you were chief of station, you and your people dealt with them in a very savage and brutal fashion. Any comments?"

"Is this conversation being recorded?"

"No. And if you want to sweep this office, I'll lend you the equipment to do it."

"This is off the record?"

"Hell, yes!"

"The Mafia, or Costa Nostra, or family, or whatever the current fashionable name is for that puke, sent thirty-one men into my territory. At first I went through channels to get rid of them. Strictly legal. Your people came down there and mucked around, trying to build a case to get them kicked out of the country. Everything by the book. By this time the Mafia was interfering in my operations. They got one of my men killed and several wounded; another four were exposed. They began killing innocent people down there—good, solid citizens of that country who were fighting organized crime by writing about it in the newspapers and reporting about it on the television. Women with babies were blown up or machine-gunned by the Mafia and their hired goons. I got tired of you people jacking around so I set up a meet with the thugs and goons. We killed them all, cut off their heads with chainsaws, wrapped the heads in heavy plastic, and packed them in a crate. We sent the crate back to the *capo* in New York City. I got lead in both my legs on that operation. I'm retiring on disability."

Simmons' mouth dropped open. "Jesus Christ!"

Matt stood up and walked to the closed door. He turned and stared at Simmons. "We had no more trouble with that crime family. That's the way you do it, Simmons. I don't give a damn if a criminal likes me or hates me, just as long as he fears me. Go back and read history, Simmons.

John Adams said it: fear is the foundation of government. And I'll add to that: once the citizens lose that fear, a government cannot enforce its laws. If you doubt that, look at what's happening in this country today."

Matt turned and opened the door, stepping out into the hall. He closed the door behind him.

Simmons slowly closed the file folder on Matt Jordan, code-named Husky.

4

Once on the street, Matt allowed himself a satisfying chuckle. He and his people had ambushed the Mafia soldiers and killed them all. But they had not cut off their heads. They had talked about it and rejected it. Too messy.

He went back to the motel and started putting the clippings and letters into chronological order.

He spent all day doing that, and just before going to bed, he knew there was no way he was going to hang around Denver for two and a half weeks doing nothing. He called Swallow and told him to get his gear out to him so he could go in early. Then he called Stapleton Field and booked the 7 A.M. flight out to Boise. By noon the next day he was driving a rented pickup truck, heading north.

He spent the night in a small motel and was up early the next morning. By eight A.M. he was on the road. The end of the line was about seventy-five miles to the east.

On the way up from Boise, he had stopped at every store he found that carried sporting goods and bought two or three boxes of .223 ammo for his Ruger Mini-14—stainless steel with folding stock. He would cache small stockpiles of ammo along the way as he went into the wilderness area.

Getting the Mini-14 in had been easy. He just folded it

45

up and stashed it in his luggage with his pistol. With his government identification, he could have easily checked weapons through legally; but he wanted to see how good American airport security was. As far as he was concerned it was a joke. Try getting weapons through in any Israeli-run airport terminal and you'd be flat on your back looking up at the muzzles of Uzis.

He drove to the end of the line: no more roads ran east from this point all the way over to the Montana state line. He paid for his room at the small lodge—they had only seven rooms—cash in advance, reserving it for six weeks, and told the man he'd be in and out, mostly out. The manager assured him that his vehicle and personal belongings would be safe there. And would Mr. Jordan like to arrange for a guide?

"No. Just a saddle horse and packhorse."

"Ah . . . sir, there are historic trails you can take that are well marked and safe. But the closest one is some miles south of here."

"I'm not interested in historic trails. I also want to rent the horses for six weeks. You have a stable here for them?"

"Oh, yes, sir. Mr. Jordan, have you ever been in this area?"

"No."

"It's rugged country out there, sir. Lots of people get turned around and lost."

Matt looked at the concerned manager and smiled. "You ever spent much time in the jungles around the Amazon River?"

"No, sir. Never been there."

"I have."

The man smiled. Message received.

Matt stuck out his hand and the man introduced himself as the owner of the lodge. Five minutes later, Matt was in his room and on the horn to Langley requesting a hurried-up check on the lodge owner.

46

It came back late that evening. "He's clean, Husky. He's a good solid type. Not a blemish on him anywhere, and we accessed the Idaho State Police files to get his social security number. He's clean with the IRS, too."

"Thanks, man."

"No problem. Watch your ass going in."

"Bright and early in the morning."

"Did you notify the Bureau backup team?"

"No. I can take care of myself. I want the Bureau in place when I go in with the amateurs."

"Understandable." The man in Langley hung up.

Matt checked his equipment, then showered and went to bed. He was looking forward to entering the wilderness area.

He saddled up right after breakfast. The lodge owner watched him for a few minutes as Matt loaded the pack horse and tied the tarp-covered equipment down. Satisfied that Matt knew what he was doing, though still a little concerned about Matt going in alone, he nodded and walked back to the lodge.

Matt rode about a thousand meters from the lodge, dismounted, and took his compass from a plastic side pouch on his belt. He shot an azimuth, carefully marking the bearings. His watch was a Revue Thommen Landmark; in addition to being a fine timepiece, it was also a solar compass that located the cardinal points of direction in relation to the sun.

Now Matt knew to the precise degree where his entry point was. Getting back would be easy. It was doubtful he would lose both his watch and the other compass.

Out of sight of the lodge, Matt took his Mini-14 from under the tarp, slipped a 30-round clip into its belly, and jacked in a round. He put the weapon on safety, slung it, and rode on.

He stayed off any trail as he headed east. His plan was to spend ten days in the area, first riding over to the Selway

River—as close to it as time permitted—then cutting toward the Salmon River, known as the River of No Return. He would then work his way back to the lodge. Matt didn't think he would be able to complete that schedule, but he was going to cover as much ground as possible. If nothing else was accomplished, he would at least get the lay of the land.

He crossed canyons and meadows and creeks, plunging deeper into the wilderness, stopping every now and then to check his bearings. He rode easy and slow, his eyes always moving as the wilderness closed in around him. The feeling of solitude struck him hard. This land was primitive, pristine in its beauty and silent in the danger it presented to any amateur who dared venture into it.

He chose his campsite for the evening carefully. If anybody out there was stalking him, they could approach his camp by only two directions, and he secured them with perimeter alerts, running the black wire at ankle, waist, and shoulder levels. If a wire was violated, a series of very loud pops and bangs would warn Matt that his camp was being penetrated and give him the necessary seconds to prepare.

He also knew that a good horse was just as good or better than a watchdog. It, too, would warn him if anyone approached the camp.

But that night no one did. Matt was up with the sun, making coffee and frying bacon. He carefully put out his fire and saddled up, moving toward the east.

Midmorning of the second day out, he stopped to let his horses water and to eat some rations. He had picketed his horses and loosened the cinches to let them blow and was finishing his snack when he suddenly got the feeling he was being watched.

He gave no indication that he had sensed whatever it was tracking him. But what bothered him even more was that the horses were not alarmed by the intruder or intruders. They continued to graze contentedly, pawing and munching. Was it just his imagination? He didn't think so. He'd been in too many tight spots not to trust his intuition. He lifted his watch as if to check the time, and, using the black-faced timepiece as a mirror, scanned the area behind him. He could find nothing.

Using his sheath knife, a Gerber sawback with a nine-inch blade, he buried the paper that had held his rations and then stood up, picking up his rifle but not slinging it. He stretched and suddenly jumped out of his campsite. He ran for about fifty yards, then cut back in the direction he had just come, but north of where he had rested.

He heard a shout. It did not sound human. It had more of a gutteral, animal-like quality to it. Matt dove into some thick underbrush and lay still, his ears picking up the sounds of faint movement some distance in front of him.

Then he saw a small tree move.

A tree—move?

Yes. The tree had been there one second; the next it was gone—limbs, leaves, trunk, and all.

He dared not lift his head nor move his arms or legs, for to a skilled hunter, movement attracts more attention than sound. He moved only his eyes and picked up on the very slight movement of a branch about a hundred yards away, slightly to his right. But the branch was out of place. It was sticking straight up instead growing out of the trunk.

He estimated that he was probably twenty to twenty-five miles east of the lodge, and about five miles north of a nature trail. But in this country, that was about the same as being on the moon.

Every instinct that had been trained and honed to its sharpest edge silently screamed for him to shoot. He had a target, but still he held his fire. There was no doubt in his mind that whoever was stalking him meant him no good. But until that was proved to his satisfaction he would not

49

use lethal force. So far, his stalkers had shown no sign of hostility or aggression.

So, Matt thought, what now?

His adversaries answered that for him. A slender arrow with a stone tip embedded itself in a tree just inches above his head and to his left. Matt smiled, slipped the Mini-14 off safety with just a flick of one finger, and lay still. He always carried the weapon with a round chambered. Matt abruptly jumped to his feet, exposing himself for a heartbeat. He threw himself to one side and came to rest at the base of a thick tree.

He heard a guttural noise pushed out of a throat—he still did not know what manner of throat it might be—but to Matt, it had a ring of command to it. He heard the rustle of brush as whoever it was stalking him began advancing. He jumped to his boots and ran toward the north, his weapon carried in combat position. He jumped over fallen logs and dodged around brush and trees, then suddenly cut to the west just as another slender arrow slammed into a tree, missing him by about a foot.

He saw movement to his right, strange movement, like small, thick trees ducking through the woods. He slid to a panting halt, leveled his Mini-14, and triggered off half a dozen quick rounds. The rifle was equipped with a good sound suppressor, and he carried spares in his pack. The .223 rounds made only a huffing sound as they left the muzzle; the working of the bolt made more noise than the muffled muzzle blast.

He saw one treelike object stumble, recover, and lurch off into the timber, staggering. The stalker's clothing—whatever it was; Matt suspected tree bark—blended in with the vegetation and the figure was gone.

Matt quickly changed locations and hit the ground, lying as still as the earth beneath him. His clothing was camouflage, designed for this terrain, and as long as he remained still he would not be spotted.

His stalkers were gone. The returning of the birds, singing and chirping, and the squirrels popping out of their dens told him he was alone, as did his own senses, still working overtime.

Matt did not move. He lay still for five more minutes, until the birds and the small animals of the forest were once more at play or in search of food. Only then did he rise from the ground and begin his search for sign. He found blood on a leaf, and more blood a few feet away from that. A lot of blood. That told him he had made a right-eous hit. He returned to his packhorse and retrieved a kit. He collected blood samples and carefully sealed the slides in plastic. He found bits of bloodied bark with what appeared to be very coarse human hair on them, and collected them. He searched for more evidence to be sent back to Washington and found where somebody or something had lain belly-down on the ground, leaving behind sweat or saliva. That was collected and sealed. He backtracked and found one of the arrows that had been fired at him. Just one. The other had been removed . . . by someone. Or something.

He wanted to get what he had into a lab as quickly as possible, so after checking his bearings, he began the ride back to the lodge. He made his camp secure for the night—very secure, now that he knew his stalkers were dangerous—and was back at the lodge the next day. There had been no further incidents. Although he had not been as far from the lodge as he'd first thought, he was pleased when he came out only a few yards south of where he had gone in.

Matt had stowed the Mini-14, but had his .380 holstered on his web belt when he rode in. The lodge owner noticed it, but said nothing. If he had any thoughts about Matt, he kept them to himself. He had already put one call through to Washington—or more precisely, Langley, Virginia—and one did not need to be a student of government

51

agencies to know that something was going on. He put another call through to the same place, five minutes after Mr. Jordan entered his room.

Matt drove away that afternoon and met the single-engine plane at an airstrip west of the lodge.

"We have a fighter waiting at an air force base south of us," the pilot told him. "This will be in the lab this evening."

"Thanks."

The pilot nodded and was gone.

Frank and Cathy Nichols looked at the mound of supplies in their den and together shook their heads, both of them wondering how in the world they were going to pack all this stuff over to the campsite . . . wherever that was.

"Do you suppose Nancy has arranged for horses?" Cathy asked.

"God, I hope so!"

"When is the last time you rode a horse, Frank?"

He shook his head. "I think it was about thirty years ago."

Then they both started laughing.

Dennis Feldman looked at his youngest, fourteen-year-old Walter, and sighed with a sigh that only a parent can bring forth. "You're going to like it out there, Walter. I promise you. You'll love it."

The boy looked at his father, a dubious expression on his face. "Sleeping on the ground and swatting bugs? God, I bet we won't even be able to pick up a decent radio station way out there in the jungle."

"Lack of what currently passes for music would be worth the trip by itself," Milli muttered.

"It isn't jungle, Walter," Dennis told him. "It's forests

and mountains and rivers and lakes. I think."

"See, you don't even know," the boy pointed out.

"You got two choices, boy," the father said. "Go with us, or go to your grandparents'."

"Some choice," Walter said. "Spend two weeks at Geriatric City or go stomping around in the hinterlands."

Dennis pointed a finger at him. "There is a third choice, boy, and it's called the back of my hand."

"So, awright, awready!" the boy said, smiling; he had his father's good sense of humor. Besides, he knew his dad would give him a smack in the mouth if he offered up anymore lip. "It'll be worth it to see you fall off your horse."

Norman and Polly Hunt had taken a different tack with their two kids, and both Judy and Johnny were looking forward to the camping trip. The four of them had gone over their supplies twice and were now packing them up. Polly had walked out to the garage in time to see her husband slip an automatic pistol and two boxes of cartridges into a knapsack. They were shipping their gear straight to the lodge.

"Norm?"

He turned to face her.

"Why are you taking a gun?"

"Because I'll feel better with it, that's why."

"I thought your friend Matt was coming along."

"Just to the reunion and dance, I think. I'd love for him to come camping with us. Hey, I think I'll call Nance and get his number; give him a call and invite him." He buckled a strap on the knapsack and turned to his wife. "Why did you make some correlation between Matt and a gun?"

"He works for the CIA, doesn't he?"

"Last I heard, yes."

"So he'll have a gun, won't he? Why do you have to take one? They scare me, Norm."

He grinned at her. "Matt have a gun, baby? Naw, he won't have a gun."

"He won't?" she asked, puzzled.

Norm laughed. "Not Matt. He'll probably have half a dozen of them!"

Frank, alarmed at the mound of supplies they had accumulated, got on the phone to Nancy. He could not remember the name of the lodge and had lost the phone number. "Nance, what is the name of that lodge where we jump off to the woods?"

She gave it to him. "Why, Frank? I've already made our reservations."

"Nance, we can't carry all this stuff in. Cathy and me alone have about a ton between us."

Her laugh was delightful over the phone, and Frank grinned. "Relax, Frankie. I've arranged for packhorses to be there."

Frank sighed with relief. "You're a sweetheart, Nance. See you in a couple of weeks."

"You think we can still dance to 'Louie, Louie,' Frankie?"

He groaned across the miles. "I don't know. But we'll give it our best shot . . . provided there is a doctor in attendance!"

Laughing, she hung up.

She still had her hand on the phone when it rang. *Norman.* "Nance, do you have a number where Matt can be reached?"

"No, I don't, Norm. Sorry. Just an address. Why don't you write to him and ask him to come along on our camping trip? You're the only one he's kept in contact with over the years."

"You're reading my mind, Nance. But as far as Matt keeping in touch, I haven't heard from him in three or four years. I used to get Christmas cards from him, all from South America. Always with a different address, or no address at all."

"Matt Jordan, man of mystery. Oh, by the way, your room number at the lodge is three. I was about to call everyone and advise them to telephone the lodge and confirm when Frank called, all in a sweat."

"Anything wrong?"

They shared a laugh over Frank's call and both of them groaned over the prospect of riding horses. Neither of them had ridden in years.

"OK, Nance. I'll call the lodge today. See you."

At the lodge, Matt was sitting in the small registration area talking with the owner.

"You're real lucky you got your room when you did," he told Matt. "It was the only one I had left open. Got a group coming in to go camping in a couple of weeks. They have all the other rooms booked."

Matt kept his expression bland. Could it be? If it was, that would solve the problem of wrangling an invitation to go camping. "Oh? From back East?"

"From all over." He flipped open the registration book. "L.A. San Jose. New York State. Denver, and San Francisco. Some of them bringing their kids, too."

Damn! Matt had to hide his frown. He had not expected any of his old classmates to bring their children. This cast everything in a new light. He wondered if Richard had known the kids would be along when he set up the operation.

"Yeah," the owner was saying. "The woman who made the reservations was all excited. Said this was going to be a part of a class reunion. All of them graduated from a high school in Denver back in '67. Mrs. Nancy Lavelle, she was."

There it was. "How about that? So did I. Nancy is an old friend of mine."

"You're kidding!"

"Nope. Class of '67. Denver. We're having a big dance in Denver to celebrate. I knew some of the old gang was planning a camping trip; I didn't know where."

"Talk about coincidence! I'll be darned."

Matt went outside to take a walk. As he was walking, Norman Hunt called the lodge.

"Yes, sir, Mr. Hunt. Your room will be ready and waiting for you. I've arranged for horses to ride and pack animals to carry your gear in. Oh, no problem, sir. I'll show you all how to saddle up and pack the gear. A guide will take you in and then come get you in two weeks. Oh, by the way—an old classmate of yours is here. He has a room booked for six weeks. Yes, that's right. Real nice fellow, name of Matt Jordan. That's right. Sure is a coincidence, isn't it? Hang on, let me buzz his room." He let the phone ring ten times. "I'm sorry, Mr. Hunt. I guess he's out for a walk. You want me to tell him you called?"

"No," Norman said after a short pause. "No. Let's keep it a surprise."

"Right. I understand." But he really didn't. Odd bunch of people, he thought. What surprise? Matt knew they were coming in, now they knew he was here. Weird.

Norm called Nancy. "He's there, Nance."

"Who is where, Norman?"

"Matt. He's at the lodge in Idaho right now. Out walking around. I just talked to the desk clerk. Matt booked a room for six weeks."

"Six *weeks!* I don't understand, Norm."

"That makes at least two of us. Matt must have found out about the camping trip and plans to surprise us."

"From whom? I certainly didn't mention anything about it in my invitation to the reunion; we didn't know we were going then. And I'm the only one who knew how to get in touch with him."

"I don't know, Nance. All I know is, he's there."

"Maybe it's another Matt Jordan?"

"Class of '67, Denver, Colorado. That pretty well narrows it down."

Nancy laughed nervously. "Well, he does work for the CIA, right?"

Norman got a good laugh out of that. "Nance, the CIA is not interested in our class reunion. But I can tell you this: I was around some of those Agency spooks in Nam." Norman was the only one of the group besides Matt to have served in Vietnam. "And they can be pretty damned weird. I tried to stay away from them as much as possible."

"I'm not sure I like the idea of the CIA knowing every aspect of my life."

"Nance," he said, and she could just see the smile on his face. "The CIA does not know every aspect of our lives. The IRS, maybe. But not the Agency. We're just little, everyday people. They're not interested in our rather mundane lives."

"Are you sure of that, Norm?"

"I'm sure, Nance."

"I'm sounding paranoid. Hey, see you in a couple of weeks!"

After he'd hung up, she sat and stared at the phone for a few minutes. She put out her hand and pulled it back from the receiver several times before making up her mind and punching out Susan's number.

Maybe all this business about Matt was just pure coincidence. She hoped it was.

But she didn't think so.

5

"Are you ready for this, Matt?" Richard asked over the phone.

"After twenty-one years with the Company, I'm ready for anything."

"It's human blood and saliva—sort of."

Matt sighed. He was in no mood for games. Sort of? "Now what the hell kind of statement is that, Richard? Sort of?"

"Let me lead you into this, Matt. We all think it's a very exciting find. You've seen a dog lick a cut on its paw, of course?"

"Yes, Richard. They have an enzyme in their saliva that helps to clot the blood and promote healing . . . something like that."

"Yes. Something like that. These people who attacked you have basically the same type of saliva."

Matt tried to mentally digest that. "Scientists say we lost that ability thousands of years ago."

"These people didn't. These . . . *things* you encountered in the wilderness, they've never been innoculated for anything. They've got more germs than a garbage dump. And that arrow is something out of the Stone Age."

"Are they rabid?" Matt asked sarcastically. He still felt

he was dealing with a group of excellent woodsmen who were a part of some wacko survivalist group.

"Take this more seriously, Matt, please," the number two man urged. "Our lab people are all excited about the samples you sent back."

"Tell them to calm down. The last time they got all excited they came up with an incendiary cigar that was supposed to set Castro's beard on fire. It didn't work."

"Matt!"

"Okay, okay, Richard. So what are these people I'm up against?"

"They're not people."

That stopped Matt for a few seconds. "Would you like to elaborate on that?"

"Certainly. They are of the species *homo sapiens*, that much we can be sure of. This bunch just didn't evolve. That's theory, Matt. We can't be sure until you bring us one."

"Bring you one?"

"I'm leveling with you, Matt. We want one alive."

Matt muttered something extremely profane under his breath. "Providing I can snare one, what the hell are you going to do with it? Sell it to a sideshow?"

"We want to study it."

"Richard, I have good reason to believe that these . . . creatures not only seize people, but that they eat them as well . . ."

"Ummm. Yes," Richard broke in. "That might explain some inconsistencies our lab people found while doing the bloodwork. Please continue."

"Thank you. And that they've been practicing cannibalism for over a hundred years. Maybe forever. How the hell do I know? Look, I'm one man up against God only knows how many of these . . . *things;* I can do only so much. And while we're on the subject, why didn't you tell me my old classmates are bringing their kids along on

59

this trip?"

Richard was silent for a moment. "Damn! That is unfortunate. I didn't know, Matt. I promise you, I wasn't aware of that."

Matt believed him. He knew that during his years in the field Richard's one weakness—if it could be called that—was his love of children. Several of his operations had been scrapped at the last minute because of the danger of kids getting hurt. Matt had done the same thing; he was just a little bit better at hiding his feelings.

"It's got to be called off, Richard. Using adults as bait is one thing; kids are something else."

"I agree with you. But how do we do it? If we were to level with your old classmates, how many would believe us? Any of them? Doubtful. How many would go straight to the press? It would take only one. Besides, a deal has been struck with . . . certain people. The lid stays on and the operation proceeds, Matt. And it goes higher than this office or agency."

"And people call us cold-blooded."

"Yes. I share your feelings. Matt, how did you come by this knowledge of cannibalism?"

"I did some snooping."

"You're not telling me the truth."

"How long have you been with the Agency, Rich?"

"Thirty years."

"Then that's how long you've been lied to. You should be used to it by now."

"Good luck, Matt."

"Yeah, thanks."

After hanging up, Matt stretched out on the bed and stared at the ceiling for a time. If he knew where the happy campers were going to pitch their tents, he could go back into the wilderness and neutralize the area for several miles around the campsite. But he didn't know—and wouldn't until he was with his old classmates. They probably didn't even know yet. They would probably tell the guide to take them to some breathtakingly beautiful spot and leave it up to him.

Matt walked back to the office. "Where is the guide who'll be taking my classmates to the campsite?"

"Nick Tanner? I think he's visiting his daughter and family over in Washington. Don't worry. He's a good man."

"Oh, I'm sure he is. I was just curious, since I might try to wrangle an invitation to go along."

"I don't think you really need a guide, Mr. Jordan," the man said dryly.

"Oh?" Matt said with a smile.

"I saw you leave, and I saw you return. You weren't ten feet off your entry point. That tells me something about you. Anything you'd like to add?"

"Such as what?" Matt sat down and accepted the mug of coffee the man offered.

"Where'd you learn to ride like you do? You're no newcomer to a saddle."

"I'm Colorado-born and -bred."

"Bein' from Denver don't make you a cowboy. But you ride like one."

"I spent a good many years in South America. We ride a lot down there."

"What line of work are you in, Mr. Jordan?"

"Matt. I'm retired."

The owner of the lodge smiled.

"I'm serious. I *am* retired. I spent twenty-one years with the company, got injured, and pulled the pin. Disability."

"You don't look disabled to me. They must have a good retirement plan."

"Oh, they do."

"You got half your life ahead of you, Matt. What are you going to do, just wander?"

"For a year. Then I'll take odd jobs here and there. You

61

must know this area around here as well as anybody. You told me earlier you were born and reared here."

"I know the country. I only left here once for any length of time, from '41 to late '45. My mother was a French Canadian, so I spoke the language. I got shot down over France in late '42 and stayed with the French Underground until Paris was liberated. And if you're wondering why that didn't show up when you ran a check on me, I never was formally with the OSS. Wild Bill Donovan asked me to stay on. I'd had enough. He came out here in, oh, '47, I think it was, right after the CIA was formed. Wanted me to come back. But I was ranching then—I just bought this lodge a few years ago—and I told him I'd had enough excitement to last me for the rest of my life. He laughed and said he didn't blame me a bit. Told me he wasn't going to have any formal role with the Agency. And as far as I know, he didn't."

"Not much of one," Matt said. "You don't mind if I verify what you just told me, do you, Mr. Watson?"

"Call me Dan. You go right ahead, Matt. Use the phone here. And then we can sit down and you can ask any questions you like about that bunch of kooks that train in the wilderness and about that strange tribe of people who are rumored to live in the primitive area."

"It's no rumor, Dan. They attacked me. I got lead into one of them."

The old man's face hardened. "Did you kill it, Matt?"

"No. But it was a righteous hit."

"A what kind of hit?"

"A good body hit." He had noticed Dan's face changing and guessed that the old man knew the Unseen were more than just a rumor.

"Where were you when they struck?"

"About eighteen miles due east of here."

"Damn! That means they've crossed the river. Many of them, Matt?"

62

"I'd say a good half dozen, at least. You don't act surprised."

"I got to get me a drink." He gave Matt his military service number and his social security number. "You call in and run your check on my military background. The reason your boss didn't catch it first time around was 'cause my records got burned up in that fire at Fifth Army Headquarters in St. Louis some years back. You want a taste of bourbon and water?"

"That would hit the spot. Thanks."

Matt called in and held on while Dan Watson's military records at the Pentagon were computer accessed. Everything was as the man had said.

"Let's sit outside," Dan suggested, coming back with two very dark drinks in very tall glasses.

"That's a taste?" Matt kidded him.

"You'll probably want another 'fore I get through telling about those things out yonder."

They sat on the rustic front porch of the small lodge on the edge of the Great Primitive Area. Dan was silent for a few moments, and Matt did not push him.

"My daddy was a rancher and a miner," Dan began. "We ranched over on the Clearwater, west of here. Daddy used to hunt just east of that river you crossed when you left here: the Red." He sighed and took a sip of his drink. "Must have been, oh, 1925 or so, I reckon, when Daddy and about fifty other men rode off one morning. I was just a little shaver; but I remember how grim faced they were. All of them. Like they knew they had something awful to do and none of them really wanted to see it done.

"The story goes, Matt, that way back, a hundred years before Lewis and Clark come in here in 1800 or so, a whole passel of settlers come into the wilderness area east of here—hell, it was all wilderness back then—and they got snowed in. I don't know where they came from. No one knows. A lot of them died during that winter. The strong

63

ones survived. And multiplied. Nearest town was three hundred miles away. So they just formed their own community. Well, they started inbreeding after a time. They stole Indian women and bred with them. Maybe they were always cannibals, I don't know. No one does. All that in yonder, Matt," he waved his hand, "stayed isolated for damn near the next two hundred years. Maybe these people were throwbacks when they came into this country. Maybe they weren't settlers but people who had lived here since time began. The problem is, Matt, no one knows. Anyhow, up to the time my daddy and the other men rode in to wipe them out, the tribe had pretty much stayed by themselves and left other people alone. They were pretty well concentrated between the Montana line and the Selway River. They must have had a population explosion—that's what my daddy figured happened—and it was years before he'd talk about that week he was gone with the other men. Hell, I was a grown man before he told me about it."

Dan took another sip of his drink. "My daddy and the other men knew they hadn't wiped them all out. But they also knew they had cut the population down to where they posed no more threat. Daddy said it was the bloodiest week he'd ever experienced. He never hunted after that and didn't like us kids hunting. And he wouldn't let us go past the Selway."

Dan fell silent.

"Have you ever personally viewed any of the Unseen?" Matt asked.

"The what?" Dan turned his head to look at Matt.

"That's what they're being called. The Unseen."

"Good name for them. Yes. I've seen them. I've killed half a dozen. Maybe one every five or six years. But I never went hunting those who stayed across the Selway. I only shot when they strayed too close to my place and were menacing. God damn it!" he suddenly cursed. "For years

64

they stayed low. For years I never heard of any further practice of cannibalism. They lived on game and plants."

Matt took a healthy slug of his drink and tried to sort through all Dan had so far told him. "Go on, Dan," he urged after a few moments.

"What do you mean?"

"How many people know of the Unseen?"

"Hell . . . lots of folks know. But they're not going to talk to you about them."

"Why?"

"Maybe it's sort of like why most people who have seen Bigfoot won't talk."

"No, it isn't, Dan. Bigfoot isn't a killer. Bigfoot doesn't, so far as I know, practice cannibalism. Does Nick Tanner know of the Unseen?"

"Oh, sure."

"Damn it!" Matt suddenly lost his temper. "How in the name of God can you people justify allowing tourists to go camping in there knowing they might be killed and eaten?"

"The guides never took people into those areas where the tribe lived. Well, that's not true. They did take people in there, but always big bunches of them. The tribe won't bother big bunches of people. At least, they never have before."

Matt sipped his drink. Some key words Dan had spoken remained with him. "You don't approve of hunting, do you, Dan?"

The old man slowly turned his head to stare at Matt. "No, sir. I don't."

"Nick Tanner?"

"He doesn't like it either. Goddamn hunters is one of the reasons the wolves don't howl anymore. Entire species have been wiped out just to satisfy a blood lust. Man doesn't have the right to tinker with the balance of nature. You've got to leave the animals' natural predators alone. The big cats and the bears and the wolves. That's how herds are maintained. Not by assholes who want to stick a dead animal's head up on a wall and brag about killing it."

"Dan, it may surprise you to learn that I am one hundred percent in agreement with you. But that doesn't solve the problem of the Unseen, does it?"

"Sure gets rid of some hunters, though."

There was a very definite note of satisfaction in Dan's voice. "So some of the guides take the hunters into areas known to be populated by the tribe—as you call them—and if they get killed, so what? Is that it?"

Dan did not acknowledge the question.

"I hate a goddamn trapper," Dan said. "That's the cruelest way for an animal to die. You ever seen an animal with his hind leg or front paw chewed off, Matt? I have. Takes a sorry son-of-a-bitch to trap an animal."

"Dan . . . I agree with you. I don't hunt. Haven't since I was a kid. I don't trap. I think it's cruel. I also think it's cruel to let people unknowingly go into areas where they might be taken alive and butchered for food."

"I'm not responsible for that, Matt. Neither is Nick or the other guides who agree with what we're doing. We're very careful about where we take decent people."

Matt was neither shocked nor surprised by Dan's feelings. He knew several men who had once been big game hunters and who had finally put up their rifles in disgust, refusing to kill another animal in the name of sport.

"Dan, the tribe, the Unseen, they must be stopped. You have to understand that. You've admitted killing them. You know what they're doing is wrong."

"I killed those who went bad. That's all this is, Matt—a few bad ones."

"God damn it, will you listen to me? How many innocent people have wandered off the nature trails and been seized by these savages? How many transients and hitchhikers have they killed and eaten? Think about it. You people can no longer protect or justify what they're doing. They're out of control."

"Not the whole tribe. I don't believe it."

"I think you do," Matt spoke softly. "I think you do. If not, you wouldn't have told me all this."

Dan sat silent for several minutes, thinking and sipping at his drink. He pulled out a battered old pipe and fired it up, filling the air with fragrant smoke. "Maybe I do," he finally spoke. "Maybe some disease has spread through the tribe. Maybe their time is over. There always was a few bad ones. But there was always some of us around to cull them."

"Your father didn't seem to have had much sympathy for them."

"Oh, you're wrong. He did. But when they moved out of the territory they had always lived in, he knew they had to be stopped. For the good of those that would remain." He looked at Matt. "Now the government's gone and stuck their nose into the matter. Four things I hate in this world: hunters, trappers, the IRS, and the goddamn CIA. I don't hate the individual field agents; you seem like a right nice young man. It's the idea of the agencies I hate. Matt, how in the hell did the CIA get involved?"

"It was taken out of the hands of the FBI and turned over—unofficially, of course—to us. Once I locate the main party of the Unseen, I am to call in the backup teams who are waiting."

"To kill them?"

"We're going to take some alive for study."

"Isn't that just grand?" Dan said sarcastically. "They paying you good money to do this, boy?"

"Enough."

"And you think I'm going to tell you where to find them?"

"You don't have to cooperate, Dan. I'll find them or they'll find me. But you think about this: my old classmates are bringing some of their children with them. You said the tribe had crossed the river, so it doesn't make any difference where the guide takes them in, the Unseen will find them. You want the blood of those people on your hands?"

The old man didn't reply. Just smoked his pipe and looked out into the not-too-distant wilderness.

"Dan, you know it's got to be political."

"Sure it is. Me and Nick have seen it coming for some time." He laid his pipe aside. "I don't have any compassion for the bad ones, Matt. Don't get me wrong . . . they're throwbacks." He cut his eyes at Matt and Matt knew that this was one old man with considerable steel in his backbone, one old man who would kill without hesitation if he felt he was being crowded. "But the tribe functions in the wilderness to give the animals a fighting chance. Who takes their place when they're gone?"

"You're the damnedest ex-rancher I've ever heard of, Dan. You're actually defending nature's predators. I just read a couple of weeks ago about some plan to reintroduce wolves to Yellowstone National Park, and the stockmen were screaming about it."

"Their losses could be kept very, very low if they work at it. I ran cattle for the first twenty years of my life, working on my daddy's ranch, and for thirty-five years after I came home from France and took over the running of the place. A man don't just move cattle out on the range and leave them, not unless he's a damned fool. You got to work them. You got to move them around and night-herd them. Look after them like children. You rest when you're dead, if you're a rancher. Ranching is hard work, boy. You ever seen a big wolf running, Matt? Beautiful. They're God's creatures, and they have a right to their place on this earth.

68

Man, now, he hollers about all the great and wonderful things that we humans have done, all the progress. Progress? Poisoning the earth and fouling the air is progress? Streams filled with dead fish due to chemicals is progress? Rivers filled with garbage is progress? Destroying forever hundreds, maybe thousands of species of wildlife and plants so a bunch of goddamn people who never grew up can come ripping and snorting through on their fancy all terrain vehicles or motorcycles is progress? Aw, hell, I'm an old man who talks too much, Matt. I'm just tired of seeing animals get the short end of the stick, that's all. Their life is hard enough. What gives us the right to make it even tougher?"

"I agree with everything you've said, Dan. You should see what they're doing to the rainforests in South America. It would make you puke. But for now, I have to keep pulling you back to the immediate problem."

"You think those friends of yours would settle for nature trails, Matt? Keep them out of harm's way."

"What did they tell you when they called, Dan?"

"That would be a Mrs. Lavelle."

"Nancy. Right."

"She said they wanted to go deep into the wilderness area and camp for two weeks. She said they didn't want to see or hear another human being during that time."

"That's your answer, then."

"You going to be with them, Matt?"

"Yes."

"I guess your boss told you that they couldn't be told nothing about this?"

"That is correct."

"Well, Nick can take them where they won't see another human being, that's a fact. It's what else they might see that worries me."

6

Matt spent a week deep in the Primitive Area. Dan had shown him on a map where Nick planned to take the campers and Matt rode through it once, picking out good defensible campsites. Norm would be the only one who might spot what Matt was doing with his choices of sites. Norm was a highly decorated Vietnam vet who had served two tours. He would understand defense positions. The other men wouldn't know a defensive position from an aardvark.

The sites set in his mind, Matt rode back toward the area where Jimmy had been camped. He had not picked up any sign of the Unseen, nor had he sensed being watched. God, but this country was big and wild and rugged. Matt spotted elk and deer, mountain goat, and several black bears. Late one afternoon he heard the scream of a mountain lion and that night the howling of wolves.

"You're right, Dan," he muttered to his dying fire. "The country belongs to the animals. It's rightfully theirs." He went to sleep under a blanket of stars.

He was frying fresh-caught trout the next morning when he heard the men come stomping and cussing and crashing out of the timber. He figured he was about to meet some representatives of the CWA.

"Well now," the voice spoke from behind him. "We got us a camper who's nice enough to fix us our breakfast, boys."

"I do believe you're right, Monroe," a second voice was added.

"But he ain't very friendly," the third and last survivalist said.

Without turning around, Matt pointed to the rushing stream below his campsite. "You want breakfast, go catch it."

"And he's right testy, too."

Matt's Mini-14 was covered by a blanket and he had turned slightly so the intruders could not see his pistol, now cocked and locked, in leather.

"You boys want coffee, you're welcome to it," Matt said. "You want something to eat, you catch it and cook it." He turned his head to look at the men and had to fight to keep from laughing. They were dressed all in camouflage, including their gloves. Their faces were painted in camouflage. They carried semiautomatic weapons, two pistols, two knives, and enough ammunition to re-wage the Tet Offensive. They looked a lot like deer hunters.

"What you find to grin about, boy?" one asked. He had a lot of ear hairs.

"You, hairy ears. Did World War Three start and somebody forget to tell me?"

The one with hairy ears stared at Matt, mustering up his best tough-guy look. He managed to look ugly, which wasn't that difficult, he already had a good start at it. "What you doin' out here, boy?"

"None of your goddamn business." Matt returned the stare. The three men he faced were of the type that immediately brought out the worst in Matt. They were ignorant and proud of it. Rednecks, bullies, bigots. They

71

browbeat their wives—physically hammered on them from time to time ("A man's got to keep his woman in line, you know")—and abused their children. They poached game out of season and bragged about it to their friends. The only rights they cared about were their own, and to hell with everybody else. "Carry your ass," Matt told the man. He took the fish from the frying pan and put them on a tin plate.

Hairy-ears flushed and began puffing up his chest, which was about the same size as his beer gut. "I think we'll just whup your ass, boy."

As Matt had explained to Richard, vocal intent to do him physical harm was enough to trigger his temper. When he moved it was very fast and very unexpected. He tossed the hot grease from the frying pan in Hairy-ears' face. Hairy-ears dropped his AK-47 and began bellowing in pain. Turning, Matt clobbered the second man with the pan, the metal clanging off his noggin. Before Number Three could close his gaping mouth, Matt hit him flush in the face with the heavy iron skillet.

Hairy-ears was on his knees, both hands covering his blistered face, screaming in pain. Number Two was staggering around, his hands on his head, which was dripping blood from the frying pan's impact with skull bone. Number Three was flat on his back, his nose broken, his lips pulped, and some teeth missing. Matt gave Number Two another whack on the noggin with the frying pan and that put him on the ground, moaning. Matt placed the skillet near the circle of rocks which held his small fire in check and then went to work.

He gathered up their guns, their ammunition, and their knives. He unloaded the assault rifles and then smashed them against boulders. He unloaded their pistols and using a rock, pounded the autoloaders into ruin. He wedged the knives, one at a time, into a crack in a boulder

72

and broke them. He dug a hole in the ground and buried their ammunition.

Then he sat down and ate his breakfast and had his coffee.

Hairy-ears lay on the ground and stared at Matt, his eyes filled with hate, hurt, and confusion. His face was horribly blistered. Number Two had managed to crawl to a tree and sit with his back against it. He moaned a lot. Number Three was looking at Matt with disbelief in his eyes. His face was bloody.

"I'll kill you for this." Hairy-ears finally gasped out the words over his burning pain.

"I doubt it," Matt told him.

"How come you attacked us?" Number Two asked.

"Me attack you?" Matt stared at him. "Who threatened whom? Who came uninvited into whose camp and started lipping off?"

"We was just kiddin' with you," Number Three said, the words slurry out of his busted mouth and swollen lips.

"A joke is only a joke if all parties involved think it funny. That's something assholes like you never quite understand."

"I'm a gonna sue you for bustin' up our guns," Hairy-ears said.

Matt chuckled and finished his breakfast. He began cleaning up his camp. The three so-called survivalists sat or lay on the ground, watching, but making no more threatening noises with the mouth.

"You a lawman?" Number Two finally asked.

"Nope." Matt carefully extinguished his fire and stirred the ashes to make certain no sparks remained. He poured water over the ashes.

After he swung into the saddle, Matt turned, looking down at the men. When he spoke, his voice was filled with contempt. "You got off lucky this time, boys. The last time

73

men like you came at me with hostile intent, I killed them and left them for the vultures. And don't you think for one second I'm kidding."

Matt rode off. He was just a dot far away before the men got up off the ground. Hairy-ears said, "The next time I see that bastard, I'm gonna kill him."

Number Two carefully shook his aching head. "Best leave that one alone, Monroe. That one's a bad man."

"Get the radio out of the pack and contact base camp," Monroe said. "Advise them of our position and tell them we need help. Move."

Number Three looked around him, a mournful expression on his battered face. "To tell you the truth, Monroe, I ain't right sure just where we is!"

Matt swung around and followed a dry creekbed back toward his last camp. He picketed his horses, took powerful binoculars from his pack, and climbed up onto the crest of a hill. He watched the three men stagger down to the creek and bathe their faces. Matt took out his compass and checked the location against his map. He sat back and began carefully scanning the treetops, looking for smoke. He finally found several thin tentacles of smoke drifting upward. The survivalists weren't very smart or they would have built smaller fires using dry wood, and they would have built them under low branches that would have broken up the smoke.

Nearly an hour passed before a half dozen men on horseback, leading three spare horses, picked their way out of the timber and up to the three men waiting by the creek. Matt watched as a lot of excited arm-waving and pointing in his direction went on. The newcomers looked at the broken rifles and pistols.

The whole passel of rednecks finally mounted up and rode off, back toward the direction of the smoke. Matt swung into the saddle and headed back to the lodge. He had reports to make and a class reunion to attend.

"That would be Monroe Bishner," the man from Langley told Matt. Matt was back in Denver, in his room at the motel. "From Alabama originally, although I'm sure the majority of residents of that state would refuse to claim him. He's a bad one, Husky. Courtmartialed out of the army for refusing to take orders from a black officer. A barroom brawler from 'way back. Half a dozen arrests for assault. One conviction. Tried for aggravated arson; he was accused of burning down a man's house with the man and his family in it. No conviction. He's been a member of one racist group or another since he was in high school. He dropped out of school in the tenth grade. He was tried for rape. No conviction. Served five years in prison for attempted murder. The next time you see him, do the world a favor and kill him."

"It'll probably come to that if we ever meet again. And I'm sure we will. How about the other two?"

"Hell, Husky, those people all look alike. They could be any of a dozen known to belong to the Citizens for a White America. They're all a bunch of jerk-offs."

"Anything new on the Unseen from the samples I sent?"

"Nothing that was reported to me."

A little warning bell started to go off in Matt's head. He'd heard it many times over the years. It played a tune that rhymed with the letters C, Y, and A. Put them together and they spelled Cover Your Ass. "Give it all to me, partner," Matt said.

"Number Two will be gone for at least a month, Husky. He's inspecting stations all around this big ol' globe."

"Well, now, if that isn't a coincidence. Just about the time things are ready to pop, the boss takes off."

"He was sent, Husky. He pulled one too many strings in

75

trying to get this operation called off on account of the kids. Persons we both know or at least are very familiar with, inside and out of this organization, and who shall remain unnamed, came down on him hard. Something is screwy about this operation, friend. And I mean big-time out of whack."

"Is that just a hunch on your part?"

"Yes. But we all have played our hunches out in the field."

"True. Could Swallow tell me anything?"

The voice a thousand miles away was silent. "You haven't checked in, right?"

"Right."

"Swallow's dead. He had an accident—ho-ho-ho—last Thursday."

"Did they get to his wife?"

"What do you mean?"

"How did he die?"

"Same old crap. A car wreck. He was buried quick. What about his wife? What the hell does she know? Talk to me, Husky."

Matt hung up. He wasn't about to talk to a voice he wasn't sure of; voices could be easily imitated. He drove to the religious bookstore. It was closed. An Out-of-Business sign hung inside the door.

Matt knew there was no point in coming back that night and slipping the lock and snooping. The place would have been cleaned out by experts.

He went next door and spoke to a clerk that looked like she might know what she was talking about. "Pardon me, miss. I'm with the American Unity and Fidelity Group Insurance Company out of New York. We hold a policy on the gentleman who ran the bookstore. You know he was killed? Yes. Terrible thing. Just awful. The highways are like a jungle, I should say. What it is, we're trying to find his next of kin . . ."

"Why, that would be his wife!"

"Yes, we know. But the address on the policy is an old one. The policy is an old one; all paid up for years. And I'm sure his wife could use the money. The problem is, we can't find her to give it to her."

"Well, she went home right after the funeral. A little town in Idaho. Let me think. Well, actually, it isn't in a town. It's a ranch they had. The town is . . . oh, what is that name! Kooskia! That's it."

Dress nicely but not flashy, be interested, look sincere, act polite, and you can get just about any type of information you want out of anybody, Matt thought.

He caught the next flight out and was heading for the county seat in a rented car after spending the night in a small Lewiston motel. He was listening to a local radio station on AM when he slowed, signaled, and pulled off onto the shoulder.

". . . the sheriff's department reports they have no leads in the brutal murder of Mrs. Gaston, who had recently returned to her home county to live after her husband was killed in a car accident in Colorado. Her badly mangled body was found yesterday afternoon. Weather is next."

Matt clicked off the radio. Badly mangled body. How about partially eaten body? Yeah, Dan, they've crossed the river all right, old son. The bastards have crossed the river, climbed the mountains, and busted out all over the goddamn place. He drove to the county sheriff's office and asked to see the sheriff.

"He's busy. Take a seat."

Matt opened a leather ID case and showed the young deputy his real ID and his federal gun permit with picture, since the Agency had stopped putting agents' photos on their IDs some time back.

"Now," Matt said.

"I never seen one of them before," the young deputy said, eyeballing the ID. He buzzed the sheriff. "There's a

CIA man out here to see you, right now, sir."

Since he had heard the radio news, all sorts of interesting ideas had been roaming around in Matt's head. It was all speculation, not one shred of proof, but it made sense to Matt. It was the only thing that made sense to him.

"I don't believe I've ever met a CIA man before, Mr. Jordan," the sheriff said, smiling at Matt.

"Oh, you've probably met a hundred and didn't know it, Sheriff." He was carefully inspecting the man's face. He wasn't sure what he was looking for, but it was something he'd seen . . .

"What can I do for you, Mr. Jordan?"

"Let me see the body of Mrs. Gaston."

The sheriff leaned forward, putting both elbows on his desk. "Now why would I want to do that, sir?"

Matt hesitated, then plunged ahead. Richard was gone, he was on his own, he wasn't even sure the FBI team was still in place, so to hell with it.

"Sheriff, my telling you this will most probably put you in danger—high-risk danger. And I'm not being melodramatic. I don't have the authority to tell you this; I'm acting on my own."

"You were studying me closely a few seconds ago, Mr. Jordan. Did I pass inspection?"

"I think so. I have to trust somebody. If you want to verify my identification, call the Denver FBI and ask for Simmons."

"Tell me your story, then I'll decide whether to call or not. Why do you want to see the body?"

"Because Gene Gaston had been with the Agency for nearly forty years. He was running a front in Denver for us. His death was no accident. Obviously, from what I heard on the radio, neither was the death of his widow."

The sheriff grunted. "Damn sure wasn't."

"Was the body partially eaten?"

That shook the man. But he recovered nicely. "Now

how in the hell would you know that?"

Matt stood up. "Let's go see the body."

It was an ugly sight. What was left of her, that is.

"Now you see why I can't release much to the press. For the time being, it's going to be a bear attack."

"It was no bear, Sheriff."

"I suppose you're going to tell me who it was?"

"No. But I can tell you *what* it was."

Fifteen minutes later, the sheriff whipped his patrol car off the road, stopped, looked at Matt, and said, "Are you fucking out of your mind?"

"No. But it's the only thing that makes any sense."

"This makes sense? To who? Not to me. I got years behind a badge and I think this is the wildest thing I ever heard of. I think you're crazy. I think you must have just broken out of some nut house. I think I am gonna call the FBI. I think . . ." He stopped his harangue and shook his head. "I been hearing those stories all my life. I never dreamed they were anything but fairy tales. I been trying to tell myself all day that was a bear attack . . . but I knew it wasn't. So does the coroner. The teeth marks don't fit a bear's. Problem is, they don't fit anything I'm familiar with. Are you a drinking man, Matt?"

"I have been known to tipple from time to time."

"Well, Mr. CIA Man, by all means, let us go tipple. After listening to you, I damn sure need some!"

7

The problem was, as the sheriff explained, that there was so much area for the Unseen—and he still was not convinced that any such tribe existed—to roam around in. And, he pointed out, that was federal land in there . . . most of it.

Matt showed him his other credentials.

"Which agency do you really work for, Matt?" the sheriff asked.

"The CIA."

The sheriff called the Denver office of the FBI and asked for agent-in-charge Simmons. He listened for a few moments, then handed the phone to Matt.

"What's going on in that area, Matt?" the Bureau man asked.

"I wish I knew for sure. Are you getting any heat?"

"Some. But nothing I can't handle. And by the way, a wreck reconstruction team has concluded that Gaston's death was no accident. Somebody offed him."

"I figured that. But thanks for confirming it."

"I liked that old man, Matt. He was a randy old rogue, but a nice guy once you got to know him. We worked closely on a lot of matters. I don't like murder anywhere; but murder in my jurisdiction offends me. And what really offends me is when I'm told to stay out of it."

"You're kidding!"

"No."

"From within your agency?"

"Let's just say that certain people, in and out of government, want this . . . tribe of whatever the hell they are . . . left alone."

"Left alone?"

"Yes. I couldn't believe it. Still can't believe it. It boggles the mind."

"But my orders were to go in and get rid of them if at all possible."

"I know. And we were to back you up. The CWA was just an excuse for the overall operation. A cover story. I know for a fact that your DCI just recently told a very powerful man in government to go fuck himself. And that if this man in government wanted a lot of publicity on this matter, just push a little bit harder. Obviously, Gene Gaston was no average field agent."

"No. He was a man who knew where a lot of bodies were buried—literally."

The sheriff's eyebrows went up at that.

"And also he knew a lot about those things in the wilderness."

"Yes. Now I have that information. It's tucked away in a very safe place. So where does this new decision leave me, I wonder?"

"From what I can get, since your number two man is out of the country, your orders stand. He was your sole contact—officially. The Bureau backup team was at first ordered to stand down. Then the director got his ass up at so much outside interference and ordered them back in position. Right now, your bureau backup is in limbo."

"What the hell is going on?" Matt yelled.

"Matt," the Denver agent said with a sigh, "I just don't know. I'm receiving so many conflicting signals it's beginning to resemble a fire drill in a lunatic asylum.''

Matt told him of his suspicions and that he had confided in the sheriff.

"That's stretching pretty far out in left field, Matt. But it's just crazy enough to make sense. Are you on a speaker phone?"

"No."

"Being taped?"

"I don't think so."

"All right. The sheriff, by the way, is a good man. I'll check him through on your theory, though, just to make sure. When you get to a secure phone, call the DCI, at home, and no one else."

"Understood."

Telling the sheriff he'd be back in touch, Matt pulled out in his rental car. He drove until after dark, then turned into a gas station and used a pay phone to call the director of central intelligence at his home.

"Is your phone clean?" the DCI asked.

"No roaches here."

"Simmons told me your theory. It fits. It's obscene, but it works. I can understand why they would want it covered up. I have been with the bureau director all afternoon, walking out in the country. Both of us are old political hands, and neither of us can remember this much pressure being exerted over one rather minor domestic operation. So you have to be correct in your assumptions and the operation must continue. Unfortunately, there is no way to dissuade the campers from going in without upsetting the apple cart, so to speak. I do not like to have my people killed. The Bureau does not like to have its people killed. This is becoming a rather personal matter. People must be taught that one does not bother the woodcutter while the woodcutter is cutting wood . . .''

That double-speak meant that if you disturbed the woodcutter, he was going to use the chainsaw on the person who bothered him.

". . . the agency team will be in place, as will the bureau team," the DCI continued. "Once you begin logging, it is going to be rather messy around here, I'm afraid. But that is not your concern. Sharpen your ax and go to work, Husky." He broke the connection.

"Time to start clearing some land," Matt said.

Back in Denver, Matt used his own money to resupply a few articles. He had thought of and rejected a dozen ways to stop the others from going into the wilderness area. He was bound by secrecy and could not divulge the danger that waited for them in the Primitive Area. If he were to level with his old friends, and they talked, Matt could be prosecuted and imprisoned for violation of the secrecy oath.

The whole thing left him with a bad taste in his mouth. But like the saying goes: Life's a bitch and then you die.

"Matt Jordan," came a voice from behind him.

Matt turned and looked at Nancy Lavelle. She ran up and hugged him for a long time in the hallway that led to the hotel ballroom. They had wanted to hold the reunion in the high school gym. But the old facility had been torn down several years back.

"Damn, boy!" she said, pulling back and hitting him on the shoulder with a small fist. "You're hard as a rock."

"And you're prettier than you were back in '67," Matt said.

Nancy rolled her eyes. "That, friend, gets you a free drink. Come on. They've got a dandy little cozy bar in this joint."

Matt had a draft beer and Nancy ordered an old-fashioned. They both sat for a time, looking at each other.

"I have to ask," Nancy broke the friendly silence. "We're all acting like a bunch of teenagers over the rumor . . ."

"Yes, I work for the CIA," Matt said with a slight smile. *And because I do, some of you or all of you just might not come back from this camping trip.*

"Are you packin' a rod?" Nancy whispered, ending it with a choked-off giggle.

"Yes," Matt laughed, then opened his specially tailored jacket so she could see the butt of the .380.

She rolled her eyes and then got serious. "It was Wade's idea that we all fly in early. Now I'm glad we did. You haven't see any of the others?"

"Not a soul. At least not to recognize."

"Oh, you'd recognize them. They really haven't changed that much. And you haven't changed at all, except . . ." She bit off the last and cut her eyes downward.

"Except what, Nance?"

"Your eyes have changed."

"Same color as before. Spit blue, one lady told me."

"Same color as before, right. But they've changed. Your lips move in a smile, but it doesn't reach your eyes."

Another lady had told him the same thing. "I'll have to get some tinted glasses so I won't look so sinister."

Nancy waved her hand and Matt twisted around in the chair. The old gang had entered the lounge. Nancy had been right. Matt knew them instantly. But his eyes were on Susan.

The men of the class of '67 all shook hands and whomped each other on the shoulder and told Matt how by-damned boy but you look in shape. The ladies all hugged and kissed him on the cheek and then Nancy suggested they move to a larger table and let's get this damn party going!

The management, wisely assuming that this bunch would eventually get noisy, suggested discreetly that they use a private room off the main lounge. Not only was it larger, but they could have full dining room services.

"You know they just kicked us out of there," Dennis said, once they had all been seated in the other room. He grinned and Matt liked him on the spot. "That means the management is the best dollars can buy and on top of things quickly. I've heard good things about this hotel."

Matt felt eyes on him and turned to stare into the gaze of Norman. Norman had been the most subdued of the bunch during their greetings, and Matt had felt that odd, since he and Norm had been the closest back in their youth.

"Something on your mind, Norm?"

The black man smiled. Actually, Norman was not black and neither was his wife, Polly. They both looked like they had good tans that never faded. "One thing about you hasn't changed, Matt. Right to the point and to hell with subtleties."

"Let's have it, buddy," Matt smiled around his words. "Or I'll tell the Bar Association about how we used to steal milk from front porches."

Norman laughed. "Yeah, but only from rich folks' porches."

"Why did you steal milk?" Nancy asked, a puzzled look on her face.

Matt looked at her. "Because sometimes our parents' paychecks just didn't stretch far enough. It was either the milk for breakfast or nothing at all."

"I never knew that," Wade and Frank both said.

Matt shrugged. "Ancient history. What's on your mind, Norm?"

"'Bout two weeks ago I called the lodge to confirm my reservation. Desk clerk said he'd been talking to another person who had graduated high school in Denver, class of '67. He said Matt Jordan had a room booked for six weeks. That sort of bothered me, Matt."

Again, Matt shrugged his shoulders. "I'm on loan-out

to another federal agency. I was working in the wilderness for them, and I'll return there after this reunion to continue working. I'm glad you brought it up."

"Why didn't you tell me this, Nance?" Susan asked.

"Hell, she didn't even tell me!" her husband said. "I bet that's the first time in her life she's been able to keep a secret for longer than ten minutes."

Everyone laughed, except Tom Dalton. He sat there like a full-gospel minister in a whore house. Matt had firmed up his opinion of the man: he didn't like him.

Norm said, "Why are you glad I brought it up, Matt?"

"Any of you people ever heard of the CWA? The Citizens for a White America?"

No one had. Or said they hadn't.

"It's a racist/survivalist group and they practice their plans for mayhem and terrorism in the wilderness area—the same place you people plan on spending two weeks camping." This was going to be his only shot, so Matt was thinking fast. "They're dangerous, gang. Very dangerous. I would like to convince you all to change your camping locations to less isolated areas. They have lovely nature trails and more secure camp sites out there."

"What government agency are you working with, Mister Jordan?" Tom Dalton asked. He put the question to him much like a king to a serf.

"Treasury Department. BATF."

"What does that mean?" Polly asked.

"Alcohol, tobacco, and firearms," her husband told her.

"What's the B stand for?" Milli asked.

"Bureau, dear," her husband said. "Matt, if they're that dangerous, you can't be working alone."

"Why not? I've worked alone in and around far more dangerous groups than this pack of rednecks."

Milli said, "But you must have . . . what's the word all the cops use on the TV? . . . backup."

"Yes, I do have backup available. But only if I decide to

86

hit the panic button."

"Then what's to worry?" Dennis said. "They bother us, we'll yell for you, and you come in with the troops."

Matt smiled, rather sadly. "Are any of you familiar with the Great Primitive Area of Idaho?"

"We've all seen pictures of it, sure," Susan said. "None of us has ever been there."

Matt had already said too much if one of them was actually funneling money to the CWA. And because of that suspicion, he couldn't tell them his backup teams were miles away—all the way across the state—and would need a day or two to get to him. He took another shot. "The man at the lodge tells me you're bringing your kids in. That's not smart, people. The CWA would hurt a child just as quickly as they would an adult."

"The children will not be allowed to leave the company of an adult, Matt," Susan said. "And we all have whistles and short-wave radios. We'll be all right, Matt. Will you be working close by?"

"If it's all right with the group, I'll camp with you."

"Great!" Dennis said. "Fine with me."

It was fine with everybody. Except for Tom Dalton. He sat scowling. Of course, Matt thought, maybe that was his normal expression.

"You'll be armed, of course?" Polly asked.

"Oh, yes," Matt assured her.

"He's armed now!" Nance said. "Nasty-looking little gun."

"What type of firearm are you carrying, Mr. Jordan?" Tom asked.

"Beretta .380."

"That doesn't have a lot of knockdown power, does it?"

"That depends on the type of ammo used. The ammunition I use is not available to the general public."

"And why is that?"

"Because it explodes on contact. At adequate pistol

range, this type of ammo gives me the same shocking power as a much larger and much heavier caliber."

"Of course, it's illegal," Tom said smugly.

"When my ass is on the line, Tom, legal doesn't mean a damn thing to me."

"We used any kind of ammo we could get our hands on in Nam," Norm said.

"That was war," Tom said. "In America, a criminal suspect should be accorded all the rights due him."

"Tom," Frank Nichols said, speaking up for the first time.

"Yes?" Tom said haughtily.

"Fuck you."

Tom's mouth dropped open and he stared across the table at the man. "I beg your pardon!"

"Let's clear the air right now," Frank said. "I am sick to death of street gangs and punks and thieves and muggers and rapists and drug dealers and murderers and off-the-wall groups like this CWA Matt just told us about operating under our noses. I think if this nation is ever going to win the fight against crime and drugs, all of us are going to have to surrender some of our rights and give the police more power. And I don't want to hear any of your back East liberal crap."

Matt gave Tom credit for some nerve. He glared across the table at the bigger man, no backup in him. "I suppose you're one of those great white hunter types with a gun in every room and the heads of dead animals you've slayed staring out from every wall."

Frank smiled. "No, sir, I do not hunt and never have. However, I do own a gun. I belong to Defenders of Wildlife and Friends of Animals and Defense of Animals and several other groups who believe that animals have rights. But if conditions continue to worsen in the streets and in the courts, I might be forced to start carrying a gun for self-protection."

Scratch Frank off your list, Richard, Matt thought. And that narrows it down considerably.

"This is certainly going to be an interesting trip," Dennis said dryly.

"I'm going to get some air," Tom said, standing up and pushing back his chair. He looked down at Susan. "Coming?"

"No."

He stalked from the room.

"Susan, honey," Milli said. "Is your husband always this charming?"

The group laughed until the management came into the room and told them they'd have to quiet down, they were bothering the other diners.

They were still laughing when they left the hotel and went looking for another place to eat.

8

After returning from dinner, Matt met the children of his former classmates. The older kids had looked after the younger ones while the parents had dinner out.

Susan's daughter, Traci, 17, had her mother's good looks and easy temperament. Tom, Jr., 11, was a well-behaved and likable kid with a good sense of humor. Wade and Nancy were taking the youngest of their three kids. Sara was 11 and cute, and Matt could see the mischief sparkling in her eyes. Dennis and Milli had brought their boy, Walter, a teenager, who was built like his father and had his mother's good looks. He was a good kid, Matt suspected, one of high intelligence and the ability to push his parents to the wall. Norman and Polly had brought their two kids, Judy and Johnny. Just approaching their teen years, the brother and sister were cute, polite, and well behaved.

Matt felt like a jerk, knowing the danger that both parents and kids would soon be facing. He excused himself and went to a pay phone to call the DCI.

"I'm not going to do it," Matt told his boss. "I refuse to put these kids in danger without their parents knowing what we're really up against."

"I see," the DCI said slowly. "Have you told them

anything about the operation?"

"Yes. Norm found out I was pre-registered at the same lodge. I had to come up with something, so I told them about the CWA."

"And they still want to go in?"

"Yes. They apparently think I can and will protect them."

"Have you found any weak links in the group?"

"Tom Dalton for sure. I think the rest of them would keep their mouths shut."

"That is something neither of us knows for certain. Here it is, Matt: either you go in, or I send someone else. Either way, this operation is green-lighted."

"And the kids be damned?"

"That is a rather vulgar way of putting it, Husky. You warned them of the CWA and they still persist. I'll make you a side bet that should you tell them of the Unseen, they will laugh in your face."

"You know I won't violate the secrecy oath, sir."

"I'm counting on it. I will make this proposition: I can have helicopters standing by to take them out at the first sign of danger. How about that?"

Most older agents do not like to use helicopters. They are too slow and too vulnerable to ground fire. Most older special operations agents don't like boats, either. Helicopters fall out of the sky and boats sink.

"Are you there, Husky?"

"All right, sir. I'll go for that."

"I'll have the choppers in place by the time you're ready to go in. Radio your exact location to the backup people as soon as you make your campsite. Good luck, Matt."

"Thank you."

The connection was broken.

He turned from the phone and spotted Susan across the hall, watching him. He walked over to her.

"Secret agent stuff, Matt?"

91

He smiled. "As a matter of fact, yes, if you want to call it that. Where's Tom?"

"Pouting in his room, probably."

"His room?"

"Yes. The kids and I are in one room, Tom is in another." She waved a hand "It's a long story and not a very happy one. I think I'll file for legal separation when we get back from Idaho. You've met him, what do you think about him?"

"I think he's pompous, arrogant, and a total asshole."

She smiled and shook her head. "That's what I remember most about you, Matt: you tell it like it is. That is an . . . apt description of Tom."

"Then why did you marry him?"

"You want to sit down out here, Matt? I really don't care much for barrooms."

"Fine."

"Like a lot of frat boys, Tom was arrogant in college. I thought he'd grow out of it. He didn't. He is very much into men's clubs and male bonding and that sort of thing. Tom is old New England money. He was privileged, pampered, spoiled. The marriage was a mistake. But . . . times rock on and we, I, rather, just rocked along with it. Now it's time to get off the boat. I suspect he'll spend two or three days camping and then leave."

Matt stared at her. "Susan, he won't be able to leave. Don't you people have any concept of where you're going? There are no roads; no vehicles allowed. If he tried to leave by himself, he'd be lost in twenty minutes. I wish to God you people would change your minds and pick a less isolated area to camp."

"Is there something you're not telling us, Matt?"

"I'm not telling you, Susan, because I can't tell you. I've told you all that you're going to be in danger. That should be enough."

"I'm sure there will be other campers with children in

the area, Matt."

He was forced to agree with that. He couldn't justify telling one group and not the other. Now he was beginning to see the bind the DCI was in. That was only one of the problems in having to operate under total secrecy: innocent people sometimes got hurt.

"All right, Susan," he finally said. "We'll play it your way."

"Dennis has a gun, Matt."

"Dennis. What kind of gun?"

"A .44 magnum. He's been taking lessons for a couple of weeks and Milli says he's pretty good with it."

"I hope to God he declared it in his luggage."

"We all had our supplies shipped to the airport in Idaho. They're in storage. We'll pick them up when we rent the cars."

Matt nodded. "I'm driving over right after the dance. You want a nightcap?"

"I don't think so. I'm tired. How about meeting for breakfast?"

"Sounds good. Eight o'clock all right?"

"I'll see you there."

He sat in the hall and watched her walk toward the elevators. A very lovely, mature woman. He put her out of his mind as best he could and walked outside for some air. He had checked out of the motel and into the hotel where the reunion would be taking place. But right now, a class reunion was the furthest thing from his mind. Deep in his guts he felt this operation was going to be a screw-up.

And there wasn't a damn thing he could do about it.

Susan stood him up for breakfast and that did not surprise Matt. After giving it some second thoughts she had probably decided she did not want to put further strain on her already shaky marriage. And she probably wanted this vacation to go as smoothly as possible, for her sake and for the sake of the kids.

The kids. They kept popping back into Matt's thoughts. Last night, after Susan had gone to her room, Matt found the others in the bar and talked to them again, trying to impress upon them the dangers they faced if they persisted in heading into a remote area of the wilderness.

After a time, he began to realize he was wasting his breath. These people simply did not believe that the government would send one man into an area to face such danger as he was describing.

Matt finally said to hell with it, had a nightcap, and went to bed.

"May I join you?" The question broke into his thoughts.

Matt looked up. Tom Dalton. "Sure. Have a seat."

Tom ordered coffee and breakfast and when the waitress had left, asked, "Why are you trying to frighten us into changing the location of this little . . . outing, Mr. Jordan?"

"The name is Matt. I am, or was, just trying to point out that this group we're investigating in the Primitive Area is big and dangerous. I think it's irresponsible to subject children to danger when it can be avoided."

"Ummm." Tom sugared and creamed his coffee. "Very commendable of you, I'm sure. I came down for a drink last night and when I passed by their table overheard the others talking about why you might be overplaying the dangers we face. Since I did not join them, I caught only a small part of the conversation."

"I assure you, I did not overplay anything. But I've had my say and I won't bring up the subject again."

"I've a good mind to check out and head back East."

"Take Susan and the kids with you when you go."

Tom paused in the lifting of coffee cup to mouth. "You're not kidding, are you, Matt? About the danger,

94

I mean."

"No."

Tom sipped and sighed, then shrugged. "Well, I have no leverage whatsoever with this group," he smiled thinly, "nor with my wife. I suspect we shall be parting ways shortly after this . . . vacation—if that is the correct terminology for one's observing the mating habits of moose and cavorting about the wilderness and communing with nature."

Matt had to chuckle. Tom was a stuffed shirt and a pompous ass, but he was trying to find some humor in all of this.

The men had little else to say to one another and Tom ate his breakfast and excused himself. Matt noticed that Tom's bill came to five dollars and fifty cents and the man left a quarter tip.

Matt wandered around the huge hotel until he found the registration area for the Denver class of 1967 and signed in. He did not know any of the people working the registration desk and they welcomed him with about as much genuine enthusiasm as a checkout clerk after a long day. The class of '67 had been a huge one, and all around the hotel little groups of middle-aged people were gathering, renewing old friendships, boring each other with pictures of their kids, and lying about how much money they were making.

Matt had a picture in his wallet of a dog he had once had while chief of station in a country in South America. A husky, naturally. Terrorists had learned Matt's real employer and had killed the dog. It takes a real brave person to kill someone's pet. There had been twelve of them in the group. Over the years Matt had found and disposed of ten. He was still looking for the other two. It had been a very nice dog.

"I feel sort of lost," Norman said, walking up to stand by Matt in the hall.

"I do know the feeling. Where is the rest of the crew?"

"Having breakfast, I guess. You look, well, fidgety, Matt."

"I am. I think I'm going to wait until the others come down, and pull out of here. I don't like these kinds of things. I don't have any old girlfriends in the group. I never was really close to anyone except for you and Susan and those in the group. So I think I'll just say to hell with it and shove off."

Like Matt, Norman had worked all during his free time in high school and had not taken part in any extracurricular activities. And, like Matt, he was no sports fan and had little patience with the rah-rah types. "I wish I could go with you," he said.

"Did you bring a piece, Norm?"

"Oh, yeah. It's with my luggage."

"What'd you bring?"

"A .32 automatic."

"I'll pick up a couple of boxes of ammo for you along the way. I also picked up some heavier firepower you can use. Just in case."

"You think it's going to come to that, Matt?"

"I tried to warn you all yesterday, partner. The smartest thing you and Polly could do is gather up your kids and go on back home."

"You're not telling us everything, are you, Matt?"

"I've told you all I can. You and me, buddy, we're the only ones in the group who ever heard a bullet whine in anger. It's going to be up to you to look after the rest of them if any kind of shitstorm flares up and I'm out of camp. Which I will be a lot of the time."

"How do you know that none of the others ever saw combat?"

"I pulled their personal files from various departments, state and federal."

"The government has that much power?"

"Oh, man. Wise up, Norm. If you've got a social security number we've got you. I'm told the IRS can access state drivers license records by computer and the state won't even know it."

"Jesus, that's unconstitutional!" The lawyer came out in the man.

Matt chuckled. "If you only knew, buddy. But I'll defend the system because it has to be. See you in Idaho, Norm."

"See you, Matt."

Matt drove straight through. He caught a few hours sleep and then began going through the supplies he had left at the lodge. Someone had carefully inspected each article and replaced them exactly as Matt had packed them. But Matt had taken tiny pebbles and put them in folded clothing, on the top of weapons and other equipment. When the pebbles fell off, there was no way the searcher could know exactly where the tiny rocks had come from.

Matt field-stripped his Mini-14 and smiled, but it was a grim smile. The firing pin was gone. He laid that one aside and went out to his Bronco. He had called Simmons in Denver and had him round up two more Mini-14's from bureau stock . . . along with some other goodies Matt felt he might need in the way of weapons. If the camp was attacked, the attackers were going to be very unhappy with the surprises Matt had in store for them.

Matt had locked his ammunition securely in metal boxes and placed tiny traps that would tell him if the boxes had been tampered with. They had not been opened. Still, he checked his ammo by going through and breaking open every tenth cartridge and pouring out the powder, checking the crimp, the case, and the primer. Everything was secure.

He checked his ropes and found tiny cuts that would

break if too much stress was put on them. He had bought extra rope in Denver. He checked everything and replaced anything that had been tampered with.

It had been Dan Watson, of course. He had given himself away that afternoon he had talked at length with Matt. The old man's hatred of hunters and trappers was not a normal thing for a man in the business of renting rooms to hunters. He had talked a bit too much of his father's sorrow at having to go in and cull out the tribe. That meant, to Matt's way of thinking, that the tribe had been, and probably still was, producing normal-appearing offspring who would leave the wilderness to become productive citizens on the outside, but always, in most cases, probably maintaining a fierce loyalty to the tribe. They were ranchers, farmers, people in all walks of life, involved in local politics, and active in state and federal government. That was the only logical answer for the pressure being put on to leave the Unseen alone.

Should he confront Dan now? Matt thought about that for a time and decided he would not. But there were people who needed to know. He took a small but very powerful high-band radio out of his Bronco and went for a walk in the woods. He strung his antenna and gave his backup people a bump on scramble.

After he had finished, the operative many miles away said, "Jesus Christ, Matt! Are you sure?"

"As sure as I can be. Let the DCI and Simmons know. Advise them I think it's going to be big and ugly."

"That's affirmative, Husky. Anything else?"

"Yeah. Tell Simmons to let the sheriff know. He'll know which one I mean. I'll monitor at regular times when I go in."

Matt shut his radio down and went back to the lodge. Dan was waiting for him.

"How was the reunion, Matt?"

"All right, I suppose. I didn't stay for the dance. Drove

straight through getting back here.''

"Why the hurry?''

"Maybe I missed your company?''

Something flickered in the old man's eyes and was gone as quickly as it came. "You find everything all right in your room?''

"Exactly as I left it. Thanks for looking after my gear. I appreciate it.''

"No sweat. The others ought to be pulling in anytime. Nick called. Said he'd be here at dawn in the morning to check the people out.''

"Yeah. They're looking forward to camping in the great outdoors.''

"I peeked in the back of your Bronco. I see you brought in some more equipment.''

"Yes. I'll need two more pack animals.''

"I'll have them for you. You're a damn fool, Jordan.''

"Oh?''

"Why don't you just take your little band of high school friends and go north instead of east in the wilderness? Tell the goddamn CIA you couldn't find anything, that it was all a hoax?''

"It's gone too far, Dan. There's been too much killing of innocent people. And you know it. You personally know it.''

Dan's face became almost savage in appearance. He visibly calmed himself. His face returned to impassiveness and his fists unclenched. "I don't know what in the hell you mean, Jordan.''

"It means cover your ass, Dan. You could kill me now; it wouldn't change a thing.'' He lifted the canvas bag containing the radio. "I just bumped my backup people. Kill me, and they'll come in. Kill them, and the government will send ten thousand troops in. It's over, Dan. I put it together. I wasn't going to let you know, but you just gave yourself away—again. So why keep it a secret? Some of you appear normal. I don't know how many. Over the years, maybe hundreds. You're in all walks of life. You're a good example of it. You . . ."

"You can't prove a goddamn thing, Jordan. You're guessing. You're farting and standing in your own stink. I suspect, Jordan, that nothing is going to happen to you or to your friends while you're camping. And you can search to your heart's content. You won't find a single member of the tribe."

"You got word to them, huh? Good for you, Dan. I'm glad. And I mean that. For the sake of the campers' kids. What did you do about the ones in the tribe who have gone bad?"

"I don't know what you're talking about."

"This is the way you're going to play it, huh?"

"Leave it alone, Jordan. Just leave it alone. You want to start a nationwide bloodbath? Is that it?"

"You're that big? There are that many of you? Is that what you mean?"

"Keep talking, CIA man. You're doing pretty well, so far."

"You're trying to breed the animal out, Dan. You don't kill and eat the people you kidnap; not right away. You breed the kidnapped men with your females, the kidnapped women with your males. It must be working. I'm looking at a member of the tribe, right?"

"You're the one flapping your gums. Go ahead. Say it all."

"Then in order to keep the bad ones happy, once a kidnap victim is no longer productive, or is injured, or becomes a problem, you give them to the cannibals among your tribe."

The look on Dan's face told Matt he had hit home.

"What do you call those people, Dan?"

"Satawsa."

"What does that mean?"

100

"It's a word in their language, Matt. It means crazy."

Matt took note that the old man said "their" instead of "our." "I hope you noticed that even though some of you are in high government positions, the pressure they exerted didn't stop me from returning."

"Goddamn CIA! You're too powerful. I hate you people. You're not untouchable, but very close to it."

"And you hate hunters and trappers because hunters have killed some of the tribe and others have been crippled by traps."

"You're very smart, Matt Jordan. Don't get too smart, though. It might be your downfall."

"Did the one I shot die, Dan?"

The man's jaw muscles bunched in thinly disguised hatred for Matt. "Yes," he finally managed to say. "After suffering for several days."

"They attacked me, Dan. Not the other way around."

"But now you're back to kill them."

"Not necessarily, I think something might be worked out."

"Like putting the people on a restricted reservation, under guard, poked and prodded by doctors? Gawked at and made fun of? Turned into sideshow freaks?"

"It's better than what they're facing, and you know it."

"I might be able to get word to them."

"I hope so. I've never hurt a soul who wasn't trying to do me harm. Oh, Dan? I replaced my Mini-14 with one that will fire. I also bought new rope and other gear. The firing pin must have fallen out and the mice must have gotten into my other equipment. But I'm a nice guy. I won't hold you responsible for the damage."

The look Matt received was one of pure savage fury.

9

The others pulled in during the middle of the afternoon and they were all, even Tom, awed into silence by the quiet grandeur surrounding them.

"I feel like I'm in the middle of nowhere," Frank said.

"You are," Matt told him. "Come on, I'll show you all the horses and you can start to get acquainted."

Dan must have called Nick immediately after talking with Matt, for the guide was over within the hour with the packhorses Matt had requested. Matt took one look at the man and knew that he, like Dan, was a normal member of the tribe. His eyes flashed hate at Matt. And it was the eyes that gave them away. They were animal eyes. That's what Matt had noticed about Dan, and it didn't register at first.

Dan came out and began assigning horses to people. He gave the oldest and gentlest animals to the women and children, and Matt was amazed at how the animals took to the man, and then to the kids. It was as if he was silently communicating with them, in their language, and, Matt thought: maybe he was.

Matt leaned against the corral rails and watched as Dan showed them all how to saddle up and rig the packs on the pack animals. Dan watched them all fumble around getting into the saddle and managed not to laugh at their awkward attempts. The kids caught on quickly, and Dan let them ride out into the pastures around the place. Susan had ridden often as a youth, and it did not take her long to get back into the swing of it. Tom bobbed up and down like a cork with a catfish on the line when he rode, as did Norman and Dennis. Frank had had some experience with riding, and he handled himself pretty well.

Nancy and Milli and Polly and Cathy made a game of it and soon were able to stay in the saddle with some ease.

"You folks will be all right, I'm thinking," Dan finally said. "Nick will set a very easy pace and you'll be surprised how many miles you'll cover in a day. I'm goin' back in and start supper. You folks ride a while longer; quit when you get ready."

Matt called a halt to it a half hour later. "You don't want to get too stiff and sore your first day. We have a lot of miles to cover in the next couple of days."

"Do you know where we're going?" Frank asked him while stripping the saddle from his mount.

"I know the general area."

"And? . . ."

"Don't get lost."

"I'll be poking along behind the group," Matt told the guide the following morning. The sun had not yet risen, and neither had the campers from the city.

"Don't get lost," Nick warned him. The guide was in his fifties, Matt guessed, but lean as a piece of rawhide, and probably just as tough. The warning, Matt figured, was an automatic response from the man, since he was 99 percent certain Nick was of the tribe and Dan had told him everything he knew about Matt.

"I know how to go in, I know how to get out," Matt replied in an easy tone of voice.

"So I been told," was Nick's response. He turned and

walked out onto the porch, taking his mug of coffee with him.

Strong, silent cowboy type, Matt thought. With the blood of savages coursing hotly through his veins.

"I'll rouse the others," Matt said to Dan.

"You do that."

Matt went from door to door, awakening the others. "Let's go, gang!" he yelled. "Head 'em up and move 'em out." he added with a smile.

"Jesus, what time is it?" Dennis said, sticking his head out the door and rubbing sleep from his eyes.

"It's 4:30," Matt told him. "Time's a-wastin'."

"This must be like the army," the man replied.

"Similar," Matt said. "But only to a very small degree." He walked on, waking the others.

The campers gathered in the dining area of the small lodge and stood staring at the biggest breakfast many of them had ever seen. There were mounds of flapjacks, piles of bacon, biscuits and gravy, scrambled eggs, country butter, and jars of home-canned jellies and preserves.

The astonished stares brought smiles from both Dan and Nick. Whatever their background, the men knew how to cook and liked to do it.

Over breakfast, Nick laid down the rules of the trail. "You get tired and want to stop, sing out. One thing we're not in is no hurry. You see a pretty flower, admire it and leave it alone. It ain't yours to pick. The only thing you shoot in yonder is a camera . . ." His eyes briefly flickered to Matt and narrowed. The others did not notice the glance. ". . . It's two days in to where I'm taking you, and two days out. That means you got ten days to fish and relax and enjoy the beauty. You start a forest fire, you pay for the damage it causes. I'll show you all how to make a safe fire for cooking and for warmth. Don't nobody wander off from the group alone. I'm told they's some among you who knows how to use a compass. That's good. Be darn sure you take your headings before we leave this area. You was good enough to spread your gear out for me last evening. You come well prepared, and you shouldn't have no trouble in the wilderness. I'll tell you other do's and don'ts as we move along. So eat up, people. We pull out at dawn and it's a long time 'til nooning."

When Matt walked to his horses, just as dawn was breaking, he had put his .380 in his saddlebags and had a big Beretta 9mm 92F in a flap holster on his web belt. Four fully loaded clips were carried just behind the holster on the right side. Each clip held fifteen rounds. The 9mm had a round chambered and the hammer down. He carried his Mini-14 in a specially made hard leather-and-aluminum saddle boot which compensated for the long, thirty-round clip. The boot was a break-open type, eliminating the need to pull the weapon up and out. Matt had designed the boot himself while working in rough country in South America.

He attached the boot to the saddle, then saw to his pack animals, fixing the lead rope from one to the other.

Nick came to him, out of earshot of the others. "There ain't no need for all that firepower, Mr. Secret Agent man." He spoke in low tones, his lips scarcely moving. "The word's done gone out. The Sataws has been rounded up and under guard. The leaders is talking over a way to come out of hiding and reveal themselves, try to work out a plan that'll be acceptable to all."

"I'm glad, Nick. I truly am. But there is still the CWA in there."

"For a fact. I keep forgetting about those nuts. You really whip hell out of three of them bare-handed?"

"Me and a frying pan."

The man allowed himself a faint smile. "Them pack animals I brought you are trained to follow the other. You shouldn't have no trouble with them. Matt, no decent one among us ever bothered a child or a camper that didn't come to kill. They's been thousands of people walked the trails and paths admiring the beauty who was left alone. It's only them that came to kill that was taken. And you was wrong about us giving them that was taken to the Sataws. Most died a natural death. The pure among us—like the one you shot—has got germs that will eventually kill a human. That's how the taken died and they was given a decent burial. Maybe not the kind that you're used to, but decent according to the tribe's ways. You see, a routine physical won't show nothing out of the ordinary among us that crossed over. But a lot of lab work would. We walk a fine line, me and Dan and the others. I ain't sayin' what we done was right or just. But it was the only way we knew to breed out the savage in us. We're just like any other race of people: we got both good and bad among us. I just wanted you to know that."

"I appreciate you telling me this. I sent word last night to my people. They're meeting now—probably met all night—with certain people in government, trying to work something out. I hope they can."

"I hope they can, too, Matt. 'Cause they's a lot of us out here with fierce ties to the tribe. And like it's said: blood is thicker than water. If we have to go down, we'll damn sure take a lot of others with us."

The campers climbed into their saddles and pulled out, heading east. Nick was at the head of the column, Matt brought up the rear. The kids were placed in the center of the column for safety's sake.

A mile from the lodge, they were already plunged into wilderness that had not changed in thousands of years. Nick took a trail that was foreign to Matt, but Matt had taken his heading and knew where he was.

"What's that?" Sara called, pointing to a fallen building.

"Call 'em wanigans," Nick told her. "They used to log in here, float the timber down the river. A wanigan is slang for a floating bunkhouse. All kind of timber in here, but some kinds don't float as good as others. Eastern oak, beech, maple, and birch have to be tied together and rafted with lighter woods. Some loggers let them dry for months so's they'll float better. They don't log in here no more, thank the gods."

Not God, Norm noted, and he seemed to be the only one who picked up on that. But "the gods." Strange.

Norm twisted in the saddle—and almost fell out of it—to see if Matt had heard the strange comment. But Matt was far back of the pack, riding like a real cowboy, the reins held in his left hand, his right hand free. Norm wondered what Matt had in those bulky packs on the horses.

When Nick finally called a halt for lunch, the kids jumped from the horses to play and the adults climbed carefully from the saddles, sure they would never be able to walk again.

"Nice horsy," Dennis said. "Stand still now."

"Ungainly brute!" Tom muttered. The horse swung its head around and stared at him. "Now, now," Tom forced a gentler tone. "I was only kidding."

Nick had them gather around and showed them the proper way to build a campfire in the wilderness. Dig a pit and circle that with stones. "Don't never build a bigger fire than you need," he warned. "Wastes fuel, cooks your food too fast, catches the grease in your skillet on fire, and throws off too many sparks. Now let's see what you-all brought to eat."

After lunch—which Nick made the campers cook and which was edible, but just barely—Matt fixed his own lunch. Nick showed them how to cut out a piece of sod, dig a hole to bury their trash, and then replace the sod. "That way it don't disturb the beauty of nature, and in two or three days you won't be able to find where you buried it."

Matt noted that whatever else Nick was, he knew what he was doing in the wilderness, he loved it, and he cared for his charges and wanted them to take care of the wilderness.

Matt lagged far behind the group, always scanning his surroundings for trouble. He did not expect any trouble from the Unseen, for he believed that wiser heads would prevail and, if at all possible, they would accept the terms offered them and come out of hiding. Matt believed the trouble would come from the CWA. They were a large group, although the entire membership was not centralized in the primitive areas of Idaho by any means, and they were a dangerous group. Monroe Bishner—"Hairy Ears"—would be gunning for Matt after the frying pan incident.

Matt put his horses into a trot when he saw the group was stopped and a half a dozen strange horses, with riders, were in front of them, facing the campers. When he rode up, Nick was facing the men, who were clad in tiger-stripe battle dress.

"What's the problem, Nick?"

"This trash," the guide said. "They seem to think they own the whole damn place."

Matt untied the rope to his pack animals and handed the free end to Norm. "Hold that, please." He rode up to the bigger and uglier of the survivalists. "What's your problem, buddy?"

"We ain't got no problem. We were just ridin' along, mindin' our own business, when cowboy here come up leadin' this bunch of niggers and Jews. I said, 'well now, would you boys just take a look at the niggers and Jews.' That's what they is, ain't they? If that chubby feller right there," he pointed to Dennis, "ain't a kike, I'll climb a tree and howl at the moon."

Dennis climbed down from the saddle and said, "Let me handle this, Matt."

"Dennis . . . ?"

"No, Matt," Milli said. "Let him. Please."

Matt looked at Nick, arched an eyebrow, and Nick did the same. Both men backed their horses out of the way.

"Kick his ass, Dad!" Walt said.

"I intend to," Dennis said.

"Son of a bitch is crazy, Luther!" One of Luther's buddies yelled. "Jump down there an' whup his ass, boy!"

"Everybody get down and picket your horses," Nick said. He pointed. "Over there. I don't want them spooked when all this fightin' starts."

Matt looked over at Dennis and changed his mind quickly about the man. Dennis had pulled off his shirt to stand in his T-shirt. The man's arms were massive, his stomach looked flat and hard, and his shoulders were wide and thickly muscled. Milli walked up to Matt.

"He was a street fighter in Brooklyn, Matt. He can take care of himself."

"I believe it. But this scum has no intention of fighting by any rules."

Milli allowed herself a small smile. "Neither does Dennis. I can assure you of that, believe me. Two thugs broke into our house last year with plans of terrorizing us. When the police got there, the two thugs were unconscious and had to be taken to the hospital. Dennis did that with his bare hands . . ."

Matt was listening to her and watching both Dennis and the bigger and taller man from the CWA get ready for a fight.

"Five years ago, Dennis worked late at his law firm and a mugger tried to rob him. Dennis broke the man's back. There have been other incidents, but you'll soon see what I mean. Several very hardened and street-wise cops have told me, off the record, that Dennis can be one mean son-of-a-bitch when he's pushed."

The five other cammie-clad survivalists had dismounted and picketed their horses. Matt had watched as Norm had taken something from his saddlebags and shoved it behind his belt, under his windbreaker. Matt had a pretty good idea what it was. He hoped none of the survivalists tried to interfere in the fight, for Matt remembered Norm as having a hair-trigger temper, and after Nam—judging from his military records—Norm would not hesitate to shoot.

The big pus-gutted CWA man was standing near his friends, laughing and making very rude remarks along racial lines when Dennis walked up to him and smashed him in the mouth with a hard right fist. Luther went down in a sprawl of arms and legs, his mouth bleeding.

Dennis didn't hesitate nor change expressions. He drew back a boot and kicked Luther in the gut. Matt relaxed a bit. Brooklyn-born and streetwise, Dennis had no illusions about fair fighting.

As if reading Matt's thoughts, Milli said, "He's also an avowed Republican."

Matt had to chuckle at that.

Luther got up cussing and hollering and swung at Dennis. Dennis ducked the punch and blasted the man two hard blows to the stomach, a left and a right. Luther staggered back, a hurt look on his unshaven face. He kept backing up, trying to catch his breath. Dennis had not said a word. He was too wise in fighting to waste his breath talking.

Dennis faked Luther and drove a left hook into the bigger man's jaw. Luther spat out blood and part of a broken tooth and back-heeled Dennis and sent him to the ground. Dennis rolled quickly, avoiding the kick, jumped to his feet and came in swinging. Luther connected with a couple of punches, but they seemed to have no effect on Dennis.

Luther's friends made movements that indicated they wanted to jump into the middle of the fight. Matt dropped

110

his right hand to the butt of his 9mm and that stopped Luther's friends before they could get started. They stood in silence and watched Luther get the shit beat out of him.

Dennis hit Luther a combination left and right to the face. The left broke the man's nose and sent blood squirting, and the right bored in and hit Luther flush on the mouth, smashing his lips.

There was a darkening mouse under Dennis' left eye and a cut on his cheek, but he paid no attention to them. He relentlessly stalked Luther, his big fists smashing the man's face and hammering at his belly.

Luther was knocked down and Dennis backed up, his fists held chest high. "Get up, you ignorant son-of-a-bitch!" Dennis spoke for the first time in the fight. "Get on your feet and fight, goddamn you!"

"He's had enough," one of the CWA men said.

"Shut your damn mouth or step over here and take a swing at me," Matt told him.

"I ain't got no quarrel with you, mister," the CWA man said.

"Then button your mouth."

The survivalist shut up.

Luther staggered to his combat boots. His face was a mess: eyes swelling closed, blood dripping from his nose and mouth. The thought managed to work its way through the maze of seldom-used gray matter in his brain that Dennis was not going to allow him to quit. If he came up with a knife, that hard-looking, pale-eyed man would shoot him. Luther didn't know how he knew that, but he knew it was a fact. There was only one way this fight was going to be over: either he'd win it, or Jew-boy would. And Luther knew he didn't have a chance in hell of winning. They'd sure misjudged this bunch of campers.

"I'll give you this much," Luther panted the words, the blood dripping from his busted mouth. "You can fight."

"Thanks," Dennis said, then stepped in and hit the man

twice, a left and right to either side of his jaw.

Luther swayed for a moment, his eyes glazing over, then dropped like a rock and didn't move. He was out cold.

Dennis walked back to his horse, got his canteen, and began cleaning up.

Nick smiled and lifted his right hand from his side. Matt had not seen him get it, but there was a long-barreled single-action pistol in the guide's hand, the hammer back. Nick lowered the hammer and stuck the gun behind his belt.

Matt walked to his horse and swung into the saddle. The others slowly followed suit. They rode off, leaving the CWA men still gathered around the prostrate Luther.

Nick chuckled as he rode ahead of the others. "I like this bunch of folks," he said to his horse. "Best group I think I ever took in. Good people. Fair-minded people with well-behaved children. And that was the best fight I've seen in many a year. I'd like to have these folks for neighbors." He turned in the saddle in time to see Tom Dalton almost fall off his horse. "Well," Nick concluded. "Most of them, anyways."

10

They made camp in mid-afternoon, Nick choosing a site by a rushing stream. "Don't drink the water without first purifying it," he warned them. "There was a time you could, but them days is long gone. The place I'm taking you is by a stream like this. It's good water, but you-all still should doctor it up 'fore you drink it, just to be on the safe side."

By themselves, Matt asked, "Nick, can you drink the water without being affected by it?"

"Not no more. When my momma and daddy and me first crossed over we could. But it didn't take civilization long to catch up with us. Once we get out here with all the chemicals in the water and in the food, it does something to our system. Changes us. And I ain't real sure it's for the better."

"How many in the tribe, Nick?"

"It's down to about six or seven hundred now. The thing I'm worried about is the Sataws breaking away. The rest of the tribe can read and write and figure and speak English." He smiled at the look on Matt's face. "Oh, yeah. We have schools. Those of us on the outside bring back books."

"Nick, what about those who killed Gene Gaston and

his wife?"

The guide sighed. "A problem there. We're all over the country, Matt. From New York City to Los Angeles. From Canada to Mexico. We been comin' out for two or three centuries. You got to try to understand the fear that many on the outside feel. If the general public was to learn they come from . . . well, hell, animal-like savages, how many would be shunned and lose their jobs or hunted down and killed? It's a problem that them still in the wilderness can't do nothing about."

"You can revert, can't you, Nick?"

"Some can," he admitted. "I can't. I . . . feel the urge to run free from time to time. But it isn't an overpowering emotion. I used to do it as a boy. Just strip off and run through the woods, talkin' to the animals and being free. My momma and daddy caught me once and whaled the livin' tar out of me. I never done it again. And as I grew older, I understood why my parents forbade me."

"The ones that are coming out now, they're, how do I say this, purer than those who came before?"

"Yeah. You see, Matt, it's kind of like when you cross a shepherd or a husky with a wolf. They call them hybrids. But you never know what you got until they grow older. Genetics, I'm talking about. You might get a 75-25 hybrid, with the dog at the low end of that percentage. As the animal matures, he or she might be almost pure dog in behavior, or they might be total wolf in behavior. It's not quite the same with us on the outside, but close. It ain't regression in a physical sense. There are no fangs protruding or hairy-clawed hands or anything like that. Not like you see in the movies. It's mental. And I've had to kill some that couldn't cope with it."

Matt stared at the man.

"Yeah. A lot of us on the outside have had to do things that we didn't really want to do in order to protect the others. It isn't easy, and it don't get any easier with time, either. We've known for a long time that Gaston had a file on us. His office in Denver was under twenty-four-hour watch. You show up there and then you show up out here and Dan made you quick. I don't know who killed the man and his wife. We got some on the outside that shouldn't be there; they slipped through our screening. Once there, they moved. They changed the names we gave them and got new social security numbers. The whole bit. They have their own network and they don't fight the urge. It's pleasant, Matt. Just go back to nature and be like a big animal. But these big animals, they like to kill. Dan told you I was visiting my kid over in Washington. I wasn't. I was helping track down and destroy those with more Sataw in them than human. And that's going to be another mark against us, I reckon."

"Did you destroy them?"

"Oh, yeah. One cell of them. But they's cells all over the damn country."

"Cannibalistic?"

"Oh, yeah. They might be high-powered executives, or mechanics or whatever during the week, and then let the urge take them during the weekend. We can see the tribe in each other, Matt . . ."

"Yeah. The eyes."

"You're a smart one. I said that already, but it bears repeating. Yeah. The eyes are a dead giveaway if you know what to look for. Them on the outside that don't fight the urge—they seek out and recruit others who are doing poorly in business or unhappy with their jobs or with their marriage or whatever. They sing a song to them, Matt. I don't mean they actually sing to them, but what they say about the urge setting them free makes sense to someone unhappy. Then they get the taste of blood in their mouth, and they're hooked forever."

"Can't you deprogram them?"

He shook his head. "No. And better people than me has

115

tried." He smiled. "Oh, yeah, Matt. We have medical doctors and psychiatrists and engineers and scientists— you name it, those on the outside are filling those jobs. The urge to run free is a strong one. If it's a weak person to start with, and the Sataw is persuasive . . ." He shrugged his shoulders. "Back to the wild."

"If those on the outside who have gone bad know I'm in here, they might return for a shot at me, right?"

"Possible. Highly possible. And they know you're here. Yeah. I'd say that's another worry you got."

"I really didn't need another one, Nick."

Chuckling, the guide moved over to the campsite to help with supper.

"This can't go unavenged," Monroe Bishner said, after looking at the battered Luther. "You said there was a hard-lookin' pale-eyed man with them, Jones?"

"Yeah. And I don't think he was some city dude come on a camping vacation neither. He was all business and looked damn fit to me."

"It's the same man." Monroe touched his still-sore face with his fingertips. He would carry some of the scars from the hot grease burn for the rest of his life. His quickly thrown up forearm had protected his eyes from the scalding grease, and he was lucky in that. "I want that bastard. I want him bad. Luddy, you and Jim Bob lay back and trail them. I want to see where they camp."

"Some fine lookin' women in that bunch," Luther was reminded. "They got a girl with 'em that looked to be about eighteen. She's prime stuff."

"Now would be the time for us to practice tactics," another said. "It'd be fun to lay out in the timber and scare them city folks."

The men gathered around grinned at the prospect of that. Then one of them who had been at the fight sobered.

"I don't know," he said, shaking his head. "That Jew-boy is strong and quick and mean. Just ask Luther. But that pale-eyed feller is the one that worries me. Me and Floyd was watchin' him all durin' the fight, wasn't we, Floyd?" Floyd bobbed his head in agreement. "He never changed expression. Didn't show no emotion a-tall. And when he told Ray to either shut up or fight him, his voice was cold. Real cold. Naw, Monroe, I'd leave this bunch alone."

"Nobody asked you, Alton. Anytime you want to haul your ass outta here, you just take off."

"I didn't say nothin' about me pullin' out," Alton said sullenly.

"Then you'll do what you're told without questioning orders. I want to know something about that pale-eyed fellow. I think he's some sort of law."

Alton wanted to say if that's what the guy was, the best thing to do would be to leave him alone, wouldn't it? But he didn't say it. He didn't want the others to think him a coward. But any man who could whup Monroe and two others with nothing more than a damn fryin' pan was someone to be left alone.

Monroe was saying, ". . . And I'm gettin' tired of this feeling of being watched all the damn time. Now by God someone is out there lookin' at us, and I want to know who it is. And don't come back here with a bunch of damn excuses about how you can't find nobody. I'm tired of hearin' it. Whitman, you and Hardin and Yates gear up and go find whoever that is sneakin' around lookin' in on us. How the hell do you think we're ever gonna take over the government when we can't even find some damn peeper? Now move out!"

Matt and Norm took their flyrods and walked over to the stream. The fish were striking at anything that jiggled on the water and between them they soon had a mess of trout—enough for everyone to have a taste. They cleaned the fish and took them back to camp, giving them to Nick.

"You folks gather around," Nick said. "I'm gonna show you how to make a batter so good it'll make you wanna slap your granny."

The kids had taken to Nick immediately and it was obvious that the man liked kids.

"You got kids of your own, Mister Nick?" Sara asked.

"A whole passel of them. Four. And I got two grandkids and another one due in the fall. Sounds like an invadin' army when they all gather at home. Now pay attention to what I'm doing here. I'm showing you a secret recipe."

They ate supper early, and all of them were surprised by their hearty appetites: they ate up everything in sight.

"This country will do it to you," Matt explained. "Not just here, but any wilderness area. You get away from smog and chemicals and smoke and pressures and begin to relax."

"What kind of rifle is that you've got, Mister Jordan?" eleven year old Tommy asked.

"Mini-14."

"Is it a machine gun?"

"No. It's a semi-automatic rifle. Some people call them assault rifles."

"The kind that a lot of people want to outlaw?"

"Yes. So I've heard. I've been out of the country for a long time, Tommy. I'm just now catching up on a lot of things that have been happening in America. But those people who are trying to disarm American citizens are wrong. That's just one person's opinion and your parents might not agree with me."

"I certainly disagree with you," Tom Dalton said.

"I could have guessed that, Tom," Matt said with a smile.

"I don't disagree with you," Dennis said. "The punks and thugs and creeps are taking over the country. The

118

police are overwhelmed, and the damn liberals want to disarm tax-paying, law-abiding citizens. It's ridiculous."

In what remained of the fast-waning sunlight, Matt caught a glimpse of movement across the stream. He cut his eyes to Nick. The guide had also seen it. Nick pointed to his chest and shook his head quickly, the minute shake telling Matt that whoever it was, it was not a member of the tribe.

Nancy said, "I think it's a national disgrace that people have to be subjected to all the gang violence that's taken over the streets. I can't understand why the police just don't go in and shoot them!"

"Nancy!" Susan looked shocked. "These are words from the most liberal democrat I ever knew?"

"No more, kid. We were young, idealistic fools back in our college days. You're looking at an avowed Republican who is sick to death of punks and street gangs and soaring crime rates."

"You stirred it up now, Susan," Wade said with a smile. "If Nancy had her way, she'd strap on six-guns and volunteer for the first firing squad to be formed."

Whoever it was across the stream had settled down and was watching the group. Matt had detected only one person so far, but he was fairly certain the watcher was not alone.

The boundaries had been laid out for the kids. They could go no further than the edge of the camp or the bank of the stream and the rules were accepted without grousing. Already the shadows were thickening and the campfire was a comforting sight to the kids. None of them seemed to want to leave the flickering light.

A high wailing note sprang out of the twilight and straightened Milli up. "What was that?"

"Wolf," Nick told her. "Relax. They won't bother you. All that crap you've been taught over the years is just that: pure garbage. I ain't never heard of a healthy, unprovoked wolf attacking a human being. If Little Red Riding Hood was eaten up by a wolf, she more than likely was pokin' the animal in the eye with a stick to get it riled."

Two men, Matt concluded after catching a sight of movement about a hundred yards north of the initial sighting. But this one had been a bit more careless than the first. Matt had caught a glimpse of camouflage in the last rays of light. The CWA was stalking them.

"When you leave us day after tomorrow, Mr. Nick," Traci said, wanting to move the conversation away from guns and politics, "won't you be afraid coming back all alone?"

Nick shook his head and smiled. "What's to be afraid of, girl? I been ridin' this country for a long, long time. I know all the secret places, all the streams and little lakes that few others have seen. I've had outlaws come at me from time to time, to take my possessions. I brung them out to the sheriff hung over the back of my packhorse."

"You killed them?" the teenager asked.

"I sure didn't give 'em a big smooch and a hug, miss. Mrs. Lavelle is right about outlaws. I know of a society where if a member steals from another member, he or she dies. They just won't tolerate it . . ."

"One of those archaic and barbarous Moslem sects," Tom Dalton said.

Darkness had fallen swiftly, and although Matt could not see Nick's face, he knew the man was smiling. And he also knew what society the man was talking about; it was a hell of a lot closer to their present location than it was to the Mideast.

"Something like that," Nick spoke from out of the darkness. He leaned forward and laid another stick on the fire.

"In the movies, they always throw it on the fire," Johnny Hunt said.

"Hollywood nonsense," Nick told him. "Tossing a

120

stick on the fire dislodges a lot of sparks. It's a dangerous and stupid thing to do anytime, but especially when you're in the timber."

"Yes, sir," the boy said. "I'll remember that."

"I know you will," the guide said. "You're a good boy. I've taken to all you kids. And I don't usually do that. You're a good bunch of people." With that, Nick rose as gracefully as Matt had ever seen any man do and stood up. "I'm gonna take me a walk. You wanna come along, Matt?"

"Yeah." Matt rose to his hiking boots. He looked at Norm. "Keep everybody close, Norm." He spoke very softly.

"Trouble?"

"Maybe. Keep everybody in sight."

A horrible scream cut the night, startling the campers and bringing them all to their feet. The screaming was followed by a roar, then a grunt, then a splatting sound. Then silence.

"What in God's name was that?" Wade asked.

"We'll find out," Nick said. "All of you, stay put! Let's go, Matt." Nick ran for his rifle while Matt popped open his rifle case and pulled out his Mini-14.

"It came from across the river," Matt said.

"Yeah. We'll cross down yonder about a hundred yards. Old tree down makes a perfect bridge."

"Luddy!" Jim Bob shouted from across the narrow but fast-moving stream. "Luddy! Where are you, boy?"

But Luddy could not hear him and would never reply. Luddy's headless torso lay crumpled like a child's tossed-away doll. One leg was bent under him, shattered by the body impacting with a tree at tremendous force.

"Luddy!" Jim Bob bellered. "You'd best answer me, boy."

Nick found the body. A dark ribbon of shiny blood on bark marked the spot where the headless body had

121

smashed against the tree and slid down.

"Luddy!" Jim Bob squalled.

Matt looked down at the broken body. "Jesus! What in hell did this?"

"Not one of ours, Matt. Look yonder; see that dark shiny smear of blood? That's a good thirty feet this man was throwed. Ain't a one of us got that much strength. The Sataws is plenty strong, but not that strong."

"Then . . ."

"Luddy! Damn it, boy, where are you?"

"Omah," Nick said softly.

"What the hell is that?"

"Oh-mo-hah is what the Indians named him, or them. It was shortened to Omah . . . I don't know when. Years ago. They're giant people, but basically gentle people who live in the wilderness areas, and not just around here. They've been spotted in areas from the Pacific coast all the way to Michigan."

"Giant people? Oh, come on, Nick!"

"Luddy! God damn it, boy, where are you?" Jim Bob hollered.

"Luddy's dead, you halfwit!" Nick yelled. "Git on over here and look at him and then carry your ass out of the wilderness."

"Where's here?" Jim Bob called. "I can't see my hand in front of my face. And who the hell are you?"

"Just follow the sound of my voice," Nick said patiently. "I'll talk you over here."

"Giant people?" Matt once again questioned.

"Speak up, man!" Jim Bob yelled. "I can't hear you."

"Come on, boy. We ain't thirty feet from the stream. Your side. Just follow it and turn right. That's north," he added dryly.

"Are you putting me on, Nick? Giant people?"

"They been here a lot longer than us, Matt. But I'm gonna tell this idiot it was a bear. As dumb as those people are, they'll believe damn near anything."

"I agree with that. Dumb but dangerous."

"You got it."

Jim Bob stumbled through the brush and pulled up short at the sight of the headless Luddy. He took a closer look, then turned his head and threw up.

"Oh, my God!" he finally gasped. "What done this?"

"Bear," Nick said. "They been known to tear the head off a person."

"Why?" Jim Bob said, disgust in his voice.

"To eat it, I reckon," Nick said with a straight face. "You go get a tarp from your horse and we'll help you wrap this fellow up. Then you can go on mindin' your own damn business and stop followin' us."

"Unless you want one of us to ride back and call the law about it," Matt said. "This is federal land, so U.S. marshals will be quick about coming in." The Marshal's Service couldn't care less about any bear attack, but Matt figured this dimwit wouldn't know that.

"Uh . . ." Jim Bob paused, thinking hard, which must have been quite a strain. "I reckon we'll take care of the seeing to the body. I'll fetch me a ground sheet for Luddy."

"Omah must have had a good reason for killin' this crud," Nick said, when Jim Bob had gone for the ground sheet. "They probably spooked him, or her, and maybe took a shot or two at it. They might have wounded one thinking it was a bear. If you see one, and the odds is strong against it, just let it be and go on about your business. They won't bother you."

"Nick, what in the hell is an Omah?"

"Oh, you been readin' about them since you was a boy, Matt. Some Indians call them Sasquatch. Most people just call them Bigfoot."

11

"Bigfoot!" Dennis was about one decibel below shouting the word. "You mean those damn things really exist?"

Nick chuckled as he fed more sticks to the fire. "Sure. But like most creatures of the forests, if you leave them alone, they'll leave you alone. That one has probably been tracking Luddy what's-his-name for no telling how long, seeking revenge for something. Most likely, Luddy shot and wounded its mate. Or he may have shot and wounded this particular Omah. I'd bet it was one or the other."

The usually unflappable Tom Dalton looked around him. "Where, uh, do you suppose this mythical beast is now? Not that I believe a word of this, you understand."

Nick sat the coffeepot on the stones to brew a fresh pot. "Long gone, Mister Dalton. No need for alarm. There are a few simple rules that you can follow in the wilderness that will help to keep you alive. If you come up on a half-eaten carcass, you get the hell gone from that area. Don't run, just walk quickly. More than likely you've come up on a bear's cache of food, and they can get right testy about their food. The same goes for the big cats in here. A grizzly is the most unpredictable of them all. They can run faster than you can. You get a grizzly on your tail, you're in a world of hurt. But bear attacks are rare if a person just uses a little common sense. You see, folks, this country ain't your country; this belongs to the animals."

"Bigfoot," Sara said. "I'd like to see one."

"Yeah, me, too," Judy Hunt echoed.

"You won't," Nick told them. "But they've seen you. Just like the wolves have seen us and the bears and the cats have seen us this day. They aren't interested in us as long as we leave them alone."

"What were those racists doing following us?" Cathy asked. "I don't like the idea of being followed by those types of people."

"Nor do I," Nancy echoed Cathy's sentiments.

Nick shrugged his shoulders.

"They want revenge for the beating I gave three of them a couple of weeks ago and for the beating Dennis handed Luther," Matt said. "And they probably suspect I'm some kind of lawman."

"You whipped three of them?" Wade asked.

"Yes. People like that rarely come at a man one on one. They're basically cowards. So put any thoughts of fair play out of your minds. It's not too late for you people to change your minds," Matt reminded the group. "You can always have Nick take you to a less isolated part of the area."

"I'd recommend it," the guide said.

"I refuse to allow crap and crud like that to ruin my vacation," Wade said. "I vote we stay on course."

It was unanimous among the group members. They would not change their plans.

Matt had no more to say on the subject. Later, when the others had gone to bed, he and Nick pulled back from the campsite and talked.

"Something's been bothering me, Nick—I'd like for you to clear it up. You said when the urge to change came, it wasn't physical, but mental. That doesn't ring true with the savage attacks. What about the fang marks on Mrs.

125

Gaston and some of the others?"

"Some of the breakaways I told you about returned to the wilderness area and lured throwbacks out. Maybe one out of ten children born are throwbacks—pure Sataw, mentally and physically. They ain't pretty to look at. The tribe voted about five years ago to start destroying those who are imperfect. It's a hard thing to do, but they all knew it was necessary for survival. Them on the outside are the older ones. The breakaways hide them out and run with them when the urge strikes."

"How widespread is it?"

"I'd say it's pretty much confined to the rural areas of this section of the country. Pretty much on the west side of the Divide."

"But you're not sure?"

"No."

"Nick, do you realize the problems facing the general public should news of this ever get out?"

"Yeah," the guide replied, a weary and sad note in his words. "I do. But the leaders know that civilization is closing in on them. They voted to do it this way rather than put it off and be discovered by some goddamn hunters or trappers and then have to face a hysterical mob of misinformed folks with blood lust runnin' hot and high."

"I believe they made the right decision, Nick."

"I hope so, Matt. If just one bobble is made, if just one person screws up, it could get bloody for a lot of people. Disregard everything Dan said about him sidin' with the tribe. He won't. He's just angry and sad and somewhat bitter. But the younger ones who haven't been on the outside long will. Bet on that. It's got to be handled on the Q.T., Matt. And I don't know how you're gonna arrange to get the tribe out of here."

"Fly them out."

Nick shook his head. "Maybe. But I don't know about

126

that. Matt, these people have never seen a helicopter or plane up close. Some of the older ones still think they're some sort of giant bird of prey. The younger ones know better, but they'd still be scared half out of their minds if one landed close."

"I guess now is as good a time as any to bump my contact and see if anything has been firmed up. Do you think we need to post a watch tonight?"

"I don't see the point in it. The Sataw ain't gonna bother us and them fools like them was trackin' us make enough noise to raise the dead. I seen you got perimeter bangers; use them after I leave you."

Matt strung his antenna, slipped on his headset, flipped the scramble toggle switch, and called in.

"The plans now are for them to be taken to an old National Guard base in Montana. It's damn near inaccessible. We've got army combat engineers moving in there now to fix the place up and troops on standby to be flown in for security. Sugar Cube has been advised, and so have members of both houses of Congress that we know can keep their damn mouths shut. Big Daddy One has warned that if anyone leaks this to the press, they will face dire consequences, and I think he convinced those in the know that he means it."

"The CWA is going to be a problem." He told his contact what happened that evening.

"Bigfoot!"

"Yes."

"Are you serious, Husky?"

"Yes."

"Can you get one for study?"

"Now, God damn it!"

"Okay, okay, Husky. Calm down. It was just a thought. This CWA bunch, do they have any redeeming qualities?"

"Hell, no."

"Stand by. I've got to check on this."

Matt waited for nearly half an hour.

"Husky?"

"Right here." Matt was an old hand at this. He activated a small tape recorder.

"You have the authority to deal with the CWA in an extremely prejudicial manner."

"Put it in plain English and make it blunt."

"Are you taping this?"

"You're damn right I am. And if a certain Marine lieutenant colonel had been smart, he'd have done the same thing. Who's giving me the authority to kill?"

"Stand by, Husky," the voice said patiently.

Matt waited for another half hour.

"Husky?"

"I haven't gone into hibernation."

"Due to the extremely sensitive nature of this operation, with hundreds, perhaps thousands of innocent lives at stake, you and all with you have the permission of both the President of the United States and the United States Congress to use deadly force to secure the completion of this operation and to protect yourselves."

"Thank you."

"You're quite welcome, Husky. Out."

Matt cut off the transceiver, took down the antenna, and stowed the rig. He wondered how Jim Bob was doing explaining the death of Luddy.

"Bear!" Monroe yelled, after looking at the headless body of Luddy. "You goddamned idiot. Bear don't tear the heads off folks and eat them. You said Luddy was flung how far 'fore he hit the tree?"

"A good thirty feet."

"Picked up off the ground and flung, huh?"

"That's right."

"That weren't no bear, Jim Bob."

"Well, what the hell could it have been, then?"

"Them . . . things that's been followin' us."

"What things, Monroe?" Floyd asked.

"Them things that I sent Yates and the others out to find, that's what things I'm talkin' about."

"Well, what is they?" Sanders asked.

"God damn it, Sanders! If I knowed what they was I wouldn't have sent Yates and Whitman and Hardin out a-lookin' to see what they was, now would I?"

"I reckon not."

"Thank you. Y'all hush up and let me think on this. I got me some suspicions about all them folks come in here supposed to be goin' campin'. It just don't add up." He held up a hand. "Don't ask me no questions. I'll ask the questions and you give me the answers." Monroe thought about that statement for a moment. Somehow, the words didn't come out exactly as he planned them to, but no matter. "First off, we got us one tough pale-eyed man come in here alone. That's fact. We don't know how long he stayed in the wilderness or what he was doin'. Fact. Then he shows up again with a bunch of Jews and niggers. Educated Jews and niggers. That's fact if what y'all told me was true."

"It's true," Alton said.

"And that Jew could fight," Luther said. "But his skin was pale like he don't get out in the sun much."

"All right," Monroe said, turning to Jim Bob. "And you tell me he come into the woods after Luddy was killed totin' a Mini-14 with a sound suppressor on it."

"That's right."

In the old cabin they had found and were using for a kitchen and headquarters building, Monroe moved to a small blackboard they used to chalk out terror tactics they used against one race or religion or writer or action group, or just anybody or anything that didn't follow along their narrow lines of thinking.

129

Monroe took a piece of chalk and printed: Hired gun? Bodyguard? Govurxxxx Gouverxxx Government Agent? "Which one fits the pale-eyed man?"

"Them last four, Monroe," Seymour said.

Monroe looked at him, sighed, and said, "You're right. Government agent. Now then, why would a government agent be escortin' a bunch of Jews and niggers into the wilderness? They all city folks, and from what y'all say, they all is as out of place as a turd in a punchbowl."

The others sat or stood in camouflaged silence.

Monroe again picked up the chalk and started to write on the blackboard. But he wasn't all that sure he knew how to spell the word. He put the chalk down and yelled, "Scientists!"

"Scientists?" Marwood said. "What in the hell would scientists be doin' in here?"

"It wasn't no bear that attacked Luddy." Monroe was getting excited. "It was the missin' link. They done discovered the missin' link!"

"The what?" Ely said.

"The missin' link. The creature that is between us and the animals in the chain of things."

"Boy," Claude said, standing up. "You beginnin' to talk like a damn communist. You speakin' words that's against the teachin's of the Good Book."

"Oh, sit down!" Monroe told him. "I ain't neither. They's some sort of creature out yonder that science can't explain, so they called it the missin' link 'cause they don't know what else to call it. Point I'm makin' is this: let's us catch the thing. The government would pay millions for it."

"Just think what one did to Luddy," Judd said, and the room fell silent.

"Get on the radio," Monroe said. "Get Yates and the others back here. Go on, do it. We got to follow them scientists. And we got to do it so's they don't see us. Now

130

then, what do we do with them outsiders when we discover the missin' links?"

"They's kids in that bunch," Duff reminded him.

"Nigger kids and Jew kids. They all inferior to the white race. Do I have to remind you of the oath we all took? We have to purify the race. We have to rid ourselves of the inferiors. And this is a damn good time to get shut of a whole bunch of them. You just keep the money that creature will be worth in your minds. That'll give you something to write home to mama about."

"I vote we go for it," Dolan said, standing up.

The rest slowly stood up and raised their hands, sealing the fates of the campers.

Monroe grinned. "And them women ain't bad lookin' neither, Alton said. Even that colored gal was a looker, weren't she, Alton?"

"Finest lookin' shine I ever put my eyes on, for a fact. High-class nigger."

"Ain't nothin' no better than brown sugar, boys. That's one thing them gals was born knowin' how to do."

"I want first dibs on her," Gerard said. "She is prime, man, prime."

"Not only is this gonna make us all rich," Monroe gloated. "But it's gonna be fun, too. I 'member the time I horsewhipped a Jew once. I whupped him slow, made it last a long time. That was more fun than the time me and some ol' boys blew up that church and killed them coons who was havin' a civil rights meetin'. And that was some fun, let me tell y'all, it was. I've had me some good times in my life, boys. Some high ol' times."

"And you done time for blowin' up that church," Monroe was reminded by a CWA member named Donny.

"Not me, boy," Monroe boasted. "Them others did, but not this ol' boy. I was way too smart and slick for them. Just like we're gonna be slicker than greased owl shit on this operation. We're a military organization, so we got to give it a name, boys. What'll it be?"

Several dozen names were tossed out and all of them rejected. Alton brought out a case of whiskey that had been carefully packed in by horse and the bottles were passed around. The men drank and thought of all the money they were going to have to spend. They could buy themselves new four-wheel drive pickup trucks with great big fat tires that would set them high off the ground and pull through any kind of mud. And they'd have smoked windows and gun racks filled with shotguns and rifles, so they could tote them around twelve months out of the year and show them off; besides, you never knew when a deer was going to pop up—in or out of season—and you could blast it.

Monroe took him a long pull from the bottle and relaxed as the raw whiskey burned its soothing way down his throat to explode in his stomach. Monroe's dreams were not elaborate like some of the others'. There wasn't much he wanted out of life. He wanted a sweet little young thing he could stroke when the feeling hit him; he wanted a return to slavery; he wanted to be the Grand Doodaddy of the Citizens for a White America; but the one overriding thought in his mind was that he wanted to slow-kill that pale-eyed man who had tossed hot grease in his face. He wanted to kill that bastard so bad when he thought about doing it he got all biled up in his stomach.

"Operation: Death!" Monroe cried out.

"Yeah!" the others yelled. "Way to go, Monroe!"

Monroe smiled. *I'm a-gonna kill you, Pale-Eyes,* he silently vowed. *And if you got a woman in that bunch of campers, I'm a-gonna mount her like a dog and make you watch.*

Monroe sat and allowed his hate to envelop him in an invisible cloud.

12

All around them mountains loomed, thrusting majestically toward the sky. The valley was lush and green, a twisting, rushing stream cutting through it. The spot Nick had chosen for them was lovely and peaceful and so quiet.

"This is it, folks," Nick told them. "You got it all right here in this valley. Hiking, camping, fishing, exploring, and relaxing."

"It's beautiful, Mr. Nick," Judy told him.

"How many people have you brought to this spot?" Susan asked.

"Not too many. This is my personal spot, I like to think. I got to really take to someone to bring them here. Come on, folks, let's get you all set up."

Matt took his bearings and marked them on a plastic-covered map. Already his mind was working, noting where helicopters could touch down; checking for the best defensive spots—and Nick had obviously had that in mind when he'd chosen this spot.

They were on the high ground, with the rocky, rushing stream below them to the front and also curving to their right as Matt stood facing west on the flat of the ridge. Behind them, far enough behind them to prevent any danger from falling rocks, was a huge upthrusting of sheer rock face.

Matt paced off the flat. It was slightly more than a hundred feet wide and about three hundred feet deep. More than enough room for a chopper to land.

Matt relieved his pack animals of their burden and stacked the unmarked boxes. He pitched his tent well away from the others and carefully ditched it. He cached some of his supplies several hundred feet from the flat, in the deep timber, and carefully covered the cache with the natural foliage he had parted to make room. With the brush back in place, the cache was not likely to be found.

Nick walked over to him after Matt returned to the main campsite. "The leaders will be contacting you, Matt. The old ones are . . . well, not like you and me. So you'll have to be careful not to hurt their feelings when you first meet them."

"Give me some idea of what I'll see, Nick."

"Heavy forehead, deep-sunk eyes, big jaw, big mouth, and some of them, the real old ones, will have teeth that are, well, larger and longer than ours."

"Fangs."

"Yes. They'll give you a start at first. Just bear in mind that they're approaching you in good faith and with trust."

"When can I expect them?"

"No later than two days from now. One of their camps is not that many miles from this spot. That's why I hardly ever brought people here."

"Any danger of these people here blundering into that camp while they're hiking?"

"No. There are sentries all around to warn them, and their sleeping and living quarters are underground, connected by passageways. Bear this in mind, Matt: they're not stupid people. Their ways are different, and many appear animal-like, but they have good minds. And they'll know if you lie to them. Just like a dog will allow ten people to pet it but growl at the eleventh person, sensing something wrong. I'm going over to the tribe's camp in the morning to tell them that you all are good people and they have nothing to fear from you. And to trust you. Matt?"

Matt met the man's golden yellow eyes.

"If you're planning something awful, I swear to God I'll kill you."

"I'm planning nothing of the sort, Nick. We'll get them out of here and over into that National Guard camp in Montana as soon as the government tells me the facility is ready to receive them."

"I believe you. I just wanted you to say it."

"Tomorrow morning I'll start making sweeps, working in an ever-widening circle. I don't trust the damn CWA, and I want to make sure they're not in here to screw things up."

Nick nodded his head in agreement. "When can I tell them to be ready for transport out?"

"Nick, just guessing, I'd say seven to ten days. I'll bump my people tonight and try to firm it up."

Nick smiled. "That's all a mule can do, Matt: just try."

Matt had hit it right on the head: his contact said between seven and ten days before the camp would be ready to receive.

"No leaks as yet?"

"No, thank God. And the damn meddling press has so far not picked up any vibes that something big is going down."

"Let's hope it stays that way. I don't like those damn people, I don't have any use for them, and they'd better not

135

get in my way."

"I swear you're going to give me an ulcer before this is over."

"Go take an antacid. When do I have permission to tell the happy campers what is really going on?"

"That is a problem, Husky."

"Not for me. They've got to know sooner or later."

"Make it later."

"Husky out."

Nick was napping, the kids were playing near the stream, and most of the other adults were exploring in the valley. Susan came over to where Matt was sitting outside his tent and sat down on the ground.

"We're being used, aren't we, Matt?" she asked.

"Not by me, Susie."

"I don't know what that means, Matt."

"It means that I tried my best to get you people to change your vacation plans and you wouldn't. It means that a government project is under way and you're caught up in the middle of it. Your choice, not mine."

"That's an odd way of looking at it, Matt."

He shrugged his shoulders. "It's the only way I can view it, Susie. I'm under orders and I can't say any more about it."

"How much danger are we in?"

"You have two very nice, well-behaved kids, Susie. I'm glad they took after you."

"I think it's unfair of you not to tell us the truth."

"Even Tom seems to be lightening up some."

"I'm going to write my congressman when I get back home and tell him of your high-handed ways."

Matt decided to take another tack. "Susan, we didn't know each other well in high school. We had a few Cokes, some hamburgers, and the few times I went with the group on outings or parties or whatever, we had some laughs.

What else do you remember about me, Susan?"

"What Norm said back in Denver. Right to the point. And there is something else: you didn't lie, Matt."

"That's right, and I'm not lying to you now when I say take your kids and your husband and your friends and get the hell out of this area. I won't warn you again."

She shook her head. "No, Matt. I think I'll stick around and see what it is you're trying to either hide or cover up."

He groaned. "Oh, Susan, I'm not the villain. I'm not the bad guy. I've just got a job to do. Then I officially pull the pin with the Agency."

"You probably aren't lying, Matt. But you're not telling the whole story, either."

"That's right, Susie. I'm not."

She studied his face for a moment. "Will you be gone from camp most of the time while we're here?"

"Probably about half the time."

"Doing what?"

"Oh, riding around, marveling at all the wonders of nature."

"Shit!" she said, and got up and walked away.

Matt whistled softly at her as she swayed away the way ladies do.

She turned and flipped him the bird. But she was smiling.

Nick woke Matt the next morning before dawn. Crouched over the campfire, Matt could see Norm making coffee.

"We'll talk, Matt. You and me and Norm."

"Suits me."

Matt dressed warmly, for the morning air was chilly, and with tin cups of coffee in their hands, the men walked away from the sleeping campers.

"I'll be pullin' out in about half an hour, boys," Nick

said. He jerked a thumb at Norm. "What does he know, Matt?"

"Nothing."

"Haven't you told any of them anything?"

"No."

"Why?"

"Because I can't risk them knowing and having it tortured out of them."

"I love it when people just ignore me," Norm said. "It makes me feel so wanted."

Nick turned to face Norm. "Did you serve in that mess over in Asia, Mr. Hunt?"

"Yes, I did. Several tours."

"Then you know what end of a gun the bullet comes out of?"

"Oh, yes. Pistol, rifle, 7.62- and .50-caliber machine gun, rocket launcher, flame thrower, Stoner . . . you want me to go on?"

"I get the picture." He turned back to Matt. "Who would want to torture any of these folks?"

"We were followed all day yesterday. I hung back a good ways; that's why you didn't see much of me. By a team of men in cammies. At sundown, I caught a glimpse of light reflecting off of glasses. Binoculars, probably. What I'm about to say is something that I don't know for a fact . . . but it could be possible. That bunch of racist nuts might have made me. If so, they could be wondering why I'm with a group of well-educated men and women; and all one has to do is listen to this bunch for a minute to know they're learned people. People who join groups like the CWA are not only stupid and bigoted, but greedy, envious—hell, they possess all the seven deadly sins. They might have it in their minds that this group is in here to seek treasure, looking to find a vein of gold—anything. If this group doesn't know what's going on, they can't tell anything, can they?"

"You're a cold bastard, Matt," the guide said.

"When I'm working, yes, I am."

"Well, you'd better level with them, Matt. A tribe member come to me last night. They's some Sataws busted loose. So it might not have been an Omah that killed that kook the other night, but a throwback."

"But you said a Sataw couldn't have thrown him that far."

"Maybe I was wrong. I been on the other side for over fifty years. I don't know all the tribes anymore, Matt."

"What in the hell are you two talking about?" Norm said.

"Yes," the voice came from behind them. "I would very much like to know myself."

Matt did not have to turn around to know it was Susan.

"What else did the visitor have to say, Nick?"

Susan walked up and stood by Norm, listening.

"Trouble. Some of the tribe don't want to relocate. 'Bout seventy-five or so broke away and left. Some who've lived on the outside long enough to know some of the dirty tricks our government has pulled now and again come back sneakin' around and convinced them it was all a trick and a trap on the part of the government."

"Nick, that's not true!" Matt said hotly. "I'm convinced of that."

The guide nodded his head. "I am too, Matt. But obviously some members of the tribe ain't."

"Indians?" Susan said. "Tribes of Indians on the warpath? In 1990?"

Matt ignored her. "You can't take them back, can you?"

"No. Dan is pullin' someone in to run the lodge and look after you-all's gear and then he's ridin' in. We got trouble, Matt. Big trouble."

"You going hunting?"

"I got no choice in the matter. Neither has Dan. What I'll do is send word back to the guides who know what's going on to keep people out of this area. Dan give me that other Mini-14 he took the pin out of. He put it back. I got it in my gear."

"Keep it, Nick. That's a lot of firepower there. I brought a spare for Norm to use."

"I knew it," the voice came out of the predawn darkness. "I just fucking knew it." Dennis Feldman. "The first real vacation I've taken in fifteen years and we're going to be attacked by a bunch of wild Indians!"

Nick had told them all to eat and then sit back, he and Matt had a story to tell them. A second cup of coffee was forgotten and left cooling on the ground as Nick told them his side of it.

"Preposterous!" Tom snorted. "There is no such thing as Bigfoot. It would be impossible for a group of people to go undetected for so many years."

"The Tasadays did in the Philippines," Frank reminded him. "They weren't discovered until the early 1970s."

"Oh, can't you people see what this is?" Tom persisted. "This is all a joke by Nick and Matt to frighten the cityfolk. Nonsense!"

"Then who tore the head off that guy?" Nancy asked.

"Oh, for heaven's sake, people, you're playing right into their hands." Tom poured a fresh cup of coffee and leaned back and laughed. "All that was part of this silly, childish hoax. No one has had their head torn off."

Nick walked to his gear and took a plastic-wrapped object out of a sack. He tossed it to Tom. "You don't think so, Mr. Dalton. Then open that up."

"You found it?" Matt asked.

"Yes. The next morning. I didn't think an Omah would tote it very far. Go ahead, Mr. Dalton. Unwrap it and take a good look."

Matt looked to see if the kids were still playing down by the stream. They were exactly where they had been sent, under the watchful eye of Traci.

Tom unwrapped the piece of plastic and the awful smell of rotting death hit him first. He took one look at the mangled head of Luddy and fainted.

13

Nick walked down to the stream to get a bucket of icy cold water while Matt rewrapped the stinking, grinning death's head of Luddy. He placed it to one side for later burial.

Nick walked back up to the flat and tossed the water in Tom's face. The lawyer came up sputtering, cussing, and waving his arms. The kids had accompanied the guide from the stream, and Tom's children stood without expression as their father was doused with the cold water.

"Go change clothes and then come back and pay attention," Matt told the man.

The expression in Tom's eyes told Matt what the lawyer thought of the man. That didn't bother Matt. He'd seen that look in the eyes of too many others for it to worry him.

Matt held nothing back from the group. There was no point in any further pretense. He felt the younger kids would be thrilled to be a part of secret-agent stuff. When the operation was over, they would be visited by child psychologists who would stress the need for secrecy. Sometimes it worked, sometimes it didn't.

Besides, Matt felt the entire operation was, in the words they used to describe a mission that no one felt would work back in Vietnam, a cluster-fuck. There were just too many things that could and more than likely would go wrong. Too many people were involved. Too much pressure was being exerted on those in power on the outside. And Matt knew only too well how big government worked. And how savage and unfeeling it could be.

Leaving the group to talk things over, Matt walked back to his equipment to radio in for choppers to take the group out.

The radio was gone.

He waved for Nick to come over.

"Radio's gone. That means we have somebody in camp siding with the breakaways in the tribe."

"Not necessarily," the guide said. "A Sataw or a tribesman could have come in here and taken it. You saw with your own eyes how animals don't spook when a tribesman approaches. There could be a Sataw or a renegade tribesman within fifty feet of us right now and the odds are we wouldn't know it. Not even me. I've had most of the animal bred out of me. *Now* are you beginning to see what we're facing?"

"Yeah but we've got to get these people out of here."

"There's a way, but it'll take two or three days. I can get word to the elders and they can send runners to your backup teams. But it's gonna take time."

"Do we have a choice?"

"None that I can see."

Matt nodded. "Get on it, Nick. I'll get these people to work pulling up small logs to build a barricade."

Nick started to protest, but Matt waved him silent. "We have no choice in the matter, Nick. The coordinates of this flat is all my people on the outside have. If we move, we're screwed."

Reluctantly, the guide agreed. "I'll be gone most of the day. Maybe up into the night."

"We'll be right here," Matt told him. "I hope."

A small stream ran out of the base of the sheer rock face

143

behind the campsite to form a table-sized pool of cold, clear water. It probably eventually fed into the stream that coursed through the valley below them. The problem of water was solved.

Nick saddled up and rode off without another word. Matt walked back to the group.

"My radio is gone," he informed them. "A renegade from the tribe slipped into our perimeter and took it." He did not voice his opinion that it might also mean that one of them was a descendant of the Unseen. Matt did not believe that a tribe member could slip unnoticed onto the flat and steal his radio. He would have had to untie the ropes, lift the tarp, and then find the small transceiver. No, it was someone in the group . . . he was sure of it.

"And that means . . . ?" Dennis asked.

"It means you people are stuck. It means I can't call in for choppers to come take you out."

"I'll file a lawsuit against the government for this," Tom said. "You had no right to endanger our lives in such a reckless manner."

"You do that, Tom," Matt told him. "But for you to do that, you have to be alive, right?"

"Are you threatening me, Jordan?"

"Oh, no, Tom. Not at all."

"What Matt is saying, Tom," Susan said, "is that we are very exposed on this . . . plain we're on, if plain is the right word. And we can't move very far from it, right, Matt?"

"That's right."

"Why can't we move?" Tom asked.

"Because Matt's backup team has these map coordinates," Dennis said. "And if we went very far from here, they'd never find us."

"That's it, Dennis," Matt said. "Oh, we could go a couple of miles from here, maybe further; we could use Susan's flare equipment to guide the choppers in. But why

144

risk it? This flat is a little exposed, but it's a good defensive position. Anyone coming at us can't do it from the rear. They have to cross the creek from two directions: north and west. Our south flank is the most exposed, and I can fix that, I assure you. So let's get cracking, gang. We've got a lot of work to do. Norm, we've got to build a fort . . . a bunker. We've got logs to pull up, stake out, and tie together. You're in charge of that. I'll get busy securing the perimeter."

Matt quickly cut branches, thumb-sized to wrist-sized and ranging in length from one to three feet, and set the kids to work sharpening one end of each. He put Walter and Traci to work digging pits for the punji stakes. Tom worked, but he did more bitching than work.

Finally Wade had listened to enough. "That's it!" the Denver businessman said. "I've had it with your complaining, Tom. Open your mouth again and I'll put a fist in it. You understand?"

The message was received and understood. Tom nodded curtly and bent his back to the ropes they used to pull the small logs up the slope to the flats.

When the kids had finished sharpening the stakes, Matt complimented them on a good job well done and said, "Now you can start filling up containers with water from the pool over at the cliff face, gang. When it gets dark, we can't risk leaving the compound."

The kids made a game of it, with one adult assigned to keep an eye on them.

Matt first chose the stakes for the punji pits, slanting the sharpened ends slightly toward the south, the most vulnerable side of their perimeter. He concealed the opening by laying light sticks across and up and down, then covering that with grass and leaves. He wished he had something lethal with which to coat the sharpened ends of the stick—to cause greater infection and, in many cases, very fast blood poisoning—but he couldn't have every-

145

thing. He knew a number of fungi which were deadly poisonous—the best rule of thumb was to look for any fungi with white gills; those were usually deadly—but didn't have time to go looking for them.

Matt moved to the timberline and began working fast but expertly. He built deadfalls, waist-high spear traps, and spring snares; but with the spring snares he substituted a sharpened stake in place of the noose.

Susan walked over and watched him work for a time. "They look hideous," she finally said.

"They are. But they work. Impress upon the kids that they are not to come near the woodline or near the crest on the south side of the perimeter. When we break, I want you to gather them here. I want to give them some simple survival lessons in case we get separated."

After a quick lunch, Matt gathered not just the kids, but everyone around him.

"OK, people," Matt said. "I'm going to go over some survival points with you. Somebody takes notes. I hope none of you has to use what I'm about to teach you, but it's a good thing to know.

"I'm going to show you four ways to tell direction. The sun, the stars, the moon, and plant growth. Now people, we're at least forty miles from where we jumped off. In case we get separated, I don't want any of you to head back west. The odds of any of you coming out anywhere near the lodge is miniscule. I want you to head south. There is a well-traveled nature trail about forty miles due south of here. It runs west and east. Take either direction. You'll run into somebody. I want you all to pack a backpack, adults and kids. I'll show you which foods to pack and what else to take. But be sure you take several pairs of socks. Your feet are very important; they might have to carry you out of this mess.

"There are fire observation towers dotting this country, manned by rangers. You all brought signal mirrors, and

146

that was a wise move unless it's raining. But not all fire towers are manned all the time. If you see one, head to it. But be damn sure you check your back trail and know which direction you were going and how to get back. Pick out landmarks and memorize them. And remember that things look very different at night."

Matt motioned the group over to a tree stump Nick had cut down only a few months back. Tom smiled and said, "I know that moss grows on the north side of a tree."

"A lot of people think that," Matt told the entire group, "but they're wrong. There is a theory that certain types of moss grow on the dampest side of a tree. In reality, moss grows all around a tree trunk. Walter, which direction are we facing?"

"South," the boy answered quickly.

"That's good. How did you know that?"

"Because I know—at least in this spot—that west is to my right and north is behind me."

"Good. Now I'll show you all another way. Look at the rings in that stump and tell me when you find those closest together."

The group looked. Judy was the first to spot it. "Right there, Mister Matt." She pointed.

"That's right. And what direction are the rings growing toward?"

"South," Susan said.

"That's right. In the northern hemisphere, the rings are closest together on the south side because that is the sunny side. Flowers tend to grow toward the sunny side. But the sun's influence will be most noticeable in a sheltered spot not affected by local shade. But don't rely on just one tree stump; check as many as you can. Mother Nature sometimes plays cruel tricks.

"Tonight I'll show you all about the pole star and Plough, Little Bear, Cassiopeia, and Orion. But if we get separated, at night I want you all to hunt a hole and stay put. If it's raining and you don't have a compass or aren't sure of your direction, build yourself a shelter, crawl under some thick underbrush, but *stay put* until the sun comes out and you can get your bearings.

"I'm not trying to frighten you, kids. Really, I'm not. I just want you all to have a fighting chance . . ." He paused. How to tell them of the extreme danger they were in? He didn't know. "I just want us all to get out of this mess that I got you in."

14

"Holy God in Heaven!" The CWA man watched the thing come out of the timber to meet with the rider he'd been tracking ever since he'd ridden away from the campsite on the flats above the creek.

"What is it? What is it?" his partner whispered.

"Monroe was right. Them people done found monsters out here. Monroe hit the mark on this one."

The second man lifted his binoculars and focused in. Horror changed his face as he looked at the manlike thing talking with Nick. Even at this distance both men could tell that whatever it was, it was not human.

"What do we do, Wilmot?"

"We don't move, that's for sure. We mark this location on the map and stay put until that rider is long gone. I think he suspects he's bein' followed, so we can't risk givin' nothin' away. He ain't what we want no-how. We got a pretty good spot here, and here is where we're gonna stay."

"What if that man heads this way?"

"We let him. We let him get as close as he wants to. We don't make a move, not a sound. The way we're set in this brush, he'd have to ride right over us 'fore he knowed we was here. So if he does come this way, we sit tight until he leaves. And then we sit tight for another couple of hours just in case he's antsy and backtracks. Come the night, we'll radio in to Monroe for orders."

"I got to piss."

"Then go piss in that crick back behind us so's it'll wash on out. We don't wanna leave no piss signs for that man to find; and he's good, he'd find them."

"He'd think it was an animal."

"No, he wouldn't, Telford. The only pee that's alike is man's and monkey's. The rest is different. Go on. Do it now. Don't break no branches, don't step on no flowers, don't leave no sign. If you leave signs and them things over yonder find us 'cause of it, I swear I'll kill you before they get me. That's a promise."

Telford looked long into the eyes of Wilmot. "All right. I believe you. I'll be careful."

That spot between Nick's shoulder blades had been itching ever since he'd left the campers on the flat. He had a nasty hunch he was being tracked, but everytime he circled back for a look, he could find nothing to confirm his suspicions. Maybe he was just jumpy, he finally concluded, even though there was still that nagging doubt in his mind. But time was running out, so he had to contact the leaders and get help for the campers. He had no choice in the matter. If he died, if Dan died, if Matt died, those were the risks of the game. But not the campers and their kids. That would be unfair.

The elder agreed that the campers must be granted safety. If Nick said they meant them no harm, then they meant them no harm. But it would take at least two days for the runners to get to the edge of civilization, and another day at least for their contacts on the outside to get to the government man's backup people.

Three days, Nick was thinking as he began his trip back to the campers. Four days, more than likely, before any help arrived. He rode out of the valley and up into the timber on the slopes, his eyes constantly searching for any sign of those he still felt were following him. He could find nothing. He circled and backtracked and circled again. Nothing. He dismounted and searched on foot, sometimes dropping to the ground, sniffing at it like a dog. But Nick was too far removed from his kin in the timber; he had lost the ability to smell out his own kind.

Swinging back into the saddle, Nick knew that if he had been followed, or was being followed, there was no point in taking a different route back to the campers. Matt was probably right in his assumption that the camp was being watched. So Nick would return the way he'd come. It was the shortest route.

Wilmot and Telford watched until Nick was just a dot, far away in the long valley. "Close," Wilmot muttered. "I thought he had us a couple of times."

"I got to shit," Telford said.

"Well, go on and shit!" Wilmot said. "I swear, I hope Monroe don't never pair us up again. You 'bout as useless as tits on a tank! Go on, I'm gonna radio in."

Wilmot called in, then put the radio back into its waterproof pouch and tucked the small but powerful transceiver under some brush. Telford had found him a log, dropped his trousers, and hung his bare ass over the other side. He sighed with relief as he emptied his bowels.

Telford was pulling up his trousers when he heard movement to his right. He cut his eyes. His mouth dropped open and his throat constricted in fright, closing off the scream of pure terror that was forming there.

His mind formed prayers and profanity all jumbled up. *Holy Jesus help me but that is one ugly motherfucker help me please God don't let that thing I pray to you Jesus Joseph Mary I swear I will be good from now on keep that whatever that son-of-a-bitch is away from me amen.*

The prayer and the scream that was lodged in his throat were now about ten feet from Telford. The Unseen had

151

ripped out Telford's throat like shredding a marshmallow and tossed the bloody mass of flesh and muscle to the ground.

Telford swayed for a moment, then crashed to the earth, his legs and arms kicking and waving as the blood poured from the massive wound. He rolled over on his back. The blood squirted several feet into the air as his heart continued to labor.

The Unseen reached down, clamped both big hands on either side of Telford's head, and squeezed.

The skull popped like an overripe watermelon.

Fifty feet away, Wilmot heard the sound and thought it was Telford having a massive bowel movement. He shook his head in disgust. Then the smell reached him, but it wasn't what he'd been expecting. He'd smelled it before and knew instantly what it was: blood.

Wilmot rolled to his knees, his AK-47 up and ready. Very powerful clawed hands closed around his throat from behind. He felt himself being bodily lifted off the ground. He dropped the assault rifle and tried to free his neck from the powerful grip, but could not. He tried to scream, but could not. The Unseen shook him like a doll and continued to shake him until his neck popped. Wilmot died with his eyes bugging out, his face a strange plum color.

The Unseen were scouts from the tribe, men who ranged several miles in all directions from the main camp. They had seen their friend Nick ride in and felt sorry for him, since it was obvious he now had so much human in him he had lost the ability to sense his followers. No matter . . . they would take care of the hostiles.

The scouts cleaned the area while others, using their clawed hands, carefully removed whole blocks of sod and then quickly scooped out a grave. They dumped the bodies and the hated guns into the hole and covered it, patting it down with their tough, bare feet. They vanished into the timber.

"Wilmot!" Monroe's voice came tinny out of the small speaker of the transceiver, in its waterproof pouch under the brush. "Wilmot, you bes' answer me, now, boy. Where you at, Wilmot?"

When there was no answer, Monroe cussed over the air.

One of the scouts picked up on the tinny transmissions and returned, finding the radio. He recognized it from a picture he'd seen in a book. He handed the radio to another scout and pointed in the direction Nick had taken. The Unseen nodded, took the radio, and ran after Nick. The radio might be important to their friend.

"Matt hasn't checked in," the contact reported to Langley.

"What else is new? He might not report in for two or three days, maybe longer."

"I don't know," the agent in charge of the Agency's backup team in Idaho said. "I been talking to Williams from the Bureau. As big as this operation is, I can't understand why Husky wasn't assigned a regular check-in time."

"Because Number Two isn't handling it. Number One is."

"Oh . . . shit!" Idaho broke off from Virginia.

[The reasoning for the disgust is that the DCI is a political appointee, while the rest of the staff are career and much more skilled in handling clandestine operations.]

The stockade looked pretty good at first glance. A second look would reveal its flaws. It certainly wasn't bulletproof, but for something that had been hurriedly thrown up in one day, it would do.

In the middle of the afternoon, Matt had taken Dennis, Walter, and Frank, and by dusk the four of them had hauled in enough small logs and cut limbs to put together a corral of sorts behind the stockade around the tents. Matt did not want to lose the horses. He wasn't worried about himself. But the kids and the women did worry him.

As the shadows began lengthening and pockets of darkness around the flats enlarged, Matt told the band of campers to get inside the crude stockade. The night was not their friend.

With everyone inside, Matt walked the edge of their perimeter, checking his perimeter bangers. He had rigged them at various heights, from ankle high to chest high. The thin black wire was invisible.

There was nothing left to do at this late hour, so Matt returned to the compound.

As soon as he entered, Tom Dalton confronted him. "First thing in the morning, I'm leaving," he announced.

"No, you're not," Matt corrected him.

"You'll have to stop me."

"That can certainly be arranged."

In the last of early summer's light, the lawyer stared at the CIA man. "You have no right to force me to remain here."

"I could debate that, but I won't. I'm trying to save your life, Tom. You wouldn't stand a chance alone out there."

"That isn't the real reason. You just don't want me to contact the press."

Matt did not bother to reply, and Tom finally shook his head and walked back to his tent.

"Tom is out as far as standing watches," Matt told the others. "I think he's going to try to slip away the first chance he gets."

"He'd die out there," Dennis said. "He doesn't even know north from south on a sunny day. He's worse in the woods than I am, and I'm terrible!"

"Nevertheless, he'll try, so keep an eye on him. Dennis, take the first watch. Frank, you take the next two hours.

Then Wade, Norm, and I will take the dogwatch. I don't know when Nick'll be back. But he'll know to approach cautiously and to sing out when he's close."

"I thought you secret-agent types had to check in at certain times," Nancy said.

"Depends on the operation. I'm known as pretty much of a lone-wolf operative. But if I haven't checked in by say, three days from now, someone should come looking. But that's only a guess."

"Let's eat, folks," Susan called. "It's ready."

"Hello, the camp!" Nick's call came out of the darkness.

Matt rolled out of his blankets and walked to the stockade gate. Wade was standing there, a club in his hand.

"Come on in, Nick," Matt called. "We have a corral of sorts in the back."

Susan fixed him a plate of food and put on fresh coffee. Nick handed the small transceiver to Matt. "Scouts from the tribe killed two CWA men. They're pretty sure the CWA guys had time to radio back to their base camp, telling them the tribe's location. So we may start getting some action tomorrow."

"Let's go over our options," Dennis said. "We're not only facing a conflict with these CWA people, but the Satanas are out to get us, too. Is that right?"

"That pretty well sums it up," the guide agreed.

Matt had inspected the small transceiver. "This has a built-in scanner. We can use it to keep track of the CWA's movements—as long as the batteries hold out, that is. I may try to bluff these crud out by advising them I'm a federal officer. But I really don't think that's going to make much of an impression."

"Does your agency have a file on these people?" Frank asked.

155

"Oh, yes. Many of them have minor criminal records. Some of them have done hard time for major crimes: assault, rape, civil rights violations, attempted murder, manslaughter, murder. They're an unsavory bunch."

"Why not make a deal with them?" Tom called from his spot in front of his tent.

"What kind of deal?" Nick asked.

"Whatever they want in exchange for our freedom to leave."

"What they probably want is to exploit the Unseen," Matt said. "They've got dollar signs in their eyes. There are certain types of people in the world who would turn the tribe members into a traveling sideshow."

"Yes. The same type who enjoys watching the abuse of animals," Cathy said.

"So?" Tom questioned.

"They're God's creatures, Tom," Susan told him, disgust evident in her voice. "Trying to survive. What you're suggesting is horrible."

"I'm trying to survive as well. We all are," Tom replied. "These tribe people are not productive members of society. Saving them makes about as much sense as these do-gooders who sob and moan about the rights of animals. Animals have no rights as far as I'm concerned."

"You'd best shut your goddamned mouth, Dalton," Nick warned him, real menace in his voice.

"Everybody go to bed," Matt suggested. "Nick's right: We need all our energy. Tomorrow we're going to need it."

The CWA was on the march. On horseback. The forty-odd members of the Citizens for a White America left shortly after Monroe tried for the last time and failed to reach Wilmot and Telford.

"They been grabbed," he told his men. "Or worse. We

156

know that they's some sort of subhuman species in the wilderness, and that pretty well tells us what the campers is doin' in here. Their kids is a smokescreen. Let's gear up and move out, boys. We got some hard ridin' ahead of us before dark. Duff, you and Ely be sure you bring them capture nets Marcel went and got. We fixin' to catch us a missin' link."

The men stuffed their pockets with all the ammunition they could carry and swung into the saddles.

"I wish we had us some kind of a flag to wave," Darnell said.

At one time the CWA was in the habit of flying Confederate flags—until several groups from Alabama, Mississippi, and Louisiana told Monroe, rather bluntly, that if they ever again saw the battle flag of the Confederacy being raised by such rednecks and white trash they'd remove it and Monroe wouldn't like where the flagpole ended up.

"Well, we ain't," Monroe said, rather testily. "So let's just go." Monroe turned in the saddle and looked back at his troops. He felt proud of his men. They was gonna wrest the government from the hands of liberals and such trash as that and run it right, by God. Monroe lifted his right arm. "Forward, ho!" he called.

There was a slight delay as Monroe's mount took that time to evacuate his bowels. Monroe waited with a sour look on his ugly face. Something like that took all the excitement out of the moment.

15

Matt did not have to wake the others. They were all up, even Tom, long before dawn. Susan was first, and she went to stand by Matt's side in the chill of predawn.

"Tell me the truth, Matt."

"Yes."

"We're really in serious trouble, aren't we?"

"Yes. It might be a week before any of my backup people are ordered in. If they try several times to contact me and can't, then they'll come in. Not before. By that time we could have been forced off this flat and be miles from the last map coordinates I gave them."

"Or dead."

"Yes. Or dead."

"I'm sorry Tom is being such an ass."

"It isn't your fault. He's just scared, Susie. He's in a situation he can't control and doesn't know how to respond to it except by running away. But in this case, that would be the worst thing to do. I wish I could make him understand that."

"I think you've already realized that Tom has tunnel vision, Matt. He sees exactly what he wants to see."

"That will get him killed out here, Susie."

She smiled. "You're the only person I ever, ever allowed

to call me Susie."

"You want me to stop?"

"Oh, no. I, uh, might as well say it: I had quite a crush on you in school, Matt."

"You're kidding! God, I was in love with you."

They shared a soft laugh in the early quiet.

"Maybe it all worked out for the best, Susie," he said, looking into her eyes. "I got the wildness out of me and you have two fine kids."

"It's over with Tom, Matt—totally, permanently, irreconcilably over. I finally realized, yesterday, that any love I might have felt for him died years ago. I'm doing my best not to hate him."

"If we ever get out of this mess, Susie, I'll put on my best duds and come calling."

"I'll be looking forward to that, Matt."

They looked at each other in the darkness. She smiled at him. "How about some coffee and breakfast?"

"I'd love it."

"Keep them folks hemmed in," Monroe ordered, after viewing the campers on the flats. He slipped his binoculars into their case. "Judd, you're the leader of the second team. Keep them people pinned down until we catch us a couple of them Links. Then we'll decide what to do with the campers."

"I already know what I'm gonna do to them women," Judd said with a grin. He shifted his chewing tobacco and spat on the ground.

"For a fact," Monroe agreed. "Let's go, boys. We got us a Link to catch."

Across the valley Matt lowered his binoculars. "They're splitting up. They're going to keep us pinned down in this valley while the others try for a member of the tribe. That's my guess, anyway."

159

"It makes as much sense as anything," Nick agreed. "But I'll tell you this: 'bout sundown you gonna see what's left of that bunch of riders comin' back in one hell of a hurry. If the tribe leaves any of them alive, that is."

"You think the breakaways are watching them?" Norm asked.

"Oh, yeah," Nick said. "They're watchin' us, too. Bet on that."

"Would the breakaways hurt you, Mr. Nick?" Sara asked.

"Just as soon as they would anyone else. I'm a traitor in their eyes, child, 'cause I'm helpin' the others in their relocation plans."

"Dan?" Matt asked.

"If he's gonna come straight in, he should be along anytime. It isn't those bums over across the valley that he'll be lookin' out for. It's the breakaways. Now if I was Dan, I'd look this situation over and then stay in the timber, out of sight of both sides, and see which way this thing shapes up. He might do that. We'll see."

Matt lifted the transceiver taken from the dead CWA men and clicked it on.

"We spotted one!" Monroe's voice came crackling out of the speaker. "Jesus God, it's a wild beast that walks upright. We're in pursuit, Judd."

"That's ten-four, Monroe. Good luck."

"He's gonna need it," Nick said solemnly. "The fool don't realize that the tribe's been in this country for centuries with only a half dozen sightings by outsiders. He's being set up for sure."

"I must confess," Wade said, "I don't know which side to root for."

"If it's the breakaways they're chasin'," Nick said, "it's a toss up. And I'm thinkin' that's who it is. The main tribe is half a day's ride from here, and they'll be holed up deep in the timber, underground, with only the scouts out. Maybe

160

we'll get lucky and they'll kill each other."

"You don't have much sympathy for the breakaways, Nick," Susan said.

"I don't have any sympathy for them," the guide corrected. "That's what's wrong with our society now: too damn many people moanin' and groanin' about the poor criminal. In the tribal society, a person is raised to know the right path. He can have one serious mistake marked against him. If he screws up again, he's in trouble . . . bad trouble."

"What happens to him then?" Frank asked.

"He gets buried," Nick said. "I was told that back in the old days, before the white man came into this area, the penalty was banishment from the tribe. All that changed after so-called civilization began moving in. The elders couldn't risk banishment—too much danger of them who was tossed out revealin' the tribe's location for spite."

"Harsh treatment," Wade said.

Nick nodded. "Keeps the crime rate down, though."

"Keep that ungodly thing in sight," Monroe hollered from the saddle. "Get them nets up here, boys. Ride him down and fling that net over his ugly ass."

"He's in the deep timber, Monroe!" came the call. "We lost him."

"Dismount!" Monroe squalled. "You and you, stay with the horses," he pointed out the guard. "Weapons at the ready like you was taught, men. Pair up and don't get separated. Let's go!"

The CWA plunged into the deep timber.

"Now they're in trouble," Nick said, after listening to the frantic radio transmissions. "They took the bait like a hungry shark. Them woods is gonna turn bloody in a few minutes. First thing I'd do is kill any guards left behind at the horses."

"Will they eat the horses?" Johnny asked.

"They might. But regular tribe members aren't red meat eaters. I never tasted meat until I come out. We lived on fish and berries and cooked tubers."

"Tubers?" the boy questioned.

"Wild potatoes and soft roots and the like. We thought of the animals as friends and family. Modern man could learn a lot from the tribe. But they won't."

"Come to think of it, Nick," Matt said, "I've never seen you eat meat."

"I don't very often. I've fixed a-plenty of it over the years for other people, but I always apologize to the animal for doin' it."

"Ridiculous!" Tom snorted. "That's like apologizing to some damn dog you run over."

Nick looked at Susan. "I have to say this, Mrs. Dalton: there ain't much to your man."

"He isn't my man, Nick. And my name is Susan. But you're right. There isn't much to him at all."

"I'm glad you finally realized that." He turned to face Tom, who was standing a safe distance away. "Don't you never get up in my face, Tom Dalton. Not for no reason. 'Cause if you do, I'll kill you."

"You're a savage," Tom told him. "You belong in a damn zoo with the wolves and bears and snakes."

"There it is!" the shout was muffled in the heavy timber and thick underbrush. "Come on, Ray. We gonna catch us a Bigfoot."

Ely looked around him. Ray was nowhere to be seen.

"Ray? Where are you, boy?"

The woods were eerily silent. Ely could hear, faintly, the sounds of other CWA men thrashing around in the brush. But none were close to his location.

Ely began folding the big capture net and slowly backing out of the timber. Rain began falling on his hat. Rain? There wasn't a cloud in the sky a few minutes ago, he thought. The rain began dripping off the brim of his hat.

Red rain.

Red rain?

A drop of blood plopped onto his nose. Ely looked up and began to scream.

Nearby, some ten feet off the ground, on a broken tree limb, Ray had been impaled. The jagged end of the limb was poking through his belly, and blood was gushing from the hideous wound. Ray's eyes were wide open and staring in death.

"Monroe!" Ely bellowed. "Oh, good God, Monroe. Come quick!"

Since Ely and Ray had been carrying one of the big capture nets, Ely's assault rifle was slung. He jerked out his .45 and jacked the hammer back as he slowly turned, his eyes searching the forest gloom.

"You got one of them things, Ely?" the faint call from Monroe reached him.

"Hell, no, I ain't. One of them done killed Ray. Get over here, quick!"

"Comin', boy. Hang in there."

Ely looked up at Ray. Ray was certainly hanging in there. Or on there. Or up there. Ely shook his head.

Ely heard the rustle of leaves behind him. He spun around, his heart hammering in his chest. He heard a growl, but it was not exactly an animal growl. He'd never heard anything like it. Something definitely was in that underbrush.

"You surrender, now, you hear?" Ely hollored.

The creature lunged out at him, all ugly and snarling, drool dripping from its mouth and onto its big hairy jaw.

163

Ely emptied his .45 into the charging . . . whatever in God's name it was. The big .45 slugs, hollow-nosed, tore into the Sataw and knocked it back as two of them hit big bones with tremendous shocking power. With shaking hands, Ely ejected the empty clip and slammed in a full one, jacking a round into the chamber.

"Monroe!" Ely squalled. "God damn it, where are you?"

"I'm a-comin,' Ely. Did you get it? Did you get it?"

"Yes, God damn it, I got it. Whatever the hell it is."

Monroe and Jim Bob and Luther crashed through the brush and came to a panting halt by Ely's side. They stood and stared at the creature lying dead on the ground.

"I believe that's the ugliest son of a bitch I ever seen in my life," Jim Bob said.

"It ain't gonna win no beauty contests, that's for sure," Luther said.

"Put a rope on it," Monroe ordered. "We're gonna drag that bastard out of here and take pitchers of it."

All of them jerked their heads up and stood rooted to the spot as wild cries began echoing all around them. They were cries like nothing any of them had ever heard before. Fingers of fear began dancing up and down their spines as the angry cries and howling intensified in volume and grew in number.

"Get a rope on it," Monroe repeated. "Get it out of here."

"What about Ray?" Ely asked.

"Where is Ray?" Jim Bob asked.

Ely stuck a finger into the air. "Up yonder."

They looked, gasped. Luther reeled and threw up on the ground.

The howling moved closer.

"There ain't nothin' we can do for him now," Monroe said. "Come on. Let's get this thing out of the woods and

164

get gone from this place."

"Sounds like there must be a hundred of them damn things," Jim Bob said.

"Damn!" Nick said, listening to the CWA's frequency on the transceiver. "Now we're in deep trouble."

"What do you mean?" Dennis asked, walking up to the group standing on the flats.

"They killed a Sataw. They'll never leave this valley alive. None of them."

"But that's good, isn't it?" Dennis asked.

"No. That's bad," Nick told him. "Sooner or later, that trash will come across to try and join us—strength in numbers and so forth. That's when we're going to be in trouble."

"This flat isn't big enough for all that bunch," Wade said.

"There won't be all that bunch in another twenty-four hours," Nick said. "But that ain't it. The Sataws already killed somebody named Ray. They killed two more yesterday. They'll get five or six tonight. That's when the leader of that half-assed bunch will try to make his run for it. When he finds that he can't leave this valley—the Sataws will have both ends plugged and he's already seen how deadly the timber on both sides is—he'll try to join us, I'm thinkin'. If we let that bunch over there join with us, the Elders will vote to stop the whole evacuation plan."

"What difference does that make?" Tom yelled from behind them. "We're talking about our lives, God damn it! There is an old saying about choosing the lesser of two evils."

"How many lives do you figure yours is worth?" Nick asked him.

"I don't know what you mean by that."

"Let me put it so maybe you can understand it, Dalton," Matt turned, facing the man. "Say that bunch of nuts and kooks over across the valley were to join us and we managed to get out of here with our skins. We, this bunch here, even you, might manage to keep our mouths shut about the Unseen. The CWA, no. They wouldn't. They'd grab the first microphone they could find and start yelling about it. Certain types of hunters would then come in to try to bag themselves a trophy. Not all hunters, not by any means, but enough of them would. And they'd kill some of the tribe members before the government could stop it—or try to stop it. And then those on the outside, those with even a drop of tribe blood still in them, those who have just one wild gene in them, those who have crossed over and taken their place in society would rise up and there would be a bloodbath in America. Am I getting through to you, Dalton?"

"You don't know that they would do that, Jordan. You're just guessing."

"Would they hurt innocent people, Mr. Nick," Sara asked.

"No. What they would do is wait until hunting and trapping seasons open and go into the woods then. No tribe member will harm an animal unless he has to in self defense. But to hate hunters and trappers is deeply instilled in them. I know men and women who have been on the outside five and six generations who have to really struggle to contain themselves when hunting season opens. Matt's right. It *would* be a bloodbath."

"What you're saying is, and please correct me if I'm wrong . . . we're all expendable?"

"That's about the size of it, Dalton," Nick told him. "But don't worry, the tribe members would see to it that no harm came to any child."

"Well, that's certainly comforting," Tom said sarcastically.

"I knew it would thrill you," Nick returned.

"Then you better kill me now," Tom said. "Because the first chance I get, I'm gone."

"Dalton," Nick said. "As far as I'm concerned, it would be good riddance. But you're not going anywhere. You know how I know? Because you're a coward. I seen that in you right off. You're a big important man sittin' in your fine office in your fancy suit and tie, but you're yellow clear through. And you know damn well you can't make it out there in the wilderness alone. You're all bluff and bluster. Go saddle your horse, bigshot. Ride on out of here. I'll give you my word that I'll stop anybody who tries to prevent you from leavin'. Go on, Dalton. Saddle up and ride!"

Tom's face turned red and he whirled around, striding swiftly to the crude corral. The group waited in silence. After a few minutes, Tom walked around to his tent. He opened the flap and went inside.

"You're better off rid of that one, Susan," Nick said.

"I can't help but feel sorry for him. He didn't want to come in the first place."

"Then why did he?"

"Because . . . I guess to show us all he could do it. Camp out, I mean."

"Then that makes him a fool *and* a coward. A man who don't know his limitations ain't never allowed himself to be put to the test. You keep guns away from him. He's liable to use one . . . on himself."

Book Two

"Contrariwise," continued Tweedledee, "if it was so, it might be; and if it were so, it would be; but as it isn't, it ain't. That's logic."

Lewis Carroll

1

"We got to get gone from this place, Monroe," Judd said. "And we got to do it now!"

"You nuts, boy. We ain't gonna make no money with a dead . . . thing. We got to get us some live ones."

"That monster's stinkin' worse than ever, Monroe," Sanborn said. "I ain't never smelled nothin' so bad. There ain't no horse gonna tote that stinkin' thing outta here."

"He's got a point," Jim Bob said.

"I think we'd best settle down and get ready for a fight," Kane said, walking up.

"What you mean by that?" Monroe asked.

"We're in a box," Kane explained. "One way in and one way out." He produced a map. "Look here—this valley is about a mile wide. Sheer cliff face at the north end. Only way we'd get out that way is go through the woods. And we all know what's waitin' for us in there. Heavy timber on both sides of the valley. Whatever them things are, they ain't stupid. You better believe they know this country and by now they've plugged up that little draw we used to come in the south end."

"You tryin' to tell me that them animal things has bottled up nearabouts fifty armed men, Kane?"

"Looks that way to me."

"What the hell we gonna do, Monroe?" Roswald asked, real fear in his voice.

B. O. Shanty then made the most intelligent statement of any CWA member that day when he said, "I think we better pray!"

"What are those nitwits across the valley doing?" Dennis asked Matt.

"I really don't know. I'm saving the batteries in the radio and relying on binoculars. So far they don't appear to be doing much of anything."

"They'd best be praying," Nick spoke up. "We're in a hell of a lot better position than they are, and we ain't got nothing to brag about."

"Are the breakaways waiting for night?" Norman asked.

"Sure. They know they're no match for guns in the daylight. They learned that a hundred and fifty years ago. Those kooks across the valley, if they stay bunched, will make it through the day. They'll lose some men come night."

"I wonder if Dan made it in," Matt remarked.

"He's probably up yonder on the ridges," Nick said, with a curt shake of his head. "But he won't skyline himself. He's probably tryin' to figure out what's the best way to help us."

"Will the tribe help us?" Susan asked.

"I don't know," the guide replied honestly. "But you can bet they're talkin' about it."

"Seems like helping us would be to their advantage," Wade said.

"Why?" Nick looked at him. "They didn't ask for this mess. If both sides kill each other, so much the better for them. There's a very slim chance they'll just go on living the way they've always lived, and in another hundred years, there won't be any of the tribe left; they'll have bred all the markings out and everyone will be on the outside, working as doctors and lawyers and shopkeepers and guides and so forth."

"Except for the Sataws," Nancy pointed out.

"That's right. And they'll stay in the deep timber helping Mother Nature . . . so to speak."

"Better get word to them that it won't work," Matt said. "They can't sit back and have this many people disappear without bringing attention to themselves."

"I done told them that."

"What'd they say?"

"They didn't say nothin'. They're scared. If we could get to their quarters, they'd take us in and help us. Look at it from their side, Matt: they got an intertribal war goin' on. As long as they stay to the ground, they know they're safe. If they surface, they're dead. They know that if the breakaways win, they'll come back home, beg for forgiveness, and ask to be allowed back in the tribe. If the breakaways lose, they'll surface and be taken out to the agreed-upon location. They win either way."

"How many prisoners do they now hold, Nick?"

"That's something I don't know. I don't even know where they're held. I'm their friend and they trust me, but only up to a point. I know how far I can go with them."

Matt squatted down on the ground. "First I'm sent in here with orders to destroy the tribe—the Unseen. Then my orders are changed and I'm to see they're safely transported out. You have some relatives in very high places, Nick."

"Planned that way. For years. We all knew the time would come when civilization would crowd us."

"How high does it go?"

But the guide would only smile and shake his head.

"Even if we do get your people out, Nick, public sentiment is going to run very strong against the tribe

173

when the kidnap victims start telling their stories about being held as slaves and breeders."

"They know that. They also know that this might very well be the last shot they're ever gonna have at comin' out. They don't have a whole lot of choice in the matter, folks. Not only is civilization closin' in on them, but time is runnin' out. Remember what I said a minute ago about there bein' a slim chance of the tribe remainin' undetected?"

"I'm not sure I understand that, Nick," Dennis said.

"I think I do," Matt said. "There are those on the outside who want their kin out, who are proud of their heritage, and those who don't want them out—who'd rather see them dead."

"Like I keep sayin', Mr. Secret Agent Man: you're a smart one. Me and Dan, we've seen this comin' for years. As those on the outside grow in number and in prestige, some of them also get a little jumpy about what might happen if their real background was to be checked too damn close. You see, a lot of them have taken a chance and bred with so-called 'normal' people . . ."

Not "married and had children," Matt noted, but "bred with." Interesting.

"Some of the babies was born real monsters. Not many of them, but a few."

"What happens to them, Nick?" Nancy asked, walking over with a fresh pot of coffee and a stack of tin camp cups.

Nick squatted down, looked far across the valley, then answered softly, "There are places around the country that take in those types of babies."

"I know there are homes for children who are . . . well, mentally disturbed and . . . disfigured physically," Milli said. "But do the parents who take them in really know what they're getting?"

"Oh, yeah," Nick said.

"Homes of ex-tribe members, Nick?" Matt asked.

"In a manner of speakin'," he said softly.

Matt sighed and stared at the man. "More and more, Nick, I'm beginning to think there are no clear-cut good and bad guys in this little play. I have to assume by your 'manner of speaking' remark that if a baby is born with clear-cut markings, that is to say, it is more tribe than . . . let's call it outsider rather than normal, once the baby is nursed . . ." He almost said "weaned." "It's given to a family, say out in the country, so it can run free when the urge strikes it. And I getting warm, Nick?"

"Right on the money, Matt. But only a small percentage of the families do that. Most families . . . ah . . ." He shook his head.

"Kill the child?" Susan said, horror in her voice.

"Yeah," the guide said. "A lot of them do that."

"How do they get away with it?" Dennis asked.

"Home births. Man, you don't think a first- or second-generation outsider would risk a hospital birth, with extensive blood tests and all that, do you? Hell, no . . . no way. When the doctor is called, he takes one look at the dead baby and says something like, 'Well, sometimes death is a blessing, Mr. and Mrs. Jones.' Usually, the first and second generation of outsiders live 'way back in the country. In the mountains, in the wilderness, away from civilization, but close enough in so their kids can get on a bus and go to school. Them that hide their tribe-marked kids in those homes I was talkin' about, those are the breakaways, the renegades, the ones who relate to the wild more than the others." His voice broke and he paused, clearing his throat. "Men like me and Dan, and we're all over the country, we're the ones who have to go in when they're found and . . ." Tears were running down the man's tanned cheeks. ". . . kill them!"

He stood up and walked away.

The attack came without warning, just as Matt had

warned the others it would. Only the screaming of Judy gave them a few second's warning. The Sataws were rappelling down long ropes, skillfully and silently coming down the sheer face of the cliff, attacking from the rear. Before the first echo of the child's screaming faded away, Matt had raised his Mini-14 and was putting lead into the Sataws. Norm soon joined in, then Nick with the Mini-14 Matt had loaned him. Those caught halfway down the ropes were wounded and fell screaming to their deaths. Those already on the ground were a different matter.

A huge, animal-faced Sataw came loping and dodging and slithering across the flats, moving so swiftly Matt could not get a shot at him. He was naked except for a loincloth, and the man-beast was heading straight for the stockade and the women.

The Sataw leaped the tall, crudely built walls of the compound, and Matt heard a dull smacking sound, followed by the crash of a body to the ground. He ran for the stockade.

Matt rounded the corner in time to see Susan standing over the Sataw with a club in her hand. Matt put a bullet in the Sataw and then noticed Cathy Nichols was right behind her, a terrible look on her face, a club in her hand, the club raised to bash Susan's brains out.

Matt lifted the assault rifle. "I'll kill you, Cathy!" he shouted. "Drop it or die!"

As Cathy turned to face him, a grotesque growling and snarling came from her throat. She flung the club to the ground just as her husband came running up.

"It's over, Matt. The rest of them ran off . . ." He pulled up short, staring at his wife's savage face. "What the hell's going on here?"

"Now we know who took the radio," Dennis said, his long-barreled .44 Magnum in his hand. He had already proved himself a man who'd stand and fight, and he'd

176

shown he could shoot with some degree of accuracy that day. He had killed or wounded at least two of the attackers.

"Cathy!" her husband said. "You're . . . I mean . . . *you* are one of . . . my God, Cathy!"

She sprang for the wall and Susan clobbered her right in the butt with her club. With a howl of pain and a snarl of anger, the woman fell to the ground. She came up fighting and decked Susan with a right hand balled into a fist. Matt stepped over and knocked her sprawling to the ground. She sprang up with amazing agility and came at him. He was not gentle with her. He punched her hard in the stomach with his fist and she doubled over and dropped gasping and choking to the ground.

Matt handed his rifle to Wade and quickly trussed her up with rope. "Where's the radio, Cathy?"

"Go to hell!" she spat at him.

Frank was ashen faced, obviously very near shock. "The kids . . . ?" he managed to say.

"They're in the network," she told him with an ugly grin. "Helping others like us."

"Then they've got to be stopped," Nick spoke.

Cathy laughed at him. "You'll never get out of here alive, you traitor."

"Traitor?" He looked at her. "Woman, this is the last shot we've got to stay alive. This relocation plan has got to work or we're doomed."

She cursed him.

"But . . . your family," Frank stuttered. "They're old and respected . . . they go back a hundred and fifty years. I don't understand this."

"Probably one of the first to come out," Nick told him. "It was easy to hide your identity back then. Names and background didn't mean anything; it was what you did that counted."

"No," Frank refused to accept the obvious. "No." He shook his head. "Our children were both born in

177

a hospital."

"A lab technician would have to know what to look for," his trussed-up wife told him. "Our blood is ninety-nine-percent pure. Someone would have to run dozens of separate tests to isolate anything abnormal."

Frank stumbled away, clearly stunned with disbelief. Matt pointed to Milli and she nodded, walking out of the stockade after Frank.

"Now maybe you can get some idea of how big this thing is," Nick said to the group.

"You'll never stop us," Cathy said calmly. "We must be allowed to maintain a level of purity. We have a right to our heritage the same as any other culture. If we do make the news, we're ready to petition the Supreme Court for our rights."

"You're foolish," Nick told her. "Woman, the tribe has kidnapped and killed over the years."

"So did the Indians. They have their place in society."

Nick shook his head. "That ain't the same. If you can't see that, then you're not thinkin' logically. Call your people off. Let the relocation go on as planned. I'm tellin' you, it's our only hope."

"You can't stop it now. No one can. We knew Matt's orders even before he did. We knew them even before the operation was handed to the CIA."

"But my orders were changed," Matt said. "You couldn't have known that would happen . . ."

Cathy grinned at him, and it was the most savage curving of the lips Matt had ever seen. "It's a movement, within a movement, within a movement," Matt said, after a few seconds.

"I'm not followin' you," Nick said.

"The original movement—and I'm guessing here—was for peace: to relocate the remaining tribe members and gradually breed the others into society. Probably through science. Your elders went along with that. But a second movement was secretly formed. That one wanted total purity to remain, to be accepted for what they are. But some of those on the outside didn't want that. They knew that could never be. The human race wouldn't tolerate a subhuman species that had kidnapped and killed in order to progress. Even though the human race has been doing that in one form or another since the beginning of time. So this third movement came up with another plan: war."

"War?" Nick said. "War?" He began pacing, walking a half dozen steps, then turning and retracing his steps. Back and forth. Back and forth. Cathy lay on the ground and watched him, a strange smile on her face. Nick said, "We have people in Congress, both state and federal. We have people in high-ranking positions in the armed forces. We have federal judges and scientists and heads of large companies and so forth. We don't need a war. With this relocation plan a success, a hundred more years of careful breeding in a controlled environment and a lot of public education and we'd all be accepted. By those who matter, that is. They'll always be somebody—like that bunch of nuts across the valley—who hate somebody else because of skin color or religious beliefs or whatever." His down-home manner of speech had disappeared, the affectation completely gone, at least for the moment. "Why the hell would anyone among us want a damned war?"

Matt looked at Cathy. She snarled at him, peeling her lips back like an animal. "Because people like her have succumbed to the call of the 'urge,' as you put it, Nick. They like it. They've probably been networking for years. Meeting in secret to run wild at night and kill. There might be two hundred of them, there might be twenty thousand or more of them. They don't want that urge bred out; they don't want it controlled by medication. They want to be exactly what they are."

"If that's true, then everything we've done for only God

179

knows how many hundreds of years has been for nothing," Nick said. He looked at Cathy. "Woman, you and your kind can't lead a double life. You got to choose."

"We have," Cathy said softly. "Oh, we have."

"Leave me alone with her for twenty minutes," Nick said, a flatness to his words. "Take the kids and go down by the stream and guard them. I'll soon know everything this bitch knows."

"No," Matt nixed that. "We've got to get her out and under supervised interrogation with chemicals. A person under intense physical torture will tell you anything just to get the torturer to stop the pain. That's no good. We need her alive to tell her story—all of it—and you and Dan to tell yours. You're correct in saying that the right people will understand. But there is something more here. Something keeps nagging at me. It's got to be something that neither you nor Cathy have admitted."

"What do you mean, Matt?" Dennis asked. "Good God, man, haven't we got enough to worry about?"

"Nick is too worried about the damage that a few hundred Unseen can inflict, and Cathy is just too damned sure of herself. All right, people, truth time. Why are you so worried about this third movement? There can't be that many of them out there."

Cathy laughed and said nothing. Nick looked uncomfortable.

"I guess your bosses are holding back on you, Matt," Nick finally said. "But you're probably used to that. The bite of a Sataw is terribly infectious . . ."

"Shut your goddamn mouth, you turncoat!" Cathy screamed at him.

"There is no known antidote."

Matt shook his head. "Nick, they'd have picked up on it and told me about something that deadly."

"Oh, you won't die from it, Matt," Nick said. "You ever been a fan of werewolf books?"

"Yes, I still enjoy reading . . . Nick, are you telling me this stuff changes people into monsters?"

"Oh, no, nothing like that. Not physically, anyway. If the bite is severe enough, and enough saliva is injected into the victim's blood, some, well, *changes* in a person's behavioral pattern can be expected."

"You son-of-a-bitch!" Cathy cursed him.

Nick allowed himself a small smile. "Maybe my grandmother, in the clinical sense of the word." To Matt: "If the wound is treated promptly, there is little danger of that change occurring. But let it become infected, and the victim is in serious trouble. The change will be so gradual, they will hardly notice it . . . until the moon is full."

Matt recalled Richard's words: "It all depends on phases of the moon."

"Cathy," Matt pleaded with her. "You, all of your kind, must have the foresight to see that your plan won't work. You won't be able to infect enough people to make a difference, not before our scientists come up with a vaccine."

"We can alter the personalities of enough to ensure the survival of those who feel the pull of the old gods," she told him. "Not breed it out, like your government wants to do."

"It'll never work," Matt told her.

"You won't be alive to see one way or the other," Cathy said with a sneer. "None of you."

2

"Them folks had a good fight over yonder, Monroe," Jim Bob said. "Twenty-five or thirty shots fired. Sounded like M-16s to me, maybe the civilian model."

Monroe nodded absently. "We got to join up with them folks, Jim Bob. I done decided on that. They's strength in numbers. Send a team over yonder and sound them out on us joinin' up with them. Whitman talks real good—he's got a high school education. Make him the spokesman."

"You mean we gonna be friends with them niggers and Jews?"

"I don't figure we got a choice in the matter. We can't use our radios to call for help. This frequency's done been assigned to us . . . in a roundabout way. 'Sides, they ain't got the range to get over the damn mountains. We ain't got no choice in the matter."

"You worryin' about tonight, ain't you, Monroe?"

"I'd be lyin' if I said I wasn't. Them folks, now, they got them a fine defensive position. That tells me the pale-eyed man knows what he's doin'. Once we get in amongst 'em and win this fight, we can kill them government people and no one'll ever be the wiser. See where I'm at, Jim Bob?"

"Oh, yeah, Monroe, yeah. And I like it. I'll get Whitman and a few others to ride on over."

"Here they come," Nick said to Matt, lowering his binoculars. "I didn't figure on them this soon."

"Get the women placed north and south to watch for the breakaways, kids to the rear of the stockade. All the men up here with us. Put a gun in every man's hand, whether or not he knows how to use it."

"Right."

Matt looked across the mile-wide valley. "There could be a hundred breakaways out there and we couldn't see them."

"True. And they probably are out there, too. Them nitwits might be ridin' into an ambush. But I doubt it."

"Because it's open country and the CWA have guns?"

"Yeah. But in the timber, that won't make a damn bit of difference."

"Howdy, folks," Whitman said, reining up about fifty feet from the crest of the hill. "How y'all doin'?"

Silence greeted his words.

Whitman shifted in the saddle. "We kind of got ourselves in a bind across the way. And judgin' from the shots we heard a while back, y'all are in the same bind. Colonel Bishner thinks we ought to join forces and maybe we'd be better off."

"*Colonel?*" Matt said with a laugh. "That stupid son-of-a-bitch couldn't command a row of fence posts to stand still. We're doing just fine, boys. Now ride on."

"It's a free country, mister," Whitman said. "We'll ride where we damn well please."

Matt leveled his Mini-14, the muzzle pointed at Whitman's chest. When he clicked the weapon off safety, Whitman started to sweat in the cool air. "Get down off the horse," Matt ordered.

Whitman got down.

"Walk up here."

Whitman walked.

"The rest of you back off a good hundred yards and sit tight," Matt told the riders, and they did.

"What are you men up to?" Matt asked Whitman.

"Ain't none of your damn business, mister."

Matt slugged him. The blow was sudden, unexpected, and very hard. Whitman's butt impacted with the ground. His eyes were glazed and his mouth was bloody.

"Do you want your face kicked in?" Matt asked.

"No, sir," Whitman mushmouthed.

"Then answer my question."

"We come after some of them missin' links. We was gonna capture some of them and sell them to the government."

Matt flipped open his wallet to his I.D. "I'm not interested in buying any of them."

"Yes, sir. Can I get up?"

"No. How many in your group?"

"Forty some-odd. I guess them links killed Wilmot and Telford. We can't find them nowhere. I know they killed Ray. Stuck him up on a broke-off limb 'bout ten foot off the ground. Awful sight to see, Colonel Bishner said. We're stuck in this valley, mister. We can't get out. And I got me a suspicion that your group can't get out neither 'cause if you could, you've have done got gone. It appears to me that our plans backfired, and so did yours."

"Tell all of it, mister."

"I don't know what you mean." The man could not meet Matt's eyes.

"You had plans for us, didn't you?"

Whitman remained silent.

"Believe me, partner," Matt said, "I'll kick you till you're dead and not lose one second's sleep over it."

"If we was to join with y'all, after we whupped the links

we was gonna kill all you folks . . . after we had our way with the women."

"There are children in this group," Matt reminded him.

"Inferiors. So that don't make no difference."

"You would kill a child because of the color of their skin or their religion?" Wade asked.

"Why not? Niggers is takin' jobs that white people ought to have. Worst thing that ever happened to this country was when slavery ended." Whitman had him a pretty good idea that this pale-eyed man was gonna kill him. He felt it in his guts. Thinking he had nothing to lose, he then unleashed his lopsided, bigoted fury on everything he felt was responsible for his current station in life. Everybody who wasn't White, Anglo-Saxon, and Protestant should be sterilized so's they couldn't breed no more, then pretty soon the race would be pure. The United States should declare war on the rest of the world. Kill 'em all. Every book except the Bible should be burned; all writers was pinko commies anyway. All actors and actresses and the like was all "commonists." Anybody who didn't pick or sing country music was a fag. There wasn't nothin' important in school 'cept sports.

He finally wound down and sat on the ground with his head bowed, waiting for the bullet he was sure was coming.

"My God," Dennis said. "You read about men like this, you hear it on the evening news, but you really don't want to believe they exist. And on the off chance they are for real, spewing their hate, you pray there is some hope for them. But there isn't any hope for men like that. They're the Nazis of this generation."

Whitman raised his head and stared at Dennis. "To hell with you. In a couple of days somebody in the CWA is gonna be butt-fuckin' your wife and a listenin' to her squall while they pump the meat to her."

Matt lifted his Mini-14 and shot the man between the

185

eyes. Whitman's head snapped back and he rolled over, trembled once, and lay still. Matt stepped forward and took the man's guns and ammo from him, then shoved the man down the slope. Whitman's body went tumbling down the hill.

"Pick up your trash and carry him with you!" Matt shouted to the startled little group of CWA men by the stream. "Stay on your side of the valley."

"If you hadn't shot him, Matt," Dennis said, "I was going to."

"Mighty cold man yonder," Monroe said, lowering his binoculars. "Mighty cold. We got to take him out. If we do that, the rest of the group will fall apart, I'm thinkin'."

"Monroe," Jones said. "Let's get the hell gone from this place." Jones had realized he was in with the wrong crowd ten minutes after he took the oath over in Indiana. Jones really didn't hate anybody, and the thought of harming a child made him sick to his stomach. Jones wanted out of the CWA. These guys were all a bunch of nuts!

And what an oath it had been. All about loving God and country, and preserving the purity of the Aryan race, and a bunch of other stuff that didn't make any sense back then and made even less sense now.

"You turning yeller on me, boy?" Monroe said, looking at Jones through hard, mean little pig eyes.

"I pulled my time in 'Nam, Monroe. As an LRRP. Two tours. Don't you call *me* yellow."

Monroe noticed that Jones had lifted the muzzle of his AR-15 ever so slightly and that he had moved his finger from the trigger guard to the trigger. Monroe knew, too, that of all the men in this contingent of the CWA, Jones was the one who had seen hard combat with the paratroopers.

"Aw, hell, Jones!" Monroe said. "Don't get your drawers in a wad, boy. We's all wound a little too tight. We can't leave now. Are you forgettin' the oath you took?"

186

I'm trying, he thought. He shook his head. "Get to it, Monroe."

"Whitman's got to be avenged. We swore a brotherhood to one another. Them folks over 'crost the valley got to go, boy. We got to get them all."

Jones stared at him for a moment, then turned and walked away.

"I'm gonna have to deal with him, I reckon," Monroe said.

"You better pack you a lunch 'fore you start," Jim Bob warned him. "When the courts turned that nigger loose who raped his wife, it took half a dozen cops to control him so's they could get him out of the courtroom. All that 'cause he wasn't read his rights or some shit while he was bein' arrested. After his wife went in-sane and finally committed suicide, Jones spent a year and all his money trackin' down that ape. Found him in Las Vegas and hauled him out in the desert and went to work on him. I heard it took that nigger about three days to die . . . and they was hard days. I'd leave Jones alone if I was you, Monroe."

"He ain't got the right attitude, Jim Bob. I can't have no breach of discipline here."

"I'll talk to him. You just leave him alone. We got to get ready for tonight; them things is gonna be comin' at us, I'm thinkin'."

Matt and the others had dragged off the Sataw's body and left it in the woods after Matt had taken pictures of it. None of them had ever seen anything like it.

"This one was a real throwback," Nick explained. "More animal than human, but with the ability to walk upright, make simple tools, and reason to some degree. That's what makes them so dangerous. You don't have to bury it. The others will be back for the body."

187

Matt reattached his perimeter bangers under the watchful eyes of Nick.

"They'll figure them out after the first night they set them off," Nick said.

"Then I'll move them," Matt replied. "I plan to add something a bit more deadly after we throw back the first night's attack."

"You real sure we will?"

"Oh, yeah, I'm sure. Let's get busy plugging up the chinks in the stockade. We've got a lot of daylight left."

Back in the stockade, he tossed a canvas bag to Norm. Norm grunted with the effort of catching the heavy bag and Matt grinned at him. "Surprises in there, buddy."

Norm unzipped and unsnapped, looked inside, and returned the grin. "All right!"

The grenades were really hand-thrown mini-Claymores, each one with an astonishing kill radius as it released its deadly shrapnel.

"We don't want to use these unless we absolutely have to, Norm. We'll see what happens after tonight. I brought some other surprises."

"I'm sure you did," his old high school buddy said dryly.

The screaming began just after dark, coming from the center of the long valley, midway between the two camps.

"They got somebody from the other camp," Nick said.

"I hope that doesn't last long," Wade said.

"It probably won't," the guide told him. "The Sataws ain't much for torture. They don't have the finesse to make it last very long."

The man's screaming intensified.

"What in God's name are they doing to him?" Polly asked.

"You really don't want to know, Mrs. Hunt."

They were pulling the man's intestines out of his stomach, slowly, after having broken his arms and legs.

"Jonathan's gone, Monroe," Luther said. "They slipped in here and took him." He swallowed hard. "Why don't they just go ahead and kill him?"

Jonathan stopped screaming. The silence was very nearly as terrifying as the man's howlings of pain.

"Will they come after us now?" Judy asked, her voice containing a trembling.

"We'll be all right, girl," Nick told her. "It'll get noisy around here, and they'll be lots of guns goin' off and shoutin' and yellin', but you young'uns will be all right."

"Mr. Nick?" Sara called softly.

"Yes, girl?"

"Your kids and grandkids, do they know what they are? I mean, you know what I mean."

"The older ones do, child. We start preparing them for the changes in the moon early."

Milli asked, "Have you had any born . . . well . . . ?"

He knew what she meant. "Yes," Nick's words were soft. "Thank the gods only one wasn't right. A boy."

"Is he in one of those caretaking places you talked about?"

"No. I destroyed it. I don't believe in those places."

"I am sorry," Milli said.

"No need to be. He wouldn't have had any kind of life, and I want all that bred out of future generations. Get ready, people, here they come."

"I don't see or hear a thing!" Dennis said.

"I can smell them," Nick said. He raised his voice to a shout and began speaking in a twisted and strange tongue. He shouted for a full minute.

After a few seconds, they could hear shouted words coming from the south side of the flat. Nick listened for a minute. A disgusted look appeared on his face. When the shouting fell silent, Nick said, "He says he was told soldiers was comin' in here. He says those on the outside told him so. They've been lied to, people. I expected it, so it don't come as any surprise."

Cathy lay in her tent and struggled against the ropes that held her and the gag that was in her mouth. But all she could do was make muffled sounds.

Nick shouted something into the darkness. He received shrill cries in return. All who listened behind the stockade could tell they were shouts of ridicule.

"Foolish, foolish creatures," Nick muttered. "So easily led."

"What happens now?" Tom asked.

"I might have bought us some time. I don't know. They mocked me, but they might pull back and think on what I said. I told them their real enemy was across the valley. Those ol' boys over yonder are in for a rough night."

Frank was sitting just outside the tent where his wife lay bound and gagged, trying to talk to her, but she was having none of it. When she scooted around on the tent floor and tried to kick him, he gave up and walked away, shaking his head.

"This is going to be a very interesting divorce," he said to Wade. "I can just see it now, me telling the judge: 'I can no longer live with this woman, your honor, she changes into a monster when the moon is full.'" He managed a sad smile.

"Maybe this camping trip was a blessing for you, Frank."

"Jesus, how?"

"You might have waked up some night to find her tearing out your throat."

Frank shuddered visibly. "She really pushed this camping trip. She had to convince me to come. They—the others like her—knew this was going to happen. My God, they *planned* it. She was going to kill me out here. I can see it in her eyes."

"You don't know that for sure, Frank," Nancy told him.

"Go look at her and then tell me you don't believe it. I just don't understand it; I don't understand how I could be married to a woman for twenty years and not know what she really is. And I wonder how many more marriages there are like mine?"

A scream turned them around and they all ran to the neat row of tents. Traci was on the ground, struggling to get up. They could all see the slickness of blood staining one side of the teenager's head, a black smear in the faint moonlight pushing through the gathering clouds.

Susan used a flashlight to inspect the cut on her daughter's head. Though bloody, it was only a small cut and did not appear serious. Nancy wet a cloth and handed it to Susan.

"She's gone!" the teenager said, sitting up. "Cathy's gone!"

Matt looked inside the tent. The ropes that had been around the woman's ankles had been chewed through. He had no way of knowing how she'd freed herself from the ropes around her wrists, but she had. Her pack was gone.

"I was walking back to check on the kids when she ran out of the tent and hit me with a club. She went over the wall like a deer jumping over a log."

"Norm?" Matt called. Norm was stationed at the rear, taking his turn at guarding the horses. "You all right?"

"I'm fine. She didn't come this way."

"Now the breakaways have a leader on site," Nick remarked. "One who knows every inch of this camp and just how vulnerable we really are."

"She also knows that Dan is out there," Dennis said.

"Oh, don't worry about Dan," the guide replied. "He can take care of himself. It's *us* you'd better worry about. Cathy can't let any of us leave here alive. She knows about the backup teams on the outside and knows they'll be in here in two or three days. They've got to destroy us within

191

that time frame. She'll work those breakaways up into a fury by telling them all sorts of lies about us. She's a smart one, and I'll bet that right now she's working on making a deal with the CWA."

"What kind of deal?" Polly asked.

Matt picked it up. "She'll convince them that if they help destroy us, she'll let them go free. But of course she won't. As soon as we're destroyed, she'll have the Sataws turn on them. And as stupid as Monroe Bishner is, he'll jump at that if it's offered."

"How about fire?" Dennis asked. "Are the Sataws afraid of fire?"

"No," Nick nixed that. "Hell, the tribe's been usin' fire for centuries to cook and heat with. We've just got to hold on until Matt's backup people can get in here."

"No way we can do that," Matt said. "Monroe's people can rush us and overwhelm us during the first wave. The Sataws would have done it if they'd had any firepower."

Clouds had begun moving in quickly and the moon was now hidden. All could smell the approaching rain.

"Shit!" Matt said.

"What's the matter?" Susan asked.

"I was going to start a forest fire to draw attention," he told her.

"You can forget that," Nick said. "It'll be pouring in minutes. Besides, unless it's a raging monster of a fire, the Forest Service usually lets smaller ones burn out. Clears the underbrush and so forth. They'd probably order a flyby to check it out. But with all the smoke, it's very doubtful we'd be spotted."

The first scattered raindrops began falling. Great big fat raindrops that chilled those it touched.

"Get to shelter," Matt ordered. "Those on watch get into rain gear. It's going to be a long, wet, miserable night, people."

"Beats being dead," Nancy said.

3

The handwritten note was wrapped in bark to keep it dry. It had been tied onto a stick and the stick tossed into the camp of the CWA men.

Monroe read the note several times. "None of them horrible things wrote this," he guessed accurately. "This was done by a human being. So them things got real people on their side. Whoever wrote this wants a meetin' with us. But where?"

"Right behind you," Cathy's voice came out of the edge of the woods.

Monroe and Luther and Jim Bob and Judd damn near shit in their underwear. They spun around, weapons at the ready. But they could see nothing.

"Who is that out there?" Monroe demanded. "Show yourself or we'll spray the woods with lead."

"You wouldn't hit anything," Cathy told him. "Don't be foolish. How about a deal?"

"What kind of deal?"

"You aren't in a very good position to ask. If you're interested, say so."

"We're interested."

She talked, her voice carrying over the slow-falling rain. Monroe began smiling, as did Luther and Jim Bob. Jones was listening, but he was not smiling. To him the deal smelled bad. He looked around. He had been sitting by his tent, near the eastern perimeter, far away from any fire. The other men had left their tents and walked toward the mysterious voice. Jones looked around him. He was alone. He pulled his pack toward him and leaned back, lying flat on the wet ground. Slowly he shifted position and allowed himself to roll over the edge of the small rise, knowing the sounds of the falling rain would cover any noise he might make.

It was about a mile across the valley to that government campsite—if it was a government campsite, and Jones had his doubts. If he didn't come up on one of those damn things out here, he'd make it. To hell with the CWA. He had allowed himself to be recruited because at that time he was filled with hatred toward the black race, flat broke, and running from the law for killing that son-of-a-bitch who'd raped and assaulted his wife . . . and walked free on a technicality. But Jones was not an unreasonable hater. He knew there were both good and bad people in every race. And he couldn't bring himself to the point of hating an entire race of people. It was stupid. How can you hate someone you don't even know?

He chanced a look back. Even at this short distance, the falling rain was obscuring the camp's fires. Jones slipped into his heavy pack and started across the valley.

"Somebody's crossin' the stream," Nick said. "And he's walkin' like a man carryin' a load."

"Jesus!" Dennis said. "I can hardly even see the damn stream, much less somebody crossing it."

"Two things most of us crossovers keep is good eyesight and a good sense of smell. My smeller is about gone, but my eyes are still good."

"What's up?" Matt asked, walking to the log-and-stake wall.

"We got company. One man."

194

"I'm awful vulnerable out here," Jones called. "I'm friendly. To hell with that bunch of nuts across the valley. And I won't blame you if you don't believe a word I'm saying."

"Come on up," Matt called. "For some reason the Sataws have gone."

"The what?"

"Links."

"They're probably with that fancy-talking woman over at the other camp. She popped up out of nowhere. Or at least her voice did. I never did see her."

"Now we know where Cathy went," Dennis said.

"I'm carrying a Colt AR-15. I got it slung. I got a Beretta 9mm in a holster, right side."

They could all hear him panting as he came closer.

"You must be carryin' a heavy load," Nick called.

"I am. I brought all the grenades I could swipe and a lot of ammo. But fear is a good part of my breathing hard. Crossing that valley will take it out of you."

Nick chuckled. "I think he's all right. He's honest about his fear, anyway."

"You see anybody else with him, Nick?" Dennis asked.

"No. He's alone."

Matt opened the gate and Jones ducked inside. The gate closed behind him on rope hinges. With a sigh of relief, he slipped out of his pack and set in on the ground. "I thought I was in good shape, but that thing must weigh a good hundred and fifty pounds." He handed his rifle to Matt. "Just to show you I'm friendly. You want my pistol?"

"I don't even want your rifle." He handed it back. "Have you eaten?"

"No, sir. I'm Hal Jones. Ex-airborne, LRRP in Nam, ex-accountant, and I'm wanted by the law for killing the man who raped my wife. The courts cut him loose on a technicality. My Betty went insane and killed herself shortly after she was raped . . . and sodomized," he added.

"I hope the son-of-a-bitch suffered for a long time," Norm said, walking up to the group.

Jones turned to face the man. "Yes, sir. He did. I kept him alive for three days out in the desert, outside Las Vegas. He was a black man. I had a lot of unreasonable hate in my heart for the black race for a time."

Norm grinned. "That's understandable. I did some LRRPing in Nam myself. What outfit were you in?"

"I was with the 82nd originally. I transfered over after LRRP school to a ranger company and volunteered for another tour."

"No kidding? I did the same damn dumb thing."

The men walked off, laughing and talking about the war.

Jones leaned back in his camp chair and smiled. The group had taken a large tarp and made a kitchen and dining area that was more or less waterproof, depending upon where one sat. "That's the best food I've had in weeks. My compliments to the cook."

"Thank you, kind sir," Polly said. "The stew was my doing."

"You don't know whether the CWA took the deal Cathy offered?" Matt asked.

"No, sir. I saw my chance and got out of there while I could."

"Knock off the 'sir'. I'm Matt. We're in too tight a situation here for formalities."

"Yes, sir . . . Matt."

"Make a guess as to Monroe's decision," Matt urged.

"Oh, he'll take it. Then just as soon as they overrun us—if they overrun us—that woman will have them all killed. I never got a look at her, but her voice chilled me." He looked across at Frank. "I'm sorry, I didn't mean . . ."

Frank waved him silent and smiled. "There is no need to apologize for the truth. I've resigned myself to what she is." He looked at Nick. "And I don't mean her heritage, either."

"I know what you mean," the guide said.

"If you don't mind telling me," Jones said, "just what is she?"

He sat very still and silent while Matt explained part of it, then let Nick finish. Jones's eyes were open wide when Nick wrapped it up.

They were all watching him closely for his reaction. Jones refilled his tin cup with coffee and sat back down. "I used to hunt when I was a kid back in Indiana. By the time I was seventeen, I'd quit it—not on moral grounds, because I know that herds have to be thinned due to the lack of the game animals' natural predators. It was a certain type of hunter that finished it for me. They wouldn't care if they were killing the last of a species. They can't wait to get out in the woods and kill something—anything. It's a blood lust with them that I never had. To kill anything. Hell, each other, sometimes. And I believe that all of God's creatures have a right to live. Including the members of this tribe you talked about, those who want to relocate and survive. Sure, I'll go along with that. But I want to tell you all now, lay it all on the table, if I'm attacked by these tribe members, I'm gonna take some with me before I go down."

Nick smiled across the way at him. "So am I, partner. Believe it."

Matt told them all to go to bed and get as much rest as possible. He believed the attack from the CWA men would come just before dawn, during his watch. They would wake up at the sound of the first perimeter banger going off.

Jones slept for a few hours, in Matt's tent, and then came out to join him on the dogwatch. The rain was still coming down, slow and steady.

"That Norman Hunt, he seems like a real nice fellow," Jones said.

"My best friend in high school. He's all right. This whole bunch, with the exception of Tom Dalton, is a very nice group of people. And they'll stand and fight, too. I saw that yesterday. Had you been married long, Jones?"

"No. I got married late. I was forty, she was thirty. We'd been married two years when that bastard grabbed her that night."

"I think I might be able to help you with that warrant that's against you. But I can't make any firm promises."

"I won't do time for killing that man," Jones said. "And that's firm with me. If we get out of this mess, I'll just drift back out of sight."

"That's no way to live. Let me see what I can do. If the right strings are pulled, it isn't as difficult as you might think to set someone up with a new identity: social security number, driver's license, background, the whole bag. Are the charges state or federal?"

"State. Nevada."

"That's even better. Just stay the hell out of Nevada." Matt lifted his rifle, hesitated, then sighted in a lump on the ground that hadn't been there an hour before. The lump lay directly in front of the stockade, about a hundred yards out. He pulled the trigger. As the slug struck it the lump howled and turned into a man wearing cammies. The wounded man lurched to his feet and Matt put another bullet into him, the slug knocking the man down. The rainy night was filled with charging CWA men coming at the stockade from three sides.

The hour before dawn was shattered by men hitting trip wires, setting off the perimeter bangers. One CWA man stumbled into an ankle-high wire and pitched forward, impaling himself on sharpened stakes. Another stepped into a punji pit, driving sharpened stakes into his foot and calf. He lay on the wet ground screaming in pain.

The defenders had fortified their positions with extra logs and rocks. Those not using weapons, especially the kids, jumped behind a three-foot enclosure in the center of the camp built of logs and rocks and dirt. It was wet and cold and soon very muddy behind the small inner fort, but the walls would stop any bullets that got past the bigger stockade.

On that wet and cold early morning Wade got his initiation into blood. Using Nick's lever-action .30-.30, he pumped lead into the air and saw one of his bullets strike a running man—quite by accident. The CWA man folded up and tumbled to the ground, both hands holding his shattered belly, and died with a scream on his lips.

Wade turned his head, vomited on the ground, and began shoving fresh loads into the rifle. He hadn't come here with violence in mind, but by God, if they wanted a fight, he'd do his best to give them one.

"Back! Back!" Monroe shouted. "Fall back, north and south."

"We can't let them stay out there and plink at us come the daylight," Matt said. "I'll take the timber on the south side. You feel like taking the north side, Norm?"

"Just try to stop me."

"Grab some grenades and let's go!" While Norm was gearing up, changing into cammies that Jones had loaned him, Matt ran across the sloppy compound ground to Nick. "Can you sense or smell any Sataws out there?"

"No. I think they laid back for this first rush and let these kooks and bums spill their blood. I'm goin' out while it's still dark and collect weapons and ammo from the dead . . . and finish off any still left alive. You be careful, Matt."

"Same to you, partner. See you."

199

Everything came rushing back to Norman Hunt as he left the stockade and belly-crawled on the ground toward the timber. All his hundreds of hours spent in life-and-death situations in Nam returned, springing loose from where he'd carefully tucked them away. The tangled jungles and rainforests and mountains and flat, dusty deadly plains of Nam came ripping back. His Mini-14 slung, he crawled forward, knife in hand.

He'd helped Matt lay out the bangers and the pits and the trip wires. He avoided them, some by just inches, as he worked his way into the timber. The ground was wet and slick, and Norm made no noise as he made his way into the brush. He muddied the blade of his knife to prevent reflection. His heart was pounding and the adrenalin raced through him. He did not realize it, but he was smiling.

Matt slithered to a halt just a few feet from the bulk of a CWA man. He waited like a great predator, animal, silently checking out that which he stalked.

"Sanborn?" came the hoarse whisper off to Matt's right. Matt lay perfectly still.

"Yeah," Sanborn softly called.

"How many got hit?"

"Bugger and Monty for sure. I seen Marcel get a slug in the leg." Sanborn left the protection of the tree and inched his way toward where Matt lay in wait.

"I seen Danny die," the second man whispered. "It was awful. A trip stake caught him in the belly. He died awful hard."

Sanborn was almost on top of Matt, crawling on his hands and knees, when Matt swung the big knife, the blade catching Sanborn in the hollow of his throat. Blood squirted out and the scream on Sanborn's tongue died there, no sound able to push past the ruined throat. Sanborn's legs kicked and jerked as Matt drove the blade deeper into his throat, twisting it, almost decapitating the man.

"Sanborn! God damn, boy. Cut out the noise! What's the matter with you? You'll get us all in trouble."

Sanborn's troubles were just beginning as he winged his way into the afterlife to face his maker. Sanborn would never make any more noise on this earth.

"I seen Nutley go down with a bullet in his shoulder. He didn't look too bad to me."

Silence.

"Sanborn?"

Matt had sheathed his knife and pulled the pin on a grenade, holding the spoon down. He waited.

"What's all that racket over yonder?" the call came about thirty feet in front of Matt.

Matt released the spoon and tossed the grenade. It exploded in a flash of fire and shrapnel. Someone had his finger on the trigger of his weapon when the full force of the explosion blew a leg off the man. The finger pulled the trigger and a full thirty-round clip was emptied into the dampness, sending CWA men diving for cover.

Matt tossed another grenade and the explosion rocked the predawn.

"Get the hell outta here!" Judd screamed. "Back into the valley, boys!"

Norm looked down into the face of the man with his throat slit and almost cut off an ear to take back for confirmation of the body count. He mentally shook himself back to reality and crawled on just as the first of Matt's grenades exploded. He sheathed his knife and pulled a Fire-Frag from his pocket, pulling the pin and holding the spoon down, his eyes searching for a target.

He soon found a target: two men crouched together behind a log, their heads sticking up. Stupid, Norm thought . . . you never look over something; you always look around it.

He tossed the grenade, the mini-Claymore striking one

of the men in the head.

"Oww!" the CWA man hollered. "God damn it, who the hell's a-chunkin' rocks?"

The grenade exploded and two more CWA men would never cause any more trouble on this earth.

Norm slipped his rifle from sling and began shooting at running shapes in the gray of dawning. He got one righteous hit and probably wounded another before the CWA men had fallen back out of range, leaving the edges of the flat and heading back across the valley.

Norm, like Matt, began collecting weapons and ammo. Norm found a wounded CWA man.

"Help me!" the man cried. "Oh, God, please help me. It hurts so bad."

I'll help you, all right, Norm thought. He shot him between the eyes.

4

"We're fucked, Monroe," Jim Bob told it like he saw it. "We both seen how at least a couple of them is like ghosts in the woods. They got grenades. They got the weapons off the dead, and that is Bugger, Monty, Danny, Sanborn, Reed, Ellsworth, and Maynard. And that gives them one hell of a lot of firepower. We got a half dozen wounded, two of them real bad off. They gonna die if we don't get them to a hospital. That's a government man over yonder, Monroe, from the damn CIA. I don't want the CIA on my ass . . ."

Monroe waved him silent. "Shut up, Jim Bob. I know all that. Don't you think I know all that? All right. We can't leave, Jim Bob. So put that out of your head. We made a deal with that . . . woman, or whatever she is, and she's gonna hold our feet to the fire and see that we keep our end of the bargain. We either kill all them folks or we die. That's as plain as I can make it. We just don't have any choice in the matter. None a-tall."

"Some of the boys is talkin' about leavin', Monroe."

"Im-press on them that they can't do that. Them links would kill them before they got a half mile from camp. How many men we got that's able to fight?"

"Right at thirty."

"Tell Judd to take ten of the boys and get around behind them people. On that cliff behind them . . . what are you shakin' your head about, Jim Bob?"

"Can't be done, Monroe. The woman said that half-breed guide, or whatever he is, picked that spot well. It ain't no wooded mountain; it's a sheer rock wall on all four sides. The links can go up and down it like monkeys—which they's probably related to—but no human can."

Monroe did some fancy cussing of the down-home variety, then finally stopped for breath and said, "We're damned if we do and damned if we don't."

"An' it don't look like this rain is ever gonna stop," Jim Bob added.

"Thanks, Jim Bob. You're a real comfort to a person."

"I figure if we can hold out another sixty hours, some of your people will be coming in," Nick said.

"Don't count on that," Matt told him. "It's all right to let the others think that to keep their morale up. But don't count on my backup teams until you actually see them."

Nick smiled. "I was just talkin' to hear myself rattle. There ain't no way we can last another sixty hours. I don't give a damn how much firepower we got . . . we don't have the people power. Oh, we'll kick the asses off them CWA people. But the breakaways are quite another matter."

"Nick, you think you could lead the group out of here if there was a diversion?"

The guide thought about it for a moment. "Maybe . . . but it'd be a slim shot at best. A one-man diversion?"

"Two—Norm and me. Jones would go with you and the group for added firepower."

"I could maybe lead them into friendly country; I'm pretty sure I could do that. I'm talking about the tribe. But

Jones had best stay back here. The tribe don't like them CWA men, and Jones might be marked."

"The three of us could create one hell of a diversion, for sure. It might buy you the time you need."

"How do you know Norman will go for it?"

"I asked him."

"Jones?"

"Him, too. He feels like he should atone for joining the CWA in the first place."

"That's crap. He's not a bad person. I'd bet on that."

"Norm and me are, Nick. With our lives."

"That's about it," Matt told the group. He had called everybody together, including the kids. The children had proved to be brave troopers about this whole mess, and Matt felt it would be unfair to exclude them. "I don't know why the Unseen, the Sataws, the breakaways, whatever you choose to call them, have let so many good opportunities to take us slide by; I'm just glad they did. But there's no way we can last another two and a half days here. And there's no guarantee that help will come if we do. It's only a matter of time before we're overwhelmed. For the moment the woods around us are clear, and I don't know why that is so. But it tells me we're up against a group of people who know little about battlefield strategy. So I'm going to suggest a pullout while we have the time. They won't be expecting anything like it to happen during the day; that's the last thing they'd anticipate. But I can't order any of you to do it. You talk it over for a time, then decide. Take a vote. I'll stand guard over by the fence."

Matt relieved Norm at the gate and told him to get with his family during the discussions. Jones stood at the north end of the compound and Matt took the south end while the family members mulled over the idea of a pullout.

It was a good day for it, Matt thought. Cool, wet, foggy, with mist hanging over the valley. Sound would be muffled. He longed for a cigarette. Once he heard a flat popping sound followed by a muffled cry coming from the group. He decided he was wrong.

It didn't take the group long to make up their minds. Less than five minutes had passed when Norm walked over to Matt. "They voted almost unanimously to go for it."

"Let me guess who voted against it: Tom Dalton."

"Right. He said we should make a deal with both sides. He was outvoted."

"Nick laid out the risks involved?"

"Yeah. He thinks Dan is tucked away out of sight across the valley, above the CWA camp, watching us through binoculars. He's pretty sure Dan will see the pullout from his vantage point and know where Nick's taking them."

"You don't have to stay, Norm. You need to be with your family. Jones and I can handle it."

Norm shook his head. "We're the only three with extensive combat experience. Hell, we're the only ones with *any* type of combat experience. No, I've got to stay. If my family makes it out, that's all that matters."

"Tell them to start packing up one at a time, with as little movement as possible. I don't want everybody to start rushing around. I can't believe we're not being watched."

"Cathy was very sure of herself, Matt. And Nick says the breakaways probably believe they have us trapped. I think we're under very loose surveillance. We just might be able to pull this off. I'll get them packed up."

It didn't take long. The tents would remain where they were pitched. Each group member was taking only a waterproof ground sheet which could be used for protection when and if they were forced to spend the night. They took foods that did not have to be heated, it would not be all that tasty, but it would keep them alive. Matt,

Nick, and Norm had stripped the dead CWA men of their camouflage jackets and shirts and those were passed around to the group. Everything that might jingle was either tied down or discarded.

Matt singled out Tom Dalton and straightened out a few points. "If you fuck up and get any member of this group hurt or killed or captured, Dalton, I'll track you down and kill you. Is that understood?"

"Are you quite through?"

"Get your shit together and get ready to ride." Matt turned away from him and walked straight to Nick.

"You about ready to pull out?"

"Sittin' on go."

"How do you want to exit the camp?"

"We'll walk the horses out one at a time, stayin' as close to the face of that rock behind us as possible. I'll go first, then the women and kids, then the men, with you personally escortin' that damn sorry Tom Dalton so's he don't attempt to make a run for it."

Nick hesitated, then said, "Once we get clear of this valley, if Dalton acts up any, I'll fall back with him and lose him. I can't risk a shot."

"Whatever you think is best, Nick."

"Best would have been for his mama to have aborted him," the guide said shortly.

"Eerie," Jones said.

The group had been gone for nearly half an hour and there had been no sounds of shots being fired or screaming or yelling. Matt figured the group had probably made the north end of the valley; Nick had said that he knew a way through what seemed to be a box canyon.

"I think they made it," Matt said. "Against all odds, I by God believe they made it out." He fed more sticks to the fire he was tending. The three of them had each built a small fire to give the appearance of a large group still in the stockade, and they had deliberately exposed themselves several times, each time wearing a different article of clothing left behind by the campers. "Let's start packing up our stuff, boys."

Matt divvied up the gear he had brought in among the three of them.

"You damn sure came prepared for war," Norm said, adding, "and ain't I glad."

"Let's get ready to go. At dusk we'll slip out the south end and work our way over to the CWA camp. Whatever we can't carry, we'll cache. I'm going to turn the horses loose just before we leave. We can't go crashing through the woods on horseback."

"Suits me," Norm said. "My butt's still sore from the ride in."

"No sign of this rain letting up," Jones said, walking to the edge of the tarp-covered cooking area and looking out, letting the rain hit his face. "That's good. Those guys over there were bitching and griping about how miserable they were when I left. They'll really be down in the dumps when we hit them."

"You mind if I ask a question?" Norm glanced at him.

"Why did I join that group?"

Norm nodded.

"You have to understand my state of mind when I joined. I was down about as far as a person can go. I'd been on the run, seeing my name in the paper and my face on TV. I was flat broke, living out of garbage cans and thrown-away food behind fast-food places, when I saw a flyer about some meeting a group was having. I went for the free food. At the meeting, there were maybe a hundred people. The food was good and there was plenty of it. The speech was . . . interesting. It really was. Emmett Trumball talked about how foreigners were taking American jobs away from Americans. He talked about the welfare state and about the decent, hardworking and law-abiding taxpayer subsidizing bastard babies who pop out of mothers like cans of beans off a belt and about mothers who refuse to work. He talked about the decline of morals in the nation and dirty songs and dirty films and dirty books and how the hands of the police are tied by liberals while criminals go free. And how the dope pushers are running loose and oftentimes when a black criminal is shot by the police there is a riot and looting immediately afterward. And I sat there and I thought: Jesus, this guy is right. Everything he is saying makes sense. If you take just those words, he's right. So there I sat, for the first time in months full of good food, dry and warm, and I thought: what the hell? Why not? Why not join this group? What has the country I fought for, was wounded twice for, and paid taxes to for years done for me? They branded me a criminal for demanding justice. I lost my business, my home, and all my savings. I lost everything because the laws in this country are so fucked up as to be unbelievable."

He had not spoken emotionally; his had not been the voice of a zealot. He was telling it as he had experienced it.

The three of them made their rounds and checked their perimeters. They were finishing packing when Jones said, "What the three of us are facing in these woods, that's nothing, boys. What's out there," he pointed his finger, "in the so-called civilized areas of America, that scares me."

5

The director of central intelligence pushed back his chair and stood up from his desk. He checked his watch. He had fifty minutes to make his luncheon engagement with the President. He buttoned his collar and straightened his tie before slipping into his suit coat. He felt lousy, worse than he had yesterday. He'd make an appointment to see his personal physician: he jotted it down on a pad on his desk. He took two steps from his desk and felt a tremendous weight slam into his chest. He went down on one knee, frantically clutching at a corner of his desk with his hands. He seemed to have no strength in his hands. They felt numb.

Jesus! he thought, *I'm having a heart attack.*

He managed to crawl around behind his desk and tried to reach the phone to punch a button, any button. He could not make his fingers do what his mind commanded. He felt a hard moment of panic at the thought of dying. He thought about his wife, his kids, his grandchildren. So much left undone; so much more in life he wanted to do. Too damn much pressure on him in this job.

Then he thought of Matt Jordan. The project code-named the Unseen. The DCI managed to knock the phone from his desk to the floor. The receiver fell off. He punched a button for an open line.

After a few seconds of anxiously calling "Sir? Sir?" his secretary ran into the office. She took one look at her boss and yelled for help.

While waiting for the EMTs to get there, the office staff managed to loosen the DCI's tie and put a throw pillow under his head. They noticed that one side of the man's face seemed frozen.

"Stroke," one of the women said softly.

"Choppers . . . Matt," the DCI muttered, slurring the words.

"What'd he say?" a woman asked.

"Sounded like he said the chopper's back."

"What chopper?"

"In some operation, I guess."

"Jesus, what operation? We've got dozens going."

"Not too many involving helicopters. Richard would know."

"Christ, Richard is in . . . where is he today? Greece, I think."

"Advise the President. Get on the horn and tell Richard we need him back here right now!"

". . . Seen," the DCI muttered. "Seen . . . choppers Batt."

"I know what he's saying," a man said, stepping around and picking up the phone. He wants the choppers to pull back from the operation Matt's on."

The DCI tried to shake his head, tried to speak, tried to tell the man it most definitely was *not* what he wanted, but only the most grotesque sounds came from his mouth. He began losing consciousness.

"That's a joint Bureau-Agency operation," another man spoke. "And one hell of a hot potato. I'm not about to give the order to pull those choppers out of that area. Husky's in there."

The DCI was unconscious.

"Well, somebody's got to give the orders! God damn it, you heard the man. Those were his orders."

"I'm not so sure," a woman said. "Maybe he was trying to say, 'Choppers, Matt.'"

"What the hell does that mean?"

She shrugged. "Beats me."

The number three man came rushing in and was brought up to date—at least as much as those in the room could tell him. "Has the President been told of this?"

"Yes, sir."

The EMTs were wheeling the DCI out of the room on a gurney, an oxygen mask over his nose and mouth.

A file folder was placed in the number three man's hands. He sat down and opened the file, reading slowly. "God damn!" he finally said.

"See what I mean?" someone said.

"Get me the President," Number Three said.

"What the hell is Operation Unseen?" the President asked.

"I beg your pardon, sir?"

"I said, what the hell is Operation Unseen?"

"Sir, it says right here that this operation was given your official go-ahead."

"Get over here. And bring that file. This conversation is between us and us alone. You understand that?"

"Yes, sir."

"Why are you handling this? Where is Richard?"

"He's . . . out of the country, doing an on-site inspection of stations."

"Who ordered that?"

"You did, sir. It says so right here."

The President strung together some words that would have caused his supporters on the evangelical right to go into hysterics. "You get Richard back into this country and do it immediately. By the fastest possible method. You bring yourself and that file to me and to me alone. Now!"

"Yes, sir."

The President punched another button on his phone. "Cancel all my appointments for the rest of the day, please. And show Mr. Manetti in as soon as he arrives."

He leaned back in his chair. "What the hell is going on?" he muttered.

The President read the report twice, then closed the folder, a look of pure astonishment on his face. "I never ordered the reopening of a National Guard base in Montana. I never heard of any tribe in the Primitive Area of Idaho. I never ordered the relocation of them. I never okayed this operation. I've never heard of *any* of this."

"Mr. President," Manetti said, "I don't know what to say. If you didn't order this, who did?"

"How the hell should I know? I want Richard in this office as soon as he lands at Andrews. I want Agent Simmons brought in from Denver! Matt Jordan. Matt Jordan. That name sure is familiar."

"You gave him a commendation when you were DCI, sir. After Operation Roses."

"Ah, yes! That Matt Jordan. Husky. Sure, good man. Why would the DCI want the helicopters recalled if he has a man in extreme danger in that area, Manetti?"

"I don't know, sir. We're not sure exactly what he said. He was either saying 'chopper's back,' or 'choppers Matt!' One or the other."

"'Choppers, Matt,' probably. He was trying to warn those in the office that he had a man in the field who was in danger. How is Husky doing in this operation?"

"I don't know, sir."

The President closed his eyes for a moment in frustration. Nothing ever changed around the Pickle Factory. Especially when Number One attempted to single-handedly run an operation. "How many helicopters are involved in this operation?"

"I don't know, sir."

The President swiveled in his chair, turning his back to the man to keep Manetti from seeing the anger and frustration building on his face. He calmed himself and slowly faced the number three man. "We appear to have an invisible government, Manetti. If you know what I mean."

"Yes, sir. Someone very powerful who is issuing orders in your name."

"Precisely. But it has to be more than one person."

"Yes, sir. May I offer a suggestion, sir?"

"Of course."

"Pull in Husky's contacts, at least by phone, and get as up to date as you can on what's going on out there in the Primitive Area."

The President nodded. "You work out of this office. This office, and tape everything that is said. Now, then, who can we trust?"

Manetti hesitated. "Some opinions and some observations, sir?"

"Say what's on your mind."

"One: we've obviously been compromised. Two: I'm not going to trust anybody in Washington except Richard. He'll be landing in about twelve hours. Three: you don't trust anybody on your staff until I can pull in some out-of-town personnel and start running extensive records' checks. Four . . ."

The President held up his hand. "What are we checking for?"

"Family history."

"I see. You think this . . . tribe really exists?"

"Yes, sir."

"You think the people issuing orders in my name are distant relatives of this tribe?"

"Yes, sir."

"Jesus Christ! Go on."

"Four: I'm going to get on the horn and pull some polygraph and PSE experts in from our stations in South

214

America. They're Argentines and Brazilians. There's no way they could be related to these . . . Unseen beings. Five: I can have them in country by dawn. With your permission, we start with your personal staff, beginning with your chief of staff."

"You have my permission."

"I'll get started."

"Manetti?"

"Yes, sir?"

"For the time being, you and I are the only ones who know about this."

"Yes, sir. The Secret Service, sir?"

"Not until they're cleared."

"Yes, sir."

Jones had been listening to a small radio left behind by one of the kids. He walked over to Matt. "Did you know the director of central intelligence, Matt?"

"I've met him. Why?"

"He just had a heart attack. He's unconscious and hasn't spoken a word since he was stricken. According to the news I just heard, the President canceled all appointments for today and something very hush-hush is going on."

"Jesus!" Matt said. "What else is going to happen?"

"Something we need to know, Matt?" Norm asked.

"The DCI—Director of Central Intelligence—took over this operation when the political heat got too much for the number two man. He's the only one back East that, so far as I know, has any knowledge of this mess."

"So . . . we might really be in trouble?" Norm opined.

"You've got that right. And you can bet that Cathy has heard the same news, or someone has heard it and got word to her. Let's cut out, boys. I'll fix the corral gate so when the horses get hungry or thirsty, they can leave easily enough."

"God damn!" Jones said, looking toward the valley below. "They're almost ready to cross the stream now, Matt. In force. And what are those? The links are with them!"

"Hit the timber, boys."

"Stand and fight?"

Matt took one quick glance through the mist and rain. It looked like a hundred shapes crossing the stream. "Hell, no!"

Dan intercepted Nick and the group. "I figured you'd take this trail, old son. Come on, we'll head for that old mining complex by the river."

"Dan, I got to get these people to our kin so's they can get underground to safety."

The old man shook his head. "No go, son. Breakaways are waiting to ambush you. Spread out all over the timber. You'd never get through. I got that information out of one early this morning."

"How'd you leave him?"

"Dead."

Nick stared at him, waiting.

"All bets are off for us and for anyone else who supports the relocation plans, partner. The breakaway told me the word's gone out nationwide. There ain't nothing any of us in here can do to prevent a bloodbath."

Dennis had worked his way to where the men were meeting. "But the breakaways can't win," he said, shifting in the saddle in an attempt to ease his sore butt. "They will eventually be destroyed. All they can do with this violence is poison the minds of the public against those tribe members who want peace."

"That's been pointed out to them. They don't seem to care. The wild urge is like dope, it seems. Their defense is

216

that the gods made them the way they are, and man ain't got no right to try to change them."

"I could tear that defense all to pieces in any court of law."

"You want the chance?"

"What do you mean?"

"The tribe's gonna need a good lawyer once they get on the outside."

"Mr. Watson, it would be a pleasure."

"They'll be pleased. Come on, folks. We got us a long and hairy ride to get to the old mine."

"Gone!" Monroe yelled in frustration. "The bastards is gone!"

"They didn't get far," Cathy said to a normal-appearing man who, with a dozen others, had joined the breakaways the night before.

"We'll catch them," the man said. He looked out over the valley. "Two more groups coming in. Look."

Cathy turned, a cruel glint in her eyes. Her lips peeled back in a snarl. At least twenty-five mounted men and women were crossing the valley. She fought back the wild animal urge that welled up within her and said, "That means the region is sealed. And that means something else too."

The man smiled. His eyes were savage. "Yes. Do we do it now?"

"It will mean taking some casualties."

"If it is a war to the finish, that is to be expected."

Cathy suddenly threw back her head and screamed like an angry panther, scaring the crap out of Monroe and everyone else. The Sataws jumped the men of the CWA, attacked them so quickly and so violently many of the men had no chance at all to defend themselves.

Claude went down to the wet earth, his throat torn out,

dying with his eyes wide open in shock and fear. Cathy knelt down and lapped at his blood while the carnage continued all around her.

Roswald was ridden to the ground by several Sataws and screamed as clawed hands tore open his stomach and pulled out his intestines. Donny got off one shot, killing a young man standing close to Cathy before the man's throat was torn from him and tossed in a bloody, quivering pile to one side.

Yates turned to run toward his horse, was tripped by a completely normal-appearing woman, and fell heavily to the ground. She leaped on his back and began gnawing at his throat while he screamed and attempted to throw her off.

Marcel yelled at his horse to move, but it was too late. A Sataw leaped flatfooted from the ground and knocked him out of the saddle. Marcel's neck was broken before he hit the ground.

Monroe, Luther, Carl, and Jim Bob made the timberline and were clear just seconds after the horrible scream sprang from Cathy's throat.

Alton was yanked screaming from his horse and his head beaten to unrecognizable pulp by a man using the butt of Alton's AK-47. A few Sataws took the opportunity to dine on raw flesh from Alton's body.

Floyd, Judd, and Kane made the timber and cut west, heading back across the valley.

Hardin, Sanders, and Duff were being bea   n to death with clubs and shovels left behind by the campers. The wet air began to stink with the odor of fresh blood and relaxed bowels and bladders.

Nutley, wounded in an earlier battle, was thrown from his horse and tried to crawl away to the timber. A very pretty young woman, dressed in designer jeans and wearing expensive jewelry, beat him unconscious with a club, then dropped down on all fours and began drinking

218

the blood gushing from his neck.

"*Oh my God up yonder in Heaven somewheres Jesus Your beloved son Mary whatever in the hell she was all the angels everywhere mama and daddy Brother Cecil of the Church I give money to all my good life somebody anybody everybody please come and save us from this fuckin' awfulness!*" a CWA man fell to his knees and prayed, running his words together while he pissed in his dirty underwear. His rifle lay in the churned-up mud and his pistol, belted around his waist, was forgotten in his wild fear.

A Sataw jammed a clawed hand into his mouth and jerked out his tongue, then stuck his mouth to the man's mouth and began sucking out the blood, holding the jerking, hunching victim by the ears while he noisily drank his fill.

Dolan made the timberline and was running for his life when a creature reared up in front of him and roared, his stinking breath foul. Dolan cut to his right. He had lost his weapon back yonder in the mud and the blood. Dolan ran right into a tree, knocking him to the ground and addling him further. His last glimpse of life on earth was slightly marred by the face of a Sataw, grinning and drooling and smacking its thick lips at the prospect of an early dinner.

Seymour, Marwood, and Ely were galloping full tilt across the valley, alternately cussing and praying as they tried to stay in the saddle.

B.O. Shanty was just a tad too slow. He made it to the edge of the flat when his horse slipped in the mud and threw him to the ground. B.O. had always enjoyed pronging his daughters. He'd been brought up for incest a number of times but the frightened little girls had always refused to testify against their daddy. B.O. would never again molest anybody. A handsome young man, fashionably dressed and wearing expensive cowboy boots and a nice smile on his pleasant face, pinned B.O. to the ground by driving a stake through his stomach.

"Oh, Lord, Lord Almighty!" B.O. squalled. "You ain't a-gonna leave me like this here, is you?" He screamed in pain and tried to pull the stake from his stomach. But his fingers were bloody and muddy and the stake was driven deep into the ground. B.O. whimpered in fear on the ground, like many of the small animals he'd trapped during his lifetime must have done while waiting for death to relieve them of the pain they could not understand and did not deserve.

"Oh, yes," the young man said.

"This ain't no Christian thing to do," B.O. gasped.

"And I am my brother's keeper, and I will fight his fight; and speak the word for beast and bird, till the world shall set things right."

"Huh?" B.O. said, looking up at the young man through pain-filled eyes.

"Ella Wheeler Wilcox," the young man said.

"I ain't never heard of her. Where'd she pick and sing?" The young man walked back to the bloody ground around the compound.

"Help!" B.O. hollered.

"Don't harm the children," Cathy said. "We can reeducate them. Kill all the others. Especially that damned CIA man. Find them. Find them!"

"Help!" B.O. hollered. "Somebody come help me."

High above, the vultures began their slow and patient circling.

6

The rundown and ramshackle old mining complex had been shut down right after World War Two. The equipment that could have been rafted out had been, and all the rest was abandoned. The buildings were rotted and dangerous, and both state and federal governments had posted signs warning people not to enter the old buildings.

Tom spoke for the first time since leaving the stockade on the flat. "Place looks dangerous."

"It is," Nick said shortly. "But what's under it ain't."

"What's under it, Mr. Nick?" Judy asked.

"Tunnels. They run all the way over to that mountain." He pointed. "The government built them back in the early thirties. I don't know why they did, but they did. I completely forgot about this place. None of the tribe will enter it, includin' Sataws."

"Why?" Sara asked.

"The mountain is sacred to them. All life is supposed to have sprung from there."

"That doesn't look much like the Garden of Eden to me," young Walter said.

Old Dan chuckled. "It ain't. And it ain't entirely safe for us either, 'cause the outsiders that's comin' in to help will

221

enter it. Come on, people. Let's get out of this rain and get dry."

"Must have been a slaughter back there," Jones said, after hearing the faint screaming and yelling and then witnessing the scared CWA men hightailing it off the flat and out into the valley. "I guessed that one right."

"And I only heard one shot," Norm said.

"They had help," Matt said. The men were taking a one minute break to catch their breath.

"Who?" Jones asked.

"My guess would be the war is on and outsiders are in helping the breakaways. Jones, you have any juice left in your transceiver?"

"Oh, yeah."

"Plug in your earpiece and see if you can find out what happened back there. I'm saving my batteries for an emergency."

Norm grinned at him. "And this ain't?"

"It'll get worse, ol' buddy."

"You sure know how to make a man's day, Matt."

Jones listened to the CWA frequency, the expression on his face growing grimmer and grimmer. He shook his head and clicked off the little transceiver.

"They're talking about all sorts of city folks joining up with the links. Real nice-talking, well-dressed folks, male and female. They said the new folks helped slaughter the CWA, then drank their blood like vampires."

"Good God!" Norm said. "But surely they must know that they can't win?"

"I don't know whether they can or not," Matt told him. "Remember, they've been coming out of this area for hundreds of years. Well, this is just confirming what I suspected. The tribe has people in government, probably

222

within the Bureau, the Agency, Treasury, Customs, House and Senate, and maybe on the President's staff.''

"How about the President himself?'' Jones asked.

"Doubtful. He's too closely investigated. He's been in the public eye for most of his life. His family has been checked out since before they left England. I think they came over on the Mayflower.''

"Mine came over by ship too,'' Norm said with a chuckle. "Chained in the hold!''

The men enjoyed a quiet laugh. Matt said, "Well, with the group safe—let's presume they are—there goes the need for any diversion, boys. Any suggestions as to what we do next?''

"Getting our asses out of here would be nice,'' Norm said.

"I'll second that,'' Jones said. "I just wish we knew exactly where Nick was taking the group so we could throw up a buffer line between those things out there and them.''

"No way of telling,'' Matt said. "Nick was intentionally vague about that. Jones, where is the nearest ranger fire tower?''

"About three days' march from here, a hard march. Over that way. I'm sure there are more, but that's the only one I'm familiar with. Monroe never really trusted me, so I didn't get away from the base camp alone very often.''

"Well,'' Matt said, standing up and looking carefully around him. "We all know what search and destroy means. So let's go search and destroy.''

"These are Secret Service people we can trust,'' Manetti said, after working at a computer for hours. A computer had been set up in a room adjoining the Oval Office and with a central codebook, Manetti had been able to access nearly any government office he desired. "Now that we know what we're looking for, I can just about say with certainty that the Secret Service has been compromised."

The President took the list and quickly scanned it. "You feel that all these names in the right-hand column are Secret Service agents somehow connected to this . . . misadventure now occurring in Idaho?"

"Yes, sir."

The President called the chief of the White House detail into the office.

"What's up, Mr. President?" James Willis said. "Sir, I can't protect you unless you level with me. If there is something . . ."

The President waved him silent. "Relax, James. Sit down. You know Manetti from the Agency. Fine. Manetti, bring him up to date."

Manetti hit the salient points quickly. When he had finished, Willis sat with his mouth hanging open. He shook his head, blinked his eyes, and said, "This is not some inside joke, Mr. President?"

"I assure you it is not, James."

Willis took the list Manetti handed him and studied it.

"What color eyes does Barnett have, James?" the CIA man asked.

"Blue."

"Hammel?"

"Umm . . . sort of a strange brown with a yellow tint. Odd eyes."

"Bell?"

"Ahhh . . . brown with that yellow tint."

"Keller?"

"Gray eyes."

"Cole?"

"Yeah," Willis said. "I see what you mean. Brown with that odd yellow tint. The same with Adams, Hancock, and

224

Walker. I just never paid any attention to that before." He reached for a cigarette then recalled that the President did not approve of smoking.

Manetti said, "Simmons is on his way in from Denver. But we have a little problem there, too. I asked him about the Bureau's backup team, which was supposed to go in with our backup team if Matt yelled for help. He pulled the files. It looks like agents Williams, Ford, Pointer, and Macky are all tribe members."

"Son-of-a-bitch!" the President said.

"Simmons is putting together a team to keep an eye on the team in place."

"This is getting complicated," Willis said. "But how about the Company's team out there?"

Manetti's expression was strained. "They fit the same profile as the Bureau's men."

"James, call in the White House physician and tell him I have ordered drug testing of all Secret Service agents, to begin immediately. Now that we know what to look for, he should be able to isolate those tribe traits quickly. Get on it."

The Secret Service man walked to a phone, gave the White House doctor his instructions, and then called some of his own people and began giving orders.

"I'll call my chief of staff in on this," the President said.

"I wouldn't," Manetti said softly.

The President turned slowly to stare at the Company man. "Do you mean . . . ?"

"Yes, sir. He fits the profile. Think about him and visualize his eyes."

The President nodded. "I can also think of three senators and a half a dozen representatives that fit it."

"That's right, sir. And also General Dawson on the Joint Chiefs. We're just touching the tip of the iceberg here. How many network news people and CEOs are a

225

part of this? How many mayors and governors and judges are a part of it? How many lower-echelon people in the CIA, Treasury, Bureau, NSA and so forth, all of them able to alter or conceal records, are a part of it? How many police chiefs and sheriffs and highway patrolmen?"

"Under no circumstances can we go public with this," Willis said. "We're going to have to go slow and easy, ferreting them out quietly."

"I agree," Manetti said. "But how many are actually enemies and how many are just people trying to live a normal life? Blending in and working within the system, obeying the law and happy to do so? According to Simmons, Matt reported that the lodge owner and the guide are both tribe members but very decent people who agreed to work with him."

The President sat down behind his desk. "We don't know if Matt Jordan is still alive. He hasn't reported in—or if he has, the Company team out there isn't passing it along. We don't know if those campers and their kids are alive or dead. We're working in the dark. What side is Atkins on?"

"I think he's probably the one giving orders in your name, sir. That means he's probably trying to save the tribe by relocation. But some things puzzle me. Why all the hurry-up on his part? He knew the plan would be exposed sooner or later, so why didn't he come to you with it?"

"Maybe he isn't trying to save the tribe," Willis said. "Maybe that isn't his plan at all. Maybe he wants to get them all together at that old NG base and then destroy them."

"That's monstrous!" the President said.

"It would be a way out for those who have crossed over," Manetti said. "But let me play devil's advocate for a moment. Maybe Atkins isn't the bad guy. Maybe he's seen a breakdown within the tribe—some disorder of the blood or the mind that is causing those on the outside to go . . . crazy and do what was done to Mrs. Gaston. Everything we have is so sketchy. We really don't have anything solid to work with."

"Are there good guys and bad guys in this thing?" Willis asked, more to himself than to the others. "Do we have a clear-cut enemy? Is national security at risk? Is the President in danger?" He looked at the President. "Let's get Atkins in here and ask him. Let's lay our cards on the table and tell him it's time for the truth."

The President looked at Manetti. "I agree."

"Do it," the President ordered.

The younger children were sleeping on pallets in a warm and dry tunnel just beneath the old mining complex. The horses had been stabled in another tunnel nearby. The adults were gathered around a small fire, waiting for the coffee to make.

"How come the smoke doesn't choke us all?" Traci Dalton asked.

"It's bein' pulled out by the breezes," Nick told her. "These tunnels are well ventilated. I think the government was goin' to use these for some sort of storage. I don't know what. Maybe it was just a make-work project during the Depression. A lot of that went on, I'm told."

"For the first time in several days I'm beginning to think we might actually get out of this alive," Frank said.

"There's a chance of that," Dan said. "But I got to say this to you, Mrs. Hunt: Your husband's chances aren't very good."

"I know," she said softly. "He explained that to me just before we left. Matt tried to get him to go with us, but Norm refused."

"I hope the government has a lot of money," Tom said.

"Because they are going to see a lawsuit over this that will make the national debt look like petty cash." He looked around the dimness of the tunnel. "Miserable goddamned place!"

The others ignored him.

"I wish that Jones was a little younger," Traci said. "I think he's cute."

"He's a little old for you, dear," Susan said. "Besides, I thought you were taken with that Nash boy."

"Ancient history, mother," the daughter replied. "Phased out to the max."

Walter took off his earphones and laid them aside. "You can forget about listening to the radio down here. All I'm getting is static."

"Coffee's ready," Milli said.

"I wish I knew what was happening with Matt and the others," Susan said.

"Damn!" Matt whispered, looking at the scene below them through binoculars. "Those people look like they just stepped out of a fashion magazine."

"Until you look at the blood all over the front of their jackets," Jones added, looking at Norm, peering through his own field glasses.

"It does take away from the in look, doesn't it?" Norm said. "Look at that pretty lady in the designer jeans, sniffing the ground like a dog."

"She'll have our scent in a few seconds," Matt said. "She's working this direction."

"What's the game plan?" Jones asked.

"I'm hoping they won't think we're right at the edge of the timberline. They don't appear to be too cautious in stalking us, so they probably think we're hiding out in deep timber. If they get our scent and advance this way, let

228

them get close and then open fire."

The woman suddenly straightened up and warbled like a bird, pointing toward the timber on the ridge above the little valley about two miles from where the vultures were now feeding on the remains of the CWA men.

"Here they come," Norm said, slipping his Mini-14 off safety. "I figure the range at about three hundred meters."

"Let them get about seventy-five yards from us," Matt said. "Noise discipline in effect, boys."

The three men waited. After a moment they could hear the civilians in the bunch talking but could not make out the words, although they could tell it was in English. And the civilians could communicate with the huge hairy Sataws traveling with them by using sign language.

This isn't a movement that just sprang up, Matt thought. Whatever their plan, they've been working on it for a long time. They work too well together for this to be the first time.

Sure, he thought: the urge that Nick talked about. Whenever the moon or the stars or whatever brought it on did so, the civilians would leave the urban areas and return to the wild, to fulfill their growing blood lust.

I've got to take one prisoner and find out how big this movement is, he thought, lifting his rifle and sighting in on the woman who appeared to be the leader.

"Now!" Matt said, and pulled the trigger, the .223 slug knocking the woman to the ground, her knee shattered.

The trio pumped lead into the startled group of civilians and half-beasts. Between them, they had ninety rounds in their clips and they turned the peaceful land into a slaughterhouse. The battle lasted less than a minute. And they knew they had not killed or wounded them all. Some would have hit the ground immediately, and they would be waiting for the men to leave their positions and come down to finish them off.

Matt and Norm and Jones remained at the timberline, listening to the moaning that drifted to them from below.

"I figure we have fifteen minutes, max, before their friends get here," Matt said. "I'd like to talk to one of the wounded."

"You take the front, Matt," Norm said. "Me and Jones will split up the flanks and the rear."

"OK."

"Dirty rotten sons-of-bitches!" a woman's voice called out. "You've killed them all!"

"Like hell we have, lady," Matt muttered. "That trick's as old as time."

"That tells me we didn't get them all," Norm whispered.

"One coming up in my perimeter," Jones spoke softly. "Don't worry about him. I have him in visual." The men had automatically reverted to military jargon.

Jones' AR-15 slammed and a short scream cut the misty air, followed by the thud of a falling body. Norm's rifle cracked just as two civilians charged Matt. Matt cut them down and the area fell silent.

"Let's see what's down there," Norm said.

"I'll point," Matt said. "Norm on my right, Jones."

"Let's do it!"

The men jumped a log and charged down the slope. A huge bloody Sataw reared up in front of Jones. The ex-paratrooper put three rounds into the beast's chest and kept running. A man jumped up from the tall grass and began running away. Norm triggered off a few rounds, knocking the man sprawling. The woman with the shattered knee leveled a pistol at Matt. Matt kicked her in the mouth with the toe of his boot. The pistol went flying out of her hand and she lost consciousness. When she opened her eyes, her hands were tied behind her back and she was looking up into the pale eyes of Matt and hearing

230

the shots as Norm and Jones finished off the more badly wounded.

"Savages!" she spat at him.

Matt grunted. "That's an interesting thing for you to call me, lady, with human blood still on your lips. What are you, a goddamned vampire?"

She stared at him.

"I want some information, lady."

"I'll tell you nothing," she hissed.

Matt took a knife from his belt. "Oh, I think you will."

7

It did not take Matt long.

Jones fought to keep down his meager lunch and Norm completely lost his while Matt was extracting information from the woman. Then they both watched as Matt left the side of what remained of the woman, walked a few steps, and vomited. He sat down on the wet earth and bathed his face with a handkerchief soaked from a canteen.

"I never liked torture," he finally said. "I've been around when it was going on more times than I like to recall, but I've always managed not to take part in it. Most of the time. You hear what she had to say, boys. Would you say that we're fucked in here?"

"Gang-shagged might be a better word," Norm said.

"I can't believe these . . . creatures have people in all the areas she claimed," Jones said. "What about security checks?"

"They've covered their back trail pretty damn well, I'd say," Matt said, standing up. "Let's get out of here. We're cutting it fine now."

"Where to?" Norm asked.

"I just remembered something," Jones said, slipping into his pack. "There's an old rundown and long-deserted mining complex on a river. It'd be . . . north and a little east of here. Big ol' place. Monroe said there was a maze of tunnels running underneath it. The CWA uses it to cache supplies."

"What river?"

"I don't know. It's more of a big creek than a river."

"Would there be radio equipment stashed there?"

Jones shook his head. "I'm sorry—I just don't know. Maybe."

"Let's try it, Matt. Let's get gone from this place," Norm said. "It's too damned open."

Jeff Atkins, the President's chief of staff, sat impassively in a chair. He had not changed expression during the President's sometimes heated barrage of words. When he still would neither confirm nor deny the charges, the President stepped forward and slapped the man across the face.

"Answer me, God damn you!"

Atkins lifted his eyes. "What happened to Hammel and Lake and the other agents supposed to be on duty at this time?"

"They're under guard until this mess is cleared up."

"It'll never be cleared up until what remains of the tribe is wiped from the face of the earth."

"That's why you used my name to order the relocation of the tribe."

"Yes."

"What were you going to do with them?"

"Another Jonestown."

"That's barbaric!"

"You don't understand. Something's happened to many of those on the outside. Something has gone wrong. More and more are running amok. Reverting to the old ways. Yielding to the primitive urges. They've got to be stopped."

"But not all of them."

"No. About ten or fifteen percent, as close as we can calculate. But they're dangerous."

"But why kill off the entire tribe because of that?"

"You don't understand. The tribe has had to shift locations many times, away from good water. Several generations have been drinking water contaminated by all the mining, the chemicals washing into the streams. It's upset the genetic balance . . . it's upset something . . . created some chemical imbalance in the brain that is passed on to the offspring. And while those who leave the tribe appear human, the brain is infected, and it gets worse with each generation. They have to be destroyed, Mr. President. There's no other way."

"How do you know? Have you sought medical opinions?"

"Yes. Many of the descendants of the tribe are physicians. We have noted scientists in the field of genetics." He reached into a breast pocket and pulled out an envelope. "I wrote this several days ago. It's my resignation. I can no longer be trusted to behave in a rational manner, Mr. President. Several nights ago I stepped out on the porch to get a breath of air and suddenly wanted to drop down on all fours and howl and rip off my clothing and run free and taste blood." He sighed. "I don't even like rare steak. You know that."

"Who sent Matt Jordan in originally?"

"I don't know. And that's the truth. It could be one of a dozen men and women in government. It's a struggle within a struggle, Mr. President. The tribe is being torn apart internally."

"General Dawson?"

"You don't have to worry about Dawson. You'll find him at his house."

"What are you talking about?"

"I just came from there. I killed him."

"You did . . . what?"

"I killed him. We've talked long about this . . . matter. He was worried about his mental state. When I got a call from him this afternoon, he was almost hysterical. I went right over, naturally. General Dawson was, by then, naked, loping through the house on all fours, ripping down drapes and overturning furniture. His wife was dead; he'd killed her and . . . had been lapping at her blood. He begged me to shoot him. I did."

Other senior members of the President's staff had quietly entered the Oval Office, with checked-out and cleared agents of various government agencies.

The President turned to members of his staff who had been cleared and briefed by Manetti and Willis. "Englund, get the Vice President home as fast as you can. Mary, get the commanding general at Fort Lewis on the phone, bring him up to date, tell him this is to be handled with the utmost secrecy, and get that ranger battalion stationed out there on the way to Matt Jordan's last known position. The press lid is clamped down tight on this matter. That is an order and I will put it in writing. Anyone who leaks a word about this matter to anyone not cleared by me will be brought up on charges. Move, people."

He turned to a Secret Service agent. "Keller, take Mr. Atkins and get the names of people in government who are affiliated in any way with this tribe." He turned to the Director of the Bureau. "Miller, send a team of agents, quietly, out to General Dawson's home and clean up the mess and bodybag the general and his wife. Have the bodies stored."

"Yes, sir."

"This is going to hit the news, people; it's inevitable. It'll probably be leaked by someone sympathetic to the tribe. We've got to have a statement ready. You stay with me, Brownie, and get to work on something."

"Right, sir."

"Are the Joint Chiefs assembled?"

"Yes, sir."

"I'll meet with them now."

"Yes, sir."

"Farnam, have plenty of fresh coffee on hand around the clock, and lots of sandwiches. There isn't going to be much sleeping for the next twenty-four to thirty-six hours."

"No point in us blundering around out here in the dark," Matt said, glancing up at the cloudy sky. The rain had stopped, at least for the moment. "Too dangerous. I figure we've got about an hour of daylight left. Let's find us a hidey-hole, secure it, and call it a day."

They had been lucky that day, and the three of them knew it. But luck has a nasty habit of running out, and they were getting tired. Tired people make mistakes. And in this game, a mistake meant death.

They found a thick stand of brush and crawled up in it, careful not to disturb the entrance. They ate field rations that had about as much flavor as the wrappers and made themselves as comfortable as possible.

"At least we're still alive," Norm summed it up.

But for how long? was the unspoken question on all their minds.

"We got troubles," Nick whispered to Dan.

"What's wrong?"

"I been explorin' some. Found a small tunnel off this one filled with survival gear. I only opened a couple of the boxes. Clothes and food. I figure the CWA's been usin' this place to cache supplies."

"That means there's a good chance that some of them will be here."

236

"Yeah, I'd say so. That is, if any escaped from the break-aways."

"Well, there *is* one way in from the north, through the complex, and a way in through the mountain. I doubt those nuts know of the mountain entrance. We're gonna have to post guards up in the old office building. Mrs. Dalton brought little radios so we can talk back and forth. Let's tell the others and start laying out shifts."

"We'll send in air strikes," a general suggested.

The President lifted his eyes heavenward and clenched his fists under the table. "No, General, we won't send in air strikes. That area is made up of thousands and thousands of acres of wilderness. We're not dealing with huge armies here. Whom did you plan to strike? A ranger battalion from Fort Lewis, Washington, is on the way in now. They have orders to find the CIA man and the campers. When that's done, they'll bring in helicopters to airlift them out."

"Are the rangers' hands tied in the matter of self-defense, sir?" an army general asked.

"No. Any military unit being sent in has orders to defend themselves using any method available. I ordered blood tests on all special operations units. The West Coast SEAL teams have been cleared. They are on the way in now. Marine force recon units are being moved in as well. I ordered a contingent from the 101st out of Fort Campbell to secure the National Guard base that will be used to house these . . . tribe members."

"What are you going to do with them, sir?" Navy asked.

The President sighed. "I don't know, Admiral. I just honest to God don't know."

The phone buzzed and the President picked it up. He listened for a half a minute, then hung up and cussed.

"That was General Lanford from the NSA. He confirmed that the National Security Agency has been compromised. We may as well assume that all departments have been penetrated and act accordingly. Testing is being done as quickly as possible, around the clock. When one section's personnel have been cleared, change the codes. Any questions?"

"These . . . tribe people on the outside can't win this thing," Air Force said. "What do they hope to gain?"

"I don't know," the President admitted. "I don't know of anybody who could answer that question."

"Don't be too sure they won't make an impact," Marine Corps said. "If they've been coming out for three or four hundred years or longer, that could conceivably mean thousands of them have taken their place in society. The bite of one is supposed to be highly infectious, with the capability of altering a normal person's behavior. If there is some genetic breakdown occurring, we could have a real bloodbath on our hands. Let's get the relocation moving and have CDC people in there doing testing on a large scale. Atkins said testing has been done; but I'll bet it was done by only a few scientists working in fear and secrecy. Maybe the CDC, working around the clock, can come up with a vaccine."

The President nodded at an aide. "Do it," he ordered.

"Monroe," Judd said, inspecting the ground near the old mining complex. "There's fresh horse droppings here."

Monroe got off his horse and knelt down.

"More over here," Woody called. "Pretty good-sized bunch came this way and not too long ago."

"Them government people?" Seymour questioned.

"Has to be. And they're headin' straight for the old minin' shacks. Cathy said that guide was part link, so he'd

238

know all about this country and them tunnels over yonder."

"Monroe, we'd be walkin' into a trap goin' in them buildin's by night," Luther pointed out.

"We ain't gonna do that. We'll split up into three five-man teams. I'll take one; Judd, you take another; Woody, you head up the third."

"How come I never get to be a leader?" Marwood said in a pouty tone.

"Shut up," Luther told him. "Stay in the timber and start gettin' into position now. Them folks is amateurs at this war business. Sooner or later one of them is gonna make a mistake and give away the guard position. Then we'll know where to strike."

"How come you call that CIA man an amateur?" Jim Bob questioned. "Him and them that was hepin' him shore done a number on our ass."

Monroe smiled. "They ain't with this group, that's why. They out yonder in the wilderness coverin' these folks' back trail. On foot."

"Them horses we seen!" Ely said.

"That's right. That CIA man and his buddies is some miles behind us. We'll take this bunch, fuck the eyeballs outta them fancy gals, git our supplies and radio in to headquarters for them to send us some help. Then we can all git the hell gone from this horrible place."

"It's startin' to rain agin," Marwood said glumly.

"I know, Marwood," Monroe said. "I know."

"I just remembered something," Jones whispered, although there was no need to with the hard driving rain that pounded their crude shelter. "There is a radio over there in that old mining complex. A real expensive rig, from what Whitman told me one time. It's stored there in

239

case of emergency."

"That's what this is, all right," Norm said.

"What band?" Matt asked.

"High band."

"That's our ticket out of here, then. Can anybody sleep?"

"Hell, no!" Norm said.

"Me, neither," Jones said.

Matt stood up and slipped into his poncho. "Let's get on the march, then. Those CWA men are hours ahead of us and they're on horseback. If they get there ahead of us, the women are in for a bad time."

They had not gone a mile before they found a horse. A dead man on the ground, a death grip on the reins. The animal was so spooked it took Matt several minutes of quiet soothing talk to calm the horse.

"Who the hell is he?" Norm asked.

"Not one of the CWA men. I never saw this guy before in my life."

Matt took the dead man's wallet out of his hip pocket. Using a tiny flashlight held between his teeth, he inspected the contents while Norm and Jones tied their heavy packs onto and behind the saddle. With the packs gone from their backs, they could make twice the time as before.

"He's a pharmacist from Oregon," Matt said. He shone the light into the dead man's wide-open eyes. They were dark brown with a yellow tint. "One of them," he muttered. "And he's been shot in the belly. Go through his saddlebags, Norm."

"Well, well," Norm said. "Would you just look at this, now." He held out a bulky object wrapped in heavy canvas.

"Let me see that thing," Matt said, standing up.

"What is it?" Jones asked.

"A fancied-up and the smallest combat net radio I have

ever seen."

"Thanks a lot, Matt," Norm said. "You really cleared that up."

Matt smiled. "Burst transmission, boys. This looks a lot like the Plessey PTR–4300 the Australian army uses."

"Is he speaking English?" Norm said to Jones.

"Beats the hell out of me, Norm."

Matt said, "See if there's an additional string antenna in the other saddlebag, please." He turned on the radio and lifted the handset to his ear, listening. He nodded as Norm showed him the wire antenna and began stringing it up. Matt punched in his backup's frequency and got them on the first bump.

"Jesus, Husky!" the voice exploded in his ear. "Where the hell have you been?"

"Who are you, pal?" Matt replied. "I don't recognize the voice."

"I'm Jaguar. We worked in Chile together."

"OK, go ahead, Jaguar. I'm a little paranoid."

"With damn good reason. Your other teams, both Agency and Bureau, were lined up with the breakaway tribe members. Two of them are now dead, and the others are being held in a safe place. The DCI had a heart attack and Manetti is running things until Richard gets back in the country. How is your situation?"

"Grim. Listen, bring me up to date. I can punch in burst transmission and digital."

"Do so. We've got to keep a lid on this damn situation."

Matt punched in burst transmission and added digital encryption. "Go, Jaguar."

"The shit's hit the fan all over. All agencies have been compromised. General Dawson reverted into some sort of animal and killed his wife. Chief of Staff Atkins killed him at his home and then confessed to Sugar Cube that he was a descendant of the tribe. The ranger battalion from

241

Fort Lewis should be arriving in your sector any time."

"I'm no longer in that sector, Jaguar. Stand by and I'll give you map coordinates. But there is no way the army is going to get choppers into this area in this heavy weather." Matt gave him map coordinates and told him everything that had happened since he'd lost radio contact.

"You want a team to converge on that old mining complex? I can find it on the map I've got."

"That's affirmative. Advise them there may be civilians there. A remote possibility."

Jones and Norm raised their eyebrows at that.

"We'll be force-marching the rest of the night to get there. I'll check in with you every hour on the hour. That's when we'll break for a rest."

"That's ten-four, Husky. The next time you call in, I'll have the ranger frequency for you so you can talk direct. Good luck."

Matt cut off the radio to conserve the batteries, since he did not know how much time was already on them.

"What's this about civilians?" Norm asked.

"That woman I extracted the information from . . . I just now made sense out of something she said before she died. I think Nick took those people away from the area of the tribe. That woman said something about the tribe being sealed off and not going anywhere. I just have a hunch we'll find our people at that mining complex."

"Who takes the point?" Norm asked, worry in his voice.

"I do," Matt said. "Let's go."

8

Because the press had started their usual indignant honking and squawking about not having full knowledge of everything that went on in the White House, the President had called the Mexican, Russian, Canadian, and British ambassadors in and leveled with them.

"You've been very lucky the press hasn't picked up on it," the Canadian said.

"But they will," the Englishman added.

"And put the American public into a panic," the Russian concluded.

"If we can get through the next twenty-four hours without that happening," the President said, "I think we can lessen the impact of the story."

"This could be the most important scientific find in history," the Mexican said.

"Oh, quite," the Englishman said.

The Russian smiled. "It's certainly going to send genealogists on a mad scramble."

Matt, Norm, and Jones stood in the timber and watched a group of Sataws and breakaways pass not fifty yards from them. The rain, the wind, the darkness all combined to help conceal the trio. Matt stood by the packhorse, stroking the animal's nose gently and praying to whatever god looks after special operations agents that the horse would not whinny and give them away.

The three men stood for five minutes more after their hunters vanished into the timber. They had a broad flat plain to cross and none of them were at all anxious to move out.

"We've got it to do," Matt whispered. "Let's do it while the rain is still heavy."

They moved out in single file, feeling more exposed than ever. They crossed the plain without incident and entered the timberline, moving up the slope. Matt led the way up, wanting more altitude before they stopped to string the antenna and contact Jaguar.

They stopped to catch their breath and Matt bumped his CIA contact.

"There is a major storm developing in your area, Husky," Jaguar told him. "High winds and heavy rains. I'm probably not telling you anything you don't already know firsthand. The choppers have been grounded. There are several SEAL teams in place and one Ranger platoon in place near your old sector. The rest of the operation has been called off until the weather calms down. I'll give you the frequencies so you can talk to them directly."

Matt set the frequencies; they would now be available to him on command.

"Husky, that 24-volt battery pack should last you through this operation if you don't lay on it too much."

"That's ten-four. What is the situation on the outside?"

"We've kept the press out of it."

"That's a damn miracle."

"I've pinpointed the mining complex. Give me your present location as close as you can, and stand by."

The men had been going full tilt for hours, and they were near exhaustion. They badly needed rest.

"Husky, you're three miles from the old complex," Jaguar told him. "There is a SEAL team at a landing strip about ten miles north of the complex. You want me to get them moving? They've got some rough country to traverse."

"That's ten-four, Jaguar. We'll move out now, get the complex in visual, and then try to get a few hours' rest before we hit it. An hour before dawn, I'll give them a bump."

"If they're close enough to try a rescue, Husky, I'm pretty sure they'd want you people to stand down and let them take it."

"They are certainly welcome to do just that, Jaguar. Husky out." He turned to Norm and Jones. "We're three miles from the complex. Let's get closer and then try to catch some rest."

"I ain't seen nothin' over yonder," Ely bitched. "I don't think them folks is there a-tall."

"Me, neither," Marwood said. "I don't see why we have to stay out here in the damn rain freezin' our asses off."

"'Cause Monroe told us to," Woody said. "That's why."

"Fuck Monroe," Darnell piped up. "Let's take that place now. I got to shit somethin' awful, and I don't wanna hang my ass over no damn log in this weather."

"OK, OK," Woody said. "I'll contact Monroe."

"I'm in-clined to agree," Monroe said. "Okay. Let's take the place. Move out. Just be careful, and don't shoot none of that pussy in yonder."

The remnants of the CWA moved out, unaware that they were being observed from the timber. Brown-yellow eyes watched them unblinking as they made their way toward the ramshackle buildings. A Sataw turned to Cathy. He pointed a clawed finger at his chest, pointed at

245

the buildings, and shook his head.

Cathy nodded her understanding. She told him in sign language that he and his kind should stand watch, and she and her bunch would see to the mining complex.

The Sataw agreed and vanished back into the gloom of the timber.

Matt and Norm and Jones were less than a half mile away, trying to get some rest before dawn.

The men of the Navy SEAL team were pushing themselves hard, setting a grueling pace, coming down from the north, while the men in the ranger platoon were pushing just as hard, coming up from the south. On the previous afternoon, the young men of the rangers had inspected the carnage on the flats, seen what was left of the CWA men, and taken pictures of the slaughter and of the crude stockade the campers had built.

The rain continued to drench the land, coming down in thick, silver sheets. The wind picked up, howling like a thousand demons over the mountains and through the passes and valleys.

Jim Bob laid the stock of his AK-47 against the back of Dennis's head and the lawyer went down, unconscious. Judd swung his weapon and busted Wade in the forehead just as the man was turning around to check out the slight noise behind him. Had he not slipped, causing the blow to be only a glancing one, the stock would have crushed his head.

Wade was trussed up and laid on the floor beside Dennis. Judd rubbed his crotch and grinned at Jim Bob, pointing downward, where they believed the women to be hiding in the tunnels.

Jim Bob returned the profane grin and squeezed his crotch.

Restless and very uncomfortable in his sleep, Matt said the hell with it and crawled out from underneath his soggy blankets. It was that gray time between the fading of night

246

and the breaking of day. His eyes caught a fleeting shape at the edge of the timberline on the ridge behind the mining complex. He gently nudged the others awake with the toe of his boot.

"We're not alone," he said, kneeling down slowly, not wishing to make any quick movement that would draw attention.

"CWA people?" Norm asked, sitting up and lacing up his boots.

"I don't think so. They looked like breakaways to me."

"Matt?" Jones whispered, his voice just carrying over the hammering rain. "CWA men going in the rear of the big building with the conveyer tower."

Matt gently parted the thick brush on the hillside and chanced a look. He could just make out the single-file line of cammie-clad men moving through the rain and disappearing into the rear of the building.

"I count eight," he said. "How many in the bunch you saw, Jones?"

"Six or seven."

Matt hurriedly set up his radio and punched up the SEAL team frequency. "This is Husky. I'm overlooking the mining complex. I've spotted CWA men entering the buildings and breakaways from the tribe on the ridges around it. How far are you from this position?"

"About a mile. But it's rough going, sir."

"Screaming from inside the complex, Matt!" Norm said. "It's faint, but I heard it. Women screaming."

"The CWA have seized the complex," Matt radioed. "The civilians are in there. We're going in. We'll have handkerchiefs tied around our upper left arms."

"Go, Husky!" The master chief petty officer turned to his team. "Out of the timber and down into that stream. We're going to run this last mile and get those civilians and kids out of that box, and God damn it, we're all going to make it. We're going to have enemy on the banks and in

247

front of us, so eyes alert. Let's go!"

The Navy SEALs left the timber and began running down the stream bank, seemingly oblivious to the heavy packs they were carrying; they were accustomed to running for miles on loose sandy beaches carrying impossibly heavy loads. Their weapons were also varied: some carried M-16s, others carried CAR-15s, Stoners, MP-5Ks, and M-14s.

"Holy fuckin' shit!" a SEAL hollered, waving those behind him to a halt. "What in the name of God is *that?*"

The entire team stopped and stared. It was certainly understandable, even for these highly trained professional fighters. A huge Sataw, well over six feet tall, with a thick, hairy body and wearing only a loincloth, stood on a bluff, looking down at the men. They could make out the animal snout and the deep-set eyes in the huge head. It roared at them.

"That's got to be one of the Sataws we were briefed about," a team member said.

"Whatever it is," the CPO panted the words. "That is one ugly motherfucker!"

A young man dressed only in jeans and boots, carrying a rifle, jumped out of the timber to stand by the huge breakaway.

"What the hell?" a SEAL said.

The young man jerked the rifle to his shoulder and took aim at the CPO. A SEAL dropped the man with one shot from his M-14. The Sataw screamed his rage and raced down the bank.

"I think he's coming to kiss you, Chief," a young SEAL said.

"I been hard up in my day, but I ain't never been *that* hard up." He lifted his CAR and stopped the howling Sataw by putting a neat row of .223 slugs in the enraged Sataw's chest. "Everybody rested?" he yelled, knowing there sure as hell was no need for noise discipline now.

"Yeah!" came the shout.

"Let's go!"

Each one of them looked at the dead Sataw as he ran past, and each inwardly shuddered . . . not so much out of fear but at the idea of not knowing what manner of man or beast they were facing.

The SEAL team raced on.

"Well, now," Ely said, pulling Sara close to him and running his free hand over her body. "Ain't this the sweet one."

"You bastard!" Nancy hissed. "She's only eleven years old!"

"Oughta be tight, then," Ely grinned.

Sara kicked back with a boot and caught the man smack on the shin. He yelled in pain and released her. She ran to her mother.

"You'll hurt for that, little girlie," Ely warned. "I'll make you scream."

Nick and Dan had been at the far end of the tunnel, near the mountain, and they were not aware of anything being wrong.

"Where's the guide?" Monroe asked.

"He left us," Susan said, doing some quick thinking. "Going for help."

"She's lying," Judd said. "The number of saddles back yonder don't match up with the number of people in here. They's two missin'."

"Easy or hard, lady," Monroe warned Susan. "Marwood yonder's got him a dick that'd put a horse to shame. You and that foxy-lookin' girl there," he stared at Traci, "kinda favor. You wanna see Marwood prong her?"

"No, I don't," Susan told him.

"Then where's the other two that belongs to them saddles back yonder?"

"They're in the tunnels somewhere," she told him. "I don't know where, and that's the truth. They told us to stay here. They said that while you won't get lost in the tunnels, it's easy to get confused in them and it might take you an hour to find your way back."

"That's the gospel truth, Monroe," Jim Bob said. "We both know that."

Monroe nodded. "Git all our shit outta here and up top. We'll blow the tunnels to seal them."

"I wanna see the titties on that one!" Marwood said, leering at Polly. "I want me some brown sugar!"

Polly met his eyes without backing down. She sensed that Marwood was not playing with a full deck. When the man brazenly unbuttoned his trousers and exposed himself, she knew he had to be low on brains. God had shorted him mentally and turned it into cock.

Nancy had turned Sara's head away from the sight.

"You like this, baby?" Marwood said, hefting his penis.

"It ain't the size of the boat," Polly told him. "It's the motion of the ocean."

The men of the CWA laughed at the expression on Marwood's face. Marwood was awful proud of his pecker, and it hurt his feelings to have someone say something bad about it. He stuck it back in his pants, buttoned up, and said, "Git your uppity ass upstairs, bitch."

"You don't talk to my mother like that!" Johnny yelled, and rushed the man, ramming his head into Marwood's stomach and driving the breath from him.

Seymour stepped forward and slugged the boy, knocking him to the floor unconscious, blood leaking from his mouth where he'd bitten his tongue.

"You sorry son of a bitch!" Frank said. "Why don't you fight me if you think you're so goddamn tough?"

Seymour laughed at him. "I think we'll slow-kill you, bigmouth. See how well you stand pain."

Marwood had caught his breath and was shoving Polly up the stairs, cussing her, goosing her in the butt with the muzzle of his AK-47, and telling her of all the things he was going to do to her. "I'm gonna fuck your ass, bitch, just to hear you squall. And I'm gonna do it in front of your kids. What do you think about that?"

"I think you're an ignorant redneck white-trash lowlife goddamn son-of-a-bitch!" Polly told him.

"Oh, boy!" Jim Bob hollered. "You got you a feisty one, Marwood."

"She ain't gonna be when I'm done with her!" Marwood hollered over his shoulder.

"You're going to kill us, aren't you?" Tom asked Monroe.

"That's right, pretty boy. We shore are."

"Maybe there's another way."

"You better tell it to me quick, 'cause we ain't got much time."

"I know Emmett Trumball personally. My law firm has represented him several times. I contribute money to the CWA. Check that out. I'm Tom Dalton."

Susan was looking at him with something between horror and disgust in her eyes. She was wondering how a woman could make such a terrible mistake in choosing a husband.

"Walk over yonder," Monroe said, pointing with the muzzle of his rifle. "I know your name for a fact. Wouldn't do to kill you. Mister Trumball wouldn't like that a-tall. Stand right there. Which woman here is yourn?"

Peyton turned at the creaking of a board behind him and lived just long enough to feel the white-hot, searing pain of Matt's knife rip into his belly and tear upward until the blade nicked his heart. Matt lowered the twitching body to the dusty floor, wiped his blade clean on Peyton's jacket, and sheathed the bloody knife. He motioned Norm and Jones forward. The three men froze as they heard Marwood cussing Polly as he prodded her up the dusty and rotten stairs.

Jones grabbed Peyton's still-warm body and dragged it

out of sight just as the sounds of gunfire reached them.

"Who's doin' all that shootin'?" Monroe hollered.

"Sounds like it's comin' from up the crick," Marwood shouted. "I'll check it out. God damn it, I wanted me some nigger pussy."

Marwood stepped out of the stairwell, shoved Polly to the floor and turned in time to see the face of Norman, savage and angry. Marwood opened his mouth to scream and Norm jammed the muzzle of his Mini-14 all the way through Marwood's throat. Marwood jerked and grunted, his boots doing a jazzy little doo-wa-diddy number on the dusty floor as he hung impaled on the muzzle of the weapon. Norm jerked the muzzle out, the sight pulling out tendons and muscles. Matt caught Marwood before he could hit the floor and cause a lot of unnecessary noise and dragged him out of sight.

Norm jerked Polly off the floor and pushed her against a far wall. "The kids?" he whispered.

"Coming up," she said. "Honey, I have never been so glad to see you."

"Stay right here," he told her. "In the shadows."

"Marwood, God damn it!" Monroe bellered. "Who the hell's doin' all that shootin'?"

Unable to speak, Marwood farted.

The sounds of shots came up from the tunnels.

"The guide's back yonder a-shootin' at us!" a CWA man yelled.

More shots.

"Both of 'em's back yonder. Oscar's been hit in the leg."

"Get up the damn stairs, all you people. Comin' up, Marwood, the government people's in front. You watch 'em, now, you hear me?"

Matt, Norm, and Jones slipped back into the shadows of the huge, empty old office. Dennis and Wade lay on the floor. Dennis was semi-conscious, but Wade was fully alert and had a smile on his face. He winked at Jones.

252

Jones returned the wink and the smile as heavy rain lashed the structure and strengthening winds shook it.

Susan was carrying Johnny, unconscious, in her arms. They were the first to climb out of the stairs and onto the ground floor. The rest of the campers quickly followed. Matt stepped from the shadows, startling the tired and scared group. He waved them to a secure corner and stepped into the doorway. He leveled his Mini-14 and started working the trigger into the candlelit gloom below him.

Matt gave the CWA thirty rounds. Sounds of moaning and screaming drifted up to the ground floor.

"We yield!" Monroe squalled. "Oh, my God, look at all the blood. We quit! We quit!"

"Nick!" Matt yelled. "You all right?"

"I'm fine," came the faint shout. "Dan's with me."

"Prod these scummy bastards up top, will you?"

"My pleasure, Matt. What's left of them, that is."

"We're surrounded by Sataws and normal-appearing people, Matt," Jones said. "I can see the SEAL team. They've been forced to take cover behind some rocks about two hundred yards upstream."

"You ladies start reinforcing these old walls," Matt said. "Those old tables in there," he pointed into an adjoining room, "will do for a start. Traci, you take charge of the kids. Keep them low and out of sight."

"Yes, sir."

Johnny was sitting up, his mouth swollen from the blow. He looked over and saw Marwood. The man was still alive, but not for long. He was jerking his legs and beating his hands and making all sorts of very disgusting sounds as he lay in his own gathering blood on the dirty and rat-shit-littered floor.

"Couldn't have happened to a nicer guy," the boy said. He followed Traci out of the room, both of them growing up very fast.

Monroe entered the ground floor, his hands behind his head. He was followed by Jim Bob, Luther, Carl, Seymour, Darnell, and the wounded Oscar.

"I got to have me some help for my leg," Oscar moaned.

"You want me to shoot you?" Matt asked him.

Oscar shut up.

"Tom is a supporter of the CWA," Susan said.

"Tie him up with the rest of these scumbags," Matt said. He opened his radio pack and bumped the SEAL team. "We've secured the mining complex . . . at least the main building. All the civilians are safe. How is your situation?"

"We're in pretty good shape, Husky. We just can't move. I talked to the ranger team. They're about five miles south of us, and pushing hard. But we're gonna have to hold out for a couple of hours at least."

"That's ten-four. We can do it. We'll spot for you and you do the same for us."

"Ten-four."

Two shots rang out from below. "I just tended to the wounded," Nick called.

"Oh, Lord, Lord!" Jim Bob hollered. "We done fell into the hands of savages!"

9

"The Sataws and breakaways won't enter the tunnel," Nick explained to Matt. "But the civilians comin' in to help them will. So me and Dan got into the CWA's supplies and rigged some surprises for any who try the tunnel through the mountain entrance. We'll know when or if they try," he added dryly.

"C-4?" Matt asked.

"Yep."

"Where'd you learn to use that stuff?"

"Watchin' the forest service people blow beaver dams." He took his binoculars and sighted in the pinned down SEAL team just two hundred yards upstream. "Them boys look like they eat rocks for breakfast," he noted. "They're in a damn good position. I think they'll fare all right."

"We've got to hold out for a couple of hours until that ranger platoon gets here," Matt told the group. "As soon as the weather breaks, we'll be airlifted out of here."

"Damn sure have plenty of ammunition and guns," Dan said. "We're in a good position. We're up high and looking down at them. I think the Sataws and breakaways and those helping them will pull out as soon as they see they can't accomplish anything by staying here. As soon as scouts get word to them about that force of rangers coming up, they'll take off. We'll just be too many for them."

"I demand that these ropes be removed from my wrists," Tom said.

"Shut up, puke!" Dan told him. "I heard you give your wife and child to these trash. Any more mouth from you and I'll personally kill you."

"What's a-gonna become of us?" Carl asked.

"You'll be tried for aggravated kidnapping, aggravated assault, aggravated battery, assault with a deadly weapon, attempted murder, attempted rape, and anything else I can think of," Dennis told him. "Or," he added, "just say the word and I'll shoot you all right here and now." He rubbed the lump on the back of his head. "I might just do it anyway."

"You don't act like no Jew I ever knowed," Darnell said. "You sure you full-blooded?"

Dennis shook his aching head in disgust. "How do people get to be that ignorant?" he tossed the question out.

"Some people say that trash begets trash," Nick said. "But that ain't always true. Tom's a good example of that. I bet his mama and daddy is fine people."

"They are," Susan said. "They're wonderful people. Tom just lost his way somehow."

"Fuck you," her husband told her. "Don't worry," he said, turning his head to look at Monroe. "You're not going to be tried for anything. The government wants the lid to remain on this entire tribe matter. If they tried you, you could blow this thing wide open. Relax, boys, you're home free."

"I lak you!" Oscar said. "That there is a fine plan, ain't it, Monroe?"

"Shore is."

Matt and Nick exchanged glances.

"Here they come!" Jones called from his lookout post. "And they're coming in one hell of a bunch."

"Get the kids on the floor and everybody into position,"

Matt yelled.

Then there was no more time for talk as the breakaway tribe members and the Sataws and the civilians rushed the complex . . . and died before they made the steps, front, sides, or rear.

The rain slackened for just a few moments, giving the men in the second floor office clear targets, and they made every shot count. Dan and Nick were together on the south side of the building, and their aim was deadly. They were fighting for their lives, and while Matt knew it must have hurt the men to kill beings whose very blood still ran in their veins, the men did not hesitate.

One Sataw climbed up the sheer face of the conveyer tower and leaped in through the windowless frame, landing on Dennis's back, knocking the man to the ground. Milli split the creature's skull with a camp ax, and he rolled off her husband to lie jerking and dying on the floor.

"Did he scratch you or bite you, son?" Dan called.

"No, sir—just scared the hell out of me."

"Check him over and be sure," Nick called, shoving a fresh clip into the belly of his weapon. "If you find a scratch, treat it promptly with alcohol or Merthiolate."

Wade and Frank dragged the dead Sataw to a window and heaved it out.

"What causes the bad odor, Nick?" Matt asked, during a break in the fighting.

"I don't know. Accordin' to my daddy, that didn't start until the late 1880s, so he was told. All the minin' that went on done something to the water in this area. Then the water done something to throw the tribe's system all out of balance."

"Then that may be the key to straightening out the urge to kill?" Susan said.

"Could be," the guide said. "But it ain't gonna help them crazy folks layin' out yonder dead in the rain, now,

257

is it?"

A tremendous explosion from far under them sent belches of dust and smoke burping out of the stairwell.

"They tried the mountain entrance," Dan said, a grim smile on his tanned face.

"Closed forever," Nick said. "And I, for one, am damned glad of it."

"That's it," Jones called a moment later from his post. "They're pulling back into the timber, civilians and . . . creatures. They've had it."

"So have I," Matt said, sinking to the floor. "I'm so goddamn tired I'm numb." He pulled the radio to him and bumped the SEAL team. "I think that's it, boys."

"Yeah, they seem to be hightailing it out of here. We felt the ground tremble a minute ago. Did you experience that?"

"Ten-four. We boobytrapped the tunnels under us with C-4. Some hostiles triggered it."

"That's ten-four. We're going to sit tight for a few more minutes and then we'll be in."

"We have you in visual," the voice popped into Matt's ear. "I'm Lieutenant Davidson, 2/75 Rangers. Is the fighting over?"

"Yes, thank God," Matt told him.

"Aw, *shit!*" said the ranger.

The storm picked up, and this time it was accompanied by some of the most wicked lightning any of them could ever remember seeing. The military dragged the dead out of the weather to take pictures, then covered up the bodies as best they could, and then bedded down wherever they could find a dry spot and settled in to eat, rest, and ride out the storm.

The military took the prisoners away, retied them, and read them the riot act as to what was going to happen to

258

their bodies should any of them try to make a break. Darnell opined, rather mournfully, that it seemed to him that the soldier boys wanted them to try to run for it.

"What about him?" the SEAL team leader asked, looking at Tom.

"Technically, he hasn't done anything," Matt said. "Except for what I told you."

"Ought to shoot the son-of-a-bitch just for that."

"I'll sue you, you goddamned ox!" Tom yelled at the man.

It took four other SEALs to restrain their team leader. Tom wisely decided to keep his mouth shut.

Matt caught a few hours' sleep that afternoon and woke to the sounds of silence. It confused him for a moment. Then he realized the storm had passed and the rain had stopped. He sat up, looking around him. Late afternoon was settling over the land. He stretched, getting the kinks out of his muscles. The others were asleep, sprawled around the room. He picked his way silently out of the big room and walked outside, then down the old steps to the ground. He joined a group of SEALs and rangers around a fire built under a roof overhang and gratefully accepted a cup of coffee.

"Choppers will be in at dawn," the SEAL team leader informed him. "We'll go out with you folks. Lieutenant Davidson and his bunch will escort Nick and Dan over to the tribe site and get them ready for evac."

So it appeared to be over in the wilderness. But Matt had a suspicion that it was far from over where the outside was concerned.

"What are you going to do about the prisoners?" Lieutenant Davidson asked.

"I don't know," Matt admitted. "But after I drink this coffee, I'm going to find out."

"Dispose of them, Husky," Jaguar told him.

"I can't do that. Lord knows they deserve it, and I've

259

been involved in assassinations before, but I'm not going to line these men up and shoot them."

"Are you experiencing some sort of midlife crisis, Husky? Male menopause, maybe?"

"No. And if the President orders me to shoot them, I will. But that order has got to come from the top."

"I could get the SEALs to put them down."

"I doubt it. Patch me through to Richard."

"Stand by, Husky."

"Richard here, Matt."

"I absolutely refuse to shoot these CWA men, Rich, even though they certainly deserve it. The story of what's going on in here will hit the news within a week and you know it. Let's keep these CWA people on ice until that happens. Then they won't have any bargaining chip to throw on the table. The government can then try them and put them in prison for the rest of their lives. If you want them dead in here, you're going to have to send someone else in to do it."

"I have a better plan."

"Let's hear it."

Matt listened, signed off, and walked over to the military. "Your boss wants you to off the CWA?" the SEAL leader asked.

"Yeah. I had an attack of conscience and refused the order. I must be getting old. He came up with an option." Matt briefed the SEAL team leader and several rangers. The men smiled.

"I think that's a very nice gesture on the part of your boss," a ranger said.

"Just lovely," the SEAL said. "Almost brings tears of joy to my eyes."

"What about that sleazebag Dalton?" Davidson asked.

"That problem is still to be resolved. Shall we go break the good news to the CWA?" Matt asked.

"I wouldn't miss it for the world."

The men of the CWA tensed as the group approached

them. They began to beg and sweat as knives were brought out. Jim Bob pissed his underwear as the big SEAL team leader stepped up to him and smiled.

"I promise I'll be good from now on!" Jim Bob blurted. "I'll go to church, I'll never call a nigger a nigger again. I . . ."

"Shut up!"

Jim Bob shut up.

The ropes binding the CWA were cut. They sat on the dusty floor and rubbed their wrists and ankles and wondered what in the hell was going on.

"Hit's a farin' squad!" Luther said. "They gonna shoot us all."

"I wanna write my mama!" Oscar said.

"I wanna go to the bathroom," Seymour said.

"This is agin the Constitution!" Monroe said. "We all got rights."

"Sure you do," Matt told him. "Stand up and get outside."

The men walked outside. Darnell started praying. Carl was shaking so bad he couldn't hold his canteen to take a drink of water. Jim Bob pissed in his pants again.

Luther hollered, "Help! Help! Somebody come help us."

"I protest this!" Tom Dalton yelled, running up and seeing what he thought was going on. "I represent these men and I demand they be tried in a court of law."

The SEAL team leader had taken an immense dislike for Tom Dalton. He stared at the man and finally controlled his more primitive urges—barely.

"Sorry, Tom," Matt told him. "But they're not going to be tried in any court of law."

"This is murder!" the lawyer yelled.

Dennis and Wade and the other civilians had gathered around.

"Murder?" Matt questioned. "Who is talking about

261

murder? I don't know what you mean."

"Yes," Davidson said. "I certainly wouldn't take part in any murder."

"Nor would I," the SEAL said. "That would be against the law. I couldn't condone anything like that. Tsk, tsk, what an appalling thought."

"Help!" Luther bellered.

"Why are you screaming for help?" the SEAL asked. "Nobody is going to hurt you."

"Whut you mean?" Monroe asked.

"You are all free to go," Matt told them.

"Lord have mercy!" Seymour hollered. "We're free at last!"

"Thank you," Norm said with a smile as Polly laughed.

"Free to go?" Monroe said, looking around him at the gloom of the timber. "Go where?"

"Anywhere you want to go," Matt told him. "But you can't stay here."

"I don't wanna stay here!" Oscar said. "I wanna git gone and go home."

Monroe stared at Matt for a moment. "You son-of-a-bitch!" Monroe cussed him. "You rotten no-good lowlife bastard!"

"Whut you cussin' him for?" Luther asked. "He's a-turnin' us loose."

"Think about it," Monroe said. "He ain't gonna give us no guns. He's sendin' us out in the timber to die. Them damn links will kill us."

"I don't know what's going to happen to you," Matt said, his voice emotionless. "But all charges against you have been dropped. As a federal agent, I've been instructed to order you all off federal land, and this is federal land. You must leave and leave now."

"So arrest us!" Monroe yelled.

"We have no facilities to hold you. Sorry, but you'll all have to leave."

"Give us our guns, man. Give us a fightin' chance!"

"Sorry. None of you seems to have a valid license to carry a gun. And since it's not hunting season, you don't have any need to carry firearms. Why don't you take up fishing?"

"At least it's a chance," Jim Bob said, shaking his pant leg. Out of piss he had made a bigger mess.

"I'd a soon they just go on an' shoot me," Seymour said. "Them links is the most horrible lookin' things I ever seen in all my life."

"I'll get out of this," Monroe said. "And when I do, I'll come lookin' for you, CIA man."

"I don't wanna go!" Oscar changed his tune.

"Move," the SEAL said.

"Come on," Monroe told his intrepid little band. "We'll hang on the edge of the timber and after the choppers come in the morning, we'll enter the tunnels and find enough guns and gear to fight our way out."

Matt's expression did not change. The SEALs and rangers had already placed explosives in what remained of the tunnels. There would be nothing left of the mining complex moments after the last helicopter lifted off.

"'At 'ere's a good idea, Monroe!" Jim Bob said. He looked at the SEAL. "You ain't got a fresh pair of britches you'd loan a man, do you?"

"Move!"

Reluctantly, hesitantly, the men began moving toward the darkness of the timber that ringed the old complex.

"I just now got my feet dry, and now I'm gonna have to wade acrost that damn stream," Jim Bob bitched. "It just ain't fair. Cain't them soldier boys see that all we's tryin' to do was save the U-nited States from niggers and Jews and other heathens?"

"I've told you fifteen times, I'm *Navy*, you ignorant son of a bitch!" the SEAL team leader roared.

"Whatever," Jim Bob replied, and vanished into the

timber with his buddies. "I just *got* to change my drawers," was the last thing any of those at the mining complex heard from him.

"You're sending those men to their deaths," Tom said. "And I'm going to testify to that effect."

"Lawyer," Matt said, turning to face him. "I have just about had all the lip I am going to take from you. Traci, take the kids back inside, please."

"Regardless of what you think of me," Tom said to Matt, "I am not a stranger to fighting. I was on the college wrestling team and was quite good at it."

The SEAL team leader looked up into the cloudy heavens and shook his head. The ranger lieutenant smiled.

"And," Tom continued, "I am *very* weary of your over-bearing and arrogant attitude. I think the time has come for you to receive your comeuppance."

"I do believe the man wants to fight, Matt," the SEAL said.

"Suits the hell out of me," Matt told him, then stepped forward and knocked Tom sprawling in the mud.

10

"Now that I have your attention, Tom," Matt said, pulling on a pair of leather riding gloves, "I'll just sweeten the pot some. We'll make this a stand-up fistfight."

"I don't know what you mean," Tom said, sitting up in the mud hole.

"Very simple, Tom. I know enough tricks to break every bone in your body. But I won't use them unless you start pulling some off-the-wall crap with me. We'll just box, if that's the way you want it."

"Fine," Tom said. He brushed himself off and tried a sneaky left at Matt's jaw. Matt bobbed his head and busted Tom in the belly with a right, then stepped back. That was not something he'd ordinarily have done.

"Does anybody want to bet on the lawyer?" a ranger said. "I'll give great odds."

He had no takers.

"You men on guard stay at your posts and keep a sharp eye out!" Lieutenant Davidson yelled.

Tom rushed Matt and tried to bear-hug him. Matt spun around and broke Tom's grasp, throwing the man to the ground. Tom plowed in, both fists flailing, but hitting only air. Matt backed up, all the while measuring the man. He saw a nice opening and drove a straight right in, catching the lawyer smack on the mouth and knocking the man back to the ground, his lips bloody and his eyes glazed.

Matt kept his word. Ordinarily he would have ended the fight right then by kicking the man in the head. Instead, he backed away a few yards and waited for Tom to shake the chirping birdies out of his head and get to his feet.

Susan and her daughter Traci stood nearby, undisguised hatred toward husband and father clearly evident on their faces. Tommy stood impassively, knowing with a child's intuition that Matt Jordan would probably soon be his stepfather. The boy had never felt love toward his real father; Tom had never allowed it. The boy knew only fear toward the man.

Tom got up and Matt smacked him again, staggering him. Tom swung and quite by accident caught Matt on the side of the head. The blow stung and Matt backed up, making Tom come after him.

Tom walked right into the next combination, a hard left and right to the jaw and belly. Tom dropped his guard and Matt popped him on the mouth. Tom sat down hard in the mud.

"You're finished, Tom," Matt said. "Give it up."

"To hell with you, Jordan!" Tom said, crawling to his hands and knees and with an effort, standing. He dived at Matt, trying to grab him by the knees and pull him down. Matt sidestepped and Tom fell face first back into the churned mud.

"Gotta give him an E for effort," a SEAL said. "He's trying."

"Yeah," a ranger said. "I don't like the son-of-a-bitch, but he's game, I'll give him that much."

Tom got up and charged, a huge mudball running toward Matt. Matt tripped him, once more sending him sprawling to the earth. Tom rolled and came to his feet, a look of hate and fury clouding what facial features could be seen through the mud.

Matt stepped in and busted the man a right and left to the jaw, staggering him, sending him back. Matt bored in, wanting an end to this nonsense. He hit Tom hard, knocking him down.

"Damn it, man, stay down!" Matt told him.

Tom crawled to hands and knees, steadily cussing Matt. He shook his head, and the mud and the blood flew with the effort. He got to his boots and raised his fists.

Matt lowered his fists. "It's over, Tom. A lot of things are over for you. Give it up."

"Fight me!" Tom screamed. "Fight me, you cowardly bastard!"

Tommy looked puzzled at that. *Cowardly?*

"Go clean up," was Matt's reply.

Tom charged him and knocked Matt down, both of them rolling and cussing and slugging in the mud like oversized schoolboys. Matt was stronger and in much better shape, and he pinned Tom, sitting on the man's chest and holding his arms to the ground.

"This is stupid, Tom," Matt panted. "It isn't proving anything."

Summoning strength from a hidden well, Tom reared up and threw Matt from him, for a moment gaining the upper hand. He kicked Matt in the side while he was down, bringing a grunt of pain from him. Matt rolled away and came to his boots, a new and savage look in his eyes.

"Okay, Tom," he said. "Now all bets are off."

Matt suddenly spun a half turn, his left leg coming up high, the side of his boot catching Tom in the face and knocking him backward. Matt followed it with a spin in the opposite direction, his right leg smashing Tom on the other side of the man's face. Tom went down, his face swelling and new blood leaking from his mouth.

Matt popped him open-handed, flashing blows with the sides and palms of his hands, to the face, chest, and neck.

Tom's head whipsawed from side to side. Matt stepped in close and brought both hands in sharply, the palms open, impacting over Tom's ears. Tom screamed as the pressure exploded in his head. Matt balled a big hand into a big fist and hit Tom on the jaw twice—short, hammering blows that sounded like a pistol discharging.

Tom fell backward and lay on the muddy ground, out cold.

Matt bent over, catching his breath. After a moment he straightened up, hands on his hips.

"Got interesting there toward the last," the SEAL team leader said.

"I wonder what the Sataws watching from the timber thought of all this nonsense," Matt said.

As if in reply, a hideous scream rose from the timber, from the direction the CWA men had taken.

"I think they've been busy doin' something else," Nick said.

The SEALs laid out an LZ for the choppers and the first helicopter set down shortly after dawn. Simmons of the FBI and Richards from the Agency stepped out. Both were dressed in BDUs and carrying M-16s.

Matt shook hands with both of them, then stepped back and eyeballed Richards. "Let me guess: I'm going to stay in here for a time?"

"For a time," his boss told him. He smiled. "If you have any good-byes to attend to, you'd better get them said."

Matt nodded and walked to Susan's side. Together they walked down to the creek.

"I don't know what's going to happen to Tom, Susie. But you can bet he's going to be kept on ice until this operation is over."

"I don't care what happens to Tom. I just don't want to lose you . . . again. We've been invited to go back to Los

268

Angeles with Milli and Dennis. I think we will. Of course, I'll have to go back and close up the house sooner or later, but that can wait. Tom told me last evening he was going to start divorce proceedings immediately. I told him to go ahead." She smiled at him. "My God, I feel positively *grimy!*"

Matt laughed at her expression. "Without being mean about it, Susie—you are."

She laughed with him. "You have the Feldmans' phone number and address?"

"Yes. Dennis gave it to me last night. Would I be out of bounds if I kissed you?"

"I've been waiting for that for twenty-three years, Matt."

Matt had kissed Traci on the cheek and shaken Tommy's hand. Then he stood and watched the campers board the choppers and lift off. When the last one had left and was no more than a dot in the sky, he turned to Richard.

"What happens to Tom Dalton and his mouth?"

"I'll let Simmons answer that."

"We have proof that Dalton was helping bankroll the CWA. We obtained a warrant to search his house and found it . . . legally. The CWA has been ruled a terrorist organization. Aiding and abetting a terrorist organization is a federal crime. In exchange for Dalton keeping his mouth shut, we'll be willing to overlook that little indiscretion on his part. He doesn't have much choice in the matter. The evidence against him is overwhelming, and he'll see that. His only other option is losing his ticket to practice law. I feel that Tom Dalton is going to be a very bitter, unhappy, silent man."

Lieutenant Davidson walked up to the men. "You fellows might want to see this," he said. "Some of my people found what was left of the CWA men. They're about a thousand yards in the timber."

The Sataws and breakaways and civilians had not been kind to the terrorists. Richard was the first to spot anything, an arm torn off at the shoulder and hurled to one side. They followed the trail of blood to the body of Seymour.

Darnell was found hanging upside down from a tree limb. They could not find his head.

Oscar had been lifted or tossed onto a broken limb, the branch impaling him through the chest.

Carl's neck had been forced into a small V between branches about six feet off the ground. His face was black and his protruding tongue was purple and swollen.

A long gray line of intestine led them to Jim Bob. The man had literally been torn apart from crotch to neck.

"Get pictures of it all," Simmons told an agent.

The men widened the search, but the bodies of Luther and Monroe could not be found.

"They might have made it out," Nick said. He and Dan were guiding the others to the tribe's home ground and staying until the relocation was complete. "If they did, they're the luckiest men on earth."

"Is that going to be a problem?" Lieutenant Davidson asked Agent Simmons.

He shook his head. "No. We have federal warrants out on both of them. They don't dare surface. This'll be old news by the time they get anyone's ear."

"How about Trumball?" Matt asked.

"He's slick. We can't tie him in directly with any crime yet. But it's only a matter of time before we do."

"What do you want done with the bodies?" a ranger asked the FBI man.

Simmons turned and with a bland expression said, "What bodies?"

When the charges went off in the tunnels, the bodies of the

270

CWA men were forever buried under tons of rubble. Tom Dalton was flown out in the last chopper to leave, escorted by an FBI agent, and he did not look at all happy about the situation. But then, Tom never looked happy about much of anything.

Matt waved. Tom spat on the ground and turned his back to him.

"You should write a book, Matt," Richard said, after witnessing Tom's dislike.

"Oh?"

"Yes. You could call it *How To Win Friends and Influence People, Part Two*." He walked away chuckling.

"Strange man," Lieutenant Davidson remarked.

"That was his idea of a joke," Matt said.

"Like I said: strange."

Matt, Simmons, and Richard rode in with Nick and Dan, while the rangers walked in, spearheading and guarding both flanks and the rear. They saw no sign of the breakaways, Sataws, or the civilians who had come in to help them.

"We won't, either," Nick said. "Too many of us for them. They've pulled back and will sit this one out. If their plan had worked, Matt, to isolate you here, without radio contact, they might have managed to convince the leaders of the tribe not to relocate. I don't think so, but there was a chance. Now they know we've won this first round. I'm lookin' for a bloodbath on the outside in round two."

Richard rode silently and properly, even though he was unaccustomed to the Western saddle. He bounced up and down as he had been taught to do in equestrian school.

Matt looked behind him at Richard. The face of the number-two man at the Agency was bland. "You know something that maybe I ought to know, Rich?"

"Not until the President makes up his mind, Husky."

The use of his code name was to warn Matt not to pursue this line any further.

As usual, Matt ignored the warning. "Until the President makes up his mind about what, Rich?"

Richard sighed. "We cannot allow a bloodbath, Husky."

"How the hell am I supposed to prevent it?"

"Must we discuss this now?"

"Yes."

"What he's trying to keep from telling you, son," Dan said, "is that he wants you to head up one of the teams that I'm sure the government is putting together as fast as they can, to go hunt down and destroy those tribe-related civilians on the outside who can't control the urge."

"Richard?" Matt said.

"Yes, Husky."

"No!"

"Don't make a hasty decision, Husky. Those people are dangerous. They have to be dealt with."

"Then round them up and vaccinate them. Goddamn, Rich, you're talking about a wholesale slaughter. Jesus, they can't help what they are anymore than a bear or a wolf or a lion or an eagle. Who came up with this brilliant idea?"

"Not us, Husky," Richard said. "And you can take that to the bank. I am on record as being adamantly opposed to us taking any further part in this . . . mess."

"Then why are you here? You're supposed to be running the shop."

"Because the President told me to come here, that's why. When the . . . creatures are safely relocated, he wants to see you."

"Who wants to see me?"

"The President! Who are we talking about here, for Christ's sake, Winston Churchill?"

"Why does he want to see me?"

"Husky! I don't know!"

"You're lying, Richard. Everytime you lie to me, your

272

ears get red."

"They do not!"

"Yes, they do. I've noticed that. I will not, repeat, *not* be a part of any Iceman team going around killing men and women and children who can't help being what God made them. But I'll seriously consider being a part of any team who'll at least make an effort to take these people alive in an attempt to save them. That's firm, Rich. Pass that along to your boss."

"I keep changing my opinion of you, Matt," Simmons said. "Sometimes reports don't do a man justice. I apologize for all the bad things I thought about you in the past."

"Just as long as you don't kiss me."

The group rode on, laughing . . . except Richard. Richard did not like crude jokes.

Book Three

Of all the creatures that were made he [man] is the most detestable. Of the entire brood he is the only one—the solitary one—that possesses malice. That is the basest of all instincts, passions, vices—the most hateful. He is the only creature that inflicts pain for sport, knowing it to be pain.

Mark Twain

1

They rode and walked for two days, camped and cooked and slept without incident. Matt radioed in to his contact twice a day and was told that the press were all about to shit a brick.

"I hope they do," Matt replied. "And it gets hung up."

The old NG base was ready to receive the Unseen.

"Wait here," Nick told the government men and the rangers on the morning of the third day. "We've been bein' watched since last night, so don't anybody get spooked and get an itchy trigger finger. These folks are not going to hurt you unless you start trouble with them. Lieutenant, stand your people down and tell them to relax. Come on, Matt. They trust you, so you go in with me and Dan."

"Trust me? How do they know they can trust me?"

"'Cause I told them about you last night. About your refusal to be a part of unnecessary killin'. They liked that. Come on. The rest of you, stay put!"

Matt was not prepared for what he saw. He had seen Sataws, more animal than human. But the sight that greeted him this day jarred him to his boots. There were some who looked to be perfectly formed human beings. There were others who had attained only about midpoint through the evolution cycle. He fought an inner struggle to keep his face expressionless and hoped it worked.

"Matt Jordan," Nick said. "This is the leader of the tribe. His name is Ty."

Ty had a human body and an animal's face, wolflike, with a shorter snout. Matt did not know whether to shake hands or just stand there.

Ty smiled and stuck out an almost perfectly formed human hand, but a lot hairier than normal. When he spoke, the words came out slow and labored but clear enough to understand.

Matt took the hand and could feel the tremendous power in the fingers.

"I understand your confusion, Matt Jordan," Ty said. "The first time I saw a human being up close their ugliness scared me half to death."

Matt had to laugh and hoped Ty and the others would understand the laughter. They did, and joined in.

"Well," Matt said, stalling for time and words, ". . . I guess the first thing we have to do is get a chopper in here and show you all there is nothing to fear from the machines."

"That would be a good first step," Ty agreed. "I personally have seen them up close. Great noisy flapping things. Yes, bring one of them in so my people can look at it, Matt Jordan."

"There is something else, Ty. Do you have any prisoners you've . . . ah, taken in the timber?"

"None. Since we were so close to attaining human form, we stopped that years ago. The Sataws are still guilty of taking prisoners, however. Those in the outside world who are supportive of them wrongly placed the blame on us."

"Ty, are you and your people fully prepared to cooperate with us in naming those who have left here and whom you suspect to be followers of the . . . 'urge,' as Nick and Dan call it?"

"The tribe members have discussed it, and we will give you the names of all those we know. But there are many out there whom we have lost track of. I don't know how much help we can be."

"That's fair. All right, here's what I'm going to do: I'm going to order helicopters in to resupply and beef up the army rangers, who will throw up a perimeter around this area to keep people out—people of my kind who might not have friendly thoughts toward you and the tribe, and also to keep out Sataws and breakaways."

"I am agreeable to that, Matt Jordan. I think I know what 'beef up' means."

Matt lifted his walkie-talkie. "All right, Richard. You and Simmons get ready to come on in. Dan is coming back to guide you in."

High overhead a passenger jet flew westward. Ty looked up. "Amazing things have happened in my lifetime. The first time I saw a plane, I thought it was a great bird of prey. I ran back underground and wouldn't come out for days."

"Would you like to ride in a jet?" Matt asked him.

"Not . . . really, Matt Jordan. My heart is pounding in my chest at the thought of riding in one of those flapping things. Will it be a long journey?"

"Several hours in the air. We have to cross the mountains."

Ty smiled. "Oh, I've crossed the mountains many times, Matt Jordan. But I've never flapped across them."

Richard paled visibly at the sight of the tribe members, but Matt gave him credit for not losing his composure. He offered the tribe food.

"We are not carnivores, Richard," Ty told him. "We have no quarrel with the animals the gods placed on the earth."

"Can you communicate with them?" Simmons asked.

"To a degree. The wolf especially. It is one of the smartest of all species. And the most misunderstood and feared by your people."

"Wrongly so?"

"Oh, yes. You people don't take time to understand an animal. You expect more out of an animal than you do from your own kind. That has always both amused and frightened us. Most animals are predictable if one takes the time to learn their ways. Most, not all."

"I think," Richard said, "that we can learn a lot from each other, Ty. If we try."

"I hope so, Richard," the tribe leader replied. "But I have very grave doubts."

"Yet despite your doubts, you agreed to be relocated."

"It had to be. Civilization—or whatever you call it—is moving toward us. Closer and closer each year. And the tribe met and agreed that the killing of the Sataws and the urge followers had to be stopped, even if it meant an end to us. And that will probably prove to be."

"You don't have much faith in the human race, Ty, yet you strive to be human."

"Yes. But since no tribe member practices war, tribe members respect animals and do not kill for sport, no tribe member steals from another, tribe members mate for life, tribe members do not engage in child abuse, and we protect the environment instead of damaging it, we concluded that our incorporation into your race could only improve it."

Richard smiled and it was genuine. "If only that would prove to be true, Ty. All we can do is hope."

"Believe me," the man-beast said, "we have done a lot of hoping since the decision was made."

"I have a suggestion," Richard said. "Let's see if we are in agreement. I am going to suggest to the President of the United States that this area, your homeland, be declared a

280

government reservation and that it be placed off limits to anyone not of the tribe. If the incorporation of the tribe into our race proves to be a failure for whatever reason, you will have a place to return and live in peace. Are you in agreement with that?"

"It sounds nice," Ty said. "But I have read of the Indians on reservations. They do not fare so well. Why would we be any different? Look at us, Richard. Look at our forms. We're trapped between worlds. There are those in your world who would consider us to be a game animal, who would come in and shoot us and mount our heads on their walls. Is this not true?"

"Well . . . ah, yes, unfortunately, it is. But we can keep those people out. I think."

"You think," Ty said with his strange animal-like smile. "But you can't be sure. Your world contains people with many strange prejudices, Richard. If a human being can have those prejudices against a fellow human being, just think how many would view us. We are part animal, Richard, and we know—have known for centuries—that your world has little or no compassion for animals. You consider yourselves far superior to animals, yet no animal kills without reason. Animals do not drag their food kills into a drunken gawking circle of like animals expecting praise for killing it, and then leave it to rot. But your people do. We've seen it countless times. Your race makes planes that fly through the heavens and land on the moon, automobiles that roar about, puking filth into the air. Very fine accomplishments, I suppose, but then you have the arrogance to think that you can tinker with nature and make it better. You kill off all the natural predators of the woods creatures to justify man's slaughter of the animals that are left . . . and all for sport. It just makes no sense to any of us."

Richard had no rebuttal; he knew there was none. He could not simply shrug this off. Finally he said, "We're not all like that, Ty."

Ty would only smile, rather sadly, Matt thought. "I approve of your reservation plan, Richard. If all else fails. When will the first helicopters arrive?"

"This afternoon."

"I will have my people ready. Please, erect your tents and be comfortable. Eat and rest. You are safe."

When the first big choppers came hammering in, the tribe members scattered like leaves in the wind. One minute there were a hundred men, women, and kids in the area. A minute later, not a one could be seen.

"Who are all those people?" Matt asked.

"Medical doctors, anthropologists, and two goddamned politicians."

"Well, that's wonderful, Richard. A politician is going to keep his mouth shut? Since when? Well, maybe it's not such a bad idea. Let Ty and others see what form of government we have. Fifteen minutes of conversation with those nitwits and Ty will order his people back underground."

"There are many good, decent, hardworking, public-minded men and women in Congress, Husky."

"Name two."

Richard walked off, muttering.

The doctors and the anthropologists were awed when the tribe members began gathering around, staring at the new arrivals. The politicians just looked scared.

The tribe parted when Ty made his entrance and one of the doctors said, "Good God!"

Ty was introduced. "What happened was we tried to breed too close," Ty explained. "From the neck down, I am pure human. You can see what I am from the neck up. I make no apologies for it. I believe it was your comic book hero Popeye who said, 'I yam what I yam.'" Ty chuckled, the sound odd coming from his animal throat and mouth.

One of the anthropologists smiled. "I would very much like to see how you and your people live, Mr. Ty. Could that be arranged?"

"Why not? I would imagine we all had best get used to being studied."

"Only with your permission, Mr. Ty," one of the doctors said. "We would like to try to learn from each other."

"A noble thought. May I pose a question?"

"Of course."

"Do you use animals in laboratory experiments?"

"No. I belong to an organization called Psychologists for the Ethical Treatment of Animals."

"Good for you. Certainly. I would be happy to show you our living quarters."

"Come along, Matt," Richard said.

"No."

Richard stopped. Turned around. "Aren't you interested?"

"I don't wish to see the sadness on the tribe members' faces, thank you."

"Whatever in the world are you talking about?"

"Ty knows they'll never see this place again."

"The President told me he approves of the plan to turn this into a reservation for them! I spoke to him not two hours ago."

"Never happen, Rich. Like a lot of things, it looks good on paper. The tribe will spend the rest of their lives confined in that old National Guard base in Montana. If it takes a hundred more years to breed the animal out of them, that's how long they'll be there. Under guard. Behind high wire. In prison. Ty knows it. He told Dan and Nick that not twenty minutes ago."

"He might suspect it, Matt. He cannot *know* it."

"Wait until the public hears of them, Rich. Some of the

more bloodthirsty ones will be swarming in here with elephant guns, hoping one of the tribe was left behind so they can kill it and mount it, stuff it, stick its head up on a den or office wall and brag to other good ol' boys about how they 'Got me a clean shot, buddy. It only lay on the ground and kicked and squalled and bellered for a couple of minutes 'fore it died.' You know what I'm saying is true, Rich."

"Go on, say it all, Matt."

"The tribe is used to running free. Some of them are not going to like being confined. They'll break out. And then here come the gun-totin' posses. And when they catch it, or before they catch it, some civilians will die."

"And what do you suggest, Rich?"

"Have Congress declare this area off-limits to everybody. No hunting, fishing, backpacking, camping—nothing. And let me pick the teams who would make those orders stand. My God, Rich, it's such a small part of such a large wilderness area. Let the tribe stay here where they belong and allow only the doctors and scientists in to do whatever. The anthropologists' study would be much more complete if the tribe could live in their natural environment."

"Umm," Richard said. "Your plan has merit, Matt. You would stay in this area and seek out and capture or kill the breakaways and Sataws; not by yourself, of course, but heading a team?"

"I would agree to that, yes."

"I can guarantee only that I will take it up with the President."

"That's all I ask."

"I'll delay the other helicopters coming in until I've spoken with the President."

"That's good enough for me, Rich."

Matt walked over to Dan and Nick and explained what he'd proposed. The men grinned and slapped him on the back. "Good for you, boy," Dan said. "If the powers that be buy it, I'll stay in here with you and help you track the bad ones down."

"Me, too," Nick said.

"Here comes Ty with the doctors," Dan said. "I'll tell them what you proposed."

The scientists were ecstatic. Matt thought one of them was actually going to try to kiss him. He backed up a couple of feet. While they were babbling happily about on-site study and fellowships and whatever, Matt winked at Ty and slipped away. Ty returned the wink. It was an odd feeling, having a wolf's head wink at him.

But a good feeling.

2

It went well for the first few days. Helicopters began ferrying in mounds of supplies for the army and the scientists who were staying indefinitely in the area code-named U-1. First camp of the Unseen, Matt supposed.

Ty and his tribe readily accepted the scientists and patiently began answering their hundreds of questions. The tribe lined up to take blood tests and to be given lengthy physicals. More equipment, including portable generators, was helicoptered in.

"Any day now," Matt told Lieutenant Davidson. "The press has to pick up on it. And when that happens, we're in trouble. Or more accurately, the tribe is in trouble. The new people in place?"

"Yes, sir. Captain Fargo is in command. We have a full company of rangers in place. But," he added glumly, "a full battalion couldn't really secure this area. It's just too damned big. What's the word from Congress?"

"A select committee is discussing the matter."

"That means the press will learn of it very soon."

"You got it."

Two weeks after the first helicopter carrying the scientists, doctors, anthropologists, and two politicians touched down near the tribe's living area, the story broke in the press.

Savage Tribe Found Living in Great Primitive Area silently screamed one headline.

Cannibals Discovered in State said another.

Watching on a satellite hookup, Matt and several of the doctors listened as a network news anchor wrapped up his commentary by saying, "And once again the government has deceived the American people. This network has, like other networks, been denied access to the tribe area. Why? If this lost tribe is harmless, as the government claims, why aren't we allowed to enter the area and film them . . . ?"

"Because it's none of your mother-fucking business, that's why," Matt muttered.

". . . And what about the recent spate of deaths of both high- and low-level government employees in and around the Washington, DC area? Confidential sources tell us the deaths are solidly connected with the lost tribe . . ."

"Idiot!" Matt said. "The tribe has been found, so how in the hell can they be *lost?*"

". . . The American people have a right to be informed. We demand that the government open up this area and allow news-gathering personnel in."

"You demand," Matt said, getting up and turning off the set. "You demand. You demand to be let in so your ratings will go up and you'll make more money. That's why you demand, you asshole."

"The acting DCI wants you on the radio, Matt," an FBI agent yelled to him.

"Yes, Richard?"

"The fat's in the fire now."

"Yes, I saw the broadcasts. Who leaked it?"

"Who knows? That's only one of our problems. Congress is very jumpy about all those rangers in the area. They're afraid some civilians are going to get hurt."

"So? All the networks have, to their credit, informed

287

people to stay out of this area. If they ignore that warning and get their asses shot off, that's their problem."

"Why must you always take such a simplistic approach to complicated problems, Matt?"

"It isn't complicated. Politicians have to make everything complicated so they can confuse the public into thinking they're doing their jobs. Who do those blithering idiots in Washington want guarding this area, the Boy Scouts? God damn it, Rich, we've still got no telling how many breakaways, Sataws, and outside sympathizers roaming this country. Now that those fucking nitwits on the networks and the newspapers have busted this story wide open, people are going to get killed. You know how the press hates us. You mark my words, Rich. Once the newspeople learn that the Agency has a hand in this, we're going to get the blame—all the blame—for anything bad that happens. It's never failed before."

"Jesus," Richard moaned. "We're not even supposed to be working domestic. How in the hell did we ever get tied up in this mess?"

"You're asking me?"

"No, no. All right, Matt. Brace yourself for a hard blow. A bad wind is coming."

"Yeah. And it's spelled R-E-P-O-R-T-E-R-S."

Simmons ran over to Matt's tent. "It's busted wide open, Matt. It's all that's on any network. The press has tied in the tribe to the disappearances, the kidnappings, and the murders over the past years. They've connected General Dawson and Chief of Staff Atkins. They've got the story about the Bureau agents and Company's agents and the Secret Service people. It's all out in the open now."

"Choppers approaching our sector now, sir!" a ranger radioman yelled. "They'll be here in about fifteen minutes."

"You want to bet me ten bucks that I'm not going to be handed this hot potato?" Matt asked the Bureau man.

"Yeah," Simmons said. "I'll take that bet. I just got off the horn with the Director. I'm the official spokesman for the Bureau out here. We're to let the choppers land and to answer the reporters' questions."

"Shit!" Matt said. "Better you than me."

"Mister Jordan?" the radioman called. "The DCI wants to talk to you."

Simmons' smile was faint. "Looks like we're both going to be on the spot, pal."

"I'll get the tribe back underground. They're not ready for this."

"Are we?"

"No. But we don't have a choice in the matter."

"Why is the CIA involved in this?" Ron Arnold asked.

Of all the network news anchors, none invoked such hatred among law enforcement people and special government agents than this one. His network was the most liberal of the big four. He and most others who worked with him moaned and sobbed and snorted and blubbered and stomped in their hankies everytime some murderer was gassed or fried. When they weren't imploring the government to seize all the privately owned weapons in the nation, they were screaming about too much government interference in the lives of American citizens.

"Because I was in place, on a camping trip with some of my high school graduating class," Matt told him. Not a lie, just not all the facts.

Matt had not shaved since he'd entered the Primitive Area. His beard would help conceal his face from the many people around the world who had him on hit lists . . . another little item that reporters never seem to give a damn about in their quest for a story.

"I find that hard to believe," Lee Peterson said.

"I don't care *what* you find hard to believe," Matt shot back. If Richard viewed the evening news, and Matt was sure he would, Richard would be eating Rolaids by the handful.

"I don't like your attitude," Ron said.

"I don't like you, period," Matt told him.

"Mr. Simmons," Jerry Kaye took it.

Matt watched out of the corner of his eye as several people wearing backpacks, including a cameraman, slipped away from the main group and headed, unnoticed by the others, into the timber. Matt turned his back on the press and walked off. He had told the Ranger CO—on orders from the White House—not to interfere with the reporters if they wanted to go stomping around in the area. Matt knew he and the others would be damned if they did and damned if they didn't in this matter. And to hell with people who ignored warnings.

He sat down in front of his tent after pouring a cup of coffee and waited. He had a hunch it was going to get interesting very quickly.

Donna Gates, a reporter whom Matt had heard was as fair in her reporting as she was allowed to be, left the main group and sought him out.

"May I join you?" she asked.

"You may. Help yourself to coffee."

"Thank you. I do not have a tape recorder on me, Mr. . . ."

"Call me Matt. Good. I'll take your word for that."

She poured coffee, sugared and stirred, and sat down in the camp chair Matt unfolded for her. "I was watching your eyes as that team of newspeople slipped out of this area. You saw them leave and did nothing to stop them."

"They're all adults. They were warned that this area was dangerous. I'm not going to hold their hands and wipe their noses."

"You don't care what happens to them?"

"On the record? Or off?"

She hesitated. Smiled. "A little of both."

He chuckled. "No, Miss Gates. I don't care what happens to them. If a person smokes cigarettes and develops a bad cough, the smart thing for him to do is to quit smoking and see a doctor. If someone tells you there's a minefield in front of you, you don't go blundering into it. See what I'm saying?"

"There are army rangers out there."

"To keep people out, not to keep people in. This isn't a prison."

"How dangerous is it?"

"Very dangerous. If they wander past the rangers' forward positions, they might not return."

"Should that happen, will you go in searching for them?"

"I won't be in any rush about it."

"You hate the press that much?"

"No—just certain members of the press who feel they should dictate foreign policy, run the country, belittle programs and individuals they disagree with or don't like, and in general stick their noses in where they shouldn't."

"In your opinion."

"Certainly. But I'm not in a position to sway the general public. You people are, and many of you do so at every opportunity."

"Will we get a chance to speak to some of these so-called tribe members?"

"Not if I have anything to say about it."

"Why?"

"Because you want to exploit them, that's why."

"That's unfair. I don't want to exploit anybody. This is a news story. I'm paid to cover the news; I'm doing my job, that's all."

Matt stared at her for a moment. "With you, and a few

others in your profession, I might be convinced of that. Captain Fargo runs everything outside this camp. Agent Simmons is the official spokesman for the camp. But I run the camp. The tribe trusts me, and that ought to tell you people something."

"That would certainly startle Ron, now, wouldn't it?"

If Ronnie-baby walks out in the wilderness, Matt thought, he won't be startled long—just dead. "I'll speak with Ty—he's the leader of the tribe. If he wants to talk with you, fine. But no film. Not yet. If—*if* you meet him, you'll see what I mean."

"Grotesquely misshapen?"

"He grows on you. Donna, it isn't the tribe that people have to fear. It's the Sataws and breakaways and outside sympathizers who have been killing. Ty and his bunch are the gentlest group of people I have ever encountered. They live as one with the forest, the land, and the animals. They don't eat meat. They're not hostile unless provoked. I'm trying to protect them, Donna."

"Strange talk coming from a CIA man."

Matt chuckled. "We're no different from other folks. Most of us have wives, kids, mortgages, bills—just like everybody else. We're not ogres, even though much of the press has painted us that way. Individually we support a wide range of groups, everything from the United Way to Defenders of Wildlife and everything in between. If the press just has to set itself up to judge—and I don't know who in the hell gave you people that power—you ought to judge us individually, not tar us all with the same brush."

It was her turn to stare at him. "You'd be a handsome man without that beard."

"As long as the press is around, the beard stays."

"And after this is over?"

"I'm through—retired."

"Is Matt your real name? All we were given was Matt, no last name."

"It won't be when I officially retire."

"It's that bad?"

"I figure I'm on about twenty hit lists—at least that many."

A young ranger walked up at a brisk pace. "Excuse me. That reporter and camera crew refused to stay within our perimeter, sir. They're out in the wilderness, alone and unarmed."

"I'd say they definitely have a problem, wouldn't you, Corporal?"

"Yes, sir. One hell of a problem."

"You warned them that they were entering a dangerous area?"

"Yes, sir. We got it on tape."

"Then we're off the hook. Don't worry about it. If they start yelling for help, then we'll go in. But we'll do so cautiously. I'll be goddamned if I'll babysit these people."

"Yes, sir," the ranger said with a grin.

"It would seem to me that those out . . . there," she cut her eyes to the deep timber, "are defeating their purpose by continuing to kill. Isn't that just bringing hardship to this peaceful tribe?"

"That's what they want. They were against the relocation. They were against any type of study that might eventually tame the wildness that springs up in them."

"The urge to kill?"

"Yes."

"Why does this part of the tribe not eat meat and those on the outside practice cannibalism?"

"I don't know. I was told it had something to do with the genes being altered by poisoned water. I don't think anybody really knows . . . yet. I'm sure the doctors and scientists and anthropologists can give you a much better answer after they've had the time to study the tribe."

"Won't they also have to study those running loose in the wilderness?"

There it is, Matt thought, keeping his expression neutral. God damn you, Rich, I'm going to break your jaw for dumping this mess in my lap. "They have some to study."

"Then you've captured some of them?"

"In a manner of speaking." He wasn't about to tell her outside agents had picked up Cathy and Frank's kids, among other people, and were holding them for observation.

"Either you did or you didn't, Matt."

"I didn't capture them myself. And they're not being held on this compound."

"I see. How far reaching is this problem? On the outside?"

"I have no idea. I have not left this area in several weeks."

"If that camera crew is not back in by night, will you search for them?"

"In the morning."

"They could be dead by then."

"If they're lucky."

3

"I demand that you launch a search for that missing crew immediately!" Ron Arnold said.

"Too late in the day," Matt told him. "We don't have that much light left."

"Those are not experienced woodsmen," Lee Peterson said.

"Then why did they ignore warnings not to go into the deep timber?"

"They're here to cover a story."

"No, they're not here, Mr. Peterson," Matt corrected. "They're out there." He pointed to the wilderness that surrounded them. "I'll start a search for the crew in the morning. First light, not before."

Ron stepped in close and stared at Matt. "I'm going to cream you, Matt Whatever-your-name-is. I'm going to smear your face over every television set in America."

"Go right ahead. It still won't start the search until the morning." He was handed a note by a smiling Agent Simmons. Matt read the note and laughed. "By orders of the Congress of the United States, and approved by the President, this area has been classified as restricted. You know the rules, boys and girls. Lieutenant Davidson, seize all cameras and expose the film."

"This is communism!" Ron hollered.

"Is that the same as commonism?" Matt asked.

"What?"

Nick laughed as he recalled the men of the CWA.

"Forget it—private joke." Matt did not read the rest of the note aloud. Jones had been given a new name, a new ID, and a complete new background. He was now getting ready to start work as an accountant for a firm outside of Washington, DC.

Something good came of this mess, anyway, Matt thought.

Donna and the rest of the reporters knew the rules and didn't bitch all that much. Ron puffed up and stormed about, making threats about what he was going to do. But it was legal, and the threats were hollow.

"Can we trust them?" Captain Fargo whispered to Matt.

"Oh, most are all right. I wouldn't trust Ron Arnold any further than I can see him. But the cameraman is not going to risk federal charges. I saw him turn over his film and his film bag."

"You think that other camera crew bought it?"

"Sure—and their killers will have planted the bodies in very conspicuous places for the reporters to see. You can make book on that."

Donna walked over to him. "We'll be back as soon as it's light, Matt. If you want to keep us out, you're going to have to arrest us. Ron is going to have his network's lawyers file suit to lift the restrictions on this area. You know there is a good chance the courts will go along with it."

"Probably."

"See you in the morning."

A smiling Ron Arnold placed the court order in Simmons'

hand an hour after daylight. Matt looked at Donna. She shrugged her shoulders.

"We can't keep them out, nor can we prevent them from taking pictures," Simmons said. "The courts ruled that the tribe does not endanger national security and is to be treated as an important anthropological find."

"So you don't have as much stroke as you think you do, right, hotshot?" Ron said to Matt.

Matt smiled thinly.

"Ron is looking to get his ashes hauled," Ken Caney said to Lee Peterson. "He's going to push that guy just a little too far."

"I tend to agree with you," Fred Salter said.

Matt and Simmons, with rangers spearheading the march and the press corps, now a hundred strong, stomping and stumbling along behind, left the safe compound and entered the quiet timber. Much to the disgust of Ron Arnold, Matt had borrowed some hair tint from one of the women doctors and dyed his hair blond the night before. It altered his looks dramatically. Donna thought it was funny, as did most of the other members of the press.

They found the cameraman's head impaled up on a limb, bits and pieces of his body scattered all about the trunk of the tree.

"That is, was, Leona's cameraman," a reporter said, after swallowing hard. "But no sign of Leona."

"They probably took her alive for a breeder," Nick told them. "The breakaways and Sataws are the only ones that still do that."

"That's obscene!" Ron said.

"So is trapping," the guide told him. "But so many of your advertisers sell and wear fur you're afraid to take a stand against it."

Ron shut his mouth momentarily. Everyone knew the

297

respite wouldn't last.

"Take pictures and bodybag the parts," Simmons told his men.

Snarling and howling and strange laughter sprang from the gloom of the timber.

"You want to go interview one of the breakaways, Ron?" Matt asked. "Just step over there about a hundred yards. I guarantee you'll run into one."

For once Ron had nothing to say.

The group pulled closer together as the howling and laughing grew louder and more derisive sounding. "His name is Matt Jordan!" Cathy shouted from the shadowed gloom. "Broadcast that."

"You know that woman?" a reporter asked.

"Her name is Cathy."

"And broadcast this!" Cathy shouted. "The goddamn government seized my children a couple of weeks ago—my kids and several hundred other offspring of men and women like me. They're experimenting on them."

"Is that true, Matt?" Donna asked.

"I don't know. I told you, I've been in here for several weeks. I don't know what's going on outside."

"Leave us alone," a male voice shouted from the forest.

"They killed or kidnapped an entire crew, and they want to be left alone," Lee said. "That doesn't make any sense. They must be crazy."

"Poor unfortunate wretches," Ron said. "They know the government is going to hunt them down and kill them. Does that make you feel like a big man, Jordan?"

"Why don't you shut your goddamn mouth, Ron?" Salter told him. "I swear you're getting more impossible day by day."

"That must be why I'm still number one and you're still number three," Ron said with a smile, referring to the ratings.

"Knock it off," Captain Fargo said. "Come on."

The body of a man was found hanging by his heels from a tree limb. Both arms had been ripped off.

"Why?" Donna asked, grimacing at the hideous sight.

"Because they're maniacs," Simmons said. "Personally, I'd like to call in helicopter gunships."

"Is that the Bureau's official stand on this matter?" Ron asked.

"No. But it's mine."

"Kids," Frank Nichols said to his children, "I had a devil of a time just getting in to see you."

The brother and sister sat at the table in the psychiatric ward of the hospital and stared at their father.

"I'm trying to get you kids out of here. You didn't help your case much by running off like you did."

"Where is our mother?" Claudia asked.

"I don't know. Still in the wilderness area, I guess."

"We've committed no crime," Rory said. "The police have no right to hold us here."

"I know. I pointed that out to them. It's a trying time for us all, believe me."

"The government is detaining people all over the country," the young woman said. "Just because we have tribe blood in us. That's not right."

"I'm trying to get you out, Claudia. I'm pulling every string I know how to pull. I should know something very shortly."

"How shortly?" Rory asked.

"Within minutes. I just spoke with Senator Martin. He was optimistic. But why did you run away?"

Brother and sister exchanged glances. The father did not pick up on the furtiveness in the look. Claudia said, "Because cops with guns came looking for us. They scared us, that's why. We knew we hadn't done anything wrong; it was a perfectly normal reaction."

Frank patted her hand. "I understand."

The door behind him was unlocked, and a man stepped into the room. "Mr. Nichols? You can take them home with you. I just got the okay to release them. Sorry for the inconvenience, kids. I hope you understand."

"Oh, we understand," Claudia said. "Believe me, we do."

The doctor smiled and winked at her. His eyes were a strange brown tinted with yellow.

Frank pulled up into the drive of the expensive home. The garage doors opened automatically. He pulled the Mercedes inside, and the doors closed behind them. He turned in the seat to smile at Claudia in the backseat, and Rory drove stiffened fingers into his father's throat. Claudia reached out and grabbed her father's head, her fingers ripping into his eyes while Rory tore out Frank's throat.

Frank Nichols, Denver graduating class of 1967, husband of Cathy and father of Claudia and Rory, gurgled and made funny little red spit bubbles as his blood drained from the hideous neck wound. His darling Claudia, the apple of his eye, leaned over the seat and sucked greedily at her father's blood. Rory shoved her out of the way, began cutting Frank's suit coat and shirt from him with a pocket knife, and then proceeded to carve them both a bloody meat treat.

When they had eaten their fill, brother and sister loped into the house, packed a few things, and rifled the huge house for cash and credit cards. They found plenty of both. They locked the house up and then shoved their father down onto the floorboards of the Mercedes.

"Your car or mine?" Rory asked.

"We'll take your four-wheel in case we have to leave the road."

"Let's go find the pack."

The press corps had pretty much run out of steam by the time they returned to the safety of the compound. Many had come into the area thinking this to be some kind of joke or hoax. Now they knew better.

Ron Arnold almost crapped his jeans when he saw Ty, standing in the center of the camp. "Holy shit!" he said.

"Amazing," Donna said.

"Come on, I'll introduce you. Obviously he wants to meet with you all. He'll probably regret that decision after he talks with Ron."

"It really doesn't bother you about those people getting killed back there, does it, Matt?"

"Nope. They were warned. Ty, this is Donna Gates. She's a network reporter. I'll let her introduce the others coming at a run."

"You don't like these people, Matt?" Ty asked.

"Not especially."

"Why's that?"

"It's a long story. I think once you're on the outside and seeing and listening to their reports you'll understand."

"Umm," Ty said as Matt walked back to his tent. "That's unfortunate, for I value Matt's opinion."

"Matt Jordan works for one of the most despicable government agencies anywhere in the world," Ron said. "They engage in illegal covert activities around the world, usually aiding some right-wing group. Do you understand what I'm saying?" Ron snapped his fingers a couple of times in Ty's face. "Is that a mask you've got on there?"

"Only the one the gods gave me, you impudent pup!" He took Donna's arm. "Come, Miss Gates. I will speak with you and only you."

"Now see here!" Ron blustered.

"I have spoken!" Ty roared. Seconds later the area was filled with tribe members forming a line between the departing Ty and Donna and the confused and badly shaken press corps—a line no one wanted to attempt to breech.

"Sir?" Ken Caney called. "Mr. Ty, sir?"

Ty stopped and turned. "Yes?"

"Do we have your permission to take pictures?"

"A polite one," Ty said. "Yes, you do. But only with the permission of the people. If they do not wish to have their images duplicated, put your cameras away."

"We have the permission of the United States government to take pictures, buddy!" Ron hollered. "We don't have to have your permission."

For a moment there was a puzzled look on Ty's face. Ty left Donna's side and walked over to Ron Arnold. Ty was far from young, but even the most unobservant could tell he was still immensely powerful. He put one hairy hand on Ron's shoulder and pushed, forcing Ron to his knees. From the expression on Ron's face, he was in some degree of pain.

"We are a polite people, loudmouth," Ty told him. "We respect the privacy of others. And we expect outsiders to do the same. I'm the elder of this tribe. My name is Ty, not Buddy. People do not raise their voices to me. And when I speak, they listen and obey me."

Ty slowly lifted Ron Arnold from his knees. With one hand, his muscles bulging, he lifted the reporter completely off his feet and put his animal's face close to Ron's. "Do you understand that?"

"Yes, sir!" Ron said, his voice breaking from fear.

Ty gently lowered Ron to the ground. "I hope so. Because if you don't, you'll be ordered from these lands. And you'll go, one way or another."

He returned to Donna, and they walked over to a

secluded area and began to talk, her crew taping and filming it all.

"Do me a favor, Ron," Lee Peterson said. "From now on, stay away from me. I don't want Ty to get the notion that I'm a friend of yours."

"Yeah, that goes for me, too," Jerry Kaye said. "What are you trying to do, screw it up for the rest of us?"

Ron was so scared he sat down on a log, afraid his legs would not support his weight. He chose not to reply to his colleagues. "No damn . . . creature threatens me," he muttered. "Every dog has his day." Ron was not known for his originality. "You just wait and see."

Ron looked around him. The others were talking with tribe members and the tapes were rolling, audio and video. A small boy, almost perfectly human in shape, walked up to him.

"You made Elder Ty angry," the boy said.

"Yes, I suppose I did." Ron suddenly realized he had a goldmine right in front of him that would probably tell it like it was. For he knew that children could be brutally honest. "I'll have to apologize to him. Would that be a good thing for me to do?"

"Oh, yes."

"My name is Ron. What's your name?"

"Charles."

"Are you afraid of having your picture taken, Charles?"

"No. Why should I be afraid of that?"

Ron waved his crew over and introduced them to the boy. "Charles here is going to talk to us, tell us all about the tribe and the way they live, aren't you, Charles?"

"Sure. If that's what you want."

The crew had worked with Ron for a long time out in the field. They knew what he was up to. They didn't like it, but they also knew they wouldn't like drawing unemployment, either. The camera began rolling as Ron led the boy into questions about tribal life and customs, laws, and methods of punishment and how they were handed out.

You sorry son of a bitch, the cameraman thought. *How damn low can one person get?*

After the interview, Ron signed off and thought: Gotcha, Ty. I'm gonna cream your ass, you goddamn savage!

4

"Those with connections to the tribe are striking all over the United States," Richard told Matt by radio. "It's turning very bloody."

"It isn't *all* those with connections, Richard," Matt corrected. "There are thousands on the outside who are living good, decent lives. It's the ones who can't control the urge to kill who are causing the problems."

"The public doesn't see it that way, Matt. And that broadcast by Ron Arnold only added fuel to the fire."

"What broadcast?"

"He aired a special last night, interviewing some child of the tribe. I suspect he deliberately scheduled it late, knowing you people would all be asleep. The boy meant no harm; he was just answering questions truthfully. My people tell me there was a lot of very skillful cutting and editing done. The boy talked about the harsh punishment for thieves among the tribe, how the Elder Ty had ordered the deaths of a lot of tribe members for what Americans would consider very minor crimes. I won't say that public sentiment has turned against the tribe, but that interview sure didn't do their cause any good."

"My fault, Rich. I should have kept a better eye on that son-of-a-bitch."

"No one expects you to do everything, Matt. You're doing a good job in there. Oh, I have some bad news that hasn't been released to the press: the FBI found the body of Frank Nichols. They believe he was killed shortly after he gained the release of his kids from a mental hospital outside of Denver. They, uh, killed him and ate him—at least parts of him."

"Damn! Where are the kids? Have they been spotted?"

"No."

"The Bureau can't sit on his death forever."

"That's right. They'll release the news later today."

"I'll get a phone patch into Susan and the others and break it to them."

"All right. Matt, wind it up in there and get ready to pull out. We need you out here."

"Ty and the tribe?"

"The rangers will stay in place. I spoke with Captain Fargo. He seems to be genuinely fond of those . . . people."

"We all are, Rich. We could learn a lot from them."

"I'll tell this to you now, Matt: Emmett Trumball has been buying air time and newspaper space around the nation. We can't prove it's him, but we know it is. He's calling for a bounty to be placed on the heads of tribe members. I don't have to tell you that there are a lot of nuts in this country who just might heed that call."

"God damn it, it's federal land here. Can't Congress send in more troops?"

"Congress is walking a tightrope on this, Matt. It's election year, you know. The senators and representatives are getting a lot of heat from the folks back home. A large percentage of their mail is saying that if a bunch of animals—meaning the tribe—is the cause of all this bloodshed, then get rid of the root source."

"God damn it, Rich!"

"I know. I know. But my hands are tied. I can only make suggestions to the President."

"I have a suggestion for Mr. Emmett Trumball: take him out."

"Very well, Matt. Why don't you?"

Matt did not minimize the danger when he spoke with Ty and the other elders. When he had finished, Ty said, "One bear goes bad and becomes a man-killer, so many of your people conclude that the only way to deal with it is to kill all bears. That is a very, ah, interesting way of looking at the problem."

"It's a very stupid way, Ty, and you know it. So I have to go back outside and help deal with the problem."

"I will miss you."

"And I'll miss you. The rangers will stay in place, Ty. And the doctors and scientists will be here. Don't be too hard on the boy, Charles. He was just being truthful."

"Oh, he will receive no punishment. He did nothing wrong."

"I'll be back as soon as I can."

"You are going to kill this Emmett Trumball, Matt Jordan?"

Matt stared at Ty. "You're very astute."

"You and I, Matt, we think alike. For any type of society to exist, there must be laws and rules. And those who break those rules must be dealt with swiftly and often harshly. It appears to me, and has for some years, that there is a breakdown in your society."

"Like you said, Ty: we think a lot alike."

Back at the lodge, Matt shampooed the dye out of his hair and carefully trimmed his beard. He put a call in to Susan and told her about Frank.

"Horrible!" she said. "Is Cathy still in the wilderness?"

"As far as I know."

"And you, Matt?"

"I have work to do. Have you had any contact with Tom?"

"He started divorce proceedings the day after he got back to New York. It's going to be uncontested and very fast."

"Good. Any post-wilderness syndrome among the kids?"

"Some, but they're dealing with it well. They're going to be all right."

"Susan, I want you and Dennis to hire private security. Around the clock. I don't mean to scare you, but I've got to think that you're targets."

"Why, Matt? And by whom?"

"The breakaways. Why? Because they're crazy and they might place part of the blame for their exposure on you and the others who were in the wilderness with me. Call this number, Susan." He gave it to her. "That group is made up largely of ex-spooks. They're very good at their jobs. Call them. Tell them I recommended them. Will you do that for me?"

"If you say so."

"I say so. I miss you, Susan. I want very much to be with you."

Her very personal reply—and Matt hoped no one else was listening—probably melted some lines along the way. He hung up with a grin on his face and an aching in his loins.

He packed up, loaded his Bronco, and pulled out. He didn't tell Susan that he was heading for the Los Angeles area, and the home—one of many—of Emmett Trumball. He wanted to get to the man before the breakaways did.

He pointed the nose of the Bronco southwest and drove for ten hours before pulling over at a motel and resting for a few hours. Then it was back behind the wheel and looking at the road. He listened to the radio a lot, mostly news programs. And the news was not at all good for the tribe.

Advocates for one group or another were screaming about the money being spent on a bunch of savages rather than spending it on them.

"Who the hell cares about a bunch of half-breeds?" hollered another loudmouth. "Let us go in and take care of them."

"Everybody in the United States should take a blood test!" yelled another one. "Everybody who has a drop of tribe blood in them should then be exterminated. And do the same thing for queers and drug addicts and liberals, too."

"Jesus!" Matt said.

"Declare open season on the tribe members!" squalled another. "Issue us hunting licenses and we'll go in and take care of the problem."

"Assholes!" Matt said. *Somebody better come up with something,* he thought, *and do it damn quick.*

The news commentator was saying, ". . . Sporting goods stores cannot keep enough rifles and shotguns and pistols in stock. The nation is arming itself at an alarming rate."

Matt turned up the volume.

". . . Authorities are fearing many will start shooting at shadows and killing innocent people. The panic and fear that has gripped the United States, Canada, and Mexico is unprecedented in this reporter's memory. The cannibalistic group called the Unseen is striking daily. To date, more than two hundred people nationwide have been attacked and eaten by these inhuman savages, and that figure is expected to soar. So far, not one of these murderers has been apprehended by the authorities. All across the nation vigilante groups are forming and are prepared to take the law into their own hands."

Matt turned off the radio. The reporter was beginning to

get emotional.

He checked into a small motel in LA and showered and shaved and watched the news on TV while eating a sandwich. The radio reporter he had listened to earlier had been correct in his assumption that the death count would rise. It had now topped three hundred nationwide. He turned off the light and was unbuttoning his shirt, preparing to lie down.

He rebuttoned his shirt at the sound of a slight scraping on the motel sidewalk. Matt screwed a silencer on his 9mm and walked quietly across the carpet to the double drapes, cracking them just a bit and looking out. He saw the room clerk, standing with several men, facing in his direction. The eyes! Matt recalled that the man had been wearing tinted glasses, although it had been completely dark when he checked in.

The man was one of them who would not fight the urge, and he was pointing out a late supper to his friends.

These damned people seemed to be everywhere.

Not wanted to be someone's meal, Matt stuck his feet back into his shoes, slipped into a light jacket, and jerked open the door. Something came silently hurtling at him from the bushes in front of the row of rooms. Matt shot it. The silenced 9mm made a huffing sound, and the slug struck the man in the center of his forehead, stopping him. He pitched forward and fell motionless on the sidewalk. The desk clerk and the others had heard nothing.

Now the tricky part: taking one of them alive for questioning—or two, preferably two. Matt quietly closed the motel room door and slipped around the back of the office, working his way close to the group of men standing by the side talking.

"That's his Bronco," the desk clerk was saying. "I checked the license plate through Ken at the sheriff's office. Good thing the Idaho cell told us what to look for. I got Roger over there watching the room."

"I hope Roger controls himself and doesn't try to entice him to come out."

"Look," the desk clerk said, "traffic will begin to thin in a couple of hours. I got four singles and eight doubles registered in. We can get it done and have the rooms cleaned out and the cars gone by daylight. Get the others and let's hit them at midnight."

"What about Roger?"

"I'll check on him in a few minutes. The switchboard is buzzing. You guys get gone and get the others. I'll see you back here in about an hour."

When the desk clerk had entered the office, Matt ran back to his room and dragged the body of Roger around to a pickup with the motel's name painted on the door and dumped him in the bed of the half-ton truck. He ran to a pay phone off the small swimming pool and called in to the LA office, bringing the voice up to date and telling him to get him some help out here and do it fast. He looked toward the office. There was no sign of the desk clerk.

Matt dialed Richard at home and got him on the second ring.

"Take one alive if you can," Richard told him. "I'll alert an interrogation crew and have them standing by with drugs. I'll be by the phone, Matt."

Matt sat in one of the poolside chairs, after pulling it into the shadows, watching the office. The desk clerk appeared to be irritated by the constant buzzing of the switchboard. He probably was anticipating a late-night snack.

The clerk finally walked out and over to Matt's room. Matt watched him walk back and forth, looking in the bushes and softly calling out Roger's name.

"You'll meet him soon enough, creep," Matt whispered. "I assure you of that."

"Roger, you son of a bitch" the desk clerk called softly. He shook his head. "Well, maybe he went to take a piss."

311

He put his ear to the motel room door and listened. "Sound asleep," he said, then walked back to the office.

The men and women from the LA office were quick in responding. Matt recognized the car that had been described to him by the voice on the phone. They began coming in shortly after the clerk returned to the office, checking in as singles or as man and wife. Six of them— four men and two women. Matt left his chair and intercepted them.

"Let's get in your room," he told the man. Inside, he faced the group and said, "I don't know how many will be coming over. Probably quite a bunch. They plan to wipe out the entire motel list. Let's do this quick and let's do it quietly, taking as many alive as we can. The desk clerk seems to be the leader. I'll take him out first, and you people drop the others." He checked his watch. "We've got about half an hour. Let's get in place."

They fanned out, the seven of them expertly placing themselves in the shadows and effectively covering the inside of the U-shaped motel. They all carried silenced handguns, ranging from the .22-caliber Colt Woodsman to the Beretta 9mm.

Matt felt sure there was more than one cell of the Unseen operating in and around LA, but he was also certain that each cell knew about the other. It was therefore imperative that he take the desk clerk alive. This could be the first good chance to break the cells in this area wide open and put an end to the killings.

The Unseen had people in the sheriff's department, so it was a sure bet they also had people in the LAPD as well. But that wasn't going to be the case long in any department, since the government, Matt had been told, had ordered massive and sudden blood testing of police and sheriff's deputies all over the country, as well as officials in local, county, state, and federal governmental bodies.

The doctors and the medics drawing the blood, as well as the technicians doing the work-up, had all either been cleared or placed under arrest or observation if found to have traces of the tribe in their blood. It was not especially fair, for only a small percentage of those on the outside felt the urge to kill, but it was the only effective method anyone could come up with to handle the situation at the moment. And Matt knew the killings were sure to become much more widespread before they began to show any signs of tapering off.

A car pulled in and four men got out, first walking to the office and then stepping back outside, to lounge by the pool. Matt recognized one of them as part of the group he'd seen talking to the desk clerk.

Two more cars pulled in, each carrying four people. If that was it, that made thirteen in all. The clerk left the office and locked the door after turning on the No Vacancy sign.

The Unseen began to spread out, moving silently around the motel.

As one of the killers moved up to a spook's position, he went down silently, the leather sap making only a small thump as it impacted with the back of his head. He was lowered to the concrete walkway and handcuffed and gagged.

Twelve to go.

Stay in your rooms, people, Matt silently implored.

One big hulk went down to his knees after being slugged but managed to call out before passing out. Matt shot the desk clerk in the knee and the man went down with a scream. Lights began flashing on in the rooms.

"Los Angeles Police!" Matt yelled. "Stay in your rooms and stay down low."

The huffing and whapping of silenced pistols echoed around the U-shaped motel. A man leaped out of the darkness and charged Matt, the primitive urges within him changing his face into that of a wild beast. Matt shot him in the chest, and the second round stopped the enraged man.

"Finish it!" Matt yelled. "Get those prisoners out of here!"

He dropped to one knee and assumed a two-handed grip on his Beretta, squeezing the trigger twice. Another night-stalker went down, falling in that boneless way that signaled a quick kill or a soon-to-be-mortal wound.

One of the agents began screaming as a woman leaped onto his back and rode him down to the concrete, her strong teeth tearing at his neck and throat. Another agent ran out of the shadows and slammed her pistol against the head of the bloodthirsty urge-follower. But it was too late. The agent fell to the walkway with his attacker, his throat torn open.

Two of the cannibals got away, running silently and swiftly into the night. None of the agents could shoot for fear of the bullet hitting one of the many innocents who had gathered on the street in front of the motel.

Matt quickly handcuffed the night clerk, gagged him so he could not bite, and dragged him to a waiting car, shoving him into the back seat. An agent jumped in the back seat with him and began putting a pressure bandage on the man's leg wound. The other wounded cannibals were dragged and shoved into other vehicles, including some of their own cars.

Matt was conscious of the many eyes on them from the people watching from behind draped motel room windows, all of them by now surely aware that Matt and the others were not LAPD cops.

"Get going," Matt told the other agents. "I'll catch up with you along the way."

"You familiar with our clinic out here?" a woman asked.

"Yeah. Richard told me. I'll find it."

"What about the paying guests?" another asked.

"They'll get a night's free lodging."

"Where are you going, Husky?"

"I've got to see a man about some rather unfair comments he's been making. And to show him it's not nice to fool with Mother Nature."

5

He was too late.

Long before he reached the walled and guarded mansion of Emmett Trumball and drove slowly to the scene, he saw the flashing lights of the police. He parked on a side street and walked up to join the people standing on the sidewalk in the ritzy neighborhood. He could see the covered bodies of the two guards who had once patrolled the entrance to the mansion.

He took from his wallet a card that identified him as a member of the press—it didn't say what press, but people never asked—and showed it to a woman who stood holding a poodle in her arms.

"Turner. CBS. What happened here?"

And as Matt knew they would, everybody started talking at once.

They had all heard faint screaming. A man had seen fast-running shapes moving around the grounds.

Another had seen the guards, sprawling in near death, their throats torn out.

"How did you know they were near death and not dead?" Matt asked.

"'Cause they were still kicking and jerking around."

Another had seen a woman kneeling down, lapping at

their blood like a wild animal. "It was awful," she said. "I barfed."

None of them had been able to hear anything coming from the mansion because it was set well back from the road. No, they couldn't see anything either, the trees obscured the mansion.

Matt thanked them and walked off a distance, watching as ambulances began arriving and leaving, carrying their grisly cargo. He walked across the road, showing the cop his ID from the Treasury Department.

"No interest in this except curiosity," Matt told him. "Anybody alive in there?"

"Only us boys and girls in blue," the cop told him. "Those damned tribe members did it, we figure. I haven't been up there, but I'm told it's a slaughterhouse. Trumball was gutted alive, they say. Nailed to a wall like Jesus Christ and his guts pulled out. Hell of a way to die."

"That would be unpleasant," Matt said dryly. "Thanks. See you around." He walked back to his Bronco and drove off, thinking that Emmett Trumball had got exactly what he so richly deserved.

He wondered when the news of the motel shootout would hit the streets.

He pulled into a shopping center and called Richard at his house, giving him the news about Emmett Trumball.

"Mere words cannot begin to express my sorrow over the demise of Emmett Trumball, Matt," the acting DCI said. "The LAPD and the county sheriff's office personnel will undergo testing beginning in the morning. Since you're in the vicinity and you've surprisingly and suddenly developed a human trait—called love—why don't you take twenty-four hours off and go see your, ah, main squeeze?"

"Main squeeze, Rich? *Main squeeze?*"

"Keep in touch, Lothario." Richard was chuckling as

he hung up the phone.

Matt laughed as he was punching out Dennis's number.

Matt was sitting in the spacious and lovely den of the Feld-man house when the news of the motel shootout broke on television. Matt sipped his drink and kept his face impassive until the newsperson said, "The police are looking for a late model, full-sized Ford Bronco, driven by a man wearing a neatly trimmed beard, about six feet tall and weighing about a hundred and eighty pounds."

"Son-of-a-bitch!" Matt said.

"Relax," Dennis said. "Take my Mercedes and park your Bronco in the garage until you can have some of your people pick it up. Were those tribe members out there, Matt?"

"Yes. It's all coming to a head, and the boil will explode any day now. Have the people in your firm tested, Dennis. It's the only way you're going to be sure."

Dennis smiled. "I started having that done yesterday. I also insisted that all our private security people here be tested. They all agreed without a bobble. Everybody at the office and here came back clean."

"Good. Susan, you and Milli get ahold of the gang— what's left of it," he added with a grimace, "and tell them to do the same with their employees and suggest it to their friends. That'll be another load off my mind. Any friend or employee who refuses, however, is not necessarily a tribe member. You all have read about the indignation concerning drug testing. The same might apply here. Tell your friends that this involves a much higher risk factor. Get yourselves tested and show them the results. Tell them that many of those urge-feelers might not have been aware of their . . . affliction until full adulthood or even middle years. If an employee still refuses, I'd suggest firing him and dropping the others off my Christmas list."

"You have a place to stay, Matt?" Milli asked.

He sighed, the weariness in him surfacing. "No, I don't."

"Yes, you do, ol' buddy," Dennis said with a smile. "And no arguments, huh?"

"None from me, friend. None at all."

Matt slept late. Dennis had been driven to work by one of the security people, and another had escorted Milli and Traci shopping. Walter and Tommy were outside by the pool. After a long and hot shower, Matt sat in the breakfast nook and watched as Susan insisted on fixing him breakfast.

"When will it be over, Matt?" she asked, not looking up from the eggs.

"I'd guess the worst'll be over in a couple of weeks. But until then it's going to be bloody. I've told you that before, but it bears repeating."

She nodded her understanding. "I tried to get Dennis to allow me to share in the security expenses. He wouldn't hear of it. Said it was all tax deductible, and since this wasn't my house, he wasn't sure I could take any of it off. I just want this over so we can pick up our lives. You and I. Matt?"

He looked up, meeting her eyes.

"Are you going to be clear of the CIA?"

"No," he told her truthfully. "I'll take jobs from time to time. I'm far too young and in too good a physical condition for them not to use me."

"Will these jobs be dangerous?"

"Some. One thing you'll have to learn, Susan, is never to ask me questions about where I'm going, what I'm going to do, where I've been, or what I did there. That way I won't have to lie to you."

She smiled. "Will we have all sorts of elaborate security

devices around the yard?"

"Probably. I'm on a lot of hit lists. I'll have to change my name, so be thinking about a name you like."

"It's that . . . complicated?"

"For a lot of us, yes."

"Then why do men like you do it?"

"Because all the other countries do it. It doesn't say much for the world, but that's the way it is."

He ate his breakfast while she bathed. The phone rang and he answered it. It was Dennis. "Matt, they hit a block away last night. They massacred a family named Feldman. Husband, wife, two kids. I don't think that was a coincidence."

"Neither do I. I think they got the wrong family. You call Wade, Dennis. I'll call Norm. Do they have security?"

"Yes—all of them. But we'd best call. How about you?"

"I'll tell my boss I'm staying put for a few days. You may have to move out, go in hiding until this is over. You know a lot of cops; some of them surely have links with the tribe. Think about it."

"And as soon as the testing starts, they'll be after blood."

"It started this morning here in LA. You'd better get home, Dennis."

Susan walked into the kitchen just as Matt was hanging up the phone. "Who was that?"

"Dennis. A family name of Feldman was slaughtered last night. They lived a block away. I suspect they'll be coming here tonight. Pack up, Susan—we'll pull out just as soon as Dennis gets here. Dennis is calling Wade; I'll call Norm. Find out from security where Milli went shopping and have them bump the guard on the radio. Get the kids inside. Move, honey!"

He called Norm and advised him to gather up his family and get ready to pull out. They would decide on a place and call him as soon as Dennis got home. He was replacing the receiver when Susan appeared by his side. "Matt?

The guards are gone. I can't find them anywhere."

He ran to his room and screwed the silencer on his 9mm. Susan had grouped the kids in the den. "Does Dennis have a phone in his car?"

Susan nodded.

"Call him. Tell him to approach the house with caution. Don't get out of his car unless I'm in the drive. Have his guard contact Milli's security. Advise them of the situation."

She picked up the phone. The line was dead. She looked at Matt, real fear in her eyes. She tried to speak. Her voice broke.

"The phone dead?"

She nodded.

"Take it easy. All of you."

A man suddenly appeared in the doorway leading from the hall to the den. He smiled faintly at Matt, but no humor lit up his strange-colored eyes.

"That's not one of our guards!" Tommy blurted.

The man stopped smiling when Matt shot him twice in the chest, the silenced 9mm making only a huffing sound.

Matt turned as he caught movement out of the corner of his eyes. He fired as the man jumped into the den. The first slug struck the urge-follower in the chest, the second slug took him in the throat. Susan screamed, spinning Matt around. A woman was struggling with her, trying to drag her from the room. Walter grabbed up a poker from the fireplace set and smashed it across the woman's back. She screamed in pain and released Susan. Walter swung the poker again, the hook driving into the woman's neck. The woman fell to the carpet and jerked her way into death. The boy worked the hook out, his face pale. He turned his head and vomited, and then nodded his head at Matt, a signal that he was all right and ready to do more battle.

"Good boy," Matt told him. "Watch my back."

The boy nodded, gripping the poker with both hands.

But the tribe-related urge-followers had pulled back. They had lost the element of surprise and had no desire to lose more people. Matt checked out the house and then cautiously walked outside.

The big house was surrounded on both sides and in the rear by a five-foot-high wooden security fence. Shrubs and trees blocked most of the view from the front. He made his way around one side of the house and found the body of a guard; the man's throat had been ripped out. He found a second guard in the rear of the house, by the security fence, a knife was sticking out of his back. Matt went back into the house.

"Hurry up and pack," he told the group, just as he heard the sound of a car pulling into the drive. He walked back outside. Milli and Traci and the guard. Matt shooed the women inside to pack and laid it out for the security guard.

"I'll call in," the guard said. "For sure we can't notify the police until the testing is complete—twenty-four hours minimum."

"I own a lodge up in the mountains," Dennis said as soon as he and Matt were alone. "It's a hard half a day's drive from here." He found a map and pointed it out. "Right there. It's big enough for us all."

"We'll call the others once we get on the road," Matt said. "We've got to get clear of this place."

"The police are looking for your Bronco," Dennis reminded him.

"For their sake, I hope they don't find it," Matt's reply was grimly spoken.

They bought supplies on the road, stopping at several stores so as not to attract too much attention, since they were buying food for a lot more than were in their small party.

Norm and Wade had been notified and they had

gathered up their families and were on the way.

Matt had several antsy moments when cops had cruised by him as they left the city. But the rash of killings had all their attention and no one pulled him over to check out the Bronco or its driver.

Daylight was fading when they pulled into the lodge in the Sierra Nevada mountain range. Matt was certain they had not been followed, but there was no way he could be sure about Norm and Wade.

"Do you want me to send in a team?" Richard had asked when Matt finally contacted with him.

"How thin are you stretched?"

"Very thin," the acting DCI replied honestly.

"Then keep the boys and girls in the field," Matt said. "I think Norm and I can handle it."

"The death count is rising," Richard informed him. "Nationwide. It's pure revenge now. They know they can't win and are going for an all-out bloodbath."

"We both anticipated that. How about Ty and the tribe?"

"They're safe. Congress has found their backbone and will officially give that area federal reservation status. That means tribal law will prevail. Anyone who goes in there will lose all protection from the government."

"That won't keep the assholes out, Rich. You know that."

"It's a start, Husky."

"Finish it, Rich."

"What do you mean?"

"The army rangers are being pulled out, aren't they?"

"Forest service personnel will take over," Richard admitted.

"That's just fucking wonderful. How many will be assigned to guard the perimeters, four?"

"Certain members of the press are screaming about the cost of keeping troops in there."

"Oh, God damn it, Rich. Don't those dunderheads realize that troops are paid wherever they are? They get the same pay sitting in the barracks as they do out in the field. It's Ron Arnold, isn't it?"

"He, ah, is certainly very vocal about it, yes."

"I'm going to kill that son-of-a-bitch when this is over, Rich."

"Husky, don't say things like that over the phone!"

"I mean it. That asshole is dead meat."

Matt hung up on Richard's frantic sputterings. The acting DCI knew only too well that Matt Jordan meant every word.

At the two-story lodge they all watched Matt as he slammed down the phone and cut loose with a stream of profanity that would have awed a drunken dockworker.

"Wow!" Walter said, as Matt finally wound down.

"Totally awesome," Traci said.

"What language was that last bit in?" Milli asked.

"Portuguese," Matt said. "Sorry, people. I usually keep a better lid on my temper."

"Cars coming up the drive," Tommy called from a front window. "Two of them."

Matt walked to the window and looked out as Norm and Wade and their families pulled up. "Well, the gang is once more united."

"Let's hope this reunion is quieter than the previous one," Susan said.

Matt picked up his Mini-14 and walked out onto the porch. He jacked a round into the chamber in reply.

"I'm pretty sure we weren't followed," Norm said. "At least, not on the last leg, anyway. I linked up with Wade in Stockton and we both were pretty careful getting there."

"We'll know in a few hours," Matt said, glancing around at the darkness that was slowly circling them.

"Come on. Let's get settled in."

The lodge was built of stone native to the area, Matt guessed. With the exception of a small bedroom downstairs—probably built with live-in help in mind—all the bedrooms were on the second floor. Matt took the downstairs bedroom. He intended to do some prowling at night if the tribe members-gone-bad found their hidey-hole.

After a supper of hot dogs, beans, and potato chips, Matt checked his perimeter bangers and the few boobytraps he'd been able to set before darkness had stopped him and then took a nap, telling the others to wake him when the last ones were ready for bed.

Susan touched his shoulder and he was wide awake. "Easy," she said. "I stayed awake while the others went to sleep. I knew you'd probably want to be up the rest of the night."

"You got that right. What time is it?"

"Midnight. How do you feel?"

"Good . . . very refreshed. Ready for some action," he added with a smile.

"Oh?" she returned the smile. "What'd you have in mind, big boy?"

He stretched out on the bed, hands behind his head, and met her gaze in the dim light coming from the other room. "It'd be a hell of a time for the breakaways to hit us."

She began unbuttoning his shirt. "I'm hoping it'd be worth the risk," she said, her voice low.

It was.

6

Matt gently untangled himself from her arms and dressed quietly. He looked at the bedside clock: 12:45. It had been a frantic first ten minutes, then a short rest, and then a slow, measured lovemaking. He made sure the window over the bed was securely locked, then picked up his Mini-14 and slipped out of the bedroom.

He was not surprised to find Norm on guard on the front porch. Norm grinned at him. "If I'd told Susan I was out here, you and she would never have had so much fun."

"Did we make that much noise?"

"Only an occasional moan or two." He laughed softly. "No, I'm just kidding. But I was about to come and get you. I saw lights down the road about five minutes ago. Several sets. Then they went dark. I think we're going to have company in about fifteen minutes. I figured the perimeter bangers would jar you from the throes of ecstasy."

"I'll stay out here if you'll double-check the windows on the first floor," Matt said. "Then you take the back."

"Will do. See you when the action is over."

"Let's hope."

Matt was alone on the darkened front porch. He clicked the Mini-14 off safety and put his back to the wall. It was reminiscent of his days in 'Nam: he knew the enemy was out there, could sense them drawing closer, but he couldn't see them. And he was too old a hand to shoot at shadows.

He wanted to tell them to give it up. They could not win. He wished he could tell them to go home, fight the killing urges that silently screamed at them, but he knew he could not do that. To call out would be to give away his position and to die. He waited.

He heard a very faint sound: a leather sole scraping against gravel. He did not move his head at the sound; only his eyes shifted. The urge-followers were about a hundred yards from the lodge, very faint shapes in the cloudy night. Was it them? Or some kids playing games in the night? Maybe some locals up in the mountains come to frighten the tourists? He just couldn't be sure.

They came in a rush and there was no more doubt. One tripped a perimeter banger, and Matt dropped to one knee at the sound of the mini-explosion and filled the night's darkness with lead death in the form of .223s.

In the rear of the lodge Norm was laying down a heavy pattern of gunfire, the reports of his rifle shattering the mountain stillness.

Matt shifted position and ejected the near-empty clip, slipping in a full thirty-round clip, jacking in a round as he moved away from the wall.

"Lights?" he heard Dennis shout the question from above him.

"Yes," Matt yelled. "Flood it."

All around the lodge floodlights clicked on, filling the area with harsh light. The lights caught the urge-followers by surprise, momentarily freezing them in the yard. Dennis and Wade had shotguns, the plug taken out of the tube and the tube filled with double-ought buckshot. Dennis ran to the front of the house, Wade to the rear. Their shotguns roared and the buckshot ripped into

327

flesh. Several men and at least one woman lay dead on the ground. Two men were screaming in pain on the rocky lawn as they bled to death in the artificially brilliant light.

A man leaped onto the porch, his shape making long shadows from the light to the gloom. Matt shot him twice and he fell over his side, one foot catching on the rail. He dangled and died. Another urge-follower made the porch, howling his rage and frustration. Matt stilled the wildness in him forever.

"Back, back!" came the call from the edge of the lighted area. Matt recognized the voice as Cathy's. He lifted his rifle and emptied a clip in her direction.

"No!" he heard someone scream. "God damn you, no!"

"Is she hit?" a voice called.

"She's dead."

Savage howling and screaming followed that.

Matt quickly changed clips and emptied that one in the direction of the screaming. The screaming stopped, fading from a painful choking gurgle into silence.

As he again changed clips, he heard running footsteps, the sounds fading away. "Hold your fire!" Matt yelled.

In a few moments, far below the lodge, one vehicle pulled away, its headlights blazing. "Call the sheriff's department, Dennis. This has to be reported."

"What if they are some of them?" Milli called.

"It has to be reported. Just keep your guns handy."

The sheriff shook his head at the carnage. He had carefully inspected Matt's credentials and handed them back to him. "I got two deputies who didn't show up for work on this shift," he said. "Now I know where one of them is." He pointed to a dead man lying on the rocky lawn. "We started blood testing yesterday afternoon. I guess he figured it was all over but the shouting."

"It's nationwide, Sheriff . . . if that's any consolation,"

328

Matt told him. "We had them in our department, too."

"Les was a pretty good cop," the sheriff said. "But looking back, he could act, well, strange at certain times."

"How do you mean?"

"He never liked to work when the moon was full. And when he did, those who were his partners said he seemed to be fascinated by it. Maybe I should have put it together . . . I don't know. You folks going to stay on here after this?"

"Right here, Sheriff."

"I was afraid you were going to say that."

"Here's Cathy!" Wade called, walking around the body-littered lawn with a deputy.

Matt walked over to the body, the sheriff with him. "You know this woman?" the lawman asked.

"She was married to a friend of ours. We graduated from high school together. His kids killed him in Denver."

"I got a teletype about that. You folks had been on a camping trip in Idaho. You're the one found that lost tribe of . . . whatever the hell they are. Frank somebody."

"Nichols." Matt looked down at Cathy. She had been shot at least half a dozen times, several of the slugs striking her in the face. She was no longer pretty. "Did the authorities ever track down her kids?"

"Not that I know of. I just hope to hell they aren't in my area. This is not the first killing tonight," the sheriff admitted.

"Nor will it be the last," Matt told him.

"You're just a real bundle of glad tidings, aren't you?" the sheriff said.

The sheriff's deputies and the city police stayed busy that night, and not just in the one county in California where Matt and the others were staying. All over the nation people were staying up, loaded guns by their sides, praying for the dawn to break to bring an end to the horror.

Lab technicians were working around the clock all over the United States, Canada, and Mexico. Hundreds of people failed to show up for work, left their homes to go to work and never returned, or stuck guns in their mouths and put an end to the nightmare they'd been living. At the sheriff's office in Los Angeles County, Ken went berserk, killing a dozen deputies and wounding a dozen more before other deputies shot him dead. At Fort Bragg, North Carolina, a paratrooper burst into the officer's club and began spraying the crowded club with M-60 fire before he was shot by an MP. An airline pilot put his jet into a dive and took more than a hundred passengers to their deaths. A bus driver spun the steering wheel and plunged over the side of a mountain in Georgia. The few survivors said he was laughing hysterically all the way down. A truck driver floorboarded his 18-wheeler and crashed into a crowded truck stop in Arkansas.

The President stayed up all night, close to a bank of phones and to his advisers. He reached the point where he would cringe each time the phone rang, knowing it was a body count as across the nation it continued to mount.

In Omaha, a man was shot dead as he went out into his back yard to check on his dog. A neighbor thought he was an urge-follower and killed him with a shotgun.

In Austin, Texas, a teenage girl was killed by a gang of vigilantes after she refused to stop her car at their illegal road block. They told police they were checking for them blood-sucking and cannibalistic monsters that might be trying to infiltrate their neighborhood. The police told them they were under arrest for murder.

In Detroit, a full-blown race riot erupted after police tried to arrest a black man who bolted after refusing to take a blood test. He was shot dead. At dawn, parts of the city were still burning as firefighters could not get close enough to fight the flames due to the many thrown bottles and bricks, and an occasional gunshot.

In Miami, a group cornered an urge-follower who had killed several people and had been run down by the mob. The urge-follower was Hispanic, the mob mainly black. Riot police—already short-handed—just sealed off the area and let them fight it out.

The President looked at the new body-count chalked onto a blackboard and shook his head. "Is this night ever going to end?"

At dawn, on the edge of the Great Primitive Area of Idaho, six men swung into their saddles and rode toward the newly declared reservation area of Ty and his tribe. An animal was an animal—whether it walked upright or on all fours (didn't none of them believe that no animal could talk English like they'd read in the newspapers and heard on the TV) and nobody had the right to tell them they couldn't hunt one. They were going to, by God, get them all a trophy to stick up on the wall.

They carried weapons ranging in power from a .30-.06 to a .458 that was capable of bringing down a rampaging Cape buffalo at full gallop.

"What'd your old lady say when you left, Al?" Art Callahan asked.

"Told me I was a fool for comin' in here. I told her to kiss my ass."

Russell Weaver laughed. "You wouldn't tell a lie, now, would you, Al?"

"Nope. I want to see her face when I drag one of these ugly bastards home with me and have it stuffed."

Steve Simpson winked at his son Sonny and said, "Since them hotshot army ranger soldier boys pulled out, we don't have nobody to fool with except the forest service people. I don't think we'll have any trouble bagging us each one of these cannibals. Last time we was in here, Sonny got him a bald eagle. Sure looks pretty, all stuffed up and sitting on that perch in his den."

"Maybe I can get another shot at a wolf," Baxter Camp-

331

ton said. "I only wounded the last one I shot at. I guess the son-of-a-bitch drug hisself off and died. I never could find him. He was a beauty, too."

"We're gonna have us a good time, boys!" Art said. "The weather's good, we got lots of booze on the pack horses, and we gonna kill us a monster apiece. Goddamn, we gonna have some fun!"

"You reckon they'll kick and squall like that bear we shot last year?" Russell asked. "That was a show all by itself, wasn't it?"

They all agreed it was indeed quite a show watching the bear die.

"Yeah," Sonny said. "Until that bunch of hunters come up and killed it. Said people like us shouldn't be allowed to hunt. Said it was wrong to allow an animal to suffer like that. Said if it was up to them we'd all be put in jail. I can't figure out why they got so upset about a damn bear. I still think we should have kicked their butts."

"Candyasses, son. That's all. Just a bunch of damned candyasses. They wasn't worth getting into a fight over. Wearing all that damn hunter orange. Hell, you could see 'em coming for a mile and a half."

"I'm with Sonny," Al said. "We should have laid down our guns and kicked some butt."

"Yeah," Baxter said. "It's people like that bunch that give huntin' a bad name."

7

Once the final tally was complete, it proved to be the bloodiest night in American history. The death count moved past five thousand just before dawn. The nation's jails, already packed to overflowing, were now jammed full of both suspected tribe-followers and those who had been taken alive during their acts of savagery and cannibalism. The ACLU was screaming in outrage and was totally ignored; the populace was in no mood for their tirades.

Blood testing was proceeding at the fastest pace possible and the doctors were learning, and passing on to the public, the fact that only about one in fifty of those whose ancestors came from the tribe were dangerous. The rest were just normal, decent, hardworking citizens who were just as frightened for their lives as anyone else.

All the military had been called out in the United States, Canada, and Mexico to assist the local authorities in keeping order and in rounding up what remained of the savage element of the tribe.

Frank and Cathy's kids had elected to go down bloody. They were killed during a raid in a home on the outskirts of Denver, along with several others of their kind.

Ron Arnold, several hours after one of his on-air and

near-screaming tirades against the tribe, the Central Intelligence Agency and the Army Rangers, was enjoying a cocktail in his luxurious New York City apartment. It was to be his last cocktail. Divorced from his third wife, and with no prospects of marriage in his future and not knowing how to boil water, he had ordered Chinese and was expecting the knock on the door. He did not get his Chinese food. He threw open the door, opened his mouth to scream, and got a big knife blade across his throat, the savage force of it almost decapitating him. Ron Arnold died with a very surprised look on his face. The food delivery man arrived just a few moments after the police got there. He gave his box of food to a cop and got the hell gone from the apartment building. A NYC detective ate the *moo goo gai pan*. He commented that it needed just a touch more salt and then went wandering off looking for an antacid tablet.

Matt called Simmons at his Denver office. "I think we've finally got a handle on the situation, Matt. We're going to miss a few of them, and there'll be more killings, but nothing like what we've seen so far."

"That was a chancy thing the President did, declaring martial law and suspending most constitutional rights pertaining to arrest and questioning."

"A damn ballsy thing on his part. But for once the majority of the press kept their damned mouths shut about it. You heard about Ron Arnold?"

"No. What happened to the sleezebag?"

"He's dead. About an hour ago. Somebody cut his throat in his apartment."

"I hope you're not waiting for me to offer condolences."

"I don't know of any cop who's all that torn up about his demise. That man stayed on the backs of law enforcement. How's your situation out there?"

"Stable. The sheriff out here is a good man. He got the lid on his county in a hurry and didn't do it gently. As soon as things are back to normal here, I'm going back in to see how Ty is getting along."

"Let me know when and I'll go in with you."

"It's a deal."

Matt walked out on the front porch and sat down beside Susan. "It is over?" she asked.

"Just about. They'll be scattered incidents of killing by the urge-followers for a long time to come—maybe for the rest of our lives—but nothing to match what's gone on the past few days. I think maybe a couple more days here and you can all go home."

"And you, Matt?"

"I'm going back into the wilderness area. I'm worried about Ty."

"It isn't your problem anymore," she reminded him.

"It's everybody's problem. Those people have to be protected. But thanks to assholes like Ron Arnold the military was pulled away. I think most sportsmen would be appalled at the thought of doing harm to any of Ty's people. But there are types who'd like to kill one and have it stuffed."

"That's disgusting!"

"Of course it is. But it's true."

"And your going back in will accomplish what, Matt?"

"That depends entirely on whether I find any civilian in there with a gun in his hands."

"And if you do?"

He looked at her.

She got the message.

"I get the feeling that we're being watched," Al said, cutting his eyes to the timber that stood tall and silent around their camp.

"You're getting spooky," Baxter told him. "All them half-human things is still miles from here. We haven't even crossed the Selway yet."

"Maybe so," Al said. "But I still got that itchy feeling in the middle of my back."

"Maybe you got fleas?" Russell suggested.

The men laughed and settled back to eat their supper.

In California, Matt was boarding a military plane that would take him to Idaho, where a helicopter was waiting. Simmons had already left Denver and was waiting for Matt near the edge of the Great Primitive Area.

Susan and her children had returned to the suburbs of Los Angeles with Dennis and Milli. The nation was fast settling down. But the courts were in a quandary over what to do with the hundreds of tribe-related men, women, and children that were still in lockup all around the nation. Martial law had been lifted, the troops returned to bases around the country, and full constitutional rights returned to the citizens.

Since the tribe-related men and women and kids who were confined had done nothing wrong, the Supreme Court ordered them released, and Congress passed a law forbidding their harassment and guaranteeing they would be given back their jobs. Some were released with strange smiles on their faces and a peculiar glint in their strange-colored eyes. They did not return to their homes and jobs; they vanished and sought out others like them. They had lots of planning to do before the next full moon unleashed the primitive urges within them. The blood tests were not completely accurate.

Ty listened with growing concern on his face. He had known that it would happen, he just hadn't thought it would happen so soon.

Hunters.

"Have you spoken with the doctors?"

"Yes. And they are as concerned as we are. They are going to speak with our new guards."

"Why do you say guards and not protectors?"

336

"I felt safe with the army here. These new people are nice people—for pure humans—but they do not appear to be as, well, how do I say this? Ready for a fight as the rangers, I suppose."

"Elder," a young man spoke, using their native tongue. It would be several more generations before the animal would be bred out of his family. "Is it not true that the government has given this land to us with the understanding that we could continue governing as before?"

Ty knew exactly what the young man was leading up to. Many of the tribe looked more animal than human, but none of them were stupid. "Say what is on your mind," Ty told him.

"The outside laws mean nothing on these lands."

"So?"

"Why give the hunters the chance to attack us."

"You want to kill the men?"

"I won't want to, Elder. But the new people who have come to guard us are not nearly enough. Not one is even in camp at this time."

"You know that since I became the elder of this tribe there have been no unwarranted killing of those who came to hunt or fish or camp in accordance with outside laws?"

"You gave me an opening, Elder," the young man said. "These people who approach are not in accordance with outside laws, or with the laws of this tribe. They are in violation of all law."

"We don't know that they're here to do any of us harm," Ty protested.

"Our scouts have listened to them talk. They boast of killing eagles and wolves and bears. They boast of watching an animal die slowly while they enjoy its pain. They talk about killing some of us and of preserving the carcass for trophy. How much more do you want, Elder?"

Ty sighed. All they wanted was to live in peace with the land and the animals. Those on the outside who refused to fight the urges and reverted back to the wild had caused them all much grief. Now this. Ty knew that no tribal adult was without sin—sin according to the rules of the outside world. They had killed humans—but only those who were lawless in their hunting or trapping practices or who threatened the tribe's safety. He stood up.

"I will speak to Nick and Dan." He found them at the doctors' tent and told them of the scouts' reports.

"I was afraid of something like this," a scientist said. "We've got to notify the authorities."

Nick and Dan exchanged glances, both of them knowing it would accomplish about as much as spitting into the wind. Tribal law was harsh compared to the laws on the outside, but it was damned effective. The tribe could prove conclusively that the death penalty worked in preventing crime. It was simply a matter of getting it done while the crime was still fresh in the minds of the innocents.

Neither of them voiced his thoughts while the doctors and scientists were present, not wanting them to run babbling hysterically to the few federal officers on the reservation. When the doctors had left, Dan said, "We'll take care of this, Ty."

"No!" Ty said sharply.

The men looked at him.

"No more killing. I have spoken. Let us live in peace with all things—whether or not all things want peace with us."

"Noble thoughts, Ty," Nick said. "But it doesn't work on the outside. Most folks on the outside don't give a damn what happens to animals. And you and your people are in that classification. Damn few of them on the outside are goin' to give a shit what happens to the tribe. Especially after all the killin' that's gone on."

"But we had nothing to do with that!"

"Most won't take that into consideration. Folks on the

338

outside will spend ten billion dollars a year to see games while stepping over a hungry, homeless person getting to the stadium."

"No!"

"He's telling you the truth, Ty," Dan said. "It's a whole different set of values outside this reservation. Why do you think so many who leave here have such a difficult time adjusting? Why do so many of them kill themselves?"

The sounds of a helicopter interrupted their conversation. Matt and FBI agent Simmons stepped down and unloaded their equipment. After they had settled in, Ty explained the problem.

"Where are the forest service people?" Simmons asked.

"Out there somewhere," Ty said, waving a hand toward the timber.

"The Sataws and breakaways?" Matt asked.

"They have gone. There's no trace of them anywhere near here. I believe they've split up and are seeking a new area in which to live."

"What do you want us to do, Ty?" Matt asked.

"I don't know. But I do have this thought: Let me speak to these men who hunt us for sport. Let me try to make them understand our position in the scheme of things."

Simmons grunted and Matt looked sad. Both men knew the types of those coming illegally into the area. Any attempted meaningful conversation with one of them would be about as productive as debating the writings of Voltaire with a tree stump.

"It would be a waste of time, Ty," Matt told him. "These people aren't interested in the advancement of science or the preservation of a species. They enjoy killing things simply for the sake of killing. When the last wolf is gone, they'll start on the eagles. When those are gone, they'll find something else. They just don't care."

"What a strange society you live in, Matt," Elder Ty said. "It is beyond my comprehension. If certain people

339

refuse to live by tried and true rules, why not dispose of them? Wouldn't it make your society a better place?"

"Of course it would," Matt said. "But that isn't going to happen. And talking about it doesn't do anything toward solving the immediate problem. Let me talk to my boss. Maybe he can come up with something."

"The only thing I can do is suggest that more game wardens be sent in to patrol the outer edges of the reservation," Richard told Matt. "The military is not going to be sent back in there, and I need you out here."

"My job is finished, Rich. I've officially pulled the pin with the agency. Look, get in touch with Donna Gates. Yes, that Donna Gates. See if her network is still interested in this story. Get it before the American people. Damn it, the tribe members in here are thinking, speaking beings. They are not trophies to be stuck up on a fucking wall."

"No time, ol' hoss," Nick said. "Ty's gone to meet with the hunters."

"God damn it!" Matt tossed the microphone to the table. "They'll kill him, Nick."

Nick shrugged. "He said he had to try, Matt. He had to see through his own eyes what manner of people lived on the outside."

"But these people are not representative of the majority," Matt said.

"Really?" the guide said dryly.

8

Matt was saddling his horse when Simmons walked up to the corral. "I'll go with you," the FBI man said.

"You'd better not."

"Why not? I'm a federal officer. I can stop these men . . . legally," he added.

"I don't give a shit for legal," Matt replied. "And I'm going to stop them—*permanently.*"

"If that's your feeling, Matt, then you're no better than those poachers coming in."

"That depends on which side of the issue you're standing on, doesn't it?" Matt swung into the saddle and looked down at Simmons. "You're needed here, partner. I'll take care of this situation."

Nick and Dan were already in the saddle. They turned their horses and moved toward the timber.

"If Ty don't want us to spot him, we won't," Dan called over his shoulder. "I expect he's already covered a couple of miles and he ain't using any trail the horses could follow."

"Simmons' comin' up behind us," Nick said. "Totin' a camera, looks like."

"That's so if anything happens, he can keep it nice and legal," Matt said.

341

Nick and Dan merely grunted at that.

Simmons rode up to the group. "You can't keep me from coming along," he said stubbornly.

"I wouldn't think of trying," Matt said.

"There's Ty," Nick pointed out. "And there are the poachers." He pointed to a line of horsemen about a hundred yards outside the timber, in a meadow.

Ty was about five hundred yards ahead of the group when the first shot rang out.

"Shit!" Matt cussed as he watched Ty stumble, grab at a tree for support, and then slump to the ground. He put his horse to a trot and the others followed.

"I got him!" They all heard the shout as they reached Ty. "Did you see the ugly bastard fall? I did. I got him. I got him."

Matt knelt down beside Ty. The being had been hit in the chest, and hit hard. "Don't kill them, Matt Jordan," Ty said. "There's been enough killing."

Matt said nothing.

"Promise me, Matt."

"All right, Ty. I give you my word I will not kill them."

"Thank you."

Nick gave Dan a glance and the man mounted up and rode off, back to the encampment.

"I only wanted to speak with them," Ty said, the words pushing painfully and laboriously out of his animal mouth. "I meant them no harm."

"Did you see that son-of-a-bitch kick when he hit the ground?" Sonny hollered.

"You got him, Sonny. He's yours. Hey!" Steve yelled. "You people get the hell away from our kill!"

"Our kill," Ty said. "I am somebody's kill. I wonder what they plan to do with me? Stuff me and frighten children?"

Nick knelt down and took Ty's hand. "It'll be a long journey, old friend. But one with a happy ending."

"For me, yes—but not for my people."

"Dan knows. He's gone back."

Simmons wondered what in hell they were talking about.

Matt thought he knew.

"We knew each other for only a very brief time, Matt Jordan," Ty said. "But I thank you for being my friend."

"The pleasure was mine, Ty."

Ty smiled. The smile no longer looked strange on the animal face. "Despite what you think of yourself, Matt, you're a good man at heart."

Matt only nodded, not trusting himself to speak. Ty held out a hand and Matt gently gripped it. Ty closed his eyes and died.

"You gave your word," Simmons reminded Matt.

Matt released Ty's hand and placed the hand on the being's chest. He stood up slowly. "I know what I said. I have no intention of killing the son-of-a-bitch."

Simmons looked at his tense stance. "You damn sure have intentions of doing something."

"You can accurately say that, yes."

"Hey!" Al Bagby yelled. "You goddamn guys get away from our kill."

"You the one who shot Ty?" Matt asked as the group of men walked into the timber.

"Ty? Who the hell is Ty?" Art asked.

"This dead being, that's who."

"You mean the goddamn thing had a name?"

"Did you shoot him?"

"Naw, I did," Sonny said. "He's mine, and I'm gonna take him and have him stuffed and mounted."

"You think that's what you're going to do, huh?"

"Yeah. And you ain't man enough to stop me."

Matt hit him. The blow was fast and landed exactly where Matt intended, flush on the mouth, and Sonny went down in a sprawl of arms and legs. Nick and Simmons

343

both leveled their weapons at the poachers.

"Drop them," Nick ordered. "Or die where you stand."

Five rifles hit the ground.

Sonny was getting up off the ground when Matt kicked him in the face. The toe of his boot impacted with teeth and pearlies went flying from the young man's mouth. Matt then proceeded to kick in Sonny's face. He stopped just short of killing the man. Sonny's face would bear the scars of this day until the day he finally did the world a favor and exited it.

"Wallets on the ground," Simmons said. "Get their IDs, Nick. I want to keep them on file in case they fuck up again sometime during their miserable lives."

Five wallets hit the ground.

"My poor boy needs a doctor!" Steve moaned, holding Sonny's bloody head in his lap. "God damn, he didn't do nothing except shoot a wild animal."

Matt was busy smashing the men's rifles to pieces against a boulder.

It was all Simmons could do to keep from pistol-whipping the poacher. "Get out of here," the FBI agent said tightly, "before I kill you myself."

Matt smiled at him. "You have human emotions after all."

"Sometimes, Husky. Sometimes."

A crowd of doctors and scientists and technicians gathered around them when they returned to the encampment. "They're gone!" a woman yelled. "Dan rode in and everybody left within fifteen minutes. They just packed up and left."

"One said the human race would be contacted someday, when the tribe felt we were advanced enough to deal with them. I'm sorry about Ty. Is that why they left?"

"I'm sure of it," Matt said.

"Aren't you going after them?" another asked him. "Please go after them."

"No."

"No! Why? Where is Ty's body? I don't understand any of this."

"I'm not going after them because our society won't protect them while you people study them. A group of tribe members took Ty's body for secret burial. I'll call in for helicopters. You people had better pack up if you're going out. It's all over here."

Matt turned his back to them and walked to the radio tent. He was again wondering, for about the thousandth time in his adult life, why the United States government always seemed to fuck up a good thing.

9

"Why did you just drop out of sight, Matt?" Richard asked. "Oh, by the way, we're holding your retirement checks."

"Susan and I left the country. Took the kids with us. I didn't think you'd have my papers processed so quickly."

"The young man you very nearly kicked to death in the wilderness is going to live."

"I don't care one way or the other, Rich."

Richard did his best to look hurt, but he didn't quite pull it off. "However, he is going to be horribly disfigured for the rest of his life."

"Maybe somebody will mistake him for an animal and shoot him."

Richard sighed. "We have a job for you, Matt. And this isn't a request."

Matt waited. He knew that a lot of not-so-subtle pressure could be exerted if he refused a job.

"You've been out of the country for several months, Matt. A lot has happened during that time." He held up thumb and forefinger about a half inch apart. "Congress is this close to passing a bill guaranteeing the protection of the tribe if they surface again."

"How?"

"United States marshals and other federal law enforcement people. The bill also has a provision that would make it a federal crime for anyone to violate the reservation area, punishable by a minimum sentence of twenty-five years."

"No."

Richard looked pained. "What do you mean, *no?* Jesus, Husky, what do you want?"

"Violators shot on sight."

Richard sighed. "Why must you be so difficult?" he muttered. He cleared his throat. "You know Congress will never go along with that."

"There's a saying that covers that pretty well."

"I am loathe to ask what that might be."

"Tough shit!"

"The tribe trusts you, Matt."

"Which is exactly why I will not approach them with any offers until their safety is absolutely, positively, one-hundred-percent guaranteed. In writing. By law. Passed by both Houses of Congress and signed by the President of the United States and approved by the Supreme Court."

"Matt, listen to me—please. You probably don't know that while the doctors were packing up, waiting for the helicopters to arrive that afternoon, someone, probably a tribe member, slipped back into camp and stole every blood sample they had taken. They took records, tape recordings . . . *everything*. We've got to have those samples."

"Why? You've got hundreds of urge-followers in jail, and hundreds more who are related to the tribe out in the civilian sector. You don't need more blood from the tribe. So don't give me any patriotic bullshit about needing their blood samples to save lives. If you want to jack around with my pension, Rich, okay—go ahead. I married a very

347

wealthy woman. I've made good investments over the years. You won't hurt me financially. You let me tell you something, Rich. I'll go in and try to find the tribe, on these conditions: I am in charge of security. Me. Personally. I have carte blanche in dealing with intruders . . ."

Richard winced at that.

". . . I personally handpick security. Only when I am satisfied do I reveal the location of the tribe. That is, if I can find it. You have a map of Idaho? Give it to me. You see this area here, Rich, the central and eastern part of the Selway-Bitteroot Wilderness area? That belongs to the tribe. All of it!"

"Jesus Christ, Matt!" Richard yelled. "Do you know how many hunter groups will be up in arms—figuratively speaking, I hope—if that went through?"

"I don't care, Rich. Sit down, I'm not finished. I want a federal law, on the books and enforced, prohibiting the killing of wolves in any part of the United States. I want the wolf reintroduced into the larger national parks. We can work out which parks after Congress approves all this."

Matt smiled, knowing how Ty would have approved of all that he had just proposed.

Richard sighed again. Scientists and statesmen from all over the world had been on the backs of the State Department deploring what had happened to the lost tribe and why it was allowed to happen. The President was on the defensive and getting testy. Knowing that Matt had gained the trust of the tribe, he had tossed the whole matter into Richard's lap with the orders, "Just get it done, Richard. I don't care what you have to promise Matt Jordan. Just *get it done!*"

"Is there anything else you want, Matt?" Richard asked wearily.

"Oh, yes!"

"Why did I have to ask? What else, Matt?"

Matt began speaking. He spoke for five minutes. When he had finished, Richard's jaw was very nearly touching the desk. "Are you out of your goddamned mind, Matt?"

"No. I think I found it, actually."

"When did you become such an animal activist? There's nothing in your jacket about it."

"Do you know what happens to a lot of greyhounds when their racing days are over?"

"No."

"If somebody doesn't adopt them, they're either killed or sold to labs for use in experiments."

"I didn't know that." Richard grimaced. "That's *disgusting!*"

"Yes, it is, isn't it? I didn't know it either until Traci told me. I did a little investigating and found it to be true." Matt held up a hand. "I've told you what I want, Rich. You know how to reach me. I'll be waiting for your call."

"I think it would be neat," Tommy said. "Living in the wilderness. And the best part is no school."

"Wrong," Matt told the boy. "A school is being built now. It'll be ready for next year's term."

Tommy's face showed his disgust. "Well . . . I still think it'll be neat."

Matt looked at Traci. "Honey, you'll go to school in New York. Your mother and I would love to have you closer, but with all the death threats coming at us, it wouldn't be wise. Have you thought of a name you like?"

"Brown."

Matt smiled. "That's a safe choice. Traci Brown. You're going to have to live with it for four years. You understand that? Okay. You can never tell anyone who you

349

really are or that I'm your stepfather or that you know anything about Project Unseen. There are a lot of nuts and wackos out there claiming to represent one group or another, and they wouldn't hesitate to hurt you to get to me. The ranching industry is howling mad about the reintroduction of wolves in certain areas—even though money has been set aside to compensate them for any loss; the racing industry is screaming about the new legislation concerning the treatment of greyhounds once their racing days are through; and a certain type of hunter is killing mad about the land we've placed off limits to them in Idaho and in all large national parks. Some of those people are nuts, honey. You've got to be careful."

"I'll be careful. I promise."

"Good girl."

"You've never told us, Matt," Susan said. "You did locate the tribe?"

"They located me. Yes. And I'm forced to change my opinion of many members of the press. They've done a very fair job of covering this issue." He smiled. "Of course, it's a politically liberal issue, so they would."

Even Tommy joined in the laughter at that.

"You all packed up?" Matt asked Susan.

"Yes. When do I join you?"

"In the spring. I'll come out several times and fly east to see you all. I promise we'll spend Christmas together."

Traci and Tommy left to pack up a few remaining articles.

"They didn't mention their father, Susan."

"They never loved him, Matt. Neither of them shed a tear when they learned he'd been killed. You think his death was tribe related?"

"Yes. We have teams tracking down the cells. We'll eventually get them all, but it's going to take some time. I've arranged security for you and Tommy, and loose

350

security for Traci. It'll be tense for a couple of years, then the furor will die down. What's so funny about the whole thing is that I've been branded an anti-hunter by some nut groups."

"I fail to see the humor in it, Matt."

"Hell, honey. I've been a member of the National Rifle Association for over twenty years!"

THE BEGINNING

A wolf's howl echoed over the cold and snowy land. Another wolf joined in, then a third and a fourth.

"It's almost as if they know they're safe," Matt said to Ty's son, standing beside him in the winter's frozen beauty.

"They do," the half-man, half-beast said. "We told them."

Dear Reader,

Zebra Books welcomes your comments about this book or any other Zebra horror book you have read recently. Please address your comments to:

Zebra Books, Dept. WM
475 Park Avenue South
New York, NY 10016

Thank you for your interest.

Sincerely,
The Editorial Department
Zebra Books